David Gemmell's first novel, *Legend*, was published in 1984. He has written many bestsellers, including the Drenai saga, the Jon Shannow novels and the Stones of Power sequence. Widely acclaimed as Britain's king of heroic fantasy, David Gemmell died in 2006.

Find out more about David Gemmell and other Orbit authors by registering for the free montly newsletter at www.orbitbooks.net

By David Gemmell

LEGEND
THE KING BEYOND THE GATE
WAYLANDER
QUEST FOR LOST HEROES
WAYLANDER II
THE FIRST CHRONICLES OF
DRUSS THE LEGEND
DRENAI TALES: OMNIBUS ONE
DRENAI TALES: OMNIBUS TWO

WOLF IN SHADOW
THE LAST GUARDIAN
BLOODSTONE

GHOST KING
LAST SWORD OF POWER

LION OF MACEDON
DARK PRINCE

IRONHAND'S DAUGHTER
THE HAWK ETERNAL

KNIGHTS OF DARK RENOWN

MORNINGSTAR

WAYLANDER

David A. Gemmell

www.orbitbooks.net

ORBIT

First published in Great Britain by Century Hutchinson 1986
Reprinted by Orbit 1997, 1998, 1999 (twice),
2000, 2001, 2002, 2003, 2004, 2005, 2006, 2007

A CIP catalogue record for this book
is available from the British Library.

ISBN 978-1-85723-621-7

Papers used by Orbit are natural, recyclable products made from
wood grown in sustainable forests and certified in accordance with
the rules of the Forest Stewardship Council.

Printed and bound in Great Britain by
Mackays of Chatham PLC, Chatham, Kent
Paper supplied by Hellefoss AS, Norway

Orbit
An imprint of
Little, Brown Book Group
Brettenham House
Lancaster Place
London WC2E 7EN

A Member of the Hachette Livre Group of Companies

www.orbitbooks.net

Acknowledgements

My thanks go to my agent Leslie Flood, whose support carried me through the lean years; my local editor, Ross Lempriere, without whom Waylander would not have stalked the dark woods; Stella Graham, the finest of proof-readers, and Liza Reeves, Jean Maund, Shane Jarvis, Jonathan Poore, Stewart Dunn, Julia Laidlaw and Tom Taylor.

Special thanks to Robert Breare for the fun of it all, and for holding the fortress against the odds.

This book is dedicated with love to Denis and Audrey Ballard, my parents-in-law, for the friendship of two decades.

And to their daughter Valerie, who changed my world on December 22 1965.

Prologue

The monster watched from the shadows as the armed men, torches aloft, entered the darkness of the mountain. He backed away as they advanced, keeping his huge bulk from the glare.

The men made their way to a rough-hewn chamber and placed the torches in rusty iron brackets on the granite walls.

At the centre of the twenty-strong group was a figure in armour of bronze, which caught the torchlight and seemed to blaze like fashioned flames. He removed his winged helm and two retainers erected a wooden skeleton frame. The warrior placed the helm atop the frame and unbuckled his breastplate. He was past middle age, but still strong – his hair thinning, his eyes squinting in the flickering light. He passed the armoured breastplate to a retainer who laid it on the frame, rebuckling the straps.

'Are you sure of this plan, my lord?' asked an elderly figure, slender and blue-robed.

'As sure as I am of anything, Derian. The dream has been with me now for a year and I believe in it.'

'But the Armour means so much to the Drenai.'

'That is why it is here.'

'Could you not – even now – reconsider? Niallad is a young man and he could wait at least two more years. You are still strong, my lord.'

'My eyes are failing, Derian. Soon I shall be blind. You think that a good trait in a King renowned for his skill in war?'

'I do not wish to lose you, my lord.' said Derian. 'It may be that I am speaking out of turn, but your son . . .'

'I know of his weaknesses,' snapped the King, 'as I know his future. We are facing the end of all we have fought for. Not now . . . not in five years. But soon will come the days of blood and then the Drenai must have some hope. This Armour is that hope.'

'But, my lord, is not magical. *You* were magical. This is merely metal which you chose to wear. It could have been silver, or gold, or leather. It is Orien the King who has built the Drenai. And now you will leave us.'

The King, dressed now in a brown tunic of doeskin, placed his hands on the statesman's shoulders.

'I have been much troubled these past few years, but always I have been guided by your good counsel. I trust you, Derian, and I know you will look to Niallad and guide him where you can. But in the days of blood he will be beyond your advice. My vision is black indeed: I see a terrible army falling upon the Drenai people; I see our forces sundered and in hiding – and I see this Armour shining like a torch, drawing men to it, giving them faith.'

'And do you see victory, my lord?'

'I see victory for some. Death for others.'

'But what if your vision is not true? What if it is merely a deceit fashioned by the Spirit of Chaos?'

'Look to the Armour, Derian,' said Orien, leading him forward.

It glinted in the torchlight still, but now had gained an ethereal quality which puzzled the eye. 'Reach

8

out and touch it,' ordered the King. When Derian did so, his hand passed through the image and he recoiled as if stung.

'What have you done?'

'I have done nothing, but it is the first promise of the dream. Only the Chosen One can claim the Armour.'

'There may be some who can undo the spell and steal the Armour?'

'Indeed there may, Derian. But look beyond the torchlight.'

The statesman turned to see scores of eyes blinking at him from the darkness. He stepped back. 'Gods! What are they?'

'Once they were human, it is said. But the tribes who live in this area talk of a stream that runs black in the summer. Water from this stream is all there is, but when drunk by pregnant women it becomes a rare poison which deforms the child in the womb. The Nadir leave the babes on the mountain to die . . . obviously not all have done so.'

Derian tugged a torch from its bracket and advanced on the doorway, but the King stopped him.

'Don't look, my friend, it would haunt you to your dying day. But be assured they are ferocious in the extreme. It would need a great force to come here, and if any but the Chosen One attempts to remove the Armour he will be torn to pieces by the beasts who dwell in the darkness.'

'And what will you do now, my lord?'

'I will say farewell.'

'Where will you go?'

'Where no one will know me as a king.'

There were tears in Derian's eyes as he dropped

9

to his knees before Orien, but the King pulled him to his feet.

'Put aside rank, old friend. Let us part as comrades.'

The two men embraced.

1

They had begun to torture the priest when the stranger stepped from the shadows of the trees.

'You stole my horse,' he said quietly. The five men spun round. Beyond them the young priest sagged against the ropes which held him, raising his head to squint through swollen eyes at the newcomer. The man was tall and broad-shouldered and a black leather cloak was drawn about him.

'Where is my horse?' he asked.

'Who is to say? A horse is a horse and the owner is the man who rides him,' answered Dectas. When the stranger first spoke Dectas had felt the thrill of fear course through him, expecting to find several men armed and ready. But now, as he scanned the trees in the gathering dusk, he knew the man was alone. Alone and mad. The priest had proved but sorry sport, gritting his teeth against the pain and offering neither curse nor plea. But this one would sing his song of pain long into the night.

'Fetch the horse,' said the man, a note of boredom in his deep voice.

'Take him!' ordered Dectas and swords sang into the air as the five men attacked. Swiftly the new-comer swept his cloak over one shoulder and lifted his right arm. A black bolt tore into the chest of the nearest man, a second entered the belly of a burly warrior with upraised sword. The stranger dropped

11

the small double crossbow and lightly leapt back. One of his attackers was dead and a second knelt clutching the bolt in his belly.

The newcomer loosened the thong which held his cloak, allowing it to fall to the ground behind him. From twin sheaths he produced two black-bladed knives.

'Fetch the horse!' he ordered.

The remaining two hesitated, glancing to Dectas for guidance. Black blades hissed through the air and both men dropped without a sound.

Dectas was alone.

'You can have the horse,' he said, biting his lip and backing towards the trees. The man shook his head.

'Too late,' he answered softly.

Dectas turned and sprinted for the trees, but a sharp blow in the back caused him to lose balance and his face ploughed the soft earth. Pushing his hands beneath him, he struggled to rise. Had the newcomer thrown a rock, he wondered? Weakness flowed through him and he slumped to the ground . . . the earth was soft as a feather-bed and sweet-smelling like lavender. His leg twitched.

The newcomer recovered his cloak and brushed the dirt from its folds before fastening the thongs at the shoulder. Then he recovered his three knives, wiping them clean on the clothes of the dead. Lastly he collected his bolts, despatching the wounded man with a swift knife-cut across the throat. He picked up his crossbow and checked the mechanism for dirt before clipping it to his broad black belt. Without a backward glance he strode to the horses.

'Wait!' called the priest. 'Release me. *Please!*'

The man turned. 'Why?' he asked.

The question was so casually put that the priest found himself momentarily unable to phrase an answer.

'I will die if you leave me here,' he said, at last.

'Not good enough,' said the man, shrugging. He walked to the horses, finding that his own mount and saddlebags were as he had left them. Satisfied, he untied his horse and walked back to the clearing.

For several moments he stared at the priest, then he cursed softly and cut him free. The man sagged forward into his arms. He had been badly beaten and his chest had been repeatedly cut; the flesh hung in narrow strips and his blue robes were stained with blood. The warrior rolled the priest to his back, ripping open the robes, then walked to his horse and returned with a leather canteen. Twisting the cap he poured water on the wounds. The priest writhed but made no sound. Expertly the warrior smoothed the strips of skin back into place.

'Lie still for a moment,' he ordered. Taking needle and thread from a small saddlebag, he neatly stitched the flaps. 'I need a fire,' he said. 'I can't see a damned thing!'

The fire once lit, the priest watched as the warrior went about his work. The man's eyes were narrowed in concentration, but the priest noted that they were extraordinarily dark, deep sable-brown with flashing gold flecks. The warrior was unshaven, and the beard around his chin was speckled with grey.

Then the priest slept . . .

When he awoke, he groaned as the pain from his beating roared back at him like a snarling dog. He sat up, wincing as the stitches in his chest pulled tight. His robes were gone and beside him lay clothes

13

obviously taken from the dead men, for brown blood stained the jerkin which lay beside them.

The warrior was packing his saddlebags and tying his blanket to his saddle.

'Where are my robes?' demanded the priest.

'I burned them.'

'How dare you! Those were sacred garments.'

'They were merely blue cotton. And you can get more in any town or village.' The warrior returned to the priest and squatted beside him. 'I spent two hours patching your soft body, priest. It would please me if you allowed it to live for a few days before hurling yourself on the fires of martyrdom. All across the country your brethren are burning, or hanged, or dismembered. And all because they don't have the courage to remove those damned robes.'

'We will not hide,' said the priest defiantly.

'Then you will die.'

'Is that so terrible?'

'I don't know, priest, you tell me. You were close to it last evening.'

'But you came.'

'Looking for my horse. Don't read too much into it.'

'And a horse is worth more than a man in today's market?'

'It always was, priest.'

'Not to me.'

'So if I had been tied to the tree, you would have rescued me?'

'I would have tried.'

'And we would both have been dead. As it is, you are alive and, more importantly, I have my horse.'

'I will find more robes.'

14

'I don't doubt that you will. And now I must go. If you wish to ride with me, you are welcome.'

'I don't think that I do.'

The man shrugged and rose. 'In that case, farewell.'

'Wait!' said the priest, forcing himself to his feet. 'I did not wish to sound ungrateful and I thank you most sincerely for your help. It is just that were I to be with you, it would put you in danger.'

'That's very thoughtful of you,' answered the man. 'As you wish, then.'

He walked to his horse, tightened the saddle cinch and climbed into the saddle, sweeping out his cloak behind him.

'I am Dardalion,' called the priest.

The warrior leaned forward on the pommel of his saddle.

'And I am Waylander,' he said. The priest jerked as if struck. 'I see you have heard of me.'

'I have heard nothing that is good,' replied Dardalion.

'Then you have heard only what is true. Farewell.'

'Wait! I will travel with you.'

Waylander drew back on the reins. 'What about the danger?' he asked.

'Only the Vagrian conquerors want me dead, but at least I have some friends – which is more than can be said for Waylander the Slayer. Half the world would pay to spit on your grave.'

'It is always comforting to be appreciated,' said Waylander. 'Now, Dardalion – if you are coming, put on those clothes and then we must be away.'

Dardalion knelt by the clothes and reached for a woollen shirt, but as his fingers touched it he recoiled and the colour drained from his face.

Waylander slid from his saddle and approached the priest. 'Do your wounds trouble you?' he asked.

Dardalion shook his head, and when he looked up Waylander was surprised to see tears in his eyes. It shocked the warrior, for he had watched this man suffer torture without showing pain. Now he wept like a child, yet there was nothing to torment him.

Dardalion took a shuddering breath. 'I cannot wear these clothes.'

'There are no lice, and I have scraped away most of the blood.'

'They carry memories, Waylander . . . horrible memories . . . rape, murder, foulness indescribable. I am sullied even by touching them and I cannot wear them.'

'You are a mystic, then?'

'Yes. A mystic.' Dardalion sat back upon the blanket shivering in the morning sunshine. Waylander scratched his chin and returned to his horse, where he removed a spare shirt, leggings and a pair of moccasins from his saddlebag.

'These are clean, priest. But the memories they carry may be no less painful for you,' he said, tossing the clothes before Dardalion. Hesitantly the young priest reached for the woollen shirt. As he touched the garment he felt no evil, only a wave of emotional pain that transcended anguish. He closed his eyes and calmed his mind, then looked up and smiled.

'Thank you, Waylander. These I can wear.'

Their eyes met and the warrior smiled wryly. 'Now you know all my secrets, I suppose?'

'No. Only your pain.'

'Pain is relative,' said Waylander.

Throughout the morning they rode through hills and

valleys torn by the horns of war. To the east pillars of smoke spiralled to join the clouds. Cities were burning, souls departing to the Void. Around them in the woods and fields were scattered corpses, many now stripped of their armour and weapons, while overhead crows banked in black-winged hordes, their greedy eyes scanning the now fertile earth below. The harvest of death was ripening.

Burnt-out villages met the riders' eyes in every vale and Dardalion's face took on a haunted look. Waylander ignored the evidence of war but he rode warily, constantly stopping to study the back-trails and scanning the distant hills to the south.

'Are you being followed?' asked Dardalion.

'Always,' answered the warrior grimly.

Dardalion had last ridden a horse five years before when he left his father's cliff-top villa for the five-mile ride to the temple at Sardia. Now, with the pain of his wounds increasing and his legs chafing against the mare's flanks, he fought against the rising agony. Forcing his mind to concentrate, Dardalion focused his gaze on the warrior riding ahead, noting the easy way he sat his saddle and the fact that he held the reins with his left hand, his right never straying far from the broad black belt hung with weapons of death. For a while, as the road widened, they rode side by side and the priest studied the warrior's face. It was strong-boned and even handsome after a fashion, but the mouth was a grim line and the eyes hard and piercing. Beneath his cloak the warrior wore a chain-mail shoulder-guard over a leather vest which bore many gashes and dents and carefully repaired tears.

'You have lived long in the ways of war?' asked Dardalion.

'Too long,' answered Waylander, stopping once more to study the trail.

'You mentioned the deaths of the priests and you said they died because they lacked the courage to remove their robes. What did you mean?'

'Was it not obvious?'

'It would seem to be the highest courage to die for one's beliefs,' said Dardalion.

Waylander laughed. 'Courage? It takes no courage to die. But living takes nerve.'

'You are a strange man. Do you not fear death?'

'I fear everything, priest – everything that walks, crawls or flies. But save your talk for the camp-fire. I need to think.' Touching his booted heels to his horse's flanks, he moved ahead into a small wood where, finding a clearing in a secluded hollow by a gently flowing stream, he dismounted and loosened the saddle cinch. The horse was anxious to drink, but Waylander walked him round slowly, allowing him to cool after the long ride before taking him to the stream. Then he removed the saddle and fed the beast with oats and grain from a sack tied to the pommel. With the horses tethered Waylander set a small fire by a ring of boulders and spread his blanket beside it. Following a meal of cold meat – which Dardalion refused – and some dried apples, Waylander looked to his weapons. Three knives hung from his belt and these he sharpened with a small whetstone. The half-sized double crossbow he dismantled and cleaned.

'An interesting weapon,' observed Dardalion.

'Yes, made for me in Ventria. It can be very useful; it looses two bolts and is deadly up to twenty feet.'

'Then you need to be close to your victim.'

Waylander's sombre eyes locked on to Dardalion's gaze. 'Do not seek to judge me, priest.'

'It was merely an observation. How did you come to lose your horse?'

'I was with a woman.'

'I see.'

Waylander grinned. 'Gods, it always looks ridiculous when a young man assumes a pompous expression! Have you never had a woman?'

'No. Nor have I eaten meat these last five years. Nor tasted spirits.'

'A dull life but a happy one,' observed the warrior.

'Neither has my life been dull. There is more to living than sating bodily appetites.'

'Of that I am sure. Still, it does no harm to sate them now and again.'

Dardalion said nothing. What purpose would it serve to explain to a warrior the harmony of a life spent building the strength of the spirit? The joys of soaring high upon the solar breezes weightless and free, journeying to distant suns and seeing the birth of new stars? Or the effortless leaps through the misty corridors of time?

'What are you thinking?' asked Waylander.

'I was wondering why you burned my robes,' said Dardalion, suddenly aware that the question had been nagging at him throughout the long day.

'I did it on a whim, there is nothing more to it. I have been long without company and I yearned for it.'

Dardalion nodded and added two sticks to the fire.

'Is that all?' asked the warrior. 'No more questions?'

'Are you disappointed?'

'I suppose that I am,' admitted Waylander. 'I wonder why?'

'Shall I tell you?'

'No, I like mysteries. What will you do now?'

'I shall find others of my order and return to my duties.'

'In other words you will die.'

'Perhaps.'

'It makes no sense to me,' said Waylander, 'but then life itself makes no sense. So it becomes reasonable.'

'Did life ever make sense to you, Waylander?'

'Yes. A long time ago before I learned about eagles.'

'I do not understand you.'

'That pleases me,' said the warrior, pillowing his head on his saddle and closing his eyes.

'Please explain,' urged Dardalion. Waylander rolled to his back and opened his eyes, staring out beyond the stars.

'Once I loved life and the sun was a golden joy. But joy is sometimes short-lived, priest. And when it dies a man will seek inside himself and ask: Why? Why is hate so much stronger than love? Why do the wicked reap such rich rewards? Why does strength and speed count for more than morality and kindness? And then the man realises . . . there are no answers. None. And for the sake of his sanity the man must change perceptions. Once I was a lamb, playing in a green field. Then the wolves came. Now I am an eagle and I fly in a different universe.'

'And now you kill the lambs,' whispered Dardalion.

Waylander chuckled and turned over.

'No, priest. No one pays for lambs.'

2

The mercenaries rode off, leaving the dead behind them. Seventeen bodies littered the roadside; eight men, four women and five children. The men and the children had died swiftly. Of the five carts which the refugees had been hauling, four were burning fiercely and the fifth smouldered quietly. As the killers crested the hills to the south a young red-haired woman pushed herself clear of the screen of bushes by the road and led three children to the smouldering cart.

'Put out the fire, Culas,' she told the oldest boy. He stood staring at the corpses, his wide blue eyes blank with shock and terror. 'The fire, Culas. Help the others put out the fire.' But he saw the body of Sheera and groaned.

'Grandmother . . .' muttered Culas, stepping forward on shaking legs. Then the young woman ran to him, taking him in her arms and burying his head against her shoulder.

'She is dead and she can feel no pain. Come with me and put out the fire.' She led him to the cart and handed him a blanket. The two younger children – twin girls of seven – stood hand in hand, their backs turned to the dead.

'Come now, children. Help your brother. And then we'll be going.'

'Where can we go, Danyal?' asked Krylla.

21

'North. The general Egel is in the north, they say, with a great army. We'll go there.'

'I don't like soldiers,' said Miriel.

'Help your brother. Quickly, now!'

Danyal turned away from them, shielding them from her tears. Vile, vile world! Three months back, when the war had begun, word had reached the village that the Hounds of Chaos were marching on Drenan. The men had laughed at the news, confident of speedy victory.

Not so the women, who instinctively knew that any army revelling in the title Hounds of Chaos would be bitter foes. But how bitter few had realised. Subjugation Danyal could understand – what woman could not? But the Hounds brought more than this; they brought wholesale death and terror, torture, mutilation and horror beyond belief.

Source priests were hunted down and slain, their order outlawed by the new masters. And yet the Source priests offered no resistance to any government, preaching only peace, harmony and respect for authority. What threat did they pose?

Farming communities were burnt out and destroyed. So who would gather the crops in the Fall?

Rape, pillage and murder without end. It was incomprehensibly savage and beyond Danyal's ability to understand. Three times now she had been raped. Once by six soldiers – that they had not killed her was testimony to her skills as an actress, for she had feigned enjoyment and on each occasion they had let her leave, bruised and humiliated but always smiling. Some instinct had told her that today would be different and when the riders first appeared she had gathered the children and fled to the bushes.

The riders were not seeking rape, only plunder and wanton destruction.

Twenty armed men who stopped to butcher a group of refugees.

'The fire is out, Danyal,' called the boy Culas. Danyal climbed into the cart, sorting out blankets and provisions left by the raiders as being too humble for booty. With lengths of hide she tied three blankets into rucksacks for the children, then gathered up leather canteens of water which she hung over her shoulder.

'We must go,' she said, and led the trio off towards the north.

They had not moved far when the sound of horses' hooves came drumming to their ears and Danyal panicked, for they were on open ground. The two girls began to cry, but young Culas produced a long-bladed dagger from a sheath hidden in his blanket roll.

'Give me that!' yelled Danyal, snatching the blade and hurling it far away from the road while Culas watched in horror. 'It will avail us nothing. Listen to me. Whatever they do to me, you just sit quietly. You understand? Do not shout or scream. You promise?'

Two riders rounded the bend in the road. The first was a dark-haired warrior of a type she was coming to know too well; his face was hard, his eyes harder. The second was a surprise, for he was slender and ascetic, fine-boned and seemingly gentle of countenance. Danyal tossed her long red hair over her shoulder and smoothed the folds of her green tunic as they approached, forcing a smile of welcome to her lips.

'You were with the refugees?' asked the warrior.

'No. We just passed that way.'

The young one with the gentle face stepped carefully from the saddle, wincing as if in pain. He approached Danyal and held out his hands.

'You need not lie to us, sister, we are not of that ilk. I am sorry for your pain.'

'You are a priest?'

'Yes.' He turned to the children. 'Come to me, come to Dardalion,' he said, kneeling and opening his arms. Amazingly they responded, the little girls first. His slender arms touched all three. 'You are safe for a little while,' he said. 'I bring you no more than that.'

'They killed grandmother,' said the boy.

'I know, Culas. But you and Krylla and Miriel are still alive. You have run a long way. And now we will help you. We will take you to Gan Egel in the north.'

His voice was soft and persuasive, the sentences short, simple and easily understood. Danyal stood by, transfixed at the power he exerted over them. And she did not doubt him, but her eyes were drawn to the dark-haired warrior who still sat his mount.

'You are not a priest,' she said.

'No. And you are not a whore.'

'How would you know?'

'I spend my life around whores,' he answered. Lifting his leg over the pommel of his saddle he slid to the ground and approached her. He smelt of stale sweat and horseflesh and close up he was as terrifying as any of the raiders she had known. Yet strangely she viewed the terror from a distance as if she were watching a play, knowing that the villain is terrible but comforted by the thought that he cannot

24

leave the stage. The power in him encompassed her without threat.

'You hid in the bushes,' he said. 'Wise. Very wise.'

'You were watching?'

'No. I read the tracks. We hid from the same raiders an hour back. Mercenaries – not true Hounds.'

'*True* Hounds? What more do they need to do to serve their apprenticeship?'

'They were sloppy – they left you alive. You would not escape the Hounds so easily.'

'How is it,' asked Danyal, 'that a man like you travels with a priest of the Source?'

'A man like me? How swiftly you judge, woman,' he answered equably. 'Perhaps I should have shaved.'

She turned from him as Dardalion approached.

'We must find a place to camp,' said the priest. 'The children need sleep.'

'It is only three hours after noon,' said Waylander.

'They need a special kind of sleep,' said Dardalion. 'Trust me. Can you find a place?'

'Walk with me aways,' said the warrior, moving some thirty feet down the trail. Dardalion joined him. 'What is the matter with you? We cannot saddle ourselves with them. We have two horses and the Hounds are everywhere. And where they are not, there are mercenaries.'

'I cannot leave them. But you are right – you go.'

'What have you done to me, priest?' snapped the warrior.

'I? Nothing.'

'Have you put a spell on me? Answer me!'

'I know no spells. You are free to do as you please, obey whatever whims you care to.'

'I don't like children. And I don't like women I can't pay for.'

'We must find a resting place where I can ease their torment. Will you do that before you go?'

'Go? Where should I go?'

'I thought you wanted to leave, to be free of us.'

'I cannot be free. Gods, if I thought you had put a spell on me I would kill you. I swear it!'

'But I have not,' said Dardalion. 'Nor would I if I could.'

Muttering dark curses under his breath, Waylander walked back to Danyal and the children. As he approached the girls clutched Danyal's skirt, their eyes wide with fear.

He waited by his horse until Dardalion was with the children. 'Anyone want to ride with me?' he asked. There was no answer and he chuckled, 'I thought not. Follow me into the trees yonder. I will find a place.'

Later, as Dardalion sat with the children telling them wondrous tales of elder magic, his voice softly hypnotic, Waylander lay by the fire watching the woman.

'You want me?' she asked suddenly, breaking his concentration.

'How much?' he asked.

'For you, nothing.'

'Then I don't want you. Your eyes don't lie as well as your mouth.'

'What does that mean?'

'It means you loathe me. I don't mind that; I've slept with women aplenty who've loathed me.'

'I don't doubt it.'

'Honesty at last?'

'I don't want any harm to come to the children.'

'You think I would harm them?'

'If you could.'

'You misjudge me, woman.'

'And you underestimate my intelligence. Did you not seek to stop the priest from aiding us? Well?'

'Yes, but . . .'

'There are no buts. Without aid our chance of survival is next to nothing. You don't call that harm?'

'Woman, you have a tongue like a whip. I owe you nothing and you have no right to criticise me.'

'I don't criticise you. That would suggest I cared enough to improve you. I despise you and all your loathsome brethren. Leave me alone, damn you!'

Dardalion sat with the children until the last was asleep, then he placed his hand on each brow in turn and whispered the Prayer of Peace. The two girls lay with arms entwined under a single blanket, while Culas was stretched out beside them with his head pillowed on his arm. The priest concluded his prayer and sat back exhausted. Somehow it was hard to concentrate while wearing Waylander's clothes. The blurred images of pain and tragedy had softened now, but still they kept Dardalion from the uppermost pathways of the Road to the Source.

A distant scream pulled him to the present. Somewhere out in the darkness another soul was suffering.

Dardalion shivered and moved to the fireside where the young woman Danyal was sitting alone. Waylander was gone.

'I insulted him,' said Danyal as the priest sat opposite her. 'He is so cold. So hard. So fitted to the times.'

27

'Yes, he is,' agreed Dardalion, 'but he is also the man who can lead us to safety.'

'I know. Do you think he will come back?'

'I think so. Where are you from?'

Danyal shrugged. 'Here and there. I was born in Drenan.'

'A pleasant city with many libraries.'

'Yes.'

'Tell me about your days as an actress,' said Dardalion.

'How did you . . . oh yes, there are no secrets from the Source.'

'Nothing so magical, Danyal. The children told me; they said you once performed the Spirit of Circea before King Niallad.'

'I played the sixth daughter and had three lines,' she said, smiling. 'But it was an experience to remember. They say the King is dead, slain by traitors.'

'So I have heard,' said Dardalion. 'Still, let us not concentrate on such things. The night is clear, the stars are beautiful, the children sleep dreaming sweet dreams. Tomorrow we will worry about death and despair.'

'I cannot stop from thinking about it,' she said. 'Fate is cruel. At any moment raiders may run from the trees and the terror will begin again. You know it is two hundred miles to the Delnoch range where Egel trains his army?'

'I kno .'

'Will you fight for us? Or will you stand by and let them kill us?'

'I do not fight, Danyal. But I will stand with you.'

'But your friend will fight?'

'Yes. It is all he knows.'

'He is a killer,' said Danyal, lifting her blanket around her shoulders. 'He is no different from the mercenaries or the Vagrians. And yet I hope he comes back – is that not strange?'

'Try to sleep,' urged Dardalion. 'And I will see that your dreams are untroubled.'

'That would be nice – and of a magic I could warm to.'

She lay by the fire and closed her eyes. Dardalion breathed deeply and entered once more into concentration, summoning the Prayer of Peace and projecting it silently to shroud her body. Her breathing deepened. Dardalion released the chains of his spirit and soared into the night sky, twisting over and over in the bright moonlight, leaving his body hunched by the fire.

Free!

Alone with the Void.

Stopping his upward spiral with an effort, he scanned the earth below for sign of Waylander.

Far to the south-east the burning cities illuminated the night sky in a jagged crimson arc, while to the north and west watch-fires burned, their regular setting identifying them as Vagrian sentry fires. To the south a single blaze twinkled in a small wood and, curious, Dardalion swooped towards it.

Six men slept around the fire while a seventh sat upon a rock spooning mouthfuls of stew from a copper pot. Dardalion hovered above them, an edge of fear seeping into him. He sensed great evil and prepared to depart.

Suddenly the seated man glanced up at him and grinned.

'We will find you, priest,' he whispered.

Dardalion did not move. The man placed the

29

copper pot by his feet and closed his eyes . . . and Dardalion was no longer alone. Hovering beside him was an armed warrior, bearing shield and black sword. The young priest darted for the skies, but the warrior spirit was faster, touching him lightly on the back as he passed. Pain lanced Dardalion and he cried out.

The warrior hovered before him, grinning.

'I will not kill you *yet*, priest. I want Waylander. Give him to me and you can live.'

'Who are you? whispered Dardalion, fighting for time.

'My name would mean nothing to you. But I am of the Brotherhood and my task is set. Waylander must die.'

'The Brotherhood? You are a priest?'

'Priest? In a way you would never understand, you pious pig! Strength, guile, cunning, terror – these are the things I worship, for they bring power. True power.'

'You serve the Darkness then?' said Dardalion.

'Darkness or Light . . . word tricks of confusion. I serve the Prince of Lies, the Creator of Chaos.'

'Why do you hunt Waylander? He is not a mystic.'

'He killed the wrong man, though doubtless the death was well-deserved. And now it is decreed that *he* must die. Will you deliver him to me?'

'I cannot.'

'Go your way then, worm. Your passivity offends me. I shall kill you tomorrow – just after dark. I will seek out your spirit wherever it hides and I will destroy it.'

'Why? What will you gain?'

'Only pleasure,' answered the warrior. 'But that is enough.'

'Then I will await you.'

'Of course you will. Your kind like to suffer – it makes you holy.'

Waylander was angry, which surprised him, leaving him uneasy and ridiculously resentful. He rode his horse to a wooded hill and dismounted. How can you resent the truth, he asked himself?

And yet it hurt to be bracketed with the likes of mercenaries who raped and plundered the innocent, for despite his awesome reputation as a bringer of death he had never killed a woman or a child. Neither had he ever raped nor humiliated anyone. So why did the woman make him feel so sullied? Why did he now see himself in such dark light?

The priest.

The damned priest!

Waylander had lived the last twenty years in the shadows, but Dardalion was like a lantern illuminating the dark corners of his soul.

He sat down on the grass. The night was cool and clear, the air sweet.

Twenty years. Vanished into the vacuum of memory. Twenty years without anger as Waylander clung like a leech to the ungiving rock of life.

But what now?

'You are going to die, you fool,' he said aloud. 'The priest will kill you with his purity.'

Was that it? Was that the spell he feared so much?

For twenty years Waylander had ridden the mountains and plains of the civilised nations, the Steppes and outlands of the Nadir savages and the far deserts of the nomads. In that time he had allowed himself no friends. No one had touched him. Like a mobile fortress, deep-walled and safe, Waylander had ghosted through life as alone as a man could be.

Why had he rescued the priest? The question tormented him. His fortress had crumbled and his defences fallen apart like wet parchment.

Instinct told him to mount up and leave the little group – and he trusted his instincts, for they were honed by the danger his occupation aroused. Mobility and speed had kept him alive; he could strike like a snake and be gone before the dawn.

Waylander the Slayer, a prince among assassins. Only by chance could he ever be captured, for he had no home – only a random list of contacts who held contracts for him in a score of cities. In the deepest darkness he would appear, claim his contracts or his fees and then depart before the dawn. Always hunted and hated, the Slayer moved among shadows, haunting the dark places.

Even now he knew his pursuers were close. Now, more than ever, he needed to vanish into the outlands or across the sea to Ventria and the eastern kingdoms.

'You fool,' he whispered. 'Do you want to die?'

Yet the priest held him with his uncast spell.

'You have clipped the eagle's wings, Dardalion,' he said softly.

There had been a flower-garden at the farm, bright with hyacinths and tulips and ageing daffodils. His son had looked so peaceful lying there and the blood had not seemed out of place among the blooms. The pain tore into him; memories jagged like broken glass. Tanya had been tied to the bed and then gutted like a fish. The two girls . . . babes . . .

Waylander wept for the lost years . . .

He returned to the camp-site in the hour before

32

dawn and found them all sleeping. He shook his head at their stupidity and stirred the fire to life, preparing a meal of hot oats in a copper pan. Dardalion was the first to wake; he smiled a greeting and stretched.

'I am glad you came back,' he said, moving to the fire.

'We will need to find some food,' said Waylander, 'for our supplies are low. I doubt we'll find a village unburned, so it means hunting meat. You may have to forget your principles, priest, if you don't want to collapse from hunger.'

'May I speak with you?' asked Dardalion.

'An odd request. I thought we were speaking?'

Dardalion moved away from the fire and Waylander sighed and removed the copper pot from the heat before joining him.

'Why so downcast? Are you regretting saddling us with the woman and her get?'

'No. I . . . I need to ask a favour of you. I have no right . . .'

'Out with it, man. What is wrong with you.'

'Will you see them safely to Egel?'

'I thought that was the plan. Are you all right, Dardalion?'

'Yes . . . No . . . I am going to die, you see.' Dardalion turned away from him and walked up the slope to the crest of the hollow. Waylander followed. Once there Dardalion told him of his spirit meeting with the hunter and the other listened in silence. The ways of mystics were closed to him, but he knew of their powers and doubted not that Dardalion was speaking the literal truth. He was not surprised that the hunters were on his heels. After all, he had killed one of their number.

'So you see,' concluded the priest, 'once I am gone I was hoping you would still guide Danyal and the children to safety.'

'Are you so well trained in defeat, Dardalion?'

'I cannot kill – and that is the only way to stop him.'

'Where was their camp?'

'To the south, But you cannot go there – there are seven of them.'

'But only one, you think, with the Power?'

'As far as I could tell; he said he would kill me just after dark. Please don't go, Waylander. I do not wish to be the cause of anyone's death.'

'These men are hunting me, priest and I don't have many choices. If I promise to stay with the woman, then they will find me anyway. Better that I find them and fight on my terms. Today you must stay here. Wait for me. If I do not return by morning, set off for the north.'

Waylander gathered his saddlebags and gear and rode away to the south just as the dawn was breaking. Swinging in the saddle he called out, 'And kill the fire – the smoke can be seen for miles. Don't light it again until dusk.'

Dardalion stared gloomily after him.

'Where is he going?' asked Danyal, coming to stand beside the priest.

'He is going to save my life,' said Dardalion, and once more he told the story of his spirit travels. The woman seemed to understand and he saw the pity in her eyes. He realised in that moment that he was engaged in confession and knew that he had compromised himself badly. In telling Waylander he had forced the man to fight for him.

'Don't blame yourself,' said Danyal.

'I should have said nothing.'

'Would that not have doomed us all? He had to know they were hunting him.'

'I told him so that he would save me.'

'I don't doubt it. But he had to know. You had to tell him.'

'Yes. But there was only selfishness in my mind.'

'You are a man, Dardalion, as well as a priest. You are too hard on yourself. How old are you?'

'Twenty-five. And you?'

'Twenty. How long have you been a priest?'

'Five years. I was trained as an architect by my father, but my heart was never in it. Always I wanted to serve the Source. And as a child I would often have visions. My parents were embarrassed by them.' Dardalion grinned suddenly and shook his head. 'My father was convinced I was possessed and when I was eight he took me to the Source temple at Sardia to have me exorcised. He was furious when they told him I was merely gifted! From then on I attended the temple school. I should have become an acolyte at fifteen, but father insisted I stay at home and learn about business. By the time I had talked him round, I was twenty.'

'Is your father still alive?'

'I don't know. The Vagrians burned Sardia and murdered the priests. I assume they did the same with neighbouring townsfolk.'

'How did you escape?'

'I was not there for the horror; the Abbot sent me to Skoda with messages for the Mountain Monastery, but when I arrived that also was burning. I was on my way back when I was captured, then Waylander rescued me.'

'He does not seem like a man who would bother to rescue anyone.'

Dardalion chuckled. 'Well, no. He was actually recovering his horse which the mercenaries had stolen and I was, somewhat ignominiously, part of the package.'

Dardalion laughed once more, then took Danyal by the hand. 'My thanks to you, sister.'

'For what?'

'For taking the time to lead me away from the paths of self-pity. I'm sorry I burdened you.'

'It was no burden. You are a kind man and you are helping us.'

'You are very wise and I am glad we met,' said Dardalion, kissing her hand. 'Come, let us wake the children.'

Throughout the day Dardalion and Danyal played with the children in the woods. The priest told them stories while Danyal led them on a treasure hunt, collecting flowers and threading garlands. The sun shone for most of the morning, but the sky darkened in mid-afternoon and rain drove the group back to the camp-site to shelter beneath a spreading pine. Here they ate the last of the bread and some dried fruit left by Waylander.

'It's getting dark,' said Danyal. 'Do you think it's safe to light the fire?'

Dardalion did not reply. His eyes were fixed on the seven men advancing through the trees, swords in hand.

3

Wearily Dardalion pushed himself to his feet. The
stitches pulled tight against the skin of his chest and
the bruises around his ribs made him wince. Even
were he a warrior, he could not have stood alone
against even one of the men walking slowly towards
him.

Leading them was the man who had filled him
with fear the night before, smiling as he approached.
Behind him, advancing in a half-circle, were six soldiers with their long blue cloaks fastened over black
breastplates. Their helms covered their faces and
only their eyes were visible through rectangular slits
in the metal.

Behind Dardalion Danyal had turned away from
the warriors and put her arms around the children,
pulling them in close to her so that, at the very least,
they would be spared the terror of the kill.

The priest felt a terrible hopelessness seep into
him. Only days before, he had been willing to bear
torture – torture and death. But now he could feel
the children's fear, and he wished he had a sword
or bow to defend them.

The advancing line stopped and the lead warrior
swung away from Dardalion, staring across the
hollow. Dardalion looked back.

There in the fading red glow of dusk stood Waylander, his cloak drawn close about him. The sun was

setting behind him and the warrior was silhouetted against the blood-red sky – a still figure, yet so powerful that he laid a spell upon the scene. His leather cloak glistened in the dying light and Dardalion's heart leapt at the sight of him. He had seen this drama played out once before and knew that beneath his cloak Waylander carried the murderous crossbow, strung and ready.

But even as hope flared, so it died. For where before there had been five unsuspecting mercenaries, here there were seven warriors in full armour. Trained killers. The Vagrian Hounds of Chaos.

Waylander could not stand against such as these.

In those first frozen moments Dardalion found himself wondering just why the warrior had come back on such a hopeless mission. Waylander had no cause to give his life for any of them – he had no beliefs, no strongly-held convictions.

But there he stood, like a forest statue.

The silence was unnerving, more so for the Vagrians than for Dardalion. The warriors knew that in scant seconds lives would be lost, death would strike in the clearing and blood seep through the soft loam. For they were men of war who walked with death as a constant companion, holding him at bay with skill or with rage, quelling their fears in blood-lust. But here they were caught cold . . . and each felt alone.

The dark priest of the Brotherhood licked his lips, his sword heavy in his hand. He knew that the odds favoured his force, knew with certainty that Waylander would die if he gave the word to attack. But the double-edged knowledge held a second certainty . . . that the moment he spoke, he would die.

Danyal could stand the suspense no longer and, twisting round, she saw Waylander. Her movement caused Miriel to open her eyes and the first thing the child saw were the warriors in their helms.

She screamed.

The spell broke . . .

Waylander's cloak flickered and the dark priest of the Brotherhood pitched backwards with a black bolt through one eye. For several seconds he writhed and then was still.

The six warriors stood their ground, then the man in the centre slowly sheathed his sword and the others followed suit. With infinite care they backed away into the gathering darkness of the trees.

Waylander did not move.

'Fetch the horses,' he said quietly, 'and gather the blankets.'

An hour later they were camped in high ground in a shallow cave; the children were sleeping and Danyal lay awake beside them as Dardalion and the warrior sat together under the stars.

After a while Dardalion came into the cave and stirred the small fire to life. The smoke drifted up through a crack in the roof of the cave, but still their small shelter smelt of burning pine. It was a comforting scent. The priest moved to where Danyal lay and, seeing she was awake, sat beside her.

'Are you well?' he asked.

'I feel strange,' she admitted. 'I was so prepared for death that all fear left me. Yet I am alive. Why did he come back?'

'I do not know. He does not know.'

'Why did they go away?'

Dardalion leaned his back against the cave wall, stretching his legs towards the fire.

'I am not sure. I have given much thought to it and I think perhaps it is the nature of soldiers. They are trained to fight and kill upon a given order – to obey unquestioningly. They do not act as individuals. And when a battle comes it is usually clearcut: there is a city which must be captured or a force which must be overcome. The order is given, excitement grows – dulling fear – and they attack in a mass, drawing strength from the mob around them.

'But today there was no order and Waylander, in remaining still, gave them no cause to fire their blood.'

'But Waylander could not have known they would run away,' she insisted.

'No. He didn't care.'

'I don't understand.'

'In truth I am not sure that I do. But I sensed it during those moments. He didn't care . . . and they knew it. But they cared, they cared very much. They didn't want to die and they were not charged up to fight.'

'But they could have killed him . . . killed us all.'

'*Could* have, yes. But they didn't – and for that I am thankful. Go to sleep, sister. We have won another night.'

Outside Waylander watched the stars. He was still numbed from the encounter and ran the memories through time and again.

He had found their camp deserted and had followed them, a growing fear eating at him. Dismounting below the woods, he had made his way to the clearing, only to see the Hounds advancing. He had strung his crossbow, and then stopped. To advance was to die and every instinct screamed at him to go back.

Yet he had advanced, throwing aside years of caution, to give away his life for a nonsense.

Why in the name of Hell had they walked away? No matter how many times he considered it, an answer always eluded him.

A movement to his left jerked him from his reverie and he turned to see one of the the children walking from the cave. She looked neither to right nor left. Waylander went to her and touched her lightly on the arm, but she moved on, unaware of him. Stooping, he lifted her. Her eyes were closed and her head drooped to his shoulder. She was very light in his arms as he walked back to the cave, ready to lay her beside her sister. But then he stopped in the cave mouth and sat with his back against the wall, drawing her close with his cloak about her.

For several hours he stayed quietly, feeling the warmth of her breath against his neck. Twice she woke, then snuggled down once more. As dawn lightened the sky he took her back into the cave and laid her beside her sister.

Then he returned to the cave mouth . . .

Alone.

Danyal's scream snatched Waylander from sleep, his heart pounding. Rolling to his feet with knife in hand he ran into the cave to find the woman kneeling beside Dardalion's still form. Waylander dropped to his knees and lifted the priest's wrist. The man was dead.

'How?' whispered Danyal.

'Damn you, priest!' shouted Waylander. Dardalion's face was white and waxen, his skin cold to the touch. 'He must have had a weak heart,' said Waylander bitterly.

'He was fighting the man,' said Miriel. Waylander turned to the child, who was sitting at the back of the cave holding hands with her sister.

'Fighting?' he asked. 'Who was he fighting?' But Miriel looked away.

'Come along, Miriel,' urged Danyal. 'Who was he fighting?'

'The man with the arrow in his eye,' she said.

Danyal turned to Waylander. 'It was just a dream; it means nothing. What are we to do?'

Waylander did not reply. Throughout the questioning of the child he had held on to Dardalion's wrist and now he felt the weakest of pulses.

'He is not dead,' he whispered, 'Go and talk to the child. Find out about the dream – quickly, now!'

For some minutes Danyal sat quietly with the girl, then she returned. 'She says that the man you killed took hold of her and made her cry. Then the priest came and the man shouted at him; he had a sword and was trying to kill the priest. And they were flying – higher than the stars. That is all there is.'

'He feared this man,' said Waylander, 'believing he had demonic powers. If he was right, then maybe death did not stop him. Perhaps even now he is being hunted.'

'Can he survive?'

'How?' snapped Waylander. 'The man won't fight.' Danyal leaned forward, placing her hand on Waylander's arm. The muscles were tensed and quivering. 'Take your hand from me, woman, or I'll cut it off at the wrist. No one touches me!' Danyal jerked back with green eyes ablaze, but she mastered her anger and moved back to the children.

'Damn you all!' hissed Waylander. He took a deep breath, quelling the fury boiling inside him. Danyal and the children sat quietly, watching him intently. Danyal knew what was tormenting him: the priest was in danger and the warrior, for all his deadly skill, was powerless. A battle was taking place in another world and Waylander was a useless bystander.

'How could you be so stupid, Dardalion?' whispered the warrior. 'All life fights to survive. You say the Source made the world? Then he created the tiger and the deer, the eagle and the lamb. You think he made the eagle to eat grass?'

For some minutes he lapsed into silence, remembering the priest as he had knelt naked by the robbers' clothes.

'I cannot wear these, Waylander . . .'

He transferred his grip from the priest's arm to his hand and as their fingers touched, there came an almost imperceptible movement. Waylander's eyes narrowed. As he gripped the priest's hand more firmly, Dardalion's arm jerked spasmodically and his face twisted in pain.

'What is happening to you, priest? Where in Hell's name are you?'

At the name of Hell Dardalion jerked again, and moaned softly.

'Wherever he is, he is suffering,' said Danyal, moving forward to kneel beside the priest.

'It was when our hands touched,' said Waylander. 'Fetch the crossbow, woman – there, by the cave mouth.' Danyal moved to the weapon and carried it to Waylander. 'Put it in his right hand and close his fingers about it.' Danyal opened Dardalion's hand, and curled his fingers around the ebony hilt. The priest screamed; his fingers jerked open and the crossbow clattered to the ground. 'Hold his fingers around it.'

'But it is causing him pain. Why are you doing this?'

'Pain is life, Danyal. We must get him back into his body – you understand? The corpse-spirit cannot touch him there. We must draw him back.'

'But he is a priest, a man of purity.'

'So?'

'You will sully his soul.'

Waylander laughed. 'I may not be a mystic, but I do believe in souls. What you are holding is merely wood and metal. Dardalion will be stung by it, but I do not believe his soul is so fragile that it will kill him. But his enemy will – so you decide!'

'I believe that I hate you,' said Danyal, opening Dardalion's hand and forcing him to grip the ebony handle once more. The priest twisted and screamed. Waylander pulled a knife from his belt and sliced a cut across the flesh of his forearm. Blood oozed and then gushed from the wound. As Waylander held his arm over Dardalion's face, blood spattered to his skin, flowed over his closed eyes and down – coursing over his lips and into his throat.

A last terrible scream ripped from the priest and his eyes snapped open. Then he smiled, and his eyes closed again. A deep shuddering breath swelled his lungs and he slept. Waylander checked his pulse – it was strong and even.

'Sweet Lord of Light!' said Danyal. '*Why*? Why the blood?'

'According to the Source no priest shall taste blood, for it carries the soul,' explained Waylander softly. 'The weapon was not enough, but the blood brought him back.'

'I don't understand you. And I do not wish to,' she said.

'He is alive, woman. What more do you want?'

'From you, nothing.'

Waylander smiled and pushed himself to his feet. Taking a small canvas sack from his saddlebag, he removed a length of linen bandage and clumsily wound it around the shallow cut in his arm.

'Would you mind tying a knot in this?' he asked her.

'I'm afraid not,' she answered. 'It would mean touching you and I do not want my hand cut off at the wrist!'

'I am sorry for that. It should not have been said.'

Without waiting for a reply, Waylander left the cave, tucking the bandage under its own folds as he went.

The day was bright and cool, the mountain breezes sharp with the snow of the Skoda peaks as Waylander walked to the crest of a nearby hill and gazed into the blue distance. The Delnoch mountains were still too far off to be seen by the naked eye.

For the next three or four days the trail would be easy, moving from wood to forest to wood, with only short stretches of open ground. But thereafter the Sentran Plain would lie before them, flat and formless.

To cross that emptiness unobserved would take more luck than a man had any right to ask. Six people and two horses! At the pace they must travel they would be on the Plain for nigh a week – a week without fires or hot food. Waylander scanned the possible trails to the north-east, towards Purdol, the City by the Sea. It was said that a Vagrian fleet had berthed at the harbour mouth, landing an army to besiege the citadel. If that were true - and Waylander thought it likely – then Vagrian outriders would be scouring the countryside for food and supplies. To the north-west was Vagria itself and the citadel of Segril, but from here troops were pouring into the Drenai lands. The Sentran Plain was due north, and beyond it Skultik forest and the mountains said to be the last Drenai stronghold west of Purdol.

But did Egel still hold Skultik?

Could anyone hold together the remnants of a defeated army against the Hounds of Chaos? Waylander doubted it . . . yet beyond the doubts there was a spark of hope. Egel was the most able Drenai general of the age, unspectacular but sound – a stern disciplinarian, unlike the courtiers King Niallad normally placed in charge of his troops. Egel was a northerner, uncultured and at times uncouth, but a man of charisma and strength. Waylander had seen him once during a parade in Drenan and the man had stood out like a boar amongst gazelle.

Now the boar had gone to ground in Skultik.

Waylander hoped he could hold, at least until he delivered the woman and the children.

If he *could* deliver them.

Waylander killed a small deer during the afternoon. Hanging the carcass from a nearby tree, he cut prime sections and then carried the meat back to the cave. It was growing dark when he arrived and the priest still slept. Danyal set the fire while Waylander rigged a rough spit to roast the venison. The children sat close to the fire, watching the drops of fat splash into the flames – their stomachs tight, their eyes greedy.

Lifting the meat from the spit, Waylander laid it

to rest on a flat rock to cool; then he sliced sections for the children and lastly Danyal.

'It is a little tough,' complained the woman.

'The deer saw me just as I loosed the shaft,' said Waylander. 'Its muscles were bunched to run.'

'It tastes good all the same,' she admitted.

'Why is Dardalion still asleep?' asked Miriel, smiling at Waylander and tipping her head to one side so that her long fair hair fell across her face.

'He was very tired,' answered the warrior, 'after his tussle with the man you saw.'

'He cut him into little bits,' said the child.

'Yes, I'm sure he did,' said Danyal. 'But children shouldn't make up stories – especially nasty stories. You'll frighten your sister.'

'We saw him,' said Krylla and Miriel nodded agreement. 'When you were sitting with Dardalion, we closed our eyes and watched. He was all silver and he had a shining sword – he chased the bad man and cut him into little bits. And he was laughing!'

'What can you see when you close your eyes?' asked Waylander.

'Where?' asked Miriel.

'Outside the cave,' said the warrior softly.

Miriel closed her eyes. 'There's nothing out there,' she said, her eyes still closed.

'Go further down the trail, near the big oak. Now what do you see?'

'Nothing. Trees. A little stream. Oh!'

'What is it?' asked Waylander.

'Two wolves. They're jumping by a tree – like they're dancing.'

'Go closer.'

'The wolves will get me,' Miriel protested.

'No, they won't – not with me here. They won't see you. Go closer.'

'They are jumping after a poor little deer that's in the tree; he's hanging there.'

'Good. Come back now, and open your eyes.'

Miriel looked up and yawned. 'I'm tired,' she said.

'Yes,' said Waylander softly. 'But tell me first – like a bedtime story – about Dardalion and the other man.'

'You tell him, Krylla. You're better at telling stories.'

'Well,' said Krylla, leaning forward, 'the nasty man with the arrow in his eye caught hold of Miriel and me. He was hurting us. Then Dardalion came and the man let us go. And a big sword appeared in the man's hand. And we ran away, didn't we, Miriel? We went and slept in your lap, Waylander. And we were safe there. But Dardalion was being cut a lot and he was flying very fast. And we couldn't catch up. But we saw him again, when you and Danyal were holding him. He seemed to grow very tall, and silver armour covered him up, and his robes caught fire and burned away. Then he had a sword and he was laughing. The other man's sword was black – and it broke, didn't it, Miriel?

'Then he fell on his knees and began to weep. And Dardalion cut off his arms and legs and he just disappeared. After that Dardalion laughed even more. Then he disappeared and came home to where his body lives. And we are all right now.'

'Yes, we are all right now,' agreed Waylander. 'I think it is time to sleep now. Are you tired, Culas?' The boy nodded glumly.

'What is wrong, boy?'

'Nothing.'

'Come, tell me.'

'No.'

'He's angry because he cannot fly with us,' said Miriel, giggling.

'No, I'm not,' snapped Culas. 'Anyway, you are making it up.'

'Listen, Culas,' said Waylander, 'I can't fly either and it doesn't worry me. Now let's stop the arguing and sleep. Tomorrow will be a long day.'

With the children huddled together by the far wall, Danyal moved alongside Waylander.

'Were they speaking the truth, do you think?' she asked.

'Yes, for Miriel saw where I hid the deer.'

'Then Dardalion did kill his enemy?'

'It would appear so.'

'It makes me feel uneasy – I don't know why.'

'It was a spirit of evil. What else would you expect a priest to do? Bless it?'

'Why are you always so unpleasant, Waylander?'

'Because I choose to be.'

'In that case, I don't suppose you have many friends.'

'I don't have *any* friends.'

'Does that make you lonely?'

'No. It keeps me alive.'

'And what a life it must be for you, full of fun and laughter!' she mocked. 'I'm surprised you're not a poet.'

'Why so angry?' he asked. 'Why should it affect you?'

'Because you are part of our lives. Because for as long as we live, you will remain in our memories. Speaking for myself, I would have preferred another saviour.'

'Yes, I have seen the arena-plays,' said Waylander. 'The hero has golden hair and a white cloak. Well, I am not a hero, woman – I am a man trapped in the priest's web. You think he has been sullied? Well, so have I. The difference is that he needed my darkness to survive. But his Light will destroy me.'

'Will you two never stop rowing?' asked Dardalion, sitting up and stretching his arms.

Danyal ran to his side. 'How do you feel?'

'Ravenous!' He threw aside the blanket and moved to the fire, casually spearing two strips of venison with the spit. Laying it in place, he added fuel to the dwindling blaze.

Waylander said nothing, but sadness settled on him like a dark cloak.

4

Waylander woke first and made his way from the cave. Stripping off his shirt and leggings, he stepped into the icy steam and lay flat on his back, allowing the water to flow over him. The stream was mere inches deep, running over rounded rocks, but the force of the flow was strong and he felt himself gently sliding down the sloping stream-bed. Rolling over, he splashed his face and beard and stood up before clambering from the water, where he sat on the grass waiting for the dawn breezes to dry his skin.

'You look like a three-day-dead fish,' said Danyal.

'And you're beginning to smell like one,' he responded, grinning. 'Go on, wash yourself!'

For a moment she looked at him closely, then she shrugged and removed the green woollen tunic dress. Waylander leaned back and watched her. Her waist was slim, her hips smooth, her skin . . .

He turned away to watch a red squirrel leaping in the branches nearby, then stood and stretched. Near the stream was a thick screen of bushes, and within it a small clump of lemon balm. Pulling free a handful of the shield-shaped leaves, he carried them back to where Danyal sat.

'Here, crush these in your hand and wipe them on your skin.'

'Thank you,' she said, reaching up.

Suddenly aware of his nakedness, Waylander

51

found his clothes and dressed. He wished he still had a spare shirt, but the priest wore it and he was uncomfortably aware of the dust in his own.

Once dressed, Waylander returned to the cave and looped his chain-mail shoulder-guard in place over his black leather jerkin. Taking his boots, he removed the two spare knives and sharpened them with his whetstone before replacing them carefully in the sheaths stitched inside each boot.

Dardalion watched him, noting the care with which he handled his weapons.

'Could you spare me a knife?' he asked.

'Of course. Heavy or light?'

'Heavy.'

Waylander picked up his belt and pulled clear a dark sheath complete with ebony-handled blade. 'This should suffice. The blade is keen enough to shave with and double-edged.'

Dardalion threaded his narrow belt through the sheath and settled it in place against his right hip.

'Are you left-handed?' asked Waylander.

'No.'

'Then angle it on your left hip. That way, when you pull it clear the blade will face your enemy.'

'Thank you.'

Waylander buckled his own belt in place, then rubbed his chin. 'You worry me, priest,' he said.

'Why?'

'Yesterday you would have walked around a crawling bug. Now you are ready to kill a man. Was your faith so weak?'

'My faith remains, Waylander. But now I see things a little more clearly. You gave me that with your blood.'

'I wonder. Was it a gift – or a theft? I feel I have robbed you of something precious.'

'If you have, then be assured I do not miss it.'

'Time will tell, priest.'

'Call me Dardalion. You know that is my name.'

'Is "priest" no longer good enough for you?'

'Not at all. Would you prefer it if I called you "assassin"?'

'Call me what you like. Nothing you say will affect the way I perceive myself.'

'Have I offended you?' asked Dardalion.

'No.'

'You have not asked me about my duel with the enemy.'

'No, I have not.'

'Is it because you do not care?'

'No, Dardalion. I don't know why, but I *do* care. My reasons are far more simple. I deal in death, my friend – death which is final. You are here, therefore you killed him and he is no longer of interest to me. It disturbs me that you cut away his arms and legs, but I shall get over that, as I shall get over you once you are safely with Egel.'

'I had hoped we could be friends.'

'I have no friends. I wish for none.'

'Was it always so?'

'Always is a long time. I had friends before I became Waylander. But that was another universe, priest.'

'Tell me.'

'I see no reason why I should,' replied Waylander. 'Wake the children. We have a long day before us.'

Waylander strolled from the cave to where he had picketed the horses, then saddled them and rode his own gelding to the spot where he had hung the deer.

Taking a canvas bag, he cut several strips from the carcass and packed them away for the evening meal. Then he pulled the remains from the tree to lie on the grass for the wolves.

'Did you have friends, little doe?' he asked, staring at the blank grey eyes.

He turned his horse towards the cave, remembered the days of camaraderie at Dros Purdol. As a young officer he had excelled, though why he had no idea; he had always disliked authority, but had relished the discipline.

He and Gellan had been closer than brothers, always together whether on patrol or whoring. Gellan had been a witty companion and only in the Silver Sword tourney had they ever found themselves as opponents. Gellan always won, but then the man was inhumanly swift. They had parted when Waylander met Tanya – a merchant's daughter from Medrax Ford, a small town to the south of Skeln Pass. Waylander was in love before he knew it and had resigned his commission for life on the farm.

Gellan had been heartbroken. 'Still,' he had said on that last day, 'I expect I won't be long following you. Army life will be dreadfully dull!'

Waylander wondered if Gellan had done so. Was he a farmer somewhere? Or a merchant? Or was he dead in one of the many lost battles fought by the Drenai?

If the latter, Waylander guessed that a neat pile of corpses would surround his body, for his blade moved faster than a serpent's tongue.

'I should have stayed, Gellan,' he said. 'I really should.'

Gellan was hot and tired, sweat sliding down the

back of his neck under the chain-mail shoulder-guard and causing his spine to itch unbearably. He removed his black helm and ran his fingers through his hair. There was no breeze and he cursed softly.

Forty miles from Skultik and the relative security of Egel's camp – and the horses were tired, the men weary and dispirited. Gellan raised his right arm with fist clenched, giving the signal to 'Walk Horses'. Behind him the fifty riders dismounted; there was no conversation.

Sarvaj rode his mount alongside Gellan and the two men dismounted together. Gellan hooked his helm over the pommel of his saddle and pulled a linen cloth from his belt. Wiping the sweat from his face, he turned to Sarvaj.

'I don't think we'll find a village standing,' he said. Sarvaj nodded but did not reply. He had served under Gellan for half a year, and knew by now when the officer's comments were rhetorical.

They walked side by side for half an hour, then Gellan signalled for a rest stop and the men sat down beside their horses.

'Morale is low,' said Gellan and Sarvaj nodded. Gellan unclipped his red cloak, laying it over his saddle. Pushing his hands into the small of his back he stretched and groaned. Like most tall men, he found long hours in the saddle irksome and was plagued by continual backache.

'I stayed too long, Sarjav. I should have quit last year. Forty-one is too old for a Legion officer.'

'Dun Esterik is fifty-one,' Sarvaj commented.

Gellan grinned. 'If I had quit, you would have taken over.'

'And what a fine time to do so, with the army

crushed and the Legion skulking in the woods. No thank you!'

They had stopped in a small grove of elm and Gellan wandered off to sit alone. Sarvaj watched him go and then removed his helm; his dark brown hair was thinning badly and his scalp shone with sweat. Self-consciously he swept his hair back over the bald patches and replaced the helm. Fifteen years younger than Gellan, yet here he was looking like an old man. Then he grinned at his vanity and pulled the helm clear.

He was a stocky man – ungainly when not in the saddle – and one of the few career soldiers left in the Legion following the savage reductions of the previous autumn, when King Niallad had ordered a new militia programme. Ten thousand soldiers had been dismissed and only Gellan's determination had saved Sarvaj.

Now Niallad was dead and the Drenai all but conquered.

Sarvaj had shed no tears for the King for the man was a fool . . . worse than a fool!

'Off on his walks again?' said a voice and Sarvaj glanced up. Jonat sat down on the grass and stretched his long bony frame to full length, lying back with his head on his hands.

'He needs to think,' said Sarvaj.

'Yes. He needs to think about how to get us through the Nadir lands. I am sick of Skultik.'

'We are all sick of Skultik, but I don't see that riding north would help. It would merely mean fighting the Nadir tribes instead of the Vagrians.'

'At least we'd have a chance there. Here we have none.' Jonat scratched his thin black beard. 'If they'd

56

damn well listened to us last year, we would not be in this mess.'

'But they didn't,' said Sarvaj wearily.

'Pox-ridden courtiers! In some ways the Hounds did us a favour by butchering the whoresons.'

'Don't say that to Gellan – he lost a lot of friends in Skoda and Drenan.'

'We all lost friends,' snapped Jonat, 'and we'll lose a lot more. How long is Egel going to keep us cooped up in that damned forest?'

'I don't know, Jonat. Gellan doesn't know and I doubt if Egel himself knows.'

'We ought to strike north, through Gulgothir, and make for the eastern ports. I wouldn't mind settling down in Ventria. Always hot, plenty of women. We could hire out as mercenaries.'

'Yes,' said Sarvaj, too weary to argue. He failed to understand why Gellan had promoted Jonat to command of a Quarter – the man was full of bile ad bitterness.

But – and this was so galling – he was right. When Niallad's militia plan had first been put forward, the men in the Legion had bitterly opposed it. All the evidence indicated that the Vagrians were preparing for invasion. But Niallad claimed that the Vagrians themselves feared an attack from a strong Drenai army, and that his gesture would promote a lasting peace and a growth in trade.

'They should have roasted the bastard over a hot fire,' said Jonat.

'Who?' asked Sarvaj.

'The King, Gods rot his soul! The word is that he was killed by an assassin. They should have taken him in chains through the empire so that he could see the results of his stupidity.'

'He did what he thought was best,' said Sarvaj. 'He had the best motives.'

'Oh yes,' mocked Jonat. 'The best motives! He wanted to save money. *Our* money! If one good thing has come out of this war, it is that the noble class is gone for good.'

'Perhaps. But then Gellan is a nobleman.'

'Yes?'

'You don't hate him, do you?'

'He's no better than the rest.'

'I thought you liked him.'

'I suppose he's not a bad officer. Too soft. But underneath he still looks down on us.'

'I've never noticed it,' said Sarvaj.

'You don't look hard enough,' responded Jonat.

A horseman galloped into the grove and the men lurched to their feet with hands on sword-hilts. It was the scout, Kapra.

Gellan walked from the trees as the man dismounted. 'Anything to the east?' he asked.

'Three gutted villages, sir. A few refugees. I saw a column of Vagrian infantry – maybe two thousand. They made camp near Ostry, by the river.'

'No sign of cavalry?'

'No, sir,'

'Jonat!' called Gellan.

'Yes, sir.'

'The infantry will be expecting supplies. Take two men and scout to the east – when you see the wagons, get back here as fast as you can.'

'Yes, sir.'

'Kapra get yourself some food and then take a fresh mount and move out with Jonat. We will wait here for you.'

Sarvaj smiled. The difference in Gellan was startling now that the prospect of action loomed – his eyes were bright and alive and his voice curt and authoritative. Gone was the habitual stoop and the casually distant manner.

Egel had sent them out to find supplies to feed his beleaguered force, and so far they had been riding for three days without success. Villages had been wantonly destroyed and food stores taken or burnt. Cattle had been driven off and sheep poisoned in their fields.

'Sarvaj!'

'Sir?'

'Get the horses picketed and separate the men into five groups. There's a hollow past the thicket there and room for three fires – but none to be lit until the north star is clear and bright. You understand?'

'Yes, sir.'

'Four men to stand watch, change every four hours. You pick the places.'

'Yes, sir.'

Gellan smoothed his dark moustache and grinned boyishly.

'Let them be carrying salt beef,' he said. 'Pray for salt beef, Sarvaj!'

'And a small escort. It might be worth praying for a Ten.'

The smile faded from Gellan's face. 'Unlikely. They'll have at least a Quarter, maybe more. And then there will be the cartsmen. Still, cross that river when we reach it. When the men are resting, organise a sabre check; I want no blunted weapons when we ride.'

'Yes, sir. Why don't you get some rest?'

'I'm fine.'

'It wouldn't do any harm,' Sarvaj urged.

'You're fussing round me like an old woman. And don't think I don't appreciate it – but I am all right now, I promise.' Gellan smiled to hide the lie, but it did not fool Sarvaj.

The men were glad of the rest and without Jonat the mood lightened. Sarvaj and Gellan sat apart from the troop, chatting lightly about the past. Careful to avoid bringing up subjects which would remind Gellan of his wife and children, Sarvaj talked mainly of regimental memories.

'Do you mind if I ask you a question?' he said suddenly.

'Why should I?' answered Gellan.

'Why did you promote Jonat?'

'Because he's talented – he just doesn't realise it yet.

'He doesn't like you.'

'That doesn't matter. Watch him – he'll do well.'

'He brings the men down, lessens morale.'

'I know. Be patient.'

'He's pushing for us to run north – to break out of Skultik.'

'Stop worrying about it, Sarvaj. Trust me.'

I trust you, thought Sarvaj. I trust you to be finest swordsman in the Legion, to be a caring and careful officer and to be a firm friend. But Jonat? Jonat was a snake and Gellan was too trusting to see it. Given the time, Jonat would start a mutiny which would spread like a prairie fire through the dispirited ranks of Egel's army.

That night, as Gellan lay under his cloak away from the fire, he fell into a deep sleep and the dreams returned. He woke with a start and the tears flowed, though he swallowed the sobs that ached to be loose.

As he stood up and wandered away from camp, Sarvaj turned over and opened his eyes.

'Damn!' he whispered.

Towards dawn, Sarvaj arose and checked the sentries. This was the worst time of the night for concentration, and often a man who could stand a shift from dusk until midnight would find it impossible on another night to stay awake from midnight to dawn. Sarvaj had no idea what caused this phenomenon, but he knew what cured it; a man found sleeping on duty was lashed twenty times, and for a second offence the sentence was death. Sarvaj had no wish to see his men hung, so he made a name for himself as a nightwalker.

On this night, as he crept soundlessly through the wood, he found all four men alert and watchful. Pleased, he made his way back to his blankets where he found Gellan waiting for him. The officer looked tired, but his eyes were bright.

'You haven't slept,' said Sarvaj.

'No, I was thinking about the convoy. What we can't steal, we must destroy; the Vagrians must be taught to suffer. I don't understand the way they are conducting this war. If they left the farming villages alone there would always be sufficient supplies, but by raping and killing and burning they are making the land a wilderness. And it will turn on them. Come winter they will be on short rations and then, by all the Gods, we'll hit them.'

'How many wagons do you think there'll be?'

'For a force of two thousand? No fewer than twenty-five.'

'So,' said Sarvaj, 'if we take the convoy without loss we'll have around twenty escort riders, and three days in the open back to Skultik. That's asking for a lot of luck.'

'We are entitled to a little , my friend,' replied Gellan.

'Entitlement means nothing. I've lost at dice ten days in a row!'

'And on the eleventh?'

'I lose again. You know I never win at dice.'

'I know you never pay your debts,' said Gellan. 'You still owe me three silver pieces. Get the men together – Jonat should be back soon.'

But it was mid-morning before Jonat and the others cantered into the clearing. Gellan strode to meet them as Jonat lifted his leg over the pommel and slid to the ground.

'What news?' he asked.

'You were right, sir – there's a convoy three hours to the east. Twenty-seven wagons. But there are fifty mounted guards and two outriding scouts.'

'Were you seen?'

'I do not believe so,' replied Jonat stiffly.

'Tell me of the ground.'

'There's only one spot to take them, but it's close to Ostry and the infantry. However, the trail winds between two wooded hills; there's plenty of cover on both sides and the wagons will move slowly, for the track is muddy and steep.'

'How soon can we be there and in place?'

'Two hours. But that will leave it very tight, sir. We might even arrive as the wagons enter the trees on the far side.'

'That's *too* damned tight,' said Sarvaj, 'especially since they have scouts out.'

The risks were too great, Gellan knew, yet Egel

needed supplies desperately. What was worse, there was no time to plan, to think.

'Mount up!' he shouted.

As the troop thundered to the east, Gellan was cursing his shortcomings. What was needed before setting out was a powerful short speech to the men, something to fire their blood. But he had never been good with groups and knew the men felt him to be a cold, distant leader. Now he was uncomfortably aware that he was leading some of them – perhaps all – to their deaths on a harebrained attack best left to reckless, colourful men like Karnak or Dundas. How the men worshipped them – young, dashing and totally fearless, they led their Centuries against the Vagrians time and again, cutting and running, letting the enemy know there was still some fight in the Drenai.

They had little time for veterans like Gellan. Perhaps rightly so, he considered, as the wind tore at his face.

I should have retired, he thought. He had made up his mind to quit this autumn, but there was no quiet retirement for a Drenai officer now.

They reached the wood in under two hours and Gellan called a swift meeting with his under-officers. Two of his best bowmen were dispatched to deal with the advance scouts, and then he split his force to left and right of the track. He himself took command of the right-hand slope, giving Jonat the left, ignoring Sarvaj's disapproving glare.

With the orders given, the men settled down to wait and Gellan bit his lip, his mind racing round in infuriating circles as he struggled to find a flaw in his plan – a flaw he felt certain was there for all to see.

On the left-hand slope Jonat crouched behind a

thick bush, rubbing at his neck to ease the tension. On either side his men waited, bows ready and arrows notched,.

He wished Gellan had given this command to Sarvaj; he felt ill at ease with the responsibility.

'Why don't they come?' hissed a man to his left.

'Keep calm,' Jonat heard himself say. 'They'll come. And when they do, we'll kill them. *All* of them! We'll teach them what it means to invade Drenai lands.'

He grinned at the soldier and as the man grinned back, Jonat felt the tension ease from him. Gellan's plan was a good one, but then Jonat would expect little else from such an ice-man. To hear him talk you would think that was just another manoeuvre, but then Gellan was one of the warrior class, damn him! Not the son of a farm labourer best known for his ability to dance while drunk. Anger flared, but Jonat quelled it as the first creaking sounds of the wagons drifted up to him.

'Steady now!' he whispered. 'No one lets fly before the order. Pass the word along – I'll flay the man alive who disobeys!'

The wagons were led by six horsemen, their black horned helms down, swords in their hands. Behind them trundled the heavy wagons and carts, twenty-two horsemen filing along both sides of the track.

Slowly they came on and as the lead horsemen passed Jonat's position he notched an arrow to his bow, waiting, waiting . . .

'Now!' he yelled as the last wagons began the incline.

Black shafts flashed from the trees on both sides. Horses reared screaming and pandemonium came to the woods. One horseman tipped over the back of

64

his horse, two arrows appearing in his chest. Another pitched forward as a shaft sliced his throat.

Cartsmen dived for cover below the wagons as the massacre continued. Three horsemen galloped west, ducking low over their horses' necks. One was brought down when an arrow hammered into his mount's neck; as he scrambled to his feet, three shafts plunged into his back. The other two broke clear over the hill-top and straightened in their saddles . . .

Only to find themselves galloping towards Sarvaj and ten bowmen. Arrows peppered them and both horses fell dying, pitching their riders to the ground. Sarvaj and his men ran forward, killing the riders before they could rise.

In the woods Jonat led his men on a reckless charge to the wagons. Several of the cartsmen crawled out to meet them with hands raised, but the Drenai were in no mood for prisoners and they were despatched without mercy.

Within three minutes of the onset of the encounter, all the Vagrians were dead.

Gellan walked slowly down to the wagons. Six of the oxen used to pull the lead wagon were down and he ordered them cut clear. The action had gone better than he could have hoped for: seventy Vagrians dead and not one of his men wounded.

But now came the hard part – he had to get the wagons to Skultik.

'Good work, Jonat!' he said. 'Your timing was excellent.'

'Thank you, sir,'

'Strip the cloaks and helms from the dead – and get the bodies hidden in the woods.'

'Yes, sir,'

'We're going to be Vagrians for a little while.'
'It's a long way to Skultik,' said Jonat.
'We'll get there,' answered Gellan.

5

Waylander paused at the foot of a grass-covered hill and lifted Culas and Miriel from the saddle. The trees were thinning now and once over the crest the group would be on open ground. Waylander was tired; his limbs felt heavy and his eyes ached. A strong man, he was unused to this physical weariness and at a loss to understand it. Dardalion halted beside him and Danyal lowered Krylla into the priest's arms.

'Why are we stopping?' asked Danyal. Dardalion shrugged.

Waylander walked to the top of the hill and lay on his belly scanning the plain beyond. In the far distance a column of wagons was heading north, escorted by Vagrian cavalry. Waylander chewed at his lip and frowned.

Heading north?

Towards Egel?

This could only mean that Egel had been forced out of Skultik, or had made a run for Purdol. If either was the case, then there was little point in taking the children to the forest. But where else could they go? Waylander returned his gaze to the plain itself: thousands of square miles of flat, unending grassland, dotted with occasional trees and ground-hugging hedgerows. And yet the land was deceptive, he knew. What looked like flatlands hid scores of gullies and hollows, random dips and curves in the earth. The entire Vagrian army could be camped within the range of his sight and yet be hidden from him. He glanced back and saw the two little girls gathering bluebells. The sound of laughter echoed on the hillside. Waylander cursed softly. Moving back carefully from the crest he stood up and turned towards the group.

As he walked down the hill four men moved out of the trees.

Waylander's eyes narrowed, but he walked on. Dardalion had not seen the men and was talking to the boy, Culas.

The men spread out as Waylander approached. All four were bearded, their faces grim. Each wore a longsword and two of them carried bows. Waylander's crossbow was clipped to his belt, but it was useless, for the metal arms were snapped shut.

Dardalion turned as Waylander walked past him and saw the newcomers. The sisters ceased their flower-gathering and ran to Danyal, Culas moving alongside them as Dardalion went to stand just behind Waylander.

'Nice horses,' said the man at the centre of the group. He was taller than the others and wore a green cloak of homespun wool.

Waylander said nothing and Dardalion could feel the tension rising. He wiped his palm on his shirt and hooked his thumb in his belt close to the hilt of the knife. The green-cloaked newcomer observed the movement and smiled, his blue eyes flickering back to Waylander.

'You don't offer much in the way of greetings, my friend,' he said.

Waylander smiled. 'Did you come here to die?' he asked softly.

'Why this talk of dying? We are all Drenai here.' The man was uncomfortable now. 'My name is Baloc and these are my brothers Lak, Dujat and Meloc – he's the youngest. We're not here to cause you harm.'

'It would not matter if you were,' said Waylander. 'Tell your brothers to sit down and be comfortable.'

'I do not like your manner,' said Baloc, stiffening. He edged back a step and the brothers fanned out to form a semi-circle around Waylander and the priest.

'Your likes and dislikes are immaterial to me,' said Waylander. 'And if your brother makes one more move to the right, I'll kill him.'

The man stopped instantly and Baloc licked his lips. 'You are big on threats for a man with no sword.'

'That should tell you something,' said Waylander. 'But then you look like a stupid man, so I will spell it out for you. I don't need a sword to deal with scum like you. No, don't say a word – just listen! Today I am in a good mood. You understand? Had you arrived yesterday I would probably have killed you without all this conversation. But today I feel expansive. The sun is shining and all is well. So take your brothers and go back the way you came.'

Baloc stared into Waylander's eyes, unsure and aware of a growing unease. Two men against four and not a sword in sight. Two horses and a woman as the prize. Yet still he was unsure.

The man was so confident, so calm. Not an ounce of tension showed in his stance or his manner . . . and his eyes were cold as tombstones.

Baloc grinned suddenly and spread his arms. 'All this talk of death and killing . . . Is there not enough trouble in the world? All right, we'll leave.' As he backed away, watching Waylander, his brothers joined him and all the men disappeared back into the trees.

'Run,' said Waylander.

'What?' asked Dardalion. But the dark-haired warrior was already sprinting towards the horses, pulling his crossbow clear and snapping the hinges open.

'Lie down!' he yelled and Danyal hurled herself to the ground, dragging the sisters with her.

Black-shafted arrows hissed from the trees. One flashed by Dardalion's head and he dived for the grass; a second missed Waylander by inches. Snapping two bolts into place and stretching the bow-arms tight, he ran for the trees, zig-zagging and ducking. Arrows flew perilously close. One hissed above Dardalion; he heard a choking cry and rolled over. The boy, Culas, had remained standing but now he knelt in pain, his small hands clutching a shaft buried in his belly.

Anger roared through Dardalion and with knife in hand he followed Waylander. As he went, a scream came from the forest . . . then another. Dardalion entered the trees at a run and saw two of the men down while Waylander, a knife in each hand, faced the other pair. Baloc ran forward, his sword flashing towards Waylander's neck, but Waylander ducked under the sweeping blade and rammed his right-hand knife in to the man's groin. Baloc doubled over and fell, dragging Waylander with him. As the last robber ran forward with sword raised, Dardalion's arm came up and swept down. The black blade

70

thudded home in the robber's throat and he toppled backwards to writhe on the dark earth. Waylander wrenched his knife clear of Baloc and then, grabbing the man's hair, pulled his head back.

'There are some who never learn,' he said, opening the man's jugular.

Standing, he moved to the writhing man downed by Dardalion and, tearing the knife clear, wiped the blade on the man's jerkin before returning it to the priest. Recovering his two bolts from the other bodies, he cleaned his crossbow and pressed the bow-arms back into place alongside the handle.

'Well thrown!' he said.

'They've killed the boy,' Dardalion told him.

'Blame me,' said Waylander bitterly. 'I should have killed them instantly.'

'They may have meant no harm,' said Dardalion.

'Collect two swords and scabbards and one of the bows,' asked Waylander. 'I'll see to the boy.'

Leaving Dardalion in the woods, he walked slowly back to the horses. The sisters were sitting together, silent in shock; Danyal was crying as Culas lay with his head in her lap, his eyes open and his hands still clutching the arrow.

Waylander knelt by his side. 'Is there much pain?'

The boy nodded. He bit his lip and tears flowed. 'I'm going to die! I know I am.'

'Of course you are not,' said Danyal fiercely. 'We'll just rest for a little while, then we'll take the arrow out for you.'

Culas let go of the arrow and lifted his hand; it was drenched in blood. 'I can't feel my legs,' he wailed. Waylander reached out and took the boy's hand.

'Listen to me, Culas. There is nothing to frighten

you. In a little while you will go to sleep, that's all. Just a deep sleep . . . there will be no pain.'

'It hurts now,' said Culas. 'It's like fire.'

As Waylander gazed down on the young face, distorted now by agony, he saw again his son lying among the flowers.

'Close your eyes, Culas, and listen to my voice. A long time ago I had a farm. A lovely farm, and there was a white pony that could run like the wind . . .' And as he spoke Waylander drew his knife and touched it to Culas' thigh. The boy did not react. Waylander carried on speaking in a low, gentle voice and turned the knifepoint into Culas' groin, slicing the artery at the top of the thigh. Blood gushed from the wound and still Waylander's voice continued as Culas' face grew pale and a blue tinge appeared on his eyelids.

'Sleep softly,' whispered Waylander and the boy's head sagged sideways. Danyal blinked and looked up, seeing the knife in Waylander's hand. Her arm lashed out, catching him on the side of the head.

'You swine, you despicable swine! You killed him!'

'Yes,' he said. He stood up and touched his lip. Blood was seeping from a split at the edge of his mouth where her fist had caught him.

'Why? Why did you do it?'

'I enjoy killing boys' he said sardonically and walked to his horse. Dardalion joined him; the priest was now wearing Baloc's longsword.

'What happened?' he asked, passing a second sword and belt to Waylander.

'I killed the boy . . . he would have lingered in pain for days. Gods, priest, I wish I had never met you! Get the children mounted and head north – I'm going to scout around for a while.'

He rode for an hour, alert and watchful, until he found a shallow dip in the land. Riding down into it, he located a camp-site near a broken tree and dismounted. After feeding his horse the last of the grain, he sat down on the stump of the tree, where he stayed without moving for another hour until the light began to fade, then he walked up the slope and stood waiting for Dardalion.

The group arrived just as the sun slid behind the western mountains. Waylander led them to the camp-site and lifted the sisters from the saddle.

'There's a man coming to see you, Waylander,' said Krylla, curing her arms around his neck.

'How do you know?'

'He told me; he said he would join us for supper.'

'When did you see him?'

'A little while ago. I was nearly asleep and Danyal was holding me and I must have drifted. The man said he would see you tonight.'

'Was he a nice man?' asked Waylander.

'His eyes were on fire,' said Krylla.

Waylander lit a small fire in a circle of stones, then walked out on to the plain to see if the glare could be spotted. Satisfied that the camp-site was hidden, he made his way slowly through the long grass towards the hollow.

A cloud drifted across the moon and the plain was plunged into darkness. Waylander froze. A whisper of movement to his right saw him drop to the ground, knife in hand.

'Get up, my son,' came a voice from beside him.

Waylander rolled left and came up on one knee,

knife extended. 'You will not need your weapon. I am alone and very old.'

Waylander eased his way back along the trail and edged to the right.

'You are a cautious man,' said the voice. 'Very well, I will go on and meet you by your fire.'

The cloud passed and silver light bathed the plain. Waylander straightened. He was alone. Swiftly he scouted the area. Nothing. He returned to the fire.

Sitting beside it with hands outstretched to the warmth was an old man. Krylla and Miriel were sitting beside him, Dardalion and Danyal opposite.

Waylander approached cautiously and the man did not look up. He was bald and beardless and the skin of his face hung in slender folds. Waylander guessed from the width of his shoulders that he had once been very strong. Now he was skeletal and his eyelids were flat against the sockets.

A blind man!

'Why doesn't your face fit?' said Miriel.

'It did once,' said the old man. 'I was considered handsome in my youth, when my hair was golden and my eyes emerald green.'

'You look awful now,' said Krylla.

'I am sure that I do! Thankfully I can no longer see myself and therefore am spared great disappointment. Ah, the Wanderer returns,' said the old man, tilting his head.

'Who are you?' asked Waylander.

'A traveller like yourself.'

'You travel alone?'

'Yes . . . but not as alone as you.'

'Are you the mystic who spoke to Krylla?'

'I had that honour – and a delightful child she is.

Very gifted for one so young. She tells me that you are a saviour, a great hero.'

'She sees with the eye of a child. All is not always as it seems,' said Waylander.

'Children see many things we no longer see. If we did, would we wage war so terribly?'

'Are you a priest, man? I've had my damned fill of priests,' snapped Waylander.

'No. I am merely a student of life. I would like to have been a priest, but I fear my appetites always had the better of me. I could never resist a pretty face or a fine wine. Now that I am old I wish for other delights, but even these are now denied me.'

'How did you find us?'

'Krylla showed me the way.'

'And I suppose you would like to travel with us?'

The man smiled. 'Would that I could! No, I shall bide with you tonight, and then I must embark on another journey.'

'We do not have much food,' said Waylander.

'But you are welcome to what we have,' said Dardalion, moving to sit beside the old man.

'I am not hungry, but thank you. You are the priest?'

'Yes.'

The old man reached out and touched the hilt of Dardalion's dagger. 'An unusual object for a priest to carry?'

'These are unusual days,' answered Dardalion, his face flushing.

'They must be.' He turned his head towards Waylander. 'I cannot see you, but I feel your power. And also your anger. Are you angry with me?'

'Not yet,' said Waylander, 'but I am wondering when you will arrive at the point of your visit.'

'You think I have some ulterior motive?'

'Not at all,' said Waylander drily. 'A blind man invites himself to supper through the mystic talents of a frightened child and finds our fire in the middle of a veritable wilderness. What could be more natural? Who are you and what do you want?'

'Do you always have to be so loathsome?' said Danyal. 'I don't care who he is, he's welcome. Or perhaps you'd like to kill him? After all, you haven't killed anyone for a couple of hours.'

'Gods, woman, your prattle turns my stomach,' snarled the warrior. 'What do you want from me? So the boy died. That's what happens in wars . . . people *die*. And before you let fly with your viper responses, remind yourself of this: when I shouted to get down I see *you* managed to save yourself. Perhaps if you had thought about the boy, he wouldn't have had an arrow in his guts.'

'That's not fair!' she shouted.

'Life is like that.' He swept up his blankets and walked away from the group, his heart pounding as rage threatened to engulf him. He strode to the top of the rise and stared out over the plain. Somewhere out there were riders hunting him. They could not allow him to live. For if they failed in their quest their own lives would be forfeit. And here was Waylander trapped by a priest and a woman – caught like a monkey in a net while the lions moved in.

Folly. Sheer folly.

He should never have accepted a contract from that Vagrian serpent, Kaem. The man's name was a byword for treachery: Kaem the Cruel, Kaem the Killer of Nations – the web-weaver at the centre of the Vagrian army.

All of Waylander's instincts had screamed at him

to spurn Kaem's contract, but he had ignored them. Now the Vagrian general would have sent out groups of assassins in every direction; they would know he had not headed south or west, and the ports to the east would be closed to him. Only the north beckoned – and the killers would be watching all paths to Skultik.

Waylander cursed softly. Kaem had offered 24,000 gold pieces for the contract and, as a gesture of faith, had lodged half of the amount in Waylander's name with Cheros, the main banker in Gulgothir. Waylander had completed the contract with his customary skill, though his memory burned with the shame of it. Seeing again the arrow in flight, he squeezed shut his eyes . . .

The night was cool, the stars gleaming like spearpoints. Waylander stretched, forcing his mind to the present, but his victim's face returned again and again . . . a gentle face, haunted by failure . . . soft eyes and a kind smile. He had been stooping to pick a flower when Waylander's bolt pierced his back . . .

'No!' shouted Waylander, sitting upright, his hand lashing out as if to drive the memory from him. Think of something else . . . anything else!

After the kill he had slipped away to the east, for the journey to Vagria and the promise of Kaem's gold. While on the road he met a merchant travelling from the north who told him in conversation of the death of Cheros the Banker. Three assassins had killed him at his home and made off with a fortune in gold and gems.

Waylander had known then that he was betrayed, but some instinct – some inner compulsion – drove him on. He had arrived at Kaem's palace and scaled a high garden wall. Once inside, he killed two guard dogs and entered the main building. Locating Kaem's room had posed a problem, but he woke a serving girl and forced her at knifepoint to lead him to the general's bedchamber. Kaem was asleep in his apartments on the third floor of the palace. Waylander struck the girl on the neck, catching her as she fell and lowering her to a white fur rug on the floor. Then he went to the bed and touched his knife to Kaem's throat. The general's eyes flared open.

'Could you have not come at a more reasonable hour?' he had asked smoothly.

Waylander's knife pressed forward a fraction of an inch and blood seeped from the cut as Kaem stared into the dark eyes above him.

'I see you have heard about Cheros. I hope you don't think it was my doing.' The knife pressed deeper and this time Kaem winced.

'I know it was your doing,' hissed Waylander.

'Can we talk about it?'

'We can talk about 24,000 gold pieces.'

'Of course.'

Suddenly Kaem twisted and his arm lashed out to knock Waylander from the bed. The speed of the attack stunned the assassin and he rolled to his feet to find himself facing the wiry general who had now clambered from the bed and pulled a sword from the scabbard hanging on the bedpost.

'You're getting old, Waylander,' said Kaem.

The door burst open and a young man ran in, carrying a bow with arrow notched to the string.

Waylander's arm shot forward and the young man collapsed with a black-bladed knife in his throat. Waylander ran to the door, hurdling the corpse.

'You'll die for that!' screamed Kaem. 'You hear me? You will *die*!'

The sound of sobbing followed Waylander as he ran down the wide stairs, for the dead man was Kaem's only son . . .

And now the hunters were searching for his killer.

Wrapped in his blankets with his back against a jutting rock, Waylander heard the old man approach, the coarse cloth of his robes whispering against the long grass.

'May I join you?'

'Why not?'

'It is a glorious night, is it not?'

'How does a blind man define glorious?'

'The air is fresh and cool and the silence a mask – a cloak which hides so much life. To the right there, a hare is sitting, wondering why two men are so close to his burrow. Away to the left is a red fox – a vixen by the smell – and she is hunting the hare. And overhead the bats are out, enjoying the night as am I.'

'It's too bright for my liking,' said Waylander.

'It is always hard to be hunted.'

'I had a feeling you knew.'

'Knew what? The feeling of being hunted, or the fact that the Dark Brotherhood are seeking you?'

'Either. Both. It does not matter.'

'You were right, Waylander. I was seeking you and there is an ulterior motive. So shall we stop fencing?'

'As you wish.'

'I have a message for you.'

'From whom?'

'That is not part of my brief. And also it would

79

take more time than I have to explain it to you. Let me say only that you have been given a chance to redeem yourself.'

'Nice of you. However, there is nothing to redeem.'

'If you say so. I do not wish to argue. Soon you will reach the camp of Egel where you will find an army in disarray: a force doomed to ultimate defeat. You can aid them.'

'Are your wits addled, old man? Nothing can save Egel.'

'I did not say "save". I said "aid".'

'What is the purpose of aiding a dead man?'

'What was the purpose in saving the priest?'

'It was a whim, damn you! And it will be a long time before I allow myself another such.'

'Why are you angry?'

Waylander chuckled, but there was no humour in the sound.

'You know what has happened to you?' asked the old man. 'You have been touched by the Source and those are the chains you rail against. Once you were a fine man and knew love. But love died, and since no man lives in a vacuum you filled yourself not with hate but with emptiness. You have not been alive these past twenty years – you have been a walking corpse. Saving the priest was your first decent deed in two decades.'

'So you came to preach?'

'No, I am preaching in spite of myself. I cannot explain the Source to you. The Source is about foolishness, splendid foolishness; it is about purity and joy. But against the wisdom of the world it fails, because the Source knows nothing of greed, lust, deceit, hate, nor evil of any kind. Yet it always triumphs. For the Source always gives something for nothing: good for evil, love for hate.'

'Sophistry. A small boy died yesterday – he hated no one, but an evil whoreson cut him down. All over this land good, decent people are dying in their thousands. Don't tell me, about triumphs. Triumphs are built on the blood of innocence.'

'You see? I speak foolishness. But in meeting you I know what triumph means. I understand one more fragment.'

'I am pleased for you,' mocked Waylander, despising himself as he spoke.

'Let me explain,' said the old man softly. 'I had a son – not a dazzling boy, not the brightest of men. But he cared about many things. He had a dog that was injured in a fight with a wolf and we should have killed the dog, for it was grievously hurt. But my son would not allow it; he stitched the wounds himself and sat with the hound for five days and nights, willing it to live. But it died. And he was heartbroken, for life was precious to him. When he became a man I passed on everything I had to him. He became a steward, and I left on my travels. My son never forgot the dog and it coloured everything he did . . .'

'Is there a point to this tale?'

'That depends on you, for you enter the tale at this juncture. My son saw that everything I had left him to care for was in peril, and he tried desperately to save it. But he was too soft, and raiders came to my lands and slew my people. Then my son learnt the error of his ways and became truly a man, for he now knew that life often brings hard decisions. So he gathered his generals and worked on a plan to free his people. And then an assassin slew him.

His life was ended . . . and as he died all he could see was a failure, and a terrible despair went out from him that touched me a thousand leagues away.

'A terrible rage filled me and I thought to kill you. I could, even now. But then the Source touched me. And I am now here merely to talk.'

'You son was King Niallad?'

'Yes. I am Orien of the Two Blades. Or, more exactly, I was Orien once.'

'I am sorry for your son. But it is what I do.'

'You speak of the death of innocents. Perhaps – had my son lived – many of those innocents would also have lived.'

'I know. And I regret it . . . but I can't change it.'

'It is not important,' said Oren. 'But *you* are important. The Source has chosen you, but the choice is yours.'

'Chosen me for what? My only talent is hardly one your Source would admire.'

'It is not your only talent. You know of my early life?'

'I know you were a great warrior, never beaten in battle.'

'Have you seen the stature of me in Drenan?'

'Yes. The Armour of Bronze.'

'Indeed. The Armour. Many would like to know its whereabouts and the Brotherhood seek it, for it threatens the Vagrian empire.'

'Is it magic then?'

'No – at least, not in the sense that you mean. It was made long ago by the great Axellian. Superb workmanship and the two swords are of a metal beyond compare – a silver steel that never dulls.

With that Armour Egel has a chance – no more than that.'

'But you said it carries no magic?'

'The magic is in the minds of men. When Egel wears that Armour it will be as if Orien has returned. And Orien was never beaten. Men will flock to Egel and he will grow – he is the best of them, an iron man of indomitable will.'

'And you want me to fetch this Armour?'

'Yes.'

'I take it there is some danger involved?'

'I think that is a fair assessment.'

'But the Source will be with me?'

'Perhaps. Perhaps not.'

'I thought you said I was chosen for this task. What is the point of having aid from a God without power?'

'A good question, Waylander. I hope you learn the answer.'

'Where is the Armour?'

'I hid it in a deep cave high up the side of a tall mountain.'

'Somehow that doesn't surprise me. Where?'

'Do you know the Nadir Steppes?'

'I am not going to like this.'

'I take it that you do. Well, two hundred miles west of Gulgothir is a range of mountains . . .'

'The Mountains of the Moon.'

'Exactly. At the centre of the range is Raboas . . .'

'The Sacred Giant.'

'Yes,' said Orien, grinning. 'And that's where it is.'

'That is insane. No Drenai has ever penetrated that far into Nadir lands.'

'I did.'

'Why? What purpose could you have had?'

'I wondered that at the time. Put it down to a whim, Waylander; you know about whims. Will you fetch the Armour?'

'Tell me, Orien, how much of a mystic are you?'

'What do you mean?'

'Can you see the future?'

'In part,' admitted Orien.

'What are my chances of success?'

'That depends on who accompanies you.'

'Then let's say that the Source chooses the right company.'

The old man rubbed his ruined sockets and leaned back.

'You have no chance,' he admitted.

'That's what I thought.'

'But that is no reason to refuse.'

'You are asking me to ride a thousand miles through hostile lands swarming with savages. You tell me that the Brotherhood are also seeking the Armour? Do they know it is in Nadir lands?'

'They know.'

'So they will be hunting me also?'

'They are already hunting you.'

'Agreed. But they don't know where I'm going. If I set off on this quest of yours, they'll soon find out.'

'True.'

'So . . . there will be Nadir warriors, warrior wizards and Vagrian troops. And if I get through those I have to scale the Sacred Giant, the holiest place on the Steppes, and risk myself in the bowels of a dark mountain. Then I merely have to ride out again, burdened down with half a ton of armour.'

'Eighty pounds.'

'Whatever!'

'There are also the werebeasts who live in the caves of Raboas. They don't like fire.'

'That's comforting,' said Waylander.

'So will you go?'

'I am beginning to understand your comments concerning foolishness,' said the warrior. 'But yes, I will go.'

'Why?' asked Orien.

'Does there have to be a reason?'

'No. But I am curious.'

'Then let us say it's in memory of a dog that should not have died.'

6

Dardalion closed his eyes. Danyal was asleep beside the sisters and the young priest released his spirit to the Void. The moon was an eldritch lantern and silver light bathed the vast Sentran Plain, while the forest of Skultik spread like a stain from the Delnoch mountains.

Dardalion hovered below the clouds, his mind free of doubts and cares. Normally when he soared he found himself clothed in shimmering robes of pale blue. But now he was naked and, try as he might, no robes appeared. He didn't care. In the blink of an astral eye he was garbed in silver armour, a white cloak flowing from his shoulders. By his side hung two silver swords and as he drew them exhilaration flooded him. Far to the west, the camp-fires of a Vagrian army blazed like fallen stars. Dardalion sheathed his swords and flew towards them. More than ten thousand men were camped in the foothills of the Skoda mountains. Eight hundred tents lined the area in ranks of four and a wooden corral had been hastily erected for two thousand horses. Cattle grazed on the mountainside and a sheep-pen had been built beside a fast-moving stream.

Dardalion moved south over rivers and plains, hills and forests. A second Vagrian force was camped outside Drenan – no fewer than thirty thousand men and twenty thousand horses. The city gates of oak and bronze had been sundered, and no citizens could be seen within its walls. To the east of the city a vast trench had been carved from the earth and Dardalion swooped towards it – then veered away, repulsed. The trench was filled with bodies. Two hundred yards in length and six yards wide, the enormous grave housed more than a thousand corpses. Not one wore the armour of a soldier. Steeling himself, Dardalion returned to the trench.

It was over ten feet deep.

Returning to the night sky, the priest headed east where a Vagrian army was waiting on the borders of Lentria. The Lentrian force, only two thousand strong, was camped within a mile, waiting grimly for the invasion. North travelled Dardalion, following the line of the sea until he reached the eastern valleys and finally the sea citadel of Purdol. By torchlight the battle for Purdol was still being waged. The Drenai fleet was sunk in the harbour mouth and the Vagrian army camped in the area of the docks. The fortress of Purdol, manned by six thousand Drenai warriors, was holding back a Vagrian force of more than forty thousand led by Kaem, the Prince of War.

Here, for the first time, the Vagrians were facing a setback.

With no siege engines they could not storm the thirty-foot walls, and were relying on ladders and ropes. They were dying in their hundreds.

Dardalion soared to the west until he reached Skultik, the forest of dark legend. It was immense, thousands of square miles of trees, clearings, hills and valleys. Three towns – one verging on city status – had been built within the forest: Tonis, Preafa and Skarta. To the last of these flew Dardalion.

Here Egel was camped with four thousand Legion

warriors. As Dardalion neared the clearing he felt the presence of another mind and his swords flashed into his hand. Before him hovered a slender man in the blue robes of the Source priest.

'Do not pass me,' said the man quietly.

'If you say not, brother,' answered Dardalion.

'Who are you that calls me brother?'

'I am a priest, even as you.'

'A priest of what?'

'Of the Source.'

'A priest with swords? I think not. If you must slay me, do so.'

'I am not here to slay you. I am as I claim.'

'Then you were a priest?'

'I *am* a priest?'

'I sense death upon you. You have klled.'

'Yes. An evil man.'

'Who are you to judge?'

'I did not judge him – his own deeds did that for him. Why are you here?'

'We are watching.'

'We?'

'My brothers and I. We tell the Lord Egel when the enemy is approaching.'

'How many brothers are here?'

'Almost two hundred. There were three hundred and seven of us at the start. One hundred and twelve have joined the Source.'

'Murdered?'

'Yes,' said the man sadly. 'Murdered. The Dark Brotherhood destroyed them. We try to be careful as we soar, for they are swift and merciless.'

'One tried to kill me,' said Dardalion, 'and I learned to fight.'

'Each man choses his own path.'

'You do not approve?'

'It is not for me to approve or disapprove. I do not judge you. How can I?'

'You thought I was of the Brotherhood?'

'Yes. For you carry a sword.'

'And yet you stood before me. You have great courage.'

'It is no hardship for me to be sent to join my God.'

'What is your name?'

'Clophas. And you?'

'Dardalion.'

'May the Source bless you, Dardalion. But I think you should leave now. As the moon reaches its height, the Brotherhood take to the sky.'

'Then I shall wait with you.'

'I do not desire your company.'

'You have no choice.'

'So be it.'

They waited in silence as the moon climbed higher. Clophas refused to speak and Dardalion took to studying the forest below. Egel had camped his army outside the southern wall of Skarta and the priest could see scouts patrolling the edge of the trees. It would be no easy task for the Vagrians to conquer the Earl of the North, for few were the sites for pitched battles within Skultik. On the other hand were they to attack the towns Egel would be left with an army intact, but no one to defend. Egel himself was faced with similar problems. Staying where he was guaranteed short term safety, but could not win him the war. Leaving Skultik was suicidal for he had not the resources to conquer one Vagrian army. To stay was to lose, to leave was to die.

And while the problems mounted the lands of the Drenai were becoming the charnel house of the continent.

Dardalion found the thought depressing in the extreme, and was about to return to his body when he heard the soul scream from Clophas.

He glanced round to see that the priest had gone and five black-armoured warriors floated below him, dark swords in their hands.

Furious, Dardalion drew his swords and attacked. The five warriors did not see him until he was upon them, and two vanished into oblivion as his silver blades pierced their astral bodies. Then as the remaining three rushed him, he parried a thrust with his left-hand blade and blocked a sweeping cut with his right. His fury gave him lightning speed and his eyes blazed as he fought. Twisting his right wrist, he slid his sword under one warrior's guard, the blade piercing the man's throat. The warrior vanished. The last two pulled back from the fight and sped west, but Dardalion flew after them, catching the first just above the Skoda mountain range and killing him with a savage cut. The sole survivor returned to the sanctuary of his body with but a second to spare . . .

His eyes jerked open and he screamed. Soldiers ran to his tent and he lurched to his feet. Sprawled on the ground beside him lay his four companions, rigid in death.

'What in Hell's name is happening here?' demanded an officer, pushing men aside as he entered the tent. He gazed down at the corpses, then up at the survivor.

'The priests have learned to fight,' muttered the warrior, his breath coming in short gasps and his heart pounding.

'You are telling me that these men were killed by Source priests? It is inconceivable.'

'One priest,' said the man.

The officer waved the soldiers away and they were glad to depart. Hardened as they were to death and destruction, the Vagrian troops wanted no part of the Dark Brotherhood.

The officer sat down on a canvas-backed chair. 'You look as if you have seen a ghost, Pulis, my friend.'

'No jests, please,' said Pulis. 'The man almost killed me.'

'Well, you've killed enough of his friends these past months.'

'That is true. But nevertheless it is unsettling.'

'I know. What is the world coming to when Source priests stoop to defending themselves?'

The warrior glared at the young officer, but said nothing.

Pulis was no coward – he had proved that a score of times – but the silver priest had frightened him. Like most warriors of the Brotherhood he was not a true mystic, relying on the power of the Leaf to free him from his body. But even so, with his powers enhanced, he had experienced visions . . . flashes . . . of a premonitory nature. It had been so with the priest.

Pulis had felt a terrible danger emanating from the silver warrior – not just personal danger, but a timeless threat which would attack his cause from now until the end of time. Yet it was so nebulous, more an emotional reaction than a vision. Although he had seen something . . . what was it? He searched his memory.

That was it! A runic number hanging in the sky bathed in flames.

A number. Meaning what? Days? Months? Centuries?

'Thirty,' he said aloud.

'What?' replied the officer. 'The Thirty?'

A cold chill hit Pulis, like a demon crossing his grave.

Dawn found Waylander alone as he opened his eyes and yawned. Strange, he thought, for he could not remember falling asleep. But he did remember his promise to Orien and he shook his head, puzzled. He glanced round, but the old man had gone.

He rubbed his chin, scratching at the skin below his beard.

The Armour of Orien.

Such a grand nonsense.

'This quest will kill you,' he whispered.

Taking a knife from his belt he honed it for several minutes, then shaved with care. His skin was raw under the blade, but the morning breeze felt good on his face.

Dardalion emerged from the hollow and sat beside him. Waylander nodded, but did not speak. The priest looked tired, his eyes set deep in his face; he was thinner now, thought Waylander and subtly changed.

'The old man is dead,' said Dardalion. 'You should have spoken to him.'

'I did,' said Waylander.

'No, I mean *really* speak. Those few words at the fire were nothing. Do you know who he was?'

'Orien,' said Waylander. The look of surprise on Dardalion's face was comical.

'You recognised him?'

'No. He came to me last night.'

'He had great power,' said Dardalion softly. 'For he died without leaving the fire. He told us many tales of his life, then he lay back and slept. I was beside him and he died in his sleep.'

'You were mistaken,' said Waylander.

'I think not. What did you speak about?'

'He asked me to fetch something for him. I said that I would.'

'What was it?'

'No business of yours, priest.'

'It is too late to turn me away, warrior. When you saved my life, you opened your soul to me. When your blood was in my throat, I knew your lifee and every instant of your being flooded me. I look in a mirror now and I see you.'

'You are looking in the wrong mirrors.'

'Tell me of Dakeyras,' said Dardalion.

'Dakeyras is dead,' snapped Waylander. 'But you have made your point, Dardalion. I saved your life. Twice! You owe me the right to my solitude.'

'To allow you to return to the man you were? I do not think so. Look at yourself. Half your life has been wasted. You suffered great tragedy – and it broke you. You wanted to die, but instead you killed only part of yourself. Poor Dakeyras, lost for two decades while Waylander strode the world, slaying for gold he would never spend. All those souls sent to the Void. And for what? To lessen a pain you could not touch.'

'How dare you preach to me!' said Waylander. 'You talk of mirrors? Tell me what you have become since killing two men.'

'Six men. And there will be more,' said Dardalion.

'Yes, that is why I understand you. I may be wrong in all that I do, but I will stand before my God and I will say that I did what I felt was right – that I defended the weak against the evil strong. You taught me that. Not Waylander the man who kills for money, but Dakeyras, the man who saved the priest.'

'I do not want to talk any more,' said Waylander, staring away.

'Did Orien know that you killed his son?'

The assassin swung back. 'Yes, he knew. It was my foulest deed. But I will pay for it, priest. Orien saw to that. You know, I used to think that hatred was the most powerful force on earth. And yet last night I learned something bitter. He forgave me . . . and that is worse than hot irons on my flesh. You understand?'

'I think I do.'

'So now I will die for him, and that will settle my debts.'

'Your death will settle nothing. What did he ask you to do?'

'To fetch his Armour.'

'From Raboas, the Sacred Giant.'

'He told you?'

'Yes. He also told me that a man named Kaem would be hunting the same treasure.'

'Kaem hunts me. But he would be wise not to find me.'

Kaem's dreams were troubled. The Vagrian general had commandeered a fine house overlooking the Purdol harbour, and guards patrolled the gardens, while his two most trusted soldiers stood outside his door. The window was barred and the heat within the small room oppressive.

He came awake with a jerk and sat up scrabbling for his sword. the door opened and Dalnor ran inside, blade in hand.

'What is it, my lord?'

'It is nothing. A dream. Did I call out?'

'Yes, my lord. Shall I stay with you?'

'No.' Kaem took a linen towel from the chair beside the bed and wiped the sweat from his face and head. 'Damn you, Waylander,' he whispered.

'My lord?'

'Nothing. Leave me.' Kaem swung his legs from the bed and walked to the window. He was a thin man and totally hairless, his wrinkled skin giving him the appearance of a beached turtle robbed of his shell. Many thought him a comical figure on first sight, but most came to see him as he was: the finest strategist of the age, the man dubbed the Prince of War. His soldiers respected him, though not with the adoration reserved for some other and more charismatic generals. But that suited him, for he was uncomfortable with emotions and found such displays among the men childlike and foolish. What he wanted was obedience from his officers and courage from his men. He expected both. He *demanded* both.

Now his own courage was being tested. Waylander had killed his son and he had sworn to see him dead. But Waylander was a skilled hunter, and Kaem felt sure that one dark night he would once more wake to feel a knife at his throat.

Or worse . . . he might not wake at all. The Brotherhood were hunting the assassin, but first reports were not encouraging. A tracker dead, and talk now amongst the Brotherhood of a mystic war-rior priest who travelled with the assassin.

Kaem, for all his strategic skills, was a cautious man. As long as Waylander lived he was a threat to Kaem's plans. Such grand plans – that when this conquest was complete he would rule an area greater than Vagria itself. Lentria, Drenai, and the Sathuli lands to the north – sixteen ports, twelve major cities and the spice routes to the east.

Then the civil war could begin, and Kaem would risk his strength against the failing guile of the Emperor. Kaem wandered to the bronze mirror on the far wall and gazed at his reflection. The crown would look out of place upon his bony head, but then he would not have to wear it often.

He returned to his bed, calmer now. And slept.

He found himself on a dark mountain, under strange stars, his mind dazed and confused. Before him was an old man in ragged brown robes. His eyes were closed as he spoke:

'Welcome, general. Do you seek the Armour?'

'Armour?' asked Kaem. 'What armour?'

'The Armour of Bronze. Orien's Armour.'

'He hid it.' said Kaem. 'No man knows where.'

'I know.'

Kaem sat down opposite the old man. Like all students of modern history, he had heard of this Armour. Some claimed it had magical properties which ensured victory to the wearer, but these were simple souls, or saga-poets. Kaem had long studied the process of war and knew that Orien was merely a master strategist. And yet the Armour was a symbol and a powerful one.

'Where is it?' he asked.

The old man did not open his eyes. 'How badly do you desire it?'

'I would like it,' said Kaem, 'but it is not important.'

'How do you define importance?'

'I will win with it, or without it.'

'Are you so sure, general? Purdol resists you and Egel has an army within Skultik.'

'Purdol is mine. It may take a month, but it will fall. And Egel is trapped – he cannot harm me.'

'He can if he has the Armour.'

'How so? Is it magic, then?'

'No, it is merely metal. But it is a symbol and the Drenai will flock to the man who wears it. Even your own soldiers know of its supposed properties and their morale will suffer. You know this is true.'

'Very well,' said Kaem. 'I accept that it could harm me. Where is it?'

'In the lands of the Nadir.'

'That covers a wide area, old man.'

'It is hidden in the heart of the Mountains of the Moon.'

'Why do you tell me this? Who are you?'

'I am a dreamer within a dream – your dream, Kaem. My words are true, and your hopes rest on how you interpret them.'

'How will I find the Armour?'

'Follow the man who seeks it.'

'Who is this man?'

'Whom do you fear most in the world of flesh?'

'Waylander?'

'The same.'

'Why would he seek the Armour? He has no interest in this war.'

'He killed the King for you, Kaem. And yet you

97

hunt him. The Drenai would kill him if they knew and the Vagrians will kill him if they find him. Perhaps he seeks to bargain.'

'How does he know its whereabouts?'

'I told him.'

'Why? What game is this?'

'A game of death, Kaem.'

The old man's eyes opened and Kaem screamed as tongues of fire flashed about him.

And he woke.

For three nights Kaem's dreams were haunted by visions of bronze armour and two fabulous swords. Once he saw the Armour floating above Skultik forest, shining like a second sun. Then it dropped, so slowly, towards the trees and he saw Egel's army bathed in its light. The army grew in number as the trees themselves became men – a vast, invincible force.

On the second night he saw Waylander coming through the trees bearing one of those terrible swords, and then he realised that the assassin was stalking him. He had run, but his legs were weak and heavy and he had watched in horror as Waylander slowly dismembered him.

On the third night he saw himself clad in the Armour of Orien, mounting the marble steps to Vagria's throne. The cheering of the crowds filled him with joy, and when he looked into the eyes of his new subjects he saw adoration.

On the morning of the fourth day, he found his mind wandering as he listened to the reports from his junior generals.

Kaem forced himself to concentrate through the seemingly endless series of small problems which affect an army at war. Supplies were slow from the west, since wagons had proved more scarce than expected; new wagons were under construction. Six hundred horses had been slaughtered near Drenan after a small number had been found coughing blood; it was thought that the disease had been checked. Some breakdown in discipline among the men had been severely dealt with, but it had to be remembered that they were now on short rations.

'What about the Lentrians?' asked Kaem.

Xertes, a young officer distantly related to the Emperor, stepped forward. 'They repulsed our first attack, my lord. But we have now pushed them back.'

'You promised me that with an army of ten thousand you could take Lentria within a week.'

'The men lacked courage,' said Xertes.

'That has never been a Vagrian weakness. What they lacked was leadership.'

'Not from me,' said Xertes fiercely. 'I ordered Misalas to take the high ground on their right flank so that I could push forward with a wedge through their centre. But he failed – it was not my fault.'

'Misalas is light cavalry – leather breastplates and sabres. The enemy right flank was dug in and the hill covered with trees. How in the name of the Spirit did you expect light cavalry to take that position? They were cut to pieces by archers.'

'I will not be humiliated in this way,' shouted Xertes. 'I will write to my uncle.'

'Noble birth does not exclude you from responsibilities,' stated Kaem. 'You made many promises and have fulfilled not one. Pushed back, you say? My understanding is that the Lentrians gave you a bloody nose and then repositioned themselves ready to give you another. I told you to move into Lentria at speed, giving them no time to dig in. What did you do? You camped on their borders and had your scouts examine the land, making it clear to a blind man where you planned to attack. You have cost me two thousand men.'

'That is not fair!'

'Be silent, you worm! You are dismissed from my service. Go home, boy!'

The colour faded from Xertes' face and his hand moved close to his ornate dagger.

Kaem smiled . . .

Xertes froze, bowed swiftly and marched stiff-legged from the room. Kaem looked around the group: ten officers rigidly at attention, not one set of eyes meeting his own.

'Dismissed,' he said and when they had gone he summoned Dalnor to him. The young officer entered and Kaem offered him a chair.

'Xertes is going home,' said Kaem.

'I heard, my lord.'

'It is a dangerous journey . . . much could happen.'

'Indeed, my lord.'

'The assassin Waylander, for example?'

'Yes, my lord.'

'The Emperor would be appalled if such a man were to kill someone of royal Vagrian blood.'

'He would indeed, my lord. He would use all his resources to have him tracked down and killed.'

'Then we must ensure that nothing untoward happens to young Xertes. See that he has an escort.'

'I will, my lord.'

'And Dalnor . . .'

'Yes, my lord.'

'Waylander uses a small crossbow with bolts of black iron.'

7

The old fort had only three good walls, each twenty feet high, the fourth having been partly stripped by villagers using the stones for foundations. Now the village was deserted and the fort stood like a crippled guard over the remains. The Keep – such as it was – was damp and cold, part of the roof having fallen in some years before, and there was some evidence that the central chamber had been used as a cattle store, the stench remaining long after the animals had been moved.

Gellan had the carts moved into place against the exposed fourth wall, providing a barrier of sorts against Vagrian attack. And the rain pounded down, lashing the stone of the ancient battlements and making them glisten like marble.

Lightning blazed across the night sky and thunder rumbled in the east as Gellan drew his cloak about him and stared to the north. Sarvaj climbed the creaking, rotted steps to the battlements and moved alongside the officer.

'I hope you are right,' he said, but Gellan did not respond. His despair was almost complete.

On the first day he had been convinced the Vagrians would find them. On the second his worries had grown. On the third he had allowed himself some hope that they would arrive in Skultik to a fanfare of triumph.

Then the rain had struck, bogging down the wagons in a sea of mud. At that point he should have destroyed the supplies and made a run for the forest – he knew that now. But he had dithered too long, and the Vagrians had circled ahead of him.

There had been time to cut and run – as Jonat pointed out – but by then Gellan had become obsessed with bringing the supplies to Egel.

He had hoped there would be fewer than two hundred Vagrians opposing him and had turned the wagons west to the ruined fort at Masin. Fifty men could hold the fort for perhaps three days against a force of two hundred. In the meantime he had sent three riders to Skultik requesting urgent aid.

But Gellan's luck was running true to form. His scouts reported that the force opposing him was five hundred and the chances were they would be over-run on the first assault.

The scouts had been sent to Egel and no one at the fort knew of the enemy strength. Gellan felt like a traitor for not informing Sarvaj, but morale was a delicate beast at best.

'We can hold,' said Gellan at last, 'even if they have more men than we think.'

'The western wall is rotten. I think an angry child could push it in,' said Sarvaj. 'The wagons don't make much of a barrier.'

'They'll do.'

'So you think two hundred?'

'Maybe three,' admitted Gellan.

'I hope not.'

'Remember the manual, Sarvaj – and I quote, "Good fortifications can be held against an enemy ten times the strength of the defending force." '

'I don't like to argue with a superior officer, but didn't the manual say "five times"?'

'We'll check it when we reach Skultik.'

'Jonat is complaining again. But the men are glad to be under cover; they have a fire going in the Keep. Why don't you go inside for a while?'

'You're getting concerned about my old bones?'

'I think you should rest. Tomorrow could get a little tense.'

'Yes, you are right. Keep the sentries alert, Sarvaj.'

'I'll do my best.'

Gellan walked to the steps, then returned. 'There are over five hundred Vagrians,' he said.

'I guessed that,' said Sarvaj. 'Get some sleep. And watch out for those steps – I say a prayer every time I mount them!'

Gellan made his way gingerly down the steps and across the cobbled courtyard to the Keep. The hinges of the gates had rusted through, but the soldiers had wedged the doors in place. Gellan squeezed through and made his way to the huge hearth. The fire was welcome and he warmed his hands against the blaze. The men had fallen silent as he entered, then one of them – Vanek – approached him.

'We lit a fire for you, sir. In the eastern room. There's a pallet bed if you wanted to catch some sleep.'

'Thank you, Vanek. Jonat, will you join me for a moment?'

The tall, bony Jonat pushed himself to his feet and followed the officer. Sarvaj had been complaining again, he guessed, preparing his arguments. Once inside the small room, Gellan removed his cloak and breastplate and stood before the crackling fire.

'You know why I promoted you?' Gellan asked.

'Because you thought I could handle it?' ventured Jonat.

'More than that. I knew you could. I trust you, Jonat.'

'Thank you, sir,' said Jonat uneasily.

'So let me tell you – and I want you to keep it to yourself for tonight – that there are at least five hundred Vagrians ranged against us.'

'We'll never hold.'

'I hope that we will, for Egel needs these supplies. Three days is all it will take. I want you to hold the western wall. Pick twenty men – the best archers, the finest swordsmen – but hold it!'

'We should have cut and run; we still could.'

'Egel has four thousand men and they are short of equipment, food and medicines; the people of Skarta are going hungry to supply them. But it cannot go on. I checked the wagons tonight. You know there are over twenty thousand shafts, spare bows, swords and spears; also salt meats, dried fruits and more than old hundred thousand silver pieces.'

'One hundred . . . it's their pay!'

'Exactly. But with it Egel can open trade links even with the Nadir.'

'No wonder they sent five hundred men to recover it. I'm surprised they didn't send a thousand.'

'We'll make them wish they had,' said Gellan. 'Can you hold the western wall with twenty men?'

'I can give it a try.'

'That's all I ask.'

After Jonat had gone Gellan lay back on the pallet

bed. It smelt of dust and decay, but it felt finer than a silk-covered four-poster.

Gellan fell asleep two hours before dawn. His last waking thought was of the children, on the day he had taken them to play in the mountains.

If only he had known it was their last day together, he would have made it so different for them. He would have hugged them and told them he loved them . . .

The storm passed during the night and the dawn sky was clear of cloud, a brilliant spring blue. Gellan was awoken within the hour when riders were seen to the east. He dressed swiftly and shaved, then made his way to the wall.

Two horses could be seen in the distance, moving slowly and heavily laden. As they neared, Gellan saw that one horse carried a man and a woman, while the second bore a man and two children.

When they approached he waved them round to the ruined gates of the western wall and ordered the wagons pulled back so as to allow the horses to enter.

'Go and question them,' he ordered Sarvaj.

The young soldier descended to the courtyard as the group were dismounting, and was drawn instantly to the man in the black leather cloak. He was a tall man with dark, grey-streaked hair, and eyes so deep a brown there appeared to be no trace of pupils. His face was set and grim and he moved with care, always balanced. In his hand he held a small black crossbow, and several knives hung on his broad black belt.

'Good morning,' said Sarvaj. 'Have you travelled far?'

'Far enough,' answered the man, turning his gaze to the wagons being pulled back in place.

'It might be safer for you to move on.'

'No,' said the man quietly. 'Vagrian outriders are everywhere.'

'They are hunting us,' said Sarvaj. The man nodded and moved towards the battlements, while Sarvaj turned to the other man standing with a young woman and the two children.

'Welcome to Masin,' he said, extending his hand which Dardalion shook warmly. Sarvaj bowed to Danyal, then squatted down before the children. 'My name is Sarvaj,' he told them, removing his plumed helm. Frightened, the sisters hugged Danyal's skirt and turned their heads away.

'I've always been good with children,' he said, with a wry smile.

'They have suffered a great deal,' said Danyal, 'but they will be better in a little while. Do you have any food?'

'How remiss of me. Come this way.'

He took them into the Keep where the cook was preparing breakfast of hot oats and cold pork and they sat at the makeshift table. The cook served them with plates of oats, but the children, after one taste, pushed the dishes away.

'It's horrible,' said Miriel.

One of the men sitting nearby came to the table.

'What's wrong with it, princess?'

'It's sour,' she said.

'You have some sugar hidden in your hair. Why don't you sweeten it?'

'I haven't any sugar,' she said. The man leaned forward, ruffled her hair and then opened his hand to show a tiny leather sack sitting on his palm. He unfastened it and poured some sugar on the oats.

'Is there sugar in *my* hair?' asked Krylla eagerly.

'No, princess, but I'm sure your sister would not mind you sharing hers.' He added the rest of his small store to Krylla's plate and the sisters began to eat.

'Thank you,' said Danyal.

'A pleasure, my lady. I am Vanek.'

'You are a kind man.'

'I like children,' he said, then moved back to his table. Danyal noticed that he walked with a slight limp.

'A horse fell on him about two years ago,' said Sarvaj. 'Crushed his foot. He's a good man.'

'Do you have spare weapons here?' asked Dardalion.

'We captured some Vagrian supplies. There are swords, bows and breastplates.'

'Must you fight, Dardalion?' asked Danyal.

Reading the concern in her voice, Sarvaj switched his gaze to the young man. He looked strong enough, though his face was gentle – more of a scholar than a warrior, thought Sarvaj; he reached out and took Danyal's hand, saying nothing.

'You don't have to fight, sir,' said Sarvaj. 'It's not obligatory.'

'Thank you, but I have chosen my path. Would you help me choose a weapon? I am not skilled in such matters.'

'Of course. Tell me about your friend.'

'What would you like to hear?' asked Dardalion.

Sarvaj grinned. 'He seems more of a loner,' he said lamely. 'Not someone I would expect to see in the company of a woman and children.'

'He saved our lives,' said Dardalion, 'and that speaks more highly of him than his looks.'

'Indeed it does,' admitted Sarvaj. 'What is his name?'

'Dakeyras,' said Dardalion swiftly. Sarvaj caught the look on Danyal's face and did not press the matter; there were far more important issues at stake than a change of name. It was likely that Dakeyras was an outlaw, which six months ago would have meant something. Now it was immaterial.

'He spoke of Vagrian outriders. Did you see them?'

'There are just under five hundred soldiers,' said Dardalion. 'They were camped in a gully to the north-east.'

'Were?'

'They moved out an hour before dawn, seeking sign of your wagons.'

'You know a great deal about their movements.'

'I am a mystic, once a priest of the Source.'

'And you want weapons?'

'I have experienced a change of perspective, Sarvaj.'

'Can you see where the Vagrians are now?'

Dardalion closed his eyes, resting his head on his elbows. Seconds later he opened them again.

'They have found the tracks where you cut to the west. Now they are moving this way.'

'What regiment are they?'

'I have no idea.'

'Describe their armour.'

'Blue cloaks, black breastplates and helms that cover their faces.'

'Are the visors clear or embossed?'

'On the forehead is an image of a snarling wolf.'

'Thank you, Dardalion. Excuse me.' Sarvaj rose from the table and returned to the battlements, where Gellan was supervising the distribution of arrows to the men: quivers of fifty shafts allocated to each archer.

Sarvaj removed his helm and ran his fingers through his thinning hair.

'You trust this man?' asked Gellan, after Sarvaj had given him the news.

'I would say that he is honest. I could be wrong.'

'We will know within the hour.'

'Yes. But if he's right we are up against the Hounds.'

'They are men, Sarvaj; there's nothing supernatural about them.'

'It is not the supernatural that worries me,' said the soldier. 'It is the fact that they always win.'

Waylander unsaddled his horse, stowing his saddlebags inside the Keep. Then he took his weapons to the decaying battlements of the western wall. Six throwing knives and two quivers of bolts for his crossbow he left leaning against the ramparts. Then he saw Dardalion and Sarvaj standing at a wagon below the eastern wall; here the wagons had been drawn in a line to create a pen for the oxen.

Waylander strolled across the courtyard. Dardalion had put aside the sword and scabbard he had taken from the dead robber and had selected a sabre of blue steel. The broadsword had been too heavy for the slender priest. Sarvaj produced a breastplate from under the tarpaulin. It was wrapped in oilskin, and when he brought it out into the sunshine it shone like silver.

'A Vagrian officer of the Blue Riders,' said Sarvaj.

'Made to order. Try it on.' Delving deeper into the depths of the wagon, he pulled clear a large parcel. Ripping it open he discovered a white cloak, trimmed with leather.

'You'll stand out like a dove among crows,' said Waylander, but Dardalion merely grinned and swept the cloak over his shoulders. Shaking his head, Waylander climbed on to the wagon where he selected two short swords of blue steel in matching black scabbards; these he threaded to his belt. The edges were dulled and he moved away to the battlements to hone them.

When Dardalion joined him Waylander blinked in mock disbelief. A white horse-hair plumed helmet was buckled at the chin, and the leather-trimmed cloak lay over a shimmering breastplate embossed with a flying eagle. A leather kilt, studded with silver, protected Dardalion's thighs, while silver greaves were buckled to his calves. By his side hung a cavalry sabre, and on his left hip a long, curved knife sat in a jewelled scabbard.

'You look ridiculous,' said Waylander.

'Most probably. But will it serve?'

'It will serve to draw the Vagrians to you like flies to a cowpat.'

'I do feel rather foolish.'

'Then take it off and find yourself something less garish.'

'No. I can't explain why, but this is right.'

'Then keep away from me, priest. I want to stay alive!'

'Will you not get yourself some armour?'

'I have my mailshirt. I don't intend to stand in one place long enough to be cut.'

'I would appreciate some advice on swordsmanship,' said Dardalion.

'Gods of Mercy!' snapped Waylander. 'It takes years to learn and you have an hour, maybe two. There's nothing I can teach you – just remember throat and groin. Protect your own, slice theirs!'

'By the way, I told Sarvaj – the soldier who greeted us – that your name was Dakeyras.'

'It does not matter. But thank you anyway.'

'I am sorry that saving me has brought you to this,' said Dardalion.

'*I* brought myself to this; don't blame yourself. Just try to stay alive, priest.'

'I am in the hands of the Source.'

'Whatever. Keep the sun to your back – that way you'll blind them with your magnificence! And get yourself a canteen of water – you'll find war dries the throat.'

'Yes, I'll do that now. I . . .'

'No more speeches, Dardalion. Fetch yourself some water and position yourself down there by the wagons. That is where the action will be.'

'I feel I ought to say something. I owe you my life . . . But the words are all trapped inside me.'

'You need say nothing. You are a good man, priest – and I am glad I saved you. Now, for pity's sake, go away!'

Dardalion returned to the courtyard and Waylander strung his crossbow, testing the strings for tension. Satisfied, he laid it gently on the stone rampart. Then, taking a short length of rawhide, he tied back his hair at the nape of the neck.

A young, bearded soldier approached. 'Good morning, sir. My name is Jonat. This is my section.'

'Dakeyras,' said Waylander, extending his hand.

'Your friend looks dressed for a royal banquet.'

'It was the best he could find. But he'll stand firm.'

'I am sure that he will. Do you intend to stay up here?'

'That is what I had in mind,' said Waylander drily.

'It is just that this is the best spot to cover the gap and I would prefer to place one of my archers here.'

'I can understand that,' said Waylander, picking up his crossbow and drawing back the upper string. Snapping a bolt in place, he glanced down at the wagon blocking the ruined gate; the wagon tongue had been pushed up, making a cross with the oxen bar. Waylander pulled back the lower string, slipping a bolt into position.

'How wide would you say the bar is?' asked Waylander.

'Narrow enough to make a difficult target,' agreed Jonat.

Waylander's arm came up and a black bolt flashed through the air to punch its way through the right-hand bar. A second bolt thudded into the left side.

'Interesting,' commented Jonat. 'May I try it?'

Waylander handed him the weapon and Jonat turned it over in his hands. It was beautifully constructed. Loading only one arrow, Jonat sighted on the centre tongue and let fly. The arrow glanced from the wood and hit the cobblestones of the courtyard, sending a shower of sparks into the air.

'Nice weapon,' said Jonat. 'I would love to practise with it.'

'If anything happens to me, you can have it,' said Waylander.

Jonat nodded. 'You'll be staying here, then?'

'I think so.'

Suddenly from the eastern wall came a shout of

warning and Jonat ran to the battlement steps, joining the stream of men rushing to see the enemy. Waylander settled back against the ramparts; he had seen armies before. He took a swig from his canteen and swished the warm water around his mouth before swallowing it.

On the eastern wall Gellan and Sarvaj were joined by Jonat.

Out on the plain some six hundred Vagrian horsemen came into view and two scouts rode from the enemy ranks, galloping their horses to the western wall. Then they returned. For several minutes nothing happened as the Vagrian officers dismounted and sat together at the centre; then one rose and remounted.

'Talk time,' muttered Sarvaj.

The officer rode to the eastern wall, his hand raised. Lifting his helm from his head, he called out: 'I am Ragic. I speak for the Earl Ceoris. Who speaks for the Drenai?'

'I do,' shouted Gellan.

'Your name?'

'It is no business of yours. What do you have to say?'

'As you can see, you are vastly outnumbered. The Earl Ceoris offers you the opportunity to surrender.'

'On what conditions?'

'Once your weapons have been surrendered, you will be free to go.'

'Very generous!'

'Then you agree?'

'I have heard of the Earl Ceoris. It is said that his word is given as lightly as the promise of a Lentrian whore. The man has no honour.'

'Then you refuse?'

'I don't deal with jackals,' said Gellan.

'That is a decision you will live to rue,' shouted the herald, pulling on the reins and spurring his horse back to the enemy line.

'I think he is probably right about that,' muttered Jonat.

'Ready the men,' sad Gellan. 'The Vagrians have no ropes or siege equipment and that means they must attack the breach. Sarvaj!'

'Sir.'

'Leave only five men per wall. The rest to go with Jonat. Do it now!'

Sarvaj saluted and moved from the battlements. Jonat followed him.

'We should have cut and run,' said Jonat.

'Give your mouth a rest,' snapped Sarvaj.

The Vagrians heeled their horses to the right and cantered round to face the western wall, then advanced until they were just beyond bowshot. Dismounting, the men thrust their lances into the earth and tied their mounts to them; then lifting shields and drawing swords, they advanced slowly.

Dardalion watched them come and licked his lips. His hands were sweating and he wiped them on his cloak. Jonat grinned at him. 'Handsome whoresons, aren't they?'

Dardalion nodded. The men around him were tense and the priest realised he was not alone in his fear. Even Jonat's eyes were burning more brightly and his face was set. Dardalion glanced up to where Waylander sat with his back to the wall, setting out crossbow bolts before him. He alone was not watching the advancing soldiers. A man to the right loosed a shaft that sailed towards the Vagrians; an enemy soldier lifted his shied and the arrow glanced from it.

114

'Hold until I order it!' bellowed Jonat.

With a sudden roar the Vagrians charged. Dardalion swallowed hard and drew his swords.

With the enemy a bare thirty feet from the breach Jonat bellowed, 'Now!' Shafts hammered into the advancing line, but most were turned aside by the brass-rimmed round shields. Others glanced from black helms, but several of the enemy fell as the barbed shafts cut into unprotected necks.

A second volley sliced home as the Vagrians gained the breach. And this time more than a dozen warriors fell back. Then they were at the wagons. A burly soldier clambered over the wooden frame with sword raised, but Waylander's bolt punched through his helm above his right ear and he fell without a sound. A second bolt skewered the neck of the soldier behind him.

Jonat had placed his defenders well. A dozen knelt on the northern battlements loosing shaft after shaft into the enemy as they struggled to clear the wagons, while twenty more archers stood in the courtyard picking off the enemy with ease. The bodies mounted, but still the Vagrians pushed on.

Waylander heard a scrabbling noise behind him and swung round to see a hand grasp the ramparts as a Vagrian soldier pulled himself over the wall. Another followed . . . and another. Waylander cocked his bow and fired and the first soldier pitched backwards and rolled from the battlements. The second took a bolt through the shoulder, but ran on, screaming his hatred. The assassin dropped his bow and dragged his sword from its scabbard, blocking a downward cut; then he kicked out to catch the man in the groin. As the soldier staggered Waylander hammered a blow to his neck and with blood gushing from

115

the wound, the man toppled to the courtyard below.

Waylander dropped to his knees as another warrior aimed a vicious blow to his head. He stabbed upwards feeling the blade sink into the man's groin. Waylander kicked him from the battlements and faced another soldier, but the man suddenly pitched forward with an arrow jutting from the back of his neck. A Drenai soldier stepped from the doorway of the tower, bow in hand; he grinned at Waylander and limped forward.

Below, four Vagrians finally burst through the crossfire and leapt into the courtyard. Jonat killed the first with a reverse cut to the neck. Dardalion ran forward, heart pounding, and thrust his sword at an enemy warrior. The man brushed the blade aside and crashed his shield into the priest. Dardalion fell back, tripping on the cobbles. The Vagrian lashed out and the priest rolled clear as the blade clanged against the stones. Pushing himself to his feet, Dardalion drew his second sword and faced the warrior. The man advanced, his sword stabbing towards Dardalion's groin. The priest parried the blade with his right-hand sword, stepped forward and thrust his left-hand blade into the man's throat; blood bubbled from under the black helm and he fell to his knees.

'Look out!' yelled Waylander, but Dardalion's sword came up too late and a second Vagrian soldier ran forward crashing a blow to his head. The blade glanced from the silver helm and thundered to his shoulder. Dazed, he stumbled back and the Vagrian moved in for the kill.

Jonat despatched another man, then swung to see Dardalion in trouble. He ran forward and leapt feet-first at the attacker, catapulting him from his feet.

Jonat scrambled up and threw himself on the man's back; then, drawing a slender dagger, he tore the man's helm clear and cut his throat.

A single bugle blast pierced the battle clamour and the Vagrians pulled back out of bowshot.

'Clear away the bodies!' shouted Jonat.

Waylander retrieved his crossbow and counted the remaining bolts. Twelve. He climbed down to the courtyard and began searching the bodies, reclaiming fifteen bolts that were usable.

Dardalion sat with his back to the northern wall, dizzy and unable to stand. Waylander strolled over and knelt by his side.

'Drink,' he said.

Dardalion weakly pushed the canteen away. 'I feel sick.'

'You cannot sit there, priest; they'll be back within minutes. Get yourself to the Keep.'

Dardalion pulled his legs under him and struggled to rise. Waylander pulled him upright.

'Can you stand?'

'No.'

'Lean on me, then.'

'I did not perform too well, Waylander.'

'You killed your first man in combat. It is a start.'

Together they made their way to the Keep and Waylander laid the priest down on a bench table. Danyal ran forward, her face white with shock.

'He's not dead, merely dazed,' said Waylander. Ignoring him she moved to Dardalion, pulling his helm clear and examining the shallow cut to his head where the helm had dented.

A bugle blast echoed over the plain.

Waylander cursed softly and made for the door.

8

To free himself from pain and dizziness Dardalion released his spirit and soared, passing through the walls of the Keep and out into the bright midday sunshine.

The battle below raged on. Waylander, back on the battlements, took aim carefully and loosed bolt after bolt into the oncoming Vagrians. Jonat, full of near-maniacal energy, gathered to him twenty warriors and rushed the Vagrians who had cleared the wagons. On the battlements to left and right, Drenai archers picked their targets with care. On the eastern wall the enemy had gained a foothold by climbing the pitted outer ramparts. Here three men fought hard to hold the tide and Dardalion floated towards them.

At the centre of the three stood a middle-aged officer whose swordplay was exquisite. Not for him the wild hacking, the fanatic attack; he fought with subtle grace and style, his sword flickering into play and scarcely seeming to touch his opponents. But down they went, choking on their own blood. His face was calm, even serene, thought Dardalion, and his concentration intense.

Through his spirit eyes the priest could see the flickering auras that marked the mood of each man. Bright red pulsed the colours on all but two of the combatants.

The officer glowed with the blue of harmony, and Waylander with the purple of controlled fury.

More Vagrians cleared the battlements of the eastern wall, while Jonat and his men were being forced back from the breach on the western wall. Waylander, his bolts exhausted, drew his sword and leapt from the ramparts to the wagon below, crashing into several Vagrian soldiers and bowling them from their feet. He came up swinging his sword, killing two before they could recover their balance. A third died even as he swung his sword into play. Waylander blocked the cut and tore open the man's throat with a downward sweep.

Back in the Keep, Danyal took the sisters up the winding stair to the tower and then sat them with their backs to the ramparts. From here the sound of battle was muted, and she took the sisters in her arms.

'You are very frightened, Danyal,' said Krylla.

'Yes, I am. You'll have to look after me,' answered Danyal.

'Will they kill us?' asked Miriel.

'No . . . I don't know, little one.'

'Waylander will save us; he always does,' stated Krylla.

Danyal closed her eyes and Waylander's face filled her mind: the dark eyes, deep-set under fine brows, the angular face and square chin, the wide mouth with the faintly mocking half-smile.

The scream of a dying man echoed above the clamour of the battle.

Danyal released the children and stood leaning out over the crenellated wall.

Waylander stood with a little knot of men trying to fight their way back to the Keep, but they were almost surrounded. She could look no more and slumped down beside the girls.

Inside the Keep Dardalion roused himself and groped for his swords. He felt less groggy now, awareness of imminent death overriding the pain. He moved to the doors and hauled them open. Outside the sun was so bright it brought tears to his eyes; blinking, he saw four men rush towards him.

Fear swamped him, but instead of forcing it back, he released it, hurling it with terrible power at the four soldiers. The mind blast staggered them. One fell clutching at his heart and died within seconds; another dropped his sword and ran screaming towards the breach. The remaining two – stronger men than most – merely backed away.

Dardalion advanced on the main group, eyes wide and startlingly blue, pupils almost invisible. Growing in strength, he hurled his fear into the blue-cloaked mass of attackers. Men screamed as it hit them and panic swept through the Vagrians like a plague. They swung round, ignoring the swords of the Drenai and faced the silver warrior advancing on them. A man at the front dropped to his knees shaking uncontrollably, then he pitched forward unconscious.

Later, under the most intensive questioning, not one Vagrian soldier could describe the terror he had felt, nor the awful menace that produced it . . . though most could recall the silver warrior who shone like white fire and whose eyes radiated death and despair.

The Vagrians broke and ran, dropping their weapons behind them.

The Drenai watched in awe as Dardalion followed them to the breach, his swords in his hands.

'Gods of Light,' whispered Jonat. 'Is he a sorcerer?'

'It looks that way,' said Waylander.

The men broke ranks and ran to the priest, pounding him on the back. He staggered and almost fell, but two of the warriors hoisted him to their shoulders and he was carried back to the Keep. Waylander smiled and shook his head.

'Dak?' said a voice. 'Is it you?' And Waylander swung round to face Gellan. The officer looked older, his hair was thinning and his eyes were tired.

'Yes, it is me. How are you, Gellan?'

'You haven't changed a jot.'

'Nor you.'

'What have you been doing with yourself?'

'I've travelled a fair deal. I see you stayed with the Legion – I thought you wanted to be married and gone.'

'I married and stayed,' said Gellan and Waylander read the pain in the man's face, though Gellan fought to disguise it. 'It is good to see you. We will talk later, there is much to do.'

Gellan left him then, but the man who had first spoken to Waylander remained.

'You are old friends?' asked Sarvaj.

'What? Yes.'

'How long since you've seen him?'

'Twenty years.'

'His children died in the plague at Skoda and his wife killed herself soon after.'

'Thank you for telling me.'

'He's a good officer.'

'He always was, better than he knew.'

'He was going to retire this year – he had bought a farm near Drenan.'

121

Waylander watched Gellan directing the men to aid the wounded and clear away the bodies of the slain. Others he sent to the battlements to watch for the Vagrians.

Leaving Sarvaj in mid-sentence, Waylander strolled back to the western wall ramparts to collect his crossbow. He found a Drenai warrior sitting beside it – the man who had saved him earlier with a well-timed arrow. In no mood for conversation, Waylander stepped past him and picked up the weapon.

'Drink?' asked the man, offering Waylander a canteen.

'No.'

'It's not water,' said the soldier, grinning.

Waylander sipped it and his eyes bulged.

'They call it Lentrian Fire,' commented Vanek.

'I can see why!'

'It makes for sweet dreams,' said Vanek, stretching out and resting his head on his arms. 'Wake me if they come back, will you?'

The Vagrians had retired out of bowshot and were massed together listening to their general. Waylander could not hear his words, but the gestures spoke most powerfully. He sat on a tall grey horse, his white cloak billowing in the afternoon breeze; his fist was being waved about extravagantly, and the men were cowed. Waylander scratched his chin and took a long swallow of Lentrian Fire.

What spell had the priest cast, he wondered, that could so demoralise such excellent fighting men? He glanced at the sky and raised the canteen to the clouds.

'Maybe you have some power after all,' he acknowledged.

He drank deeply and sat down abruptly, his head spinning. Then with great care he replaced the stopper in the canteen and laid it at his side.

Stupid, he told himself. The Vagrians would be back. He chuckled. Let Dardalion handle them! He took a deep breath and leaned his head against the cold stone. The sky was bright and clear, but dark shapes wheeled and dived over the fort.

'You can smell the death, can you?' said Waylander, and the raucous cries of the crows floated back to him on the wind. Waylander shivered. He had seen these birds feast before, tearing eyes from sockets and squabbling over juicy morsels from still-warm corpses. He transferred his gaze to the courtyard.

Men were working to clear away the bodies. The Vagrians were dumped outside the breach, while the Drenai dead were laid side by side against the northern wall with their cloaks over their faces. Twenty-two bodies were laid out. Waylander counted the remaining men. Only nineteen were in view – not enough to hold the fort against another charge. A shadow fell across him and he glanced up to see Jonat carrying a small bundle of his bolts.

'I thought you might need these,' said the under-officer. Waylander accepted them with a lopsided grin.

'Drink?' he asked.

'No. Thank you.'

'It's not water,' said Waylander.

'I know, I recognised Vanek's canteen! Dun Gellan would like to see you.'

'He knows where I am.'

Jonat squatted down and smiled grimly. 'I like you, Dakeyras. It would be unseemly if I had three men drag you into the Keep – unseemly and ridiculous.'

'True. Help me up.'

Waylander's legs were unsteady, but with an effort he walked alongside Jonat, through the main hall to a small room at the rear. Gellan was sitting on a pallet bed with quill in hand, completing his reports.

Jonat saluted and backed out of the door, pulling it closed behind him. For want of a better place, Waylander sat on the floor with his back to the wall.

'I was wrong,' said Gellan. 'You have changed.'

'We all change. It's part of the process of dying.'

'I think you know what I mean.'

'You tell me – it's your fort.'

'You're cold, Dak. We were friends once. Brothers. Yet out there you greeted me like a one-time acquaintance.'

'So?'

'So tell me what's happened to you.'

'If I want confession, I can find a temple. And besides, you have more important problems to consider. Like an army waiting to destroy you.'

'Very well,' said Gellan sadly, 'we might forget our past friendship. Tell me of your friend. What vast powers does he have – and from where does he come by them?'

'Damned it I know,' said Waylander. 'He is a Source priest. I stopped some men from torturing him to death, since when he has been a positive burden to me. But I have not seen any evidence of powers before today.'

'He could be valuable to us.'

'He certainly could. Why don't you talk to him?'

'I shall. Will you be coming to Skultik?'

'Probably. If we survive.'

'Yes, if we survive. Well, if you do, do not carry that crossbow.'

'It is a good weapon,' said Waylander.

'Yes, and very unusual. All officers have been told to watch for a man bearing such a weapon; it is said he killed the King.'

Waylander said nothing, but his dark eyes met Gellan's gaze and the assassin looked away. Gellan nodded. 'Go now, Dakeyras. I wish to speak to your friend.'

'Everything is not always as it seems,' said Waylander.

'I do not want to hear it. Go now.'

As Waylander left, the door opened and Dardalion entered. Gellan stood to receive him, offering his hand. The priest shook it. The clasp was firm, but not strong, thought Gellan.

'Sit down,' said Gellan, offering Dardalion the bed. 'Tell me about your friend.'

'Dakeyras or Danyal?'

'Dakeyras.'

'He rescued me . . . all of us. He has proved a fine friend.'

'Have you always known him as Dakeyras?'

'Of what concern is that to you, sir?'

'Then you did know him by another name?'

'I shall not divulge it to you.'

'I have already spoken to the children,' said Gellan.

'Then you do not need me to corroborate.'

'No. I knew Dakeyras once – or thought I did. A man of honour.'

'He has shown himself to be such a man over the last few days,' said Dardalion. 'Let that suffice.'

Gellan smiled and nodded. 'Perhaps. Tell me about yourself and the dread powers you showed today.'

'There is little I can tell you. I am . . . was . . . a priest of the Source. I have some powers of Travel and communication.'

'But what made the enemy run?'

'Fear,' said Dardalion simply.

'Of what?'

'Merely fear. My fear hurled into their minds.'

'Make me feel fear,' said Gellan.

'Why?'

'So that I may understand?'

'But I feel no fear at this time. I have nothing to use.'

'Will the enemy return? Can you tell me that?'

'I do not think that they will. There is a man among them – his name is Ceoris – who is urging them to attack, but they are afraid. Given time he will convince them, but within the hour your reinforcements will be here.'

'Who is coming?'

'A large man named Karnak. He has four hundred riders with him.'

'That is good news indeed. You are a useful man to know, Dardalion. What are your plans?'

'Plans? I have no plans. I have not thought . . .'

'We have priests in Skultik – more than two hundred. But they won't fight like you do – if they did, the Drenai could gain much. Using your powers, magnified a hundredfold, we could set entire Vagrian armies fleeing before us.'

'Yes,' said Dardalion wearily, 'but that is not the way of the Source. I became what I am from weakness. Were I as strong as so many of my brother

126

priests I would have resisted – even as they do – such abuses of power. I cannot ask them to become what they loathe. The true power of the Source has always lain in the absence of power. Can you understand that?'

'I am not sure that I can.'

'It is like holding a spear to the chest of an enemy, then laying it aside. Even as he kills you – if such he does – he knows that he does not do it by his strength, but by your choice.'

'But – to continue with your analogy – you are still dead, yes?'

'Death is not important. You see, the Source priests believe that for life to exist there must be harmony created by balance. For every man who lives to steal or kill, there must be another who lives to give and save. Tidal love was the name they gave it at my temple; my Abbot used to teach it often. In a merchant's shop, the merchant gives you too many coins in change. You keep the coins, marvelling at your good fortune. But when you have gone he realises his mistake and is angry, both with himself and with you. So the next man who comes into the shop he cheats, to gain back his money. This man in turn realises later and he is angry, and perhaps takes out his anger on someone else. So the tide goes out, each wave affecting more and more people.

'The Source teaches us to do only kind deeds – to be honest and living, giving good for evil, to bring the tide back in.'

'All very noble,' said Gellan, 'but wondrously impractical. When a wolf raids the fold, you don't make it go away by feeding it lambs! However, this is not the time for theological debate. And you have already proved where your feelings lie.'

127

'May I ask you something, Dun Gellan?'

'Of course.'

'I watched you fight today, and you were unlike any other warrior. You were calm and at peace. Amid the slaughter and the fear you alone remained calm. How was it done?'

'I had nothing to lose,' said Gellan.

'You had your life.'

'Ah yes, my life. Was there anything else you wished to know?'

'No, but if you will forgive me, let me say this: all children are creatures of joy, and all people are capable of love. You feel you lost everything, but there was a time before your joy when your children did not exist and your wife was unknown to you. Could it not be that there is a woman somewhere who will fill your life with love, and bear you children to bring you joy?'

'Go away, priest,' said Gellan gently.

Waylander returned to the wall and watched the enemy. Their leader had finished his speech and the men were sitting, staring sullenly towards the fort. Waylander rubbed his eyes. He knew how they felt. This morning they had been confident of their skills, arrogant and proud. Now they were demoralised by the realisation of defeat.

His own thoughts echoed their despair. A week ago he had been Waylander the Slayer, secure in his talents and unaware of any guilt.

Now he felt more lonely than at any time in his life. How strange that loneliness should lay him how while he was surrounded by people, he thought. He had never sensed this emotion while living alone in the mountains or the forests. His conversation with

Gellan had hurt him deeply and he had withdrawn, as ever, into flippancy. Of all the people who thronged his memories, Gellan alone he regarded with affection.

But what could he have said to him? Well, Gellan my friend, I see you stayed with the army. Me? Oh, I became an assassin. I'll kill anyone for money – I even killed your King. It was so easy; I shot him in the back while he walked in his garden.

Or perhaps he could have mentioned the murder of his family. Would Gellan have understood his despair and what it did to him? Why should he? Had he not lost his own?

It was the damned priest. He should have left him tied to the tree. The priest had power: when he had touched the clothes of the robbers he had sensed their evil through the cloth. Waylander had turned him into a killer by staining his purity. But was such power double-edged? Had the priest returned the unholy gift by touching Waylander with goodness? Waylander smiled.

A Vagrian rider galloped from the north and dragged his mount to a halt before the general. Within minutes the Vagrians were mounted and heading east.

Waylander shook his head and loosened the strings of his crossbow. Drenai soldiers ran to the walls to watch the enemy depart and a ragged cheer went up. Waylander sat down. Vanek yawned and stretched.

'What's happening?' he asked, sitting up and yawning once more.

'The Vagrians have gone.'

'That's good. Gods, I'm hungry.'

'Do you always sleep in the middle of a battle?'

'I don't know, this is the first battle I've been in – unless you count when we captured the wagons, which was more of a massacre. I'll let you know when I've been in a few more. Did you finish my canteen?'

Waylander threw him the half-empty canteen, then rose and wandered to the Keep. A barrel of apples had been opened by the cook and Waylander took two and ate them before making his way to the winding stair and the tower, emerging into the sunlight to see Danyal leaning on the rampart and staring north.

'It's over,' said Waylander. 'You are safe now.'

She turned and smiled. 'For the while.'

'That is all anyone can ask.'

'Stay and talk,' she said. He looked at her, seeing the sunlight glinting from her red-gold hair.

'I have nothing to say.'

'I feared for you in the fighting. I didn't want you to die,' she said hurriedly, as he stepped into the shadows of the doorway. He stopped then, standing with his back to her for several seconds, then he turned.

'I am sorry about the boy,' he said softly. 'But the wound was grievous and he would have been in great pain for hours, perhaps days.'

'I know.'

'I do not enjoy killing boys. I don't know why I said it. I am not good with words . . . with people.' He wandered to the ramparts and gazed down on the soldiers harnessing the oxen to the wagons and preparing for the long ride to Skultik. Gellan was at the centre of the operation, flanked by Sarvaj and Jonat. 'I used to be an officer. I used to be many things. A husband. A father. He looked so peaceful

130

lying there among the flowers. As if he was asleep in the sunshine. Only the day before I had taught him to ride his pony over the short jumps. I went out hunting . . . he wanted to come with me.' Waylander stared down at the grey stone. 'He was seven years old. They killed him anyway. There were nineteen of them – renegades and deserters.'

He felt her hands on his shoulders and turned into her arms. Danyal had not understood much of what he said, but she read the anguish in his words. He sat back on the ramparts, pulling her to him, his face against hers, and she felt his tears upon her cheeks.

'He looked so peaceful,' said Waylander.

'Like Culas,' whispered Danyal.

'Yes. I found them all – it took years. There was a price on their heads and I used each bounty to finance my search for the others. When I caught the last, I wanted him to know why he was going to die. And when I told him who I was, he couldn't remember the killings. He died not knowing.'

'How did you feel?'

'Empty. Lost.'

'How do you feel now?'

'I don't know. It is not something I want to think about.'

Her hands came up and cupped his face, turning it towards her own. Tilting her head she kissed him, first on the cheek, then on the mouth. Then she moved back, pulling him to his feet.

'You gave us life, Dakeyras, the children and me. We will always love you for that.'

Before he could answer, another cheer went up from the walls below.

Karnak had arrived with four hundred riders.

9

Gellan ordered the wagons pulled back from the breach and Karnak rode into the fort with ten of his officers. He was a huge man, running to fat, who looked older than his thirty-two years. He dismounted beside Gellan and grinned.

'Gods man, you're a wonder!' he said. Swinging round, he unfastened his green cloak and draped it over his saddle. 'Gather round, you men,' he shouted. 'I want to see the heroes of Masin. That means you too, Vanek,' he called. 'And you, Parac!'

The twenty-five survivors came forward, grinning sheepishly. Many of them were wounded, but they bore themselves proudly before the charismatic general.

'Gods, I'm proud of you all! You've seen off a crack force of some of the best the Vagrians can offer. What's more, you've taken enough supplies to keep us for a month. But even better than that, you've shown what Drenai courage can do. Your deeds here will shine like a torch to the Drenai people – and I can promise you that this is only the beginning. At the moment we may be down, but we're not finished – not while we have men like you. We'll take this war to the enemy and make them suffer. You have my word on it. Now let's get to Skultik and I'll really show you how to celebrate.'

He moved to Gellan, throwing a brawny arm over the officer's shoulder.

'Now where's this sorcerer of yours?'

'He is in the Keep, sir. How do you know of him?'

'That's why we're here, man. He contacted one of our priests last night and told us of your plight. Damn it all, this could be a turning point for us.'

'I hope so, sir.'

'You did wonderfully well, Gellan.'

'I lost almost half my men, sir. I should have abandoned the wagons two days ago.'

'Nonsense, man! Had we not arrived in time and you had all been killed, I would have agreed with you. But the victory was worth the risk. I've got to be honest – I didn't expect it of you. Not that I doubt your courage, but you are a cautious man.'

'You use "cautious" as an insult, sir.'

'Maybe I do. But these are desperate times and they call for the odd risk. Caution won't send the Vagrians packing. And make no mistake, Gellan, what I said to the men was not mere rhetoric. We *will* win. Do you believe that?'

'It is very hard not to believe what you say, general. The men think that if you wanted the sky green instead of blue, you would climb a mountain and paint it as it passed.'

'And what do you think?'

'I am ashamed to admit that I agree with them.'

'The men need leaders, Gellan. Men with fire in their bellies. When morale goes, there can be no victory. Remember that.'

'I am aware of it, sir. But I am not good with speeches.'

'Don't worry about that, I'll handle the speeches.

You've done fine work today and I'm proud of you. You know Purdol is still holding?'

'I am glad to hear it, sir.'

'I'm going there tomorrow.'

'But it's surrounded.'

'I know, but it's important that the fortress holds. It ties down the bulk of the Vagrian force.'

'With respect, sir, it is far more important that you stay free. It is said they have put a price of 10,000 gold pieces on your head – almost as much as they've offered for Egel himself.'

'Have you forgotten so swiftly what I just said about risks?'

'But if they realise you are in Purdol, they will redouble their efforts to take it and bring in more troops.'

'Precisely!'

'I am sorry, sir, but I think it's insane.'

'That's where you and I differ, Gellan. You don't see things on the grand scale. Look at me! I'm too big to sit a horse with any confidence and I am no cavalry general – give me a fortress to hold and I'm in my element. But Egel is a strategist and a fine, wily campaigner. They don't need me in Skultik. But if I can get into Purdol the Vagrians will mass troops there, giving Egel a chance to break from the forest.'

'I see the logic and I don't want to sound like a sycophant, but we *need* you. If you are captured or killed, the Drenai cause will be close to lost.'

'Nice of you to say so. But the plan is set. How do you fancy coming with me?'

'I wouldn't miss it for the world,' said Gellan, grinning.

'That's my man,' said Karnak. 'Now where is this sorcerer?'

Gellan took the general into the Keep where Dardalion sat with the children.

'That is the sorcerer?' asked Karnak, staring at the young man in the silver armour.

'I am afraid so,' replied Gellan.

Dardalion turned as they entered and stood, bowing to the general.

'You are Dardalion?'

'I am.'

'I am Karnak.'

'I know, general. You are most welcome.'

'You are the most unlikely sorcerer I ever met.'

'I am hardly a sorcerer; I cast no spells.'

'You certainly cast one over the Vagrians – you saved the fort and every man in it. Will you ride with me?'

'I should be honoured.'

Karnak smiled at the children, but they hid behind Dardalion. 'You know, I believe the tide is turning,' said Karnak. 'If I can but avoid the soldiers around Purdol and the cursed Dark Brotherhood, I think we might just be ready to deliver a few death blows to the Vagrian hopes.'

'The Dark Brotherhood are hunting you?' asked Dardalion.

'They have been for months. And added to that, it is said that Waylander the Slayer has been hired to kill me.'

'That is most unlikely,' said Dardalion.

'Really? You are a prophet also?'

'No . . . yes . . . it is not Waylander's way.'

'You know him?' asked Karnak.

'Yes, he knows him,' said Waylander, moving into sight on the stairway with his crossbow in hand.

Karnak turned slowly and Gellan moved in front of him.

'I am Waylander, and if I wanted you dead you would *be* dead. So now all you have to worry about is the Brotherhood.'

'You think I should believe you?'

'It would be a wise move in the circumstances.'

'I have four hundred men within call.'

'But they are not here now, general.'

'That is true,' Karnak agreed. 'So you are not here to kill me?'

'No. I have other business.'

'Does it affect the Drenai cause?'

'And if it does?' asked Waylander.

'Then I will walk over to you and break your neck,' said Karnak.

'Luckily it should help your cause,' said Waylander. 'I have been asked to supply Egel with a new suit of Armour!'

They rode warily, a dozen scouts ringing the main party and the warrior general at the centre of the force shielded by six riders. Dardalion rode on his left and Gellan on the right. Behind them came the wagons, each pulled by six oxen.

Danyal and the children rode in the lead wagon alongside the warrior Vanek. She found him to be an amusing companion. At one point, as the two lead oxen pulled in opposite directions, Vanek said, straight faced: 'Highly trained these animals – obey my every command. I'm making them do this.'

Behind the wagons rode the rearguard of a hundred men led by Dundas, Karnak's aide: a young man with fair hair and a friendly open face. Beside him rode Waylander, in no doubt that he was a virtual prisoner; four riders sat their mounts close to him, hands on sword-hilts.

Waylander hid his annoyance and allowed his mind to wander as his eyes soaked in the green beauty of the Sentran Plain where it merged with the grey-blue mountains of the north. After all, what did it matter if they killed him? Had he not murdered their king? And what was so special about life that he should desire to extend his span?

None of it mattered, he realised, as the mountains loomed ever more close. How much death had these peaks seen? Who would care about this petty war in a thousand years?

'You are an undemanding companion,' remarked Dundas, lifting his helm and running his fingers through his hair.

Waylander did not reply. Swinging his horse's head to the left, he made to canter forward but his way was blocked by a rider.

'The general thinks we should hold formation while in dangerous territory,' said Dundas smoothly. 'You don't object?'

'And if I do?'

'It will not be for long, I assure you.'

As the day wore on, Dundas tired of attempting conversation with the dark-haired warrior. He didn't know why Karnak wanted him guarded and, in truth, he didn't care. But then that was Karnak's way – to explain only what was necessary and expect his orders to be carried out to the letter. At times it made him an extraordinarily aggravating man to serve under.

'What is he like?' asked Waylander suddenly.

'I am sorry, my mind was wandering,' said Dundas. 'What did you say?'

'The general – what is he like?'

'Why do you want to know?'

'Curiosity. I understand he was a First Dun officer in charge of a hill fort. Now he is a general.'

'You have not heard of Hargate and the siege?'

'No.'

'I should really let the general tell it. There are so many wonderful embellishments to the tale now that it would not surprise me to hear that dragons have been introduced. But still . . . would you like to hear it?'

'Were you there?'

'Yes.'

'Good. I prefer first-hand accounts.'

'Well, as you say, Karnak was First Dun at Hargate. The fort is not large – probably twice the size of Masin, and there is . . . was . . . a small town outside the keep. Karnak had six hundred men under his command. The Vagrians poured into Skoda and surrounded Hargate, demanding our surrender. We refused and held off their attacks for the first day, then watched as they made their night camp. We had lost sixty men during the day, but we were holding well and the Vagrians believed they had us all in their net.'

'How many of them were there?' asked Waylander.

'We estimated eight thousand. Anyway, Karnak had sent scouts to watch for the Vagrians – he never trusted their promises of peace – so we had advance warning of their attack. Do you know Hargate . . . ?' Waylander nodded. 'Then you know there is a small wood about a mile to the east.

Karnak had taken three hundred men there during the previous night. Now, as the Vagrians slept in their camp he descended on them in the darkest hours of the night, firing their tents and stampeding their horses. Our warriors made enough noise to be mistaken for a whole Drenai army, and we opened the gates and led an attack from the front. The Vagrians pulled back to re-form, but by dawn we were away to Skultik. We must have slain more than eight hundred of them.'

'Clever,' said Waylander, 'but hardly a victory.'

'What do you mean? We were outnumbered more than ten to one.'

'Exactly. When you first received news of the invasion, you could have pulled back. What point was there in fighting at all?'

'Have you no sense of honour? We gave them a bloody nose – we let them know the Drenai can fight as well as they run.'

'But still they took the fort.'

'I do not understand you, Dakeyras . . . or whatever your name is. If running means so much to you, why did you go to Masin and help Gellan and his men?'

'It was the only safe place. Or rather the safest I could find.'

'Well, you will be safe enough in Skultik. The Vagrians dare not invade.'

'I hope the Vagrians know that.'

'What does that mean?' snapped the young officer.

'Nothing at all. Tell me about Egel?'

'Why? So that you can mock *his* achievements?'

'You are young and full of fire, and you see mockery where none exists. It is not blasphemy to question a military decision. It could be, as you say, that Karnak's decision to give a bloody nose to the Vagrians was a good one; it would lift morale, for example. But it strikes me that it was a risky venture which could have whiplashed against him. What if the enemy had scouted the woods? He would have been forced to run, leaving you and three hundred men trapped.'

'But they did not.'

'Exactly – and now he is a hero. I have known many heroes. Mostly other men die to build their legends.'

'I would be proud to die for Karnak – he is a great man. And beware of insulting him, unless you wish to cross swords with any man within earshot.'

'I think your message is clear, Dundas. He is revered.'

'And rightly so. He does not send his men into danger without risking himself. He is always in the thick of the fighting.'

'Very wise,' observed Waylander.

'Even now he plans to ride to the aid of Purdol. Is that the act of a vainglorious man?'

'Purdol? It is surrounded.'

Dundas bit his lip and turned away momentarily, his face reddening. 'I would be obliged if you did not repeat that. I should not have said it.'

'I am not known for being loose-tongued,' said Waylander. 'It is forgotten.'

'Thank you, I am grateful. It is just that I was angry. He is a very great man.'

'I am sure that he is. And now that we trust each other, I am sure you will not object to my riding forward to speak with my companions?'

Dundas' face was a picture of confusion, but a resigned expression settled over his features. 'Of course not. I need to feel the wind in my face also. I will ride with you.'

The two men spurred their horses into a canter and Waylander rode to the centre of the column. Karnak swung in the saddle as he approached, followed by the young officer.

'Welcome to our group, Waylander,' said the general, grinning. 'You've just missed the tale of Hargate.'

'No, I did not. Dundas spoke of it. But were there dragons in your account?'

'Not yet, but I'm working on it,' replied Karnak. 'Come ride beside me. I understand you and Gellan are old friends?'

'We knew one another once,' said Gellan, 'but not very well.'

'No matter,' said Karnak. 'Tell me, Waylander, why do the Brotherhood hunt you?'

'I killed Kaem's son.'

'Why?'

'His father owed me money.'

'God, you sicken me!' snapped Gellan. 'Excuse me, general, but I need to ride awhile and stretch my back.' Karnak nodded and Gellan pulled his horse from the group.

'You're a strange man,' said Karnak.

Waylander smiled coldly. 'So are you, general. What are you seeking?'

'Victory. What else is there?'

'Immortality?'

Karnak smiled. 'Do not misread me, Waylander – I am no man's fool. I am vain. I am conceited. My strength is that I *know* what I am. I am the finest general you will ever know, and the greatest warrior of the age. Yes, I want immortality. And I will not be remembered as a gallant loser. Count on it.'

Although they pushed on through most of the night, a sudden storm bogged down the wagons and Karnak called a halt. Tarpaulins were hastily erected against the sides of the wagons to create makeshift tents and men huddled there together against the lashing rain.

Karnak kept Waylander close to him, but the assassin could not fail to notice the presence of two armed men who watched him constantly. Nor did he miss the venomous glance Karnak hurled at Dundas as the young officer returned to his men. Yet for all that the general remained, on the surface, in good humour. Sitting below the crude tent, his clothes wet and clinging to his body, Karnak ought – Waylander considered – to cut a ridiculous figure. The man was overweight and outlandishly garbed in clothes of green, blue and yellow. And yet he was still impressive.

'What are you thinking?' asked Karnak, drawing his cloak about his shoulders.

'I am wondering what on earth possesses you to dress like that,' said Waylander, grinning. 'Blue shirt, green cloak, yellow leggings! It seems that you dressed in stages while drunk.'

'I am not shaped for fashionable garments,' admitted Karnak. 'I dress for comfort. Now tell me about this Armour of Egel's.'

'An old man asked me to fetch it for him and I said that I would. There is no mystery to it.'

'How splendidly you understate your mission. The old man was Orien, while the Armour is legend and hidden in the lands of the Nadir.'

142

'Dardalion told you. Well then, there is no need for you to question me further. You know all there is to know.'

'I do not know why you chose to go. What does it profit you?'

'That is my business.'

'Indeed. But the Armour means a great deal to the Drenai and that *is* my concern.'

'You have come a long way in a short time, general. It is hardly the concern of a First Dun at a run-down fort.'

'Understand me, Waylander. I am a genial man with a heart of gold . . . when people humour me. Now, I like you and I am trying to forget that a man dressed in black and carrying a small crossbow killed King Niallad. Such a man would receive swift sentencing.'

'Why do you need to know?'

Karnak leaned back, his pale eyes locking to Waylander's gaze. 'I could use the Armour, it would help me.'

'It would not fit you, general.'

'It can be altered.'

'But it is promised to Egel.'

'He does not even know of it.'

'You are a man full of surprises, Karnak. Here you sit on the edge of defeat and already you plan your brilliant future. What is it to be? King Karnak? That has a ring to it. Earl Karnak, perhaps?'

'I am not looking that far ahead, Waylander. I trust my judgements. Egel is a fine warrior and a good general. Cautious, yes, but there is steel in the man. Given certain advantages, he could swing this war.'

'The Armour would be just such an advantage,' commented Waylander.

'Indeed it would. But it could be put to better use elsewhere.'

'Where?'

'Purdol,' said Karnak, leaning forward and watching Waylander intently.

'The fortress is already surrounded.'

'There is a way in.'

'What do you have in mind?'

'I will send twenty of my best men with you to fetch the Armour. You will bring it to Purdol – to me.'

'And you will stand on the battlements in Orien's Armour of Bronze and carve yourself a role in the history of the Drenai people.'

'Yes. What do you say?'

'I say forget it. Orien asked a favour of me and I said that I would attempt it. I may not be a great man, Karnak, but when I speak you can rely on my word. If it is humanly possible to retrieve the Armour, I will do so . . . and deliver it to Egel in Skultik, or wherever he may be. Does that answer the question?'

'You realise I am holding your life in the palm of my hand?'

'I do not care, general. That is the simple beauty of this quest. I do not care if it is successful – and I care even less about threats to my life. I have nothing to live for, my blood runs in no living thing. Can you understand that?'

'So I cannot tempt you with riches or with threats?'

'That is true. It makes a nonsense of my reputation, does it not?'

'Is there anything I can do to help you with your quest?'

'That is a somewhat abrupt change of stance, general.'

'I am a realist. I know when to walk away. If I cannot have the Armour, then Egel is the next best thing for the Drenai. So ask. Anything you require?'

'I require nothing. I have funds enough in Skarta.'

'But surely you cannot intend to go alone?'

'Ideally I would like to take an army – but short of that, one man has more chance of success.'

'What of Dardalion?'

'His destiny lies elsewhere. He can, and will, prove useful to you.'

'How soon do you plan to leave?'

'Soon.'

'Still you do not trust me?'

'I trust no one, general. Trust implies need, need implies caring.'

'And you care for nothing? Not even the woman and the children?'

'I care for nothing.'

'I read men as other men read tracks. You are an open book to me, Waylander, and I think you are lying – as you lied when I asked about Kaem's son. But we will let it lie; it matters not a whit, except to you. I will let you sleep now.'

The huge general pushed himself to his feet and stepped out into the night. The rain had stopped. Karnak stretched his back and moved off along the column, flanked by his two bodyguards.

'What do you make of him, Ris?' he asked the taller of the two.

'I don't know, general. They say he fought well at Masin. He's steady. Cool.'

'But would you trust him?'

'I think I would. I would certainly sooner trust him than fight him.'

'Well said.'

'I do have a question, sir, if I may?'

'Gods, man, you don't have to ask. Go ahead.'

'All that about the Armour. What would you do with it?'

'I would have sent it to Egel.'

'I do not understand. That is where he plans to take it.'

'All life is a riddle, my friend,' said Karnak.

10

The town of Skarta sprawled across a clearing between two hills in the south-west of Skultik. There were no walls around it, though hastily constructed defences were in evidence – loosely packed barriers of local rock built behind deep ditches. Soldiers were at work everywhere, increasing the height of the barricades or filling in the outfacing windows of perimeter homes.

But all work ceased as Karnak, now at the head of the column, led the wagons into the town.

'Welcome back, general!' shouted one man, sitting back on the wall he was building.

'Meat tonight. How does that sound?' yelled Karnak.

Back at the rear of the column Waylander rode with Dardalion.

'Another great Karnak victory,' observed Waylander. 'See how the crowds flock to him! You would think he defended Masin himself. Where is Gellan in this moment of triumph?'

'Why do you not like him?' asked Dardalion.

'I do not dislike him. But he is a poseur.'

'Do you not think he needs to be? He has a demoralised army – a force in need of heroes.'

'Perhaps.' Waylander cast his eyes over the defences. They were well planned, the ditches deep enough to prevent a force of horsemen from charging the town and the walls strategically placed to allow archers to inflict heavy losses on an attacking army. But they were useless in any long-term encounter, for they were neither high nor strong. Nor were they linked. It was not possible to turn Skarta into a fortress, and Waylander guessed the defences were more for the town's morale than for any genuine attempt to fight the Vagrians.

Once through the outer defences, the wagons pulled into the centre of Skultik. The buildings were mainly of white stone, hewn from the Delnoch mountains to the north. Mostly single-storey dwellings, the town was built around an old fort villa at the centre which now was the Hall of Council and Egel's headquarters.

Waylander reined in his horse as the column entered.

'I will find you later,' he called to Dardalion, then rode to the eastern quarter. Since his meeting with Karnak he was no longer guarded, but he still proceeded cautiously, checking several times to see if he was being followed. The houses were poorer here, the walls painted white to imitate the grand granite and marble homes of the northern quarter, but the stone was inferior quality.

Waylander rode to an inn near the Street of Weavers and left his mount in a stable at the rear. The inn was crowded, the air thick with the smell of stale sweat and cheap beer. He pushed his way through to the long wooden bar, his eyes raking the crowd; the barman lifted a pewter mug as he saw him approach.

'Ale?' he asked.

Waylander nodded. 'I am looking for Durmast,' he said.

'Many people look for Durmast. He must be a popular man.'

'He's a pig. But I need to find him.'

'Owe you money, does he?' The barman grinned, showing stained and broken teeth.

'I am ashamed to admit that he's a friend of mine.'

'Then you ought to know where he is.'

'Is he in that much trouble?'

The barman grinned again and filled Waylander's jug with frothing ale. 'If you are seeking him, you'll find him. Enjoy your drink.'

'How much?'

'Money's not worth that much here, friend. So we are giving it away.'

Waylander drank deeply. 'Tasting like this, you ought to pay people for drinking it!' The barman moved away and Waylander settled his arms on the bar and waited. After several minutes, a thin hatchet-faced young man tapped his arm.

'Follow me,' he said.

They moved through the crowd to a narrow door at the back of the inn, which opened on to a small courtyard and a series of alleys. The man's slight figure jogged ahead, cutting left and right through the maze until at last he stopped at a wide door studded with brass. There he knocked three times, waited, then twice more and the door was opened by a woman wearing a long green dress. Wearily she led them to a room at the back of the house and the young man knocked again. Then he grinned at Waylander and moved away.

Waylander placed his hand on the door-latch, then stopped. Moving to one side with his back against the wall, he flicked the latch and pushed the door open. A crossbow shaft hammered into the wall

149

opposite, sending a shower of sparks across the corridor.

'Is that any way to greet an old friend?' asked Waylander.

'A man has to be careful among friends,' came the reply.

'You owe me money, you reprobate!'

'Come in and collect it.'

Waylander moved away from the door to the other side of the corridor. Taking two running steps, he hurled himself head-first into the room, rolling forward to his feet with knife in hand as he hit the floor.

'Game is over and you are dead!' came the voice, this time from the doorway. Waylander turned slowly. Standing behind the door was a huge bear of a man holding a black crossbow, the bolt aimed at Waylander's stomach.

'You are getting old and slow, Waylander,' commented Durmast. Lifting the bolt from the weapon, he snapped the string forward and placed the crossbow against the wall. Waylander shook his head and sheathed his knife. Then the big man moved across the room and lifted him from his feet in a bone-crushing bear hug. He planted a kiss on Waylander's forehead before releasing him.

'You stink of onions,' said Waylander.

Durmast grinned and lowered his huge frame into a leather chair. The man was even bigger than the assassin remembered, and his brown beard was shaggy and unkempt. He was dressed as always in a mixture of green and brown homespun wool which gave him the appearance of a human tree: a thing created from sorcery. Durmast was just under seven feet tall and weighed more than three large men.

Waylander had known him for eleven years and, in as much as he trusted any living man, he trusted the giant.

'Well, get to the point,' said Durmast. 'Who are you hunting?'

'No one.'

'Then who is hunting you?'

'Just about everyone. But mainly the Brotherhood.'

'You pick your enemies well, my friend. Here, read this.' Durmast delved into an untidy mass of parchment scrolls and came up with a tightly rolled package, sealed with a black circle of wax. The seal was broken. Waylander took the scroll and read it swiftly.

'Five thousand gold pieces? It makes me valuable.'

'Only dead,' said Durmast.

'Hence the crossbow greeting.'

'Professional pride. If times get tough I can always rely on you – and the price on your wolf's head.'

'I need your help,' said Waylander, pulling up a seat opposite the giant.

'Helping you will prove costly.'

'You know I can pay. You already owe me six thousand in silver.'

'Then that is the price.'

'You don't know yet what aid I need.'

'True – but that is the price anyway.'

'And if I refuse?'

The smile faded from the giant's face. 'Then I will collect the Brotherhood's bounty on you.'

'You drive a hard bargain.'

'No harder than the one you forced me to on that

Ventrian mountainside when my leg was broken. Six thousand for a splint and a horse?'

'There were enemies close by,' said Waylander. 'Was your life worth so little?'

'Another man would have rescued me out of friendship.'

'But then men like us have no friends, Durmast.'

'So do you agree the price?'

'Yes.'

'Fine. What do you need?'

'I need someone to guide me to Raboas, the Sacred Giant.'

'Why? You know where it is.'

'I want to get back alive – and I shall be bringing something with me.'

'You intend to steal Nadir treasure from their holiest place? You don't need a guide, you need an army! Ask the Vagrians – they just might be strong enough. But I doubt it.'

'I need someone who knows the Nadir and is welcome in their camps. What I am seeking is not a Nadir treasure; it belongs to the Drenai. But I will not lie to you, Durmast, there is great danger. The Brotherhood will be on my train and they seek the same goal.'

'Valuable, is it?'

'It is worth more than a king's ransom.'

'And what percentage do you offer me?'

'Half of what I am receiving.'

'That's fair. What are you getting?'

'Nothing at all.'

'Are you telling me that this is something you promised to do for your sick mother on her deathbed?'

'No. I promised an old blind man on his.'

'I don't believe a word of this. You never did anything for nothing in your life. Gods, man, I saved you twice at cost to myself, yet when I was in trouble you charged me silver. Now you tell me you have become an altruist? Do not make me angry, Waylander. You would not like me angry.'

Waylander shrugged. 'I am surprising myself. There is little more I can tell you.'

'But there is. Tell me about the old man.'

Waylander leaned back. What could he tell him? In what way could he lay out the story so that Durmast would understand what had happened to him? No way at all. The giant was a killer, merciless and amoral – even as Waylander had been but a few short days before. How could he understand the shame the old man had inspired in Waylander? He took a deep breath and launched into the tale, allowing no embellishments. Durmast listened in silence, no flicker of expression on his wide features, no glint of emotion in his green eyes. At the conclusion Waylander spread his arms and lapsed into silence.

'The Drenai would pay all that they have to get the Armour?' asked Durmast.

'Yes.'

'And the Vagrians would pay more?'

'Indeed they would.'

'And you are going to do it for nothing?'

'With your help.'

'When do you plan to leave?'

'Tomorrow.'

'You know the grove of oaks to the north?'

'Yes.'

'I'll meet you there and we'll go out over the Delnoch Pass.'

'What about the money?' asked Waylander softly.

153

'Six thousand, you said. It wipes the slate clean.'

Waylander nodded thoughtfully. 'I had expected you to ask for more, considering the size of the task.'

'Life is full of surprises, Waylander.'

After the assassin had gone, Durmast called the hatchet-faced young man into the room.

'Did you hear all that?' he asked.

'Yes. Is he mad?'

'No, he's merely gone soft. It happens, Sorak. But do not underestimate him. He is one of the finest warriors I have ever seen and will prove a hard man to kill.'

'Why do we not just kill him for the bounty?'

'Because I want that Armour *and* the bounty.'

'So much for friendship,' said Sorak, grinning.

'You heard the man. People like us have no friends.'

Danyal took the children to a tiny schoolhouse behind the Hall of Council. It was run by three Source priests and there were more than forty children housed there, orphans of the war. A further three hundred had been billeted with the townspeople of Skarta. Krylla and Miriel seemed content enough to be left there and waved happily from the play area as Danyal walked away beside an elderly priest.

'Tell me, sister,' he asked as they halted by the wrought-iron gate, 'what do you know of Dardalion?'

'He is a priest like yourself,' she answered.

'But a priest who kills,' he said sadly.

'I cannot help you. He did what he felt was necessary to save lives – there is no evil in him.'

'There is evil in all of us, sister, and the mark of

154

a man is how he defies the evil within. Our young men talk much of Dardalion and I fear he poses a terrible threat to our Order.'

'Or perhaps he will help to save it,' she ventured.

'If we need saving by men, then all we believe is nonsense. For if Man is ultimately more powerful than God, what need have we to worship a deity at all? But I do not wish to burden you with our problems. May the Source bless you, sister.'

She left him and wandered through the white-walled streets. Her dress was filthy and torn and she felt like a beggar under the stares of the townsfolk. A short fat man approached her, offering money, but she dismissed him with an angry glare. Then a woman touched her arm as she passed.

'Did you just come in, my dear?' she asked.

'Yes.'

'Was there a man named Vanek with your party?'

'Yes, a soldier with a limp.'

The woman looked relieved. She was plump, and once must have been pretty, but now her face was lined and she had lost several teeth on the right side of her face which gave her a lopsided appearance.

'My name is Tacia. there is a bath-house next to my home and you are welcome to use it.'

The bath-house was deserted and the main bath empty, but several tubs remained in the side rooms. Tacia helped Danyal to fill a copper tub with buckets of water from a well at the rear of the bath-house, then sat down as she removed her dress and lowered herself into the cold water.

'They do not heat the water any more,' said Tacia. 'Not since the council man left. He owned the House; he went to Drenan.'

'It is fine,' said Danyal. 'Is there any soap?'

Tacia left her and returned some minutes later carrying soap, towels and a skirt and tunic top.

'It will be too large for you, but I can soon alter it,' she said.

'Are you Vanek's wife?'

'I was,' she said, 'but he lives now with a young girl from the southern quarter.'

'I am sorry.'

'Never wed a soldier – isn't that what they say? The children miss him; he is very good with children.'

'Were you married long?'

'Twelve years.'

'Maybe you'll get back together,' said Danyal.

'Maybe – if my teeth grow again and the years fall away from my face! Have you anywhere to stay?'

'No.'

'You are welcome to share our house. It isn't much, but it is comfortable – if you don't mind children.'

'Thank you, Tacia, but I am not sure I am staying in Skarta.'

'Where else is there to go? Purdol is ready to fall, I hear, despite the promises from Karnak and Egel. They must think we are stupid. No one is going to resist the Vagrians for long . . . look how swiftly they have conquered the country.'

Danyal said nothing, knowing she had no antidote to the woman's despair.

'Do you have a man?' asked Tacia.

Danyal thought instantly of Waylander, then shook her head.

'You are lucky,' said the woman. '*We* fall in love with men, *they* fall in love with soft skin and bright eyes. I really loved him, you know. I would not have

156

minded had he slept with her now and again. But why did he have to leave me for her?'

'I am sorry. I do not know what to say.'

'No. You'll know one day though, when that pretty red hair of yours streaks with grey and your skin gets hard. I wish I was young again. I wish I had pretty red hair and did not know how to answer an old woman.'

'You are not old.'

Tacia stood and laid the clothes on the chair. 'When you are ready, come next door. I have some supper prepared – vegetables only, I'm afraid, but we still have some spices to give it flavour.'

Danyal watched the woman leave, then poured soap into her hair and scrubbed away the dirt and grease. At last she stood and dried herself before a bronzed mirror at the far end of the room.

Somehow the sight of her beauty failed to lift her as it usually did.

Dardalion wandered to the outskirts of the town, crossing a curved stone bridge over a narrow stream. The trees were thinner here – elm and birch, slender and graceful compared with the giant oaks of the forest. Flowers bloomed by the stream, bluebells seeming to float above the ground like a sapphire mist. There was tranquillity here, thought Dardalion. Harmony.

The tents of the priests were spread in a meadow in an orderly circle. Nearby was a fresh graveyard, the mounds carpeted with flowers.

Uncomfortable in his armour, Dardalion walked into the meadow and watched the eyes of the priests turn towards him. A mixture of emotions stuck him forcefully: anguish, pain, disappointment, elation, pride, despair. He absorbed them, as he absorbed the mind-faces of those who projected the feelings, and he responded with love born of sorrow.

As he came near the priests gathered around him silently, leaving a path to the tent at the centre of the circle. When he approached an elderly man stepped from the tent and bowed deeply. Dardalion fell to his knees before the Abbot and bowed his head.

'Welcome, brother Dardalion,' said the old man softly.

'Thank you, Father Abbot.'

'Will you remove the garments of war and rejoin your brethren?'

'It is with regret that I must refuse.'

'Then you are no longer a priest and should not kneel before me. Stand as a man, freed of your vows.'

'I do not wish to be free of my vows.'

'The eagle does not pull a plough, Dardalion, and the Source accepts no half-way heroes.'

The old man reached down and gently pulled Dardalion to his feet. The young warrior priest looked into his eyes, seeking righteous anger but finding only sadness. The Abbot was very old, his face webbed with the weight of his life. Yet his eyes were bright, alive with intelligence.

'I do not wish to be free. I wish to follow a different path to the Source.'

'All paths lead to the Source, whether for judgement or joy.'

'Do not play word games with me, Father Abbot. I am no child. But I have seen great evil in the land and I will not sit by and watch it triumph.'

'Who is to say where triumph lies? What is life

158

but a search for God? A battleground, a cesspit, a paradise? I see the pain you see and it saddens me. And where I find pain I bring comfort, and where I find sorrow I bring promises of future joy. I exist to heal, Dardalion. There is no victory in the sword.'

Dardalion drew himself upright and glanced about him, feeling the weight of the unasked questions. All eyes were on him and he sighed and closed his eyes, praying for guidance. But his prayer was unanswered, and he felt no lifting of the burden upon him.

'I brought two children to Skarta – bright, lively youngsters with rare talents. And I have seen the deaths of evil men, and know that through their deaths other innocents will know life. And I have prayed constantly about my path, and my deeds, and my future. It seems to me, Father Abbot, that the Source required balance in the world. Hunters and hunted. The weakest calf in the herd is the one to be caught by wolves. Therefore the bloodlines remain strong in the herd. But too many wolves will destroy the herd, so the huntsmen track the wolves, catching the weakest and oldest.

'How many examples do we need to show that the Source is a God of equity? Why create the eagle and the wolf, the locust and the scorpion? At every turn there is balance. Yet when we see the evil of the Brotherhood at work, and the worshippers of Chaos stain the land, we sit in our tents and ponder the mysteries of the stars. Where is the balance there, Father Abbot?'

'We seek to teach the world that our values are those to be followed. But if all followed us in celibacy, where would the world be? Mankind would cease.'

159

'And there would be no more war,' said the Abbot. 'No more greed, lust, despair and sorrow.'

'Yes. And no love, joy, or contentment.'

'Are you content, Dardalion?'

'No. I am heartsick and lost.'

'And were you content as a priest?'

'Yes. Sublimely so.'

'And does not that show where the error lies in your thinking?'

'It does not – rather it exposes the selfishness of my soul. We seek to be altruistic, for we yearn to be blessed by the Source. But then it is not altruism, nor love, that guides us, but self-interest. We do not spread the message of love for love's sake, but for our own futures as priests of the Source. You bring comfort to those in pain? How? How can you understand their pain? We are all cerebral men, living apart from the world of reality. Even our deaths are a moral disgrace, for we welcome them as chariot rides to paradise. Where is the sacrifice? The enemy brings us what we desire and we accept death from him as a gift. A gift of Chaos – a stained, bloody, vile gratuity from the Devil himself.'

'You speak as one who has been stained by Chaos. All that you say is plausible, yet that is the strength of the Chaos Spirit. That is why he was called the Morning Star and is now the Prince of Lies. The gullible devour his promises as he devours them. I have looked inside you, Dardalion, and I find no evil. But your very purity was your downfall, when you allowed yourself to travel with the assassin Waylander. You were too confident in your purity, and the evil of the man overcame you.'

'I do not see him as evil,' said Dardalion. 'Amoral, cruel, but not evil. You are right, though, when you

160

say he affected me. But purity is not a cloak which can be stained in a storm. He merely made me question values I had accepted.'

'Nonsense!' snapped the Abbot. 'He fed you his blood and therefore his soul. And you became one with him, even as he now struggles against the stain you have placed on his evil. You are joined, Dardalion, like symbiotic twins. He struggles to do good, while you struggle to commit evil. Can you not see it? If we listen to you, then our Order is finished, our discipline gone to the winds of the desert. What you ask is selfishness, for you seek safety among the numbers of the Source priests. If we accept you, then we lessen your doubt. We will not accept you.'

'You speak of selfishness, Father Abbot. Then let me ask you this: if our lives as priests teach us to abhor selfishness, why do we allow the Brotherhood to kill us? For if unselfishness means giving up that which we desire in order to help others, then surely fighting the Brotherhood would achieve it? We do not want to fight, we want to die, therefore when we fight we are being unselfish and helping the innocents who would otherwise be slain.'

'Go away, Dardalion, you are tainted beyond my humble counsel.'

'I will fight them alone,' said Dardalion bowing stiffly.

As he turned the priests moved back to allow him a path, and he walked it without turning his head to see their faces, his mind closed to their emotions.

Clearing their ranks, he crossed the stone bridge and paused to stare at the stream. He no longer felt uncomfortable in the armour, and the burden was gone from his soul. The sound of footsteps caused him to turn and he saw a group of priests crossing

161

the bridge, all of them young. The first to come was a short, stocky man with bright blue eyes and close-cropped blond hair.

'We wish to speak with you, brother,' he said. Dardalion nodded, and they formed a half-circle around him and sat down on the grass. 'My name is Astila,' said the blond priest, 'and these of my brethren have been waiting for you. Do you object to communing with us?'

'For what purpose?'

'We wish to know of your life, and the change you have undergone. We will best understand that by sharing your memories.'

'And what of the stain to your purity?'

'There are enough of us to withstand it, if such it be.'

'Then I agree.'

The group bowed their heads and closed their eyes. Dardalion shuddered as the priests flowed into his mind and he merged into the oblivion of their mass. A kaleidoscope of memories flickered and flashed. Childhood, joy and torment. Study and dreams. The mad rush of images slowed as the mercenaries tied him to the tree and went to work with their knives, and the pain returned. Then . . .

Waylander. The rescue. The cave. The blood. The savage joy of battle and death. The walls of Masin. But through it all the constant prayers for guidance. All unanswered. Nausea swept though him as the priests returned to their bodies.

He opened his eyes and almost fell but sucking in air, he steadied himself.

'Well?' he asked. 'What did you find?'

'You were stained,' said Astila, 'in the first moments when Waylander's blood touched you. That

162

is why you cut your opponent to pieces. But since then you have struggled – as the Abbot pointed out – to restrain the evil.'

'But you think I am wrong?'

'Yes. And yet I will join you. We will all join you.'

'Why?'

'Because we are weak, even as you are weak. Poor priests we have been, despite our struggles. I am prepared to be judged by the Source for all my deeds, and if His judgement says eternal death then so be it. But I am tired of watching my brothers slain. I am sickened by the deaths of the children of the Drenai, and I am ready to destroy the Brotherhood.'

'Then why have you not done so before now?'

'That is not an easy question to answer. I can only speak for myself, but I feared that I might become as one with the Brotherhood. For my hatred was growing – I did not know if a man could retain any purity, any sense of God. You have, so I will follow you.'

'We were waiting for a leader,' said another man.

'And you have found one. How many are we?'

'With you, thirty.'

'Thirty,' said Dardalion. 'It is a beginning.'

11

Waylander dismissed the two female servants and rose from the bath, brushing flower petals from his body. Wrapping a towel around his waist, he walked to a full-length mirror and shaved slowly. His shoulder ached, the muscles were tense and knotted from the battle at Masin and an ugly bruise was flowering along his ribs. He pressed it lightly and winced. Ten years ago such a bruise would have long since vanished; ten years before that, no bruise would have flowered at all.

Time was a greater enemy than any he had faced.

He stared into his own dark brown eyes, then scanned the fine lines of his face and the grey hair fighting for dominance at his temples. His gaze flickered down. The body was still strong, but the muscles were looking stretched and thin, he thought. Not many years left for a man in his occupation.

Waylander poured himself some wine and sipped it, holding it on his tongue and enjoying the sharp, almost bitter flavour.

The door slid open and Cudin entered; he was short and fat, sweat shining on his face. Waylander nodded a greeting. The merchant was followed by a young girl carrying clothing. She laid it on a gilded chair and left the room with eyes downcast, which Cudin hovered, rubbing his hands nervously.

'Everything as you requested, my dear fellow?'

'I will also need a thousand in silver.'

'Of course.'

'Have my investments gone well?'

'Well, these are hard times, But I think you will find the interest has been substantial. I have lodged the greater part of the eight thousand in Ventria, for the spice trade, so the war should not affect it. You may collect it at Isbas, at the bank of Tyra.'

'Why so nervous, Cudin?'

'Nervous? Not I – it is the heat.' The fat man licked his lips and tried to smile, but he was not successful.

'Someone has been looking for me, yes?'

'No . . . yes. But I told them nothing.'

'Of course not; you *know* nothing of my movements. But I shall tell you what you promised them – you said that you would let them know if ever I called on you. And you told them about the bank at Tyra.'

'No,' whispered Cudin.

'Do not be afraid, merchant, I do not blame you. You are not a friend and there is no reason to risk yourself for me; I would not expect it. Indeed, I would think you a fool if you did. Have you informed them yet of my arrival?'

The merchant sat down beside the pile of clothing. His flesh seemed to sag as if the muscles of his face had suddenly ceased to function.

'Yes, I sent a messenger into Skultik. What can I say?'

'Who came to you?'

'Cadoras the Stalker. Gods, Waylander, he has the eyes of Hell. I was terrified.'

'How many men did he have with him?'

165

'I do not knoow. I remember he said "they" would be camped at the Opal Creek.'

'How long ago was this?'

'Five days. He knew you were coming.'

'Have you seen him since?'

'Yes. He was in a tavern, drinking with the giant outlaw – the one who looks like a bear. You know him?'

'I know him. Thank you, Cudin.'

'You will not kill me?'

'No. But had you not admitted it to me . . .'

'I understand. Thank you.'

'There is nothing to thank me for . . . Now on another matter – there are two children recently brought to Skarta, now lodged with the Source priests. Their names are Krylla and Miriel. You will see they are looked after? There is also a woman, Danyal; she too will have need of money. For this service you will keep the interest from my investments. You understand?'

'Yes. Krylla, Miriel, Danyal. I understand.'

'I came to you, Cudin, because of your reputation for honest dealings. Do not fail me.'

The merchant backed from the room and Waylander moved to the clothing. A fresh linen shirt lay at the top of the pile and he lifted it to his face; it smelled of roses. Slipping it on, he tied the cuffs. Next was a pair of black troos in thick cotton, and then a woollen-backed leather jerkin and a pair of thigh-length black riding boots. Moving to the window, he hefted his mailshirt and placed it over his shoulders. The rings were freshly greased, the metal cold to his body. He dressed swiftly, buckling on his knife-belt and sword. His crossbow lay on the broad bed with a fresh quiver of fifty bolts; he clipped both to his belt and left the room.

Outside in the hall the girl waited and Waylander gave her four silver pieces. She smiled and moved away, but he called her back when he saw the bruise on her upper arm.

'I am sorry for being rough on you,' he said.

'Some men are worse,' she replied. 'You didn't know you were doing it.'

'No. I did not.' He gave her another silver piece.

'You cried in your sleep,' she said softly.

'I am sorry if it wakened you. Tell me, doesHewla still live in Skarta?'

'She has a cabin north of the town.' The girl was frightened, but she gave Waylander directions and he left the merchant's house, saddled his horse and rode north.

The cabin was badly built; the unseasoned wood was beginning to warp and mud had been pushed into the cracks. The main door was poorly fitted and a curtain had been hung behind it so as to cut down the draughts. Waylander dismounted, tethered his horse to a stout bush and knocked on the door. There was no answer and he moved inside warily.

Hewla was sitting at a pine table staring into a copper dish filled to the brim with water. She was old and almost bald, and even more skeletal than the last time Waylander had visited her two years before.

'Welcome, Dark One,' she said, grinning. Her teeth were white and even, strangely out of place amidst the ruin of her face.

'You have come down in the world, Hewla.'

'All life is a pendulum. I shall return,' she answered. 'Help yourself to wine – or there is water if you prefer.'

'Wine will be fine,' he said, filling a clay goblet from a stone carafe and sitting opposite her.

'Two years ago,' he said softly, 'you warned me against Kaem. You spoke of the death of princes, and of a priest with a sword of fire. It was pretty, poetic and meaningless. Now it has meaning . . . and I wish to know more.'

'You do not believe in pre-destiny, Waylander. I cannot help you.'

'I am not a fatalist, Hewla.'

'There is a war being waged.'

'You surprise me.' His tone was ironic.

'Close your mouth, boy!' she snapped. 'You learn nothing while your lips flap.'

'I apologise. Please go on.'

'The war is on another plane, between forces whose very nature we do not understand. Some men would call these forces Good and Evil, others refer to them as Nature and Chaos. Still others believe the power is of one Source that wars on itself. But whatever the truth, the war is real. I myself tend towards the simplistic: good and evil. In this struggle there are only small triumphs and no final victory. You are now a part of this war – a mercenary who has changed sides at a crucial time.'

'Tell me of my quest,' said Waylander.

'I see the global view does not excite your interest. Very well. You have allied yourself with Durmast, a brave decision. He is a killer without conscience and in his time has slain men, women and babes. He is without morality, neither evil nor good – and he will betray you, for he has no understanding of true friendship. You are hunted by Cadoras, the

Scarred One, the Stalker, and he is deadly for, like you, he has never been bested with the sword or the bow. The Dark Brotherhood seek you, for they desire Orien's armour and your death, and the Ventrian emperor has ordered a team of assassins against you for killing his nephew.'

'I did not kill him,' said Waylander.

'No. The deed was arranged by Kaem.'

'Go on.'

Hewla gazed into the bowl of water. 'Death is being drawn to you from every side. You are trapped at the centre of a web of fate and the spiders are closing in.'

'But will I succeed?'

'It depends on your definition of success.'

'No riddles, Hewla. I have no time.'

'That is true. Very well then, let me explain about prophecy. Much depends on interpretation, nothing is clear-cut. If you were to take your knife and hurl it into the forest, what chance would you have of hitting the fox that killed my chickens?'

'None at all.'

'That is not strictly true. The law of probability says you *might* kill it. And that is the size of your task.'

'Why me, Hewla?'

'Now that is a question I have heard before. If I could lose a year for every time it has been asked, I would be sitting before you as a virgin beauty. But it was honestly asked and I will answer it. You are nothing in this game but a catalyst. Through your actions a new force has been birthed in the world. This was born the moment you saved the priest. It is invulnerable and immortal and will ride through the centuries until the end of time. But no one will remember you for it, Waylander. You will fade into the dust of history.'

'I care nothing for that. But you have not answered my question.'

'True. Why you? Because you alone have the chance, slim as it is, to change the course of this nation's history.'

'And if I refuse?'

'A pointless question – you will not.'

'Why so sure?'

'Honour, Waylander. You are cursed with it.'

'Do you not mean blessed?'

'Not in your case. It will kill you.'

'Strange. I thought I would live for ever.'

He stood to leave, but the old woman raised her hand.

'I can give you one warning: beware the love of life. Your strength is that you care not about death. The powers of Chaos are many and not all of them involve pain and sharp blades.'

'I do not understand you.'

'Love, Waylander. Beware of love. I see a red-haired woman who could bring you grief.'

'I shall not see her again, Hewla.'

'Maybe,' grunted the old woman.

As Waylander stepped from the cabin, a shadow flickered to his left and he dived forward as a sword blade whistled over his head. Hitting the ground on his shoulder, he rolled to his knees, his knife flashing through the air to take his attacker under the chin. The wounded man sank to his knees, tearing the blade loose, blood gushing from his throat as he toppled forward. Waylander swung round, scanning the trees, then rose and walked to the corpse. He had never seen the man before.

He cleaned his knife and sheathed it as Hewla stepped into the doorway.

'You are a dangerous man to know,' she said, grinning.

His dark eyes fixed on her wrinkled face. 'You knew he was here, you crone.'

'Yes. Good luck on your quest, Waylander! Walk warily.'

Waylander rode east through the darkest section of the forest, his crossbow primed and his dark eyes scanning the undergrowth for movement. Above him the branches interlaced and shafts of sunlight splayed the trees. After an hour he turned north, the tension growing within him causing his neck to ache.

Cadoras was not a man to be taken lightly. His was a name spoken in whispers in the darkest alleyways of forbidden cities: Cadoras the Stalker, the Dream Ender. It was said that none could match him for cunning and few for cruelty, but Waylander dismissed the more wild stories, for he knew how legend could add colour to the whitest of deeds.

For he, of all men, could understand Cadoras.

Waylander the Slayer, the Soul Stealer, the Chaos Blade.

Saga-poets sang dark songs about the wandering assassin, the stranger, the Waylander, choosing always to finish their tale-telling with Waylander's exploits as the fires guttered low and the tavern dwellers prepared for a walk home in the dark. Waylander had sat unnoticed in more than one inn while they entertained the crowds with his infamy. They would begin their performances with stories of golden heroes, beautiful princesses, courageous tales of shadow-haunted castles and silver knights. But as the hours passed they introduced an edge of fear, a taste of terror, and men would walk out into darkened streets with fearful eyes which searched the shadows for Cadoras the Stalker, or for Waylander.

How the poets would dance with glee when they heard that Cadoras had been paid to stalk the Slayer!

Waylander turned west along the line of the Delnoch mountains until he entered a large clearing where some thirty wagons were waiting. Men, women and children sat at breakfast fires while the giant Durmast walked among the groups collecting his payments.

Once out of the trees, Waylander relaxed and cantered in to the camp-site. He removed the bolts from the crossbow and loosed the strings; clipping the weapon to his belt, he slid from the saddle. Durmast – two leather saddlebags drooped over one huge shoulder – spotted him and waved. Moving to a nearby wagon, he heaved the bags inside and wandered back to Waylander.

'Welcome,' he said, grinning. 'This war is making for good business.'

'Refugees?' queried Waylander.

'Yes, heading for Gulgothir. With all their worldly possessions.'

'Why do they trust you?'

'Just stupidity,' said Durmast, his grin widening. 'A man could get rich very quickly!'

'I don't doubt it. When do we leave?'

'We were only waiting for you, my friend. Gulgothir in six days, then the river east and north. Say three weeks. Then Raboas and your Armour. Sounds easy, does it not?'

'As easy as milking a snake. Have you heard that Cadoras is in Skultik?'

Durmast's eyes opened wide in mock surprise. 'No!'

'He is hunting me, so I am told.'

'Let us hope he does not find you.'

'For his sake,' said Waylander. 'How many men do you have?'

'Twenty. Good men. Tough.'

'Good men?'

'Well no, scum as a matter of fact. But they can fight. Would you like to meet some of them?'

'No, I have just eaten. How many people are you taking?'

'One hundred and sixty. Some nice-looking women among them, Waylander. It should be a pleasant few days.'

Waylander nodded and glanced around the camp. Runners all of them, yet he felt pity for the families forced to trust a man like Durmast. Most of them would escape with their lives, but they would arrive in Gulgothir as paupers.

He transferred his gaze to the tree-lined hills to the south. A flash of light caught his eye and for some time he stared at the distant slopes.

'What is it?' asked Durmast.

'Perhaps nothing. Perhaps sunlight on a piece of quartz.'

'But you think it is Cadoras?'

'Who knows?' said Waylander, leading his horse away from the wagons and settling down in the shade of a spreading pine.

High in the hills, Cadoras replaced the long glass in its leather container and sat back on a fallen tree.

173

He was a tall, thin man, black-haired and angular. A scar ran from his forehead to his chin, cutting across his lips and giving him a mocking devil's smile. The eyes were cloudy grey and cold as winter mist. He wore a black mailshirt, dark leggings and riding boots, and by his hips hung two short swords.

Cadoras waited for an hour, watching the wagons hitched to oxen and then assembled into a north-pointing line. Durmast rode to the head of the column and led the way towards the mountains and the Delnoch Pass. Waylander rode at the rear.

A sound from behind him caused Cadoras to turn sharply. A young man emerged from the bushes, blinking in surprise as he saw the knife in Cadoras' raised hand.

'He didn't come,' said the man. 'We waited where you said, but he didn't come.'

'He came – but he circled you.'

'Vulvin is missing. I sent Macas to find him.'

'He will find him dead,' said Cadoras.

'How can you be sure?'

'Because I wanted him dead,' said Cadoras, walking away and staring after the wagons. Gods, why did they give him such fools? Bureaucrats! Of course Vulvin was dead. He had been ordered to watch the cabin of Hewla, but on no account to tackle Waylander. Why not, he had asked, he is only a man? Cadoras had known the fool would do something foolish, but then Vulvin was no loss.

An hour later Macas returned – short and burly, with a petulant mouth and a permanently surly manner. He moved to Cadoras, ignoring the younger man.

'Dead,' he said simply.

'Did you kill the old woman?'

'No. She had two wolves with her – they were eating Vulvin.'

'And you did not want to disturb their lunch?'

'No, Cadoras, I did not want to die.'

'Very wise. Hewla would have struck you dead in an instant; she has rare powers. By the way, there were no wolves.'

'But I saw them . . .'

'You saw what she wanted you to see. Did you ask her how Vulvin died?'

'I did not have to. She said it was pointless sending jackals after a lion – told me to tell you that.'

'She is right. But you jackals were part of the contract. Mount up.'

'You do not like us, do you?' asked Macas.

'Like you, little man? What is to like? Now mount up.'

Cadoras walked to his horse and swung smoothly into the saddle. The wagons were out of sight now and he eased his mount out on to the slope, sitting back in the saddle and keeping the beast's head up.

'Don't make it too easy, Waylander,' he whispered. 'Do not disappoint me.'

12

When Karnak entered the council chamber, the twenty officers stood and saluted. Waving them to their seats, the general moved to the head of the table and removed his cloak, draping it over the chair behind him.

'Purdol is ready to fall,' he declared, his blue eyes scanning the grim faces around the table. 'Gan Degas is old, tired and ready to crack. There are no Source priests at Purdol and the Gan has received no news for more than a month. He believes he is alone.'

Karnak waited, allowing the news to sink in and gauging the rising tension. He watched Gellan, noting the sustained absence of emotion. Not so young Sarvaj, who had leaned back with disappointment etched into his features. Jonat was whispering to Gellan, and Karnak knew what he was saying; he was harping on past mistakes. Young Dundas waited expectantly, his belief in Karnak total. The general glanced around the table. He knew every man present, their weaknesses and their strengths – the officers prone to melancholy and those whose reckless courage was more dangerous than cowardice.

'I am going to Purdol,' he said, judging the moment. A gasp went up from the men and he lifted his hand for silence. 'There are three armies ranged against us, with Purdol taking the lion's share. If the fortress falls it will release 40,000 men to invade Skultik. We cannot stand against such a force. So I am going there.'

'You will never get in,' said one officer, a bearded Legion warrior named Emden. 'The gates are sealed.'

'There is another way,' said Karnak. 'Over the mountains.'

'Sathuli lands,' muttered Jonat. 'I've been there. Treacherous passes, ice-covered ledges – it is impassable.'

'No,' said Dundas, rising to his feet. 'Not impassable – we have more than fifty men working to clear the way.'

'But the mountains do not lead into the fortress,' protested Gellan. 'There is a sheer cliff rising from the back of Purdol. It would be impossible to climb down.'

'We are not going over the mountain,' said Karnak. 'We are going *through* it. There is a deep honeycomb of caves and tunnels and one tunnel leads through to the dungeons below the main Keep; at the moment it is blocked, but we will clear it. Jonat is right: the way is difficult and there will be no room for horses. I intend to take a thousand men, each bearing sixty pounds of supplies. Then we will hold until Egel breaks out of Skultik . . .'

'But what if he doesn't?' demanded Jonat.

'Then we retreat through the mountains and disperse into small raiding groups.'

Sarvaj raised his hand. 'One question only, general. According to the fortress specifications, Purdol should be manned by 10,000 men. Even if we get through, we will only raise the defenders to a sixty-per-cent complement. Can we thus hold?'

177

'Only architects and bureaucrats work in numbers, Sarvaj. The first wall at Purdol has already fallen, which means that the harbour and the docks are already held by the Vagrians and allowing them to ship in supplies and troops. The second wall has only two gates and they are holding firm. The third wall has but one gate – and after that there is the Keep. A strong force could hold Purdol for at least three months; we will not need more than that.'

Gellan cleared his throat. 'Have we any idea,' he said, 'as to losses at Purdol?'

Karnak nodded. 'Eight hundred men. Six hundred dead, the rest too badly wounded to fight.'

'And what of Skarta?' asked Jonat. 'There are Drenai families here depending on us for protection.'

Karnak rubbed at his eyes and let the silence grow. This was the question he had feared.

'There is a time for hard decisions, and we have reached it. Our presence here may give the people hope, but it is false hope. Skarta is indefensible. Egel knows it, I know it – and that is why he raids the west, to keep the Vagrians on the move, to disconcert them and hopefully to prevent a large-scale invasion here. But we are pinning down troops desperately needed elsewhere. We will leave a token force of some 200 men . . . but that is all.'

'The people will be wiped out,' said Jonat, rising to his feet, his face flushed and angry.

'They will be wiped out anyway ,' started Karnak 'should the Vagrians attack. At the moment the enemy waits for Purdol to fall and they won't risk entering the forest. Holding Purdol is the best chance for Skarta and the other Skultik towns. Egel will be left with just under 4,000 men, but there are others coming in from the mountains of Skoda. We must win him time.'

'I know what you are thinking: that it is madness. I agree with you! But the Vagrians have all the advantages. Every major port is in their hands. The Lentrian army is being pushed back. Drenan has fallen and the routes to Mashrapur are closed. Purdol alone holds against them. If it falls before Egel breaks clear, we are finished and the Drenai will be wiped out. The Vagrian farmers are being offered choice Drenai lands, merchants are planning for the day when all of our lands will be part of Greater Vagria. We are doomed people unless we take our fate in our hands and risk everything.

'Quite simply, my friends, there is no more room for manoeuvre. Bereft of choices, we must hold the tiger by the throat and hope that he weakens before we tire. Tomorrow we ride for Purdol.'

Deep down Gellan knew the venture was perilous, moreover a tiny spark of doubt told him that Karnak's real reason for wanting to aid Purdol owed more to personal ambition than to strategic sanity. And yet . . .

Was it not better to follow a charismatic leader to the gates of Hell, rather than a mediocre general to a dull defeat?

The meeting ended at dusk and Gellan wandered to his tiny room to pack his few possessions into canvas and leather saddlebags. There were three shirts, two sets of woollen leggings, a battered leather-covered hand-written Legion manual, a jewelled dagger and an oval wooden painting of a blonde woman and two young children. He sat down on the bed, removed his helmet and studied the portrait. When it had been presented to him he had disliked it, feeling it failed to capture the reality of their smiles, the joy of their lives. Now he saw it as a work of rare genius. Carefully he wrapped the painting in oilskin and placed it in a saddlebag between the shirts. Lifting the dagger, he slid it from its scabbard; he had won it two years before when he became the first man to win the Silver Sword six times.

His children had been so proud of him at the banquet. Dressed in their best clothes, they had sat like tiny adults, their eyes wide and their smiles huge. And Karys had spilt not one drop of soup on her white dress, a fact she pointed out to him all evening. But his wife, Ania, had not attended the banquet; the noise, she had said, would only make her head ache.

Now they were dead, their souls lost to the Void. It had been hard when the children died, bitter hard. And Gellan had retreated into himself, having nothing left with which to comfort Ania. Alone she had been unable to cope and eighteen days after the tragedy she had hung herself with a silken scarf . . . Gellan had found the body. Plague had claimed his children. Suicide took his wife.

Now all he had was the Legion.

And tomorrow it would head for Purdol and the gates of Hell.

Dardalion waited silently for his visitor. An hour ago the Drenai general Karnak had arrived at the meadow, and had sat outlining his plan to aid Purdol. He had asked if Dardalion could help him, by keeping at bay the spirits of the Dark Brotherhood.

'It is vital we arrive unnoticed,' said Karnak. 'If

there is the merest whisper of my movements, the Vagrians will be waiting for us.'

'I will do what I can, Lord Karnak.'

'Do better than that, Dardalion. Kill the whoresons.'

After he had gone, Dardalion knelt on the grass before his tent and bowed his head in prayer. He had stayed thus for more than an hour when the Abbot came and knelt before him.

Dardalion sensed his presence and opened his eyes. The old man looked tired, his eyes red-rimmed and sorrowful.

'Welcome, Lord Abbot,' said Dardalion.

'What have you done?' asked the old man.

'My Lord, I am sorry for the pain you feel, but I can only do what I feel is right.'

'You have sundered my brotherhood. Twenty-nine priests are now preparing for war and death. It *cannot* be right.'

'If it is wrong, we will pay for it, for the Source is righteous and will suffer no evil.'

'Dardalion, I came to plead with you. Leave this place, find a far monastery in another land and return to your studies. The Source will show you the path.'

'He has shown me the path, my lord.'

The old man bowed his head and tears fell to the grass.

'I am powerless, then, against you?'

'Yes, my lord. Whereas I am not against you at all.'

'You are now a leader, chosen by those who would follow you. What title will you carry, Dardalion. The Abbot of Death?'

'No, I am not an abbot. We will fight without hate

and we will find no joy in the battle. And when it is won – or lost – we will return to what we were.'

'Can you not see the folly in your words? You will fight evil on its own ground, with its own weapons. You will defeat it. But will that end the war? It may stop the Brotherhood, but there are other brotherhoods and other evils. Evil does not die, Dardalion. It is a weed in the garden of life. Cut it, burn it, uproot it, yet will it return the stronger. This path of yours has no ending – the war merely changes.'

Dardalion said nothing, the truth of the Abbot's words hammering home to him.

'In this you are right, my lord. I see that. And I see also that you are correct when you name me "Abbot". We cannot merely become Soul Warriors. There must be order and our mission must be finite. I will consider your words carefully.'

'But you will not change your immediate course?'

'It is set. What I have done, I have done in faith and I will not go back on it, any more than you will break your own faith.'

'Why not, Dardalion? You have already broken faith once. You took an oath that all human life – all life, indeed – would be sacred to you. Now you have slain several men and have eaten meat. Why should one more act of "faith" concern you?'

'I cannot argue with that, my lord,' said Dardalion. 'The truth of it grieves me.'

The Abbot pushed himself to his feet. 'I hope that history does not recall you and your Thirty, Dardalion, though I fear that it will. Men are always impressed by acts of violence. Build your legend carefully, lest it destroy all we stand for.'

The Abbot walked away into the darkening dusk

where Astila and the other priests waited in silence. They bowed as he passed, but he ignored them.

The priests gathered in a ring around Dardalion and waited while he concluded his prayers. Then he looked up.

'Welcome, my friends. Tonight we must aid Lord Karnak, but above this we must learn about ourselves. There is more than a chance that the path we follow is the road to perdition, for it may be that everything we do is against the will of the Source. So we must hold in our hearts the strength of our faith and the belief in our cause. Tonight some of us may die. Let us not travel to the Source with hate in us. We will begin now by joining in prayer. We will pray for our enemies, and we will forgive them in our hearts.'

'How can we forgive them and then slay them?' asked a young priest.

'If we do not forgive, then hate will flower. But think on this: if you had a dog that became rabid, you would slay it with regret. You would not hate it. That is what I ask. Let us pray.'

As darkness closed in around them they concluded their communion, and their spirits rose into the night sky.

Dardalion glanced about him. All the priests were clothed in silver armour, shining shields upon their arms and swords of fire in their hands. The stars shone like gems in a blaze, and the mountains of the moon cast sharp shadows as The Thirty waited for the Brotherhood. All was silence.

Dardalion could feel the tension among the priests, for their minds were still linked. Doubts and uncertainties flickered and faded. The night was clear and calm, the forest below them bathed in silver light.

The hours stretched on, impossibly long, and fear ebbed and flowed among the priests to touch each of them with icy fingers.

The night grew more menacing and to the west sombre clouds gathered, staining the moonlight.

'They are coming!' pulsed Astila. 'I can sense it.'

'Be calm,' urged Dardalion.

The dark clouds drew nearer and Dardalion's sword flickered into his hand, the blade burning with white fire.

The clouds loomed and disgorged black-cloaked warriors who swept down on a wave of hatred that engulfed The Thirty. The dark emotion closed over Dardalion, but he shook himself free and soared to meet the attackers. His blade cut and sliced into their mass and his shield rang with returned blows. The Thirty flew to his aid and the battle was joined.

There were more than fifty black warriors, but they could not match the silver-armoured priests and their fiery swords, and they fell back towards the clouds. The Thirty gave chase.

Suddenly Astila screamed a mind warning and Dardalion, about to enter the clouds, veered away.

The cloud bunched in on itself – forming a bloated body, scaled and dark. Huge wings unfurled and a gaping red maw opened at the front of the beast. The Brotherhood were absorbed into its mass and it grew yet more solid.

'Back!' pulsed Dardalion, and The Thirty fled over the forest.

The beast pursued them and Dardalion halted in his flight, his mind racing. Somehow the combined

184

forces of the Brotherhood had created this thing. Was it real? Instinctively he knew that it was.

'To me!' he pulsed. The Thirty gathered around him. 'One warrior. One mind. One mission,' he intoned, and The Thirty merged. Dardalion was swamped and his mind swam as his power multiplied.

Where there had been Thirty, now there was One whose eyes blazed with fire and whose sword was jagged like frozen lightning.

With a roar of rage, the One hurled himself at the beast. The creature reared and taloned arms raked out at the warrior, but the One hammered his lightning blade across its body, severing one limb at a stroke. The beast bellowed in pain and with jaws opened wide it plunged towards its attacker. The One looked up into the giant maw, seeing row upon row of teeth, shaped like the dark swords of the Brotherhood. Hefting his blade, he threw it like a thunderbolt into the cavern of the mouth. As the weapon speared home the One created another and another, hurling them deep into the monster. The beast drew back, its form shifting and changing as the lightning blades lanced its body.

Small dark shapes fled from its mass and it shrank. Then the One spread his hands and flew like an arrow into the heart of the cloud, tearing at the astral flesh. His mind was full of screams and pain as the Brotherhood died one by one. When the cloud broke up and the surviving warriors fled for the safety of their bodies, the One hurled bolts of light at them as they went, then hovered under the stars, seeing them for the first time.

How beautiful, he thought. His far-seeing eyes scanned the planets, the shifting of colours, the swirling of distant clouds over dried-out oceans, and far off he spied a comet arcing through the galaxy. So much to see.

Within the One, Dardalion struggled for identity; his name was a lost thing to him and he fell asleep in the mass. Astila fought on, his thoughts things of mist ebbing and flowing. One. The One. More than One. Numbers. A wave of joy suffused him as he fought, and his vision was blanked by the sight of a meteor shower exploding in rainbow colours through the atmosphere. The One was mightily pleased with the display.

Astila clung to his task. Numbers. A number. No . . . not One. Slowly he forced himself to count, searching what was left of his memory for thoughts that were his alone. Then a name struck him. Dardalion. Was it *his* name? No. Another. He called out weakly, but there was no response. A number.

Thirty. That was the number of power. *Thirty.* The One shivered and Astila burst clear.

'Who are you?' asked the One.

'Astila.'

'Why have you withdrawn from me? We are One.'

'I seek Dardalion within you.'

'Dardalion?' said the One, and deep within him the young priest stirred to life. One by one Astila called the names of The Thirty and the priests came to themselves, drawing away confused and uncertain.

Dawn was near when Astila led the group home. Once more in their bodies, they slept for several hours.

Dardalion was the first to wake. He roused the others and called Astila to him

'Last night you saved us,' said Dardalion. 'You have a gift for seeing through deceptions.'

'But you created the One,' said Astila. 'Without that we would not have survived.'

'We almost did not survive. The One was as great a danger to us as the Cloudbeast and you saved us a second time. Yesterday the Abbot gave me a warning and I said I would think on his words. We need form, Astila . . . discipline. I shall be the Abbot of The Thirty. But you must have a senior part. I shall be the Voice and you will be the Eyes. Together we will find the path to the will of the Source.

13

Waylander leaned back in the saddle and stared out over the Delnoch Pass to the Nadir plains beyond. Behind him the wagons had bunched for the night, ready for the perilous descent tomorrow. The pass sloped down for over a mile in a series of treacherous scree-covered ledges, and it took a brave man to drive a wagon over the narrow winding trail. Most of the refugees had paid Durmast's men handsome sums to take over the reins for the descent, while they walked behind in comparative safety.

A cool breeze was blowing from the north and Waylander allowed himself to relax. There had been no sign of Cadoras or of the Brotherhood, and he had checked the back trails with care. Suddenly he grinned. It was said of Cadoras that when you saw him there was danger – that when you did not see him, there was death. Waylander slid from his horse's back and led the animal to the picket ropes. Stripping off the saddle, he rubbed the horse down, fed it with grain and moved into the centre of the camp where the fires crackled under iron cooking-pots.

Durmast was sitting with a group of travellers, regaling them with tales of Gulgothir. In the red firelight his face was less brutal and his smile warm and friendly. Children sat around him, gazing in awe at the giant and relishing his outrageous stories. It was hard to believe that these people were fleeing from a terrible war; that many of them had lost friends, brothers and sons. Their relief at the prospect of escape was showing itself in over-loud laughter and jests. Waylander transferred his gaze to Durmast's men, sitting in a group apart from the others. Hard men, Durmast had said, and Waylander knew their type. They were not hard, they were murderous. In days of peace and plenty, the worthy townsfolk who now laughed and sang would bolt their doors against such as these; you could not have paid them enough to travel with Durmast. Now they laughed like children, unable to see that their danger was just as great.

Waylander turned to fetch his blankets – and froze. Standing not ten feet away from him, facing a fire, was Danyal. The firelight danced in her red-gold hair, and she was wearing a new dress tunic of wool embroidered and edged with gold thread. Waylander swallowed hard and took a deep breath. Then she lifted a hand to her hair and turned, seeing him for the first time. Her smile was genuine and he hated her for it.

'So you notice me at last,' she said, moving towards him.

'I thought you were staying in Skarta with the children?'

'I left them with the Source priests. I am tired of war, Waylander. I want to go somewhere where I can sleep at night without fearing tomorrow.'

'There is no such place,' he said bitterly. 'Come, walk with me.'

'I am preparing some food.'

'Later,' he said, walking away towards the pass. She followed him to a grassy knoll where they sat on jutting boulders. 'Do you know who is leading this caravan?'

'Yes,' she answered. 'A man called Durmast.'

'He is a killer.'

'So are you.'

'You don't understand. You are in more danger here than back in Skultik.'

'But you are here.'

'What has that to do with it? Durmast and I understand one another. I need him to help me find the Armour; he knows the Nadir and I might not get through without him.'

'Will you allow him to harm us?'

'*Allow*, woman? What on earth do you think I could do to stop him? He has twenty men. Damn you, Danyal, why are you dogging my footsteps?'

'How dare you?' she stormed. 'I didn't know you were travelling with us. Your conceit is colossal.'

'That's not what I meant,' he said defensively. 'It just seems that whenever I turn round you are there.'

'How depressing for you!'

'For pity's sake, woman – can you not hold back from jumping down my throat? I do not want to fight with you.'

'In that case, let me say that you have a regrettable line in small talk.'

For a while they sat in silence, watching the moon traverse the Delnoch Pass.

'I am not going to live very long, Danyal,' he said at last. 'Maybe three weeks, maybe less. I would very much like to end my life successfully . . .'

'Just the sort of stupid remark I would expect from a man! Who is going to care if you find that Armour of yours? It is not magic, it is just metal. And not even precious metal.'

'*I* will care.'

'Why?'

'What sort of question is that?'

'Stalling for time, Waylander?'

'No, I meant it. You think men stupid when they lust after glory? So do I. But this is not about glory – it concerns honour. I have lived in shame for many years and I fell to a level I would not have believed possible. I killed a good man . . . ended his life for money. I cannot undo that act. But I can atone. I do believe in Gods who care about humans. I do not seek forgiveness from some higher authority. I want to forgive myself. I want to find the Armour for Egel and the Drenai and fulfil a promise I made Orien.'

'You do not have to die to do that,' she said softly, placing her hand gently on his.

'No, I don't – and would prefer to live. But I am a hunted man. Cadoras hunts me. The Brotherhood seek me. And Durmast will sell me when the time is right.'

'Then why stay here like a tethered goat? Strike out on your own.'

'No. I need Durmast for the first part of my journey. I have an advantage! I know my enemies and I have no one to rely on.'

'That makes no sense.'

'Only because you are a woman and cannot understand the simplicity of the words. I am alone, so there is no one to let me down. When I run – if I run – I carry no baggage. I am self-sufficient and very, very deadly.'

'Which brings us to our first point,' said Danyal. 'You are trying to tell me that I am baggage to weigh you down.'

'Yes, Durmast must not realise that we know one another, else he will use you against me.'

'It is too late for that,' said Danyal, looking away. 'I wondered why he changed his mind about allowing me to ride with the wagons when I had no money. But I thought it was my body he desired.'

'Explain,' said Waylander wearily.

'A woman I met directed me to Durmast, but he told me that with no money I was useless to him. Then he asked where I was from, as he had not seen me before in Skarta, and I told him that I came in with you. Then he changed and asked me all about you, after which he said I could come.'

'You are leaving something out.'

'Yes. I told him I loved you.'

'Why? Why would you do that?'

'Because it's true!' she snapped.

'And he asked you whether I felt the same?'

'Yes. I told him no.'

'But he did not believe you.'

'How do you know?'

'Because you are here.' Waylander lapsed into silence, remembering Hewla's words about the red-headed woman and Orien's enigmatic warning concerning companions. What was it the old man had said?

That success or failure would depend on Waylander's companions. Or rather on whom he chose to accompany him.

'What are you thinking?' she asked, seeing him smile, and the tension fade from his face.

'I was thinking that I am glad you are here. It is very selfish of me. I will die, Danyal. I am a realist and the odds are too great. But knowing you will be with me, for a few days at least, gives me pleasure.'

'Even though Durmast will use me against you?'

'Even so.'

'Do you have a small copper coin?' she asked.

He fished in his money-sack, producing a tiny coin carrying the head of Niallad which he handed to her.

'What do you want it for?'

'You once said you never took a woman you had not paid for. Now you have paid.'

Leaning over, she kissed him softly and his arms moved round her waist, pulling her in to him.

Hidden in the trees, Durmast watched the lovers move to the grass beside the boulders. The big man shook his head and smiled.

The dawn broke bright and clear, but dark clouds loomed in the north and Durmast cursed loudly.

'Rain,' he spat. 'That's all we damned well need!'

The first of the wagons was led to the crest of the Pass. Pulled by six oxen, it was some twenty feet long and heavily laden with boxes and crates. The driver licked his lips, his eyes narrowing as he gauged the dangers of the trail. Then he cracked his whip over the head of the lead oxen and the wagon lurched forward. Waylander walked behind, with Durmast and seven of his men. The first two hundred yards were steep, though relatively simple to travel for the path was wide and firm. But then it narrowed and dipped to the right. The driver hauled back on the reins and jammed the wheel-brake tight against the rim, but the wagon slid slowly sideways towards the yawning drop on the left.

'Ropes!' bellowed Durmast and the men ran forward to hook inch-thick hemp ropes about the axles. The wagon stopped its slide. Waylander, Durmast and the others took up the two ropes and gathered in the slack.

'Now!' called Durmast and the wagoner gently released the brake. The wagon inched forward, slithering to a stop some twenty paces on. The trail was angled here, and the weight of the wagon caused it to pull towards the edge. But the men on the ropes were strong, and well-used to the perils of the Delnoch Pass.

For over an hour they toiled, until at last the wagon came to level ground.

Far behind them a second wagon was making the descent, with seven more of Durmast's men hauling on ropes. The giant sat back and grinned as he watched them strain.

'They earn their money when they work with me,' he said.

Waylander nodded, too weary to speak. 'You've gone soft Waylander. A little gentle exercise and you're sweating like a pig in heat!'

'Pulling wagons is not my usual occupation,' said Waylander.

'Did you sleep well?' asked Durmast.

'Yes.'

'Alone?'

'What sort of question is that from a man who hid in the bushes and watched?'

Durmast chuckled and scratched his beard. 'You don't miss much, my friend. Soft you may be, but you eyes have lost nothing in sharpness.'

'Thank you for allowing her to come,' said Waylander. 'It will make the first few days of the journey more pleasurable.'

'The least I could do for an old friend. Are you taken with her?'

'She loves me,' replied Waylander with a grin.

'And you?'

'I shall say farewell at Gulgothir – with regret.'

'Then you are fond of her?'

'Durmast, you watched us last night. Did you see what happened before we made love?'

'I saw you pass her something.'

'You saw me give her money. *Love*? You tell me.'

Durmast leaned back, closing his eyes against the morning sun.

'You ever wished you had settled down? Raised a family?'

'I did once, they died,' said Waylander.

'Me too. Only mine didn't die – she ran off with a Ventrian trader and took my sons with her.'

'I am surprised you didn't go after her.'

Durmast sat up and stretched his back. 'I did, Waylander,' he said.

'And?'

'I gutted the trader.'

'And your wife?'

'She became a whore in the dockside taverns.'

'What a fine pair we make! I pay for my pleasures because I will never again risk love, while you are haunted by love's betrayal.'

'Who says I am haunted?' demanded the giant.

'I do. And don't let yourself get too angry, my friend, for soft though I may be you cannot handle me.'

For several seconds Durmast's angry glare remained, then it faded from his eyes and he smiled. 'At least some of the old Waylander remains,' he said. 'Come, it's time for the long climb and another wagon.'

Throughout the day the men toiled and by dusk

all the wagons were safely at the foot of the pass. Waylander had rested through the afternoon, his instincts warning him that he would need all his strength over the next few days.

The rain passed them by and by nightfall the camp-fires were blazing and the smell of cooking meat hung in the air. Waylander made his way to the wagon of the baker, Caymal, who had allowed Danyal to ride with him and his family. On his arrival he found Caymal nursing a bruised eye, his wife Lyda, beside him.

'Where is Danyal?' asked Waylander.

Caymal shrugged. His wife, a lean dark-haired woman in her late thirties, looked up.

'You animals!' she hissed.

'Where is she?'

'Wait your turn, ' said Lyda, her lip trembling.

'Listen to me, woman – I am a friend of Danyal's. Now where is she?'

'A man took her. She didn't want to go and my husband tried to stop him but he hit Cayınal with a club.'

'Which way?'

The woman pointed to a small grove of trees. Waylander lifted a rope from the back of the wagon, coiled it over his shoulder and loped off in that direction. The moon shone bright in a clear sky and he slowed his pace as he neared the grove, closing his eyes and focusing his hearing.

There! To the left was the sound of coarse cloth against tree bark. And to the right, a muffled cry. Angling towards the left Waylander moved slowly forward, bursting into a sprint just as he reached the trees.

A knife flashed past his head and he hit the ground

on one shoulder and rolled. A dark shadow detached itself from the trees, moonlight shining from a curved sword. Waylander rolled to his feet and leapt, his right foot crashed into the man's head and then – as the stranger staggered – Waylander spun on his heel, his right elbow exploding against the man's ear. He fell without a sound. Waylander crept to the right. There in a shallow hollow lay Danyal, her dress ripped open, her legs spread. A man was kneeling over her as Waylander slid the rope from his shoulder and opened the noose.

Moving forward silently he came up behind the man, slipping the noose over his head and jerking it tight. He fell back, scrabbling at the noose, but Waylander pulled him from his feet and dragged him across the hollow to a tall elm. Swiftly he hurled the rope over a branch some ten feet from the ground and hauled the struggling man to his feet. The attacker's eyes were bulging and his face above the dark beard was purple.

Waylander had never seen him before.

Then a whisper of movement from behind caused him to drop the rope and dive to his right. An arrow hissed past him to thud into the bearded attacker. The man grunted and his knees gave way. Waylander bunched his legs under him and came up running, cutting left and right to hinder the aim of the hidden assassin. Once into the trees he dropped low and began to crawl through the bushes, circling the hollow.

The sound of horse's hooves caused him to curse and he straightened, slipping his dagger into his sheath. Returning to the clearing he found Danyal unconscious. Across her naked breasts someone had laid a goose-feathered arrow. Waylander snapped it in half.

Cadoras!

Lifting Danyal, he walked back to the wagons, where he left her with the baker's wife and returned to the grove. The first man who had attacked him lay where he had fallen; Waylander had hoped to question him, but his throat had been cut. Swiftly he searched the body, but there was nothing to identify him. The second man had three gold coins in a belt pouch. Waylander took the coins back to the camp and gave them to Lyda.

'Hide them about your person,' he told her.

She nodded and lifted the canvas flap, allowing Waylander to climb into the wagon.

Danyal was awake, her lip swollen and a bruise on her cheek. Caymal sat beside her. The wagon was cramped and the baker's two young children were sleeping beside Danyal.

'Thank you,' she said, forcing a smile.

'They will not trouble you again.'

Caymal eased himself past Waylander and climbed out over the tailboard. Waylander moved up to sit beside Danyal.

'Are you hurt?' he asked.

'No. Not much anyway. Did you kill them?'

'Yes.'

'How is it you can do these things?'

'Practice,' he said.

'No, that's not what I meant. Caymal tried to stop the man . . . and Caymal is strong, but he was brushed aside like a child.'

'It is all about fear, Danyal. Do you want to rest now?'

'No, I want some air. Let's walk somewhere.'

He helped her from the wagon and they walked to the cliff face and sat on the rocks.

'Tell me about fear,' she said.

He walked away from her and stooped to lift a pebble.

'Catch this,' he said, flicking the stone towards her. Her hand snaked out and she caught the pebble deftly. 'That was easy, was it not?'

'Yes,' she admitted.

'Now if I had Krylla and Miriel here, and two men had knives at their throats and you were told that if you missed the pebble they would die, would it still be easy to catch? Think of those times in your life when you were nervous, and your movements became disjointed.

'Fear makes fools of us all. So too does anger, rage and excitement. And then we move too fast and there is no control. You follow me?'

'I think so. When I had to give my first performance before the King in Drenan, I froze. All I had to do was walk across the stage, but my legs felt as if they were carved from wood.'

'That is it. Exactly! The onset of fear makes the simplest of actions complex and difficult. No more so than when we fight . . . and I can fight better than most because I can bring all my concentration to bear on the small things. The pebble remains a pebble, no matter what hangs upon success or failure.'

'Can you teach me?'

'I don't have time.'

'You are not obeying your own maxim. This is a small thing. Forget the quest and concentrate on me, Waylander – I need to learn.'

'How to fight?'

'No – how to conquer fear. Then you can teach me to fight.'

'Very well. Start by telling me what is death?'

'An ending.'

'Make it worse.'

'Maggots and grey rotting flesh?'

'Good. And where are you?'

'Gone. Finished.'

'Do you feel anything?'

'No . . . perhaps. If there is a paradise.'

'Forget paradise.'

'Then I feel nothing. I am no longer alive.'

'This death, can you avoid it?'

'Of course not.'

'But you can delay it?'

'Yes.'

'And what will that give you?'

'The prospect of more happiness.'

'But at worst?'

'The prospect of more pain,' she said. 'Old age, wrinkles, decay.'

'Which is worse? Death or decay?'

'I am young. At the moment I fear both.'

'To conquer fear, you must realise that there is no escape from what you dread. You must absorb it. Live with it. Taste it. Understand it. Overcome it.'

'I understand that,' she said.

'Good. What do you fear most at this moment?'

'I fear losing you.'

He moved away from her and lifted a pebble. Clouds partly obscured the moonlight and she strained to see his hand.

'I am going to throw this to you,' he said. 'If you

catch it, you stay – if you miss it, you return to Skarta.'

'No, that's not fair! The light is poor.'

'Life is not fair, Danyal. If you do not agree, I shall ride away from the wagons alone.'

'Then I agree.'

Without another word he flicked the stone towards her – a bad throw, moving fast and to her left. Her hand flashed out and the pebble bounced against her palm, but she caught it at the second attempt. Relief swept through her and her eyes were triumphant.

'Why so pleased?' he asked.

'I won!'

'No. Tell me what you did.'

'I conquered my fear?'

'No.'

'Well, what then? I don't understand you.'

'But you must, if you wish to learn.'

Suddenly she smiled. 'I understand the mystery, Waylander.'

'Then tell me what you did.'

'I caught a pebble in the moonlight.'

During the first three days of travel Danyal's progress astonished Waylander. He had known she was strong and supple and quick-witted but, as he discovered, her reflexes were staggeringly swift and her ability to assimilate instructions defied belief.

'You forget,' she told him, 'I performed on the stages of Drenan. I have been trained to dance and to juggle, and I spent three months with a group of acrobats.'

Every morning they rode away from the wagons out on to the undulating terrain of the Steppes. On the first day he taught her to throw a knife; the ease

201

with which she adapted to the skill caused him to re-think his training methods. He had planned to humour her at first, but now he pushed her in earnest. Her juggling skills gave her a sense of balance which was truly extraordinary. His knives were of different weights and lengths, but in her hands they performed equally. She merely hefted the blade in her fingers, judging the weight, and then let fly at the target. Of her first five throws, only one failed to thud home into the lightning-blasted tree.

Waylander found a rock with high chalk content and outlined the figure of a man on the tree bole. Handing Danyal a knife he turned her round, facing away from the tree.

'Without pause I want you to turn and throw, aiming for the neck,' he said. Spinning on her heel, her arm flashed forward and the knife hammered into the tree just above the right shoulder of the chalk figure.

'Damn!' she said. Waylander smiled and retrieved the knife.

'I said turn, not spin. You were still moving to your left when you threw – and that carried your arm past the target. But, nevertheless, it was a fine effort.'

On the second day he borrowed a bow and quiver of arrows. She was less skilled with this weapon, but her eye was good. For some time Waylander watched her, then he bade her remove her shirt. Taking it by the sleeves, he moved behind her and tied it tightly around her, flattening her breasts against her ribs.

'That is not very comfortable,' she protested.

'I know. But you are bending your back as you

pull, to avoid the string catching your body – that affects your aim.'

But the idea was not a success and Waylander moved on to the sword. One of Durmast's men had sold him a slender sabre with an ivory hilt and a filigreed fist-shield. The weapon was well-balanced and light enough to allow Danyal's greater speed to offset her lack of strength.

'Always remember,' he told her as they sat together after an hour of work, 'that most swords are used as hacking weapons. Your enemy, in the main, will be right-handed. He will lift his sword over his right shoulder and sweep it down from right to left, aiming at your head. But the shortest distance between two points is a straight line. So thrust! Use the point of the sword. Nine times out of ten you will kill your opponent. Most men are untrained, they hack and slash in a frenzy and are easy to despatch.' Taking up two sticks he had whittled to resemble swords, he handed one to Danyal. 'Come, I will play the part of your opponent.'

On the fourth day he began to teach her the principles of unarmed combat.

'Hammer this thought into your mind: Think! Harness your emotions and act on the instincts this training will inspire. Rage is useless, so do not lash out. *Think!* Your weapons are fists, fingers, feet, elbows, and head. Your targets are eyes, throat, belly and groin. These are the areas in which a well-timed blow will disable an enemy – you have one great advantage in this kind of combat: you are a woman. Your enemies will expect, fear, terror . . . and ultimately surrender. If you stay cool you will survive – and they will die.'

On the afternoon of the fifth day, as Waylander

and Danyal rode back towards the wagons a group of Nadir warriors galloped into sight whooping and cheering. Waylander reined in his horse as they approached. There were some two hundred riders and they were heavily laden with blankets, trade goods and saddlebags bulging with coins and jewels. Danyal had never seen Nadir tribesmen, but she knew of their reputation as ferocious killers. Squat and powerful men they were, with slanted eyes and flat faces; many wore lacquered breastplates and fur-trimmed helms; most carried two swords and an assortment of knives.

The Nadir pulled up, spreading across the trail. Meanwhile Waylander sat quietly, trying to pick out the leader.

After several tense seconds a middle-aged warrior rode from the group; his eyes were dark and malicious, his smile cruel. The eyes flickered to Danyal and Waylander read his thought.

'Who are you?' asked the leader, leaning forward on the pommel of his saddle.

'I ride with Ice-eyes,' said Waylander, using the Nadir form of Durmast's name.

'You say.'

'Who is there to doubt me?'

The dark eyes fixed on Waylander and the Nadir nodded.

'We have come from Ice-eyes' wagons. Many gifts. You have gifts?'

'Only one,' said Waylander.

'Then give it to me.'

'I already have. I gave you the gift of life.'

'Who are you to give what I already possess?'

'I am the Soul Stealer,'

204

The Nadir showed no emotion. 'You ride with Ice-eyes?'

'Yes. We are brothers.'

'Of the blood?'

'No. Of the blade.'

'Ride in peace on this day,' said the Nadir. 'But remember – there will be other days.'

Lifting his arm, the Nadir leader waved on his men and the group thundered past the two riders.

'What was that all about?' asked Danyal.

'He did not want to die,' said Waylander. 'There is a lesson there, if you care to consider it.'

'I have had enough lessons for one day. What did he mean – many gifts?'

Waylander shrugged. 'Durmast betrayed the wagon folk. He took their money to lead them to Gulgothir, but he already had a deal with the Nadir. So the Nadir rob the wagons and Durmast takes a percentage. At the moment they still have their wagons, but the Nadir will come again before Gulgothir and take even those. The people who survive will arrive in Gulgothir as paupers.'

'That is despicable.'

'No. It is the way of the world. Only the weak run . . . now they must pay for their weakness.'

'Are you really that callous?'

'I am afraid so, Danyal.'

'That is a shame.'

'I agree with you.'

'You are an infuriating man!'

'And you are a very special woman – but let us think about that this evening. For now, answer me the question of the Nadir rider: Why did he let us live?'

Danyal smiled. 'Because you isolated him from

his men and threatened him as an individual. Gods, will these lessons never cease?'

'All too soon.' said Waylander.

14

Danyal and Waylander made love in a sheltered hollow away from the wagons, and the experience shook Waylander. He could not recall the moment of penetration, nor any sense of passion. He had been filled with a desire to be closer to Danyal, to somehow absorb her body into his own – or perhaps lose his own within hers. And for the first time in many years he had ceased to be aware of movement around him. He had been lost within the lovemaking.

Now alone, fear tugged at him.

What if Cadoras had crept upon them?

What if the Nadir had returned?

What if the Brotherhood . . . ?

What if?

Hewla was right. Love was a greater enemy at this time.

'You are getting old,' he told himself. 'Old and tired.'

He knew he was no longer as swift or as strong and the silver hairs were multiplying. Somewhere out in the vast blackness of the world was a young killer more swift, more deadly than the legendary Waylander. Was it Cadoras? Or one of the Brotherhood?

The moment of drama with the Nadir had been telling. Waylander had survived it on experience and bluff, for with Danyal beside him he had not wanted to die. His greatest strength had always been his lack of fear but now – when he needed all his talents – the fear was returning.

He rubbed at his eyes, aware of the need for sleep yet reluctant to give in. Sleep is the brother of Death, said the song. But it is gentle and kind. Weariness eased its warmth into his muscles, and the rock against which he sat seemed soft and welcoming. Too tired to pull his blankets over himself, he laid his head back on the rock and slept. As he fell into darkness he saw the face of Dardalion; the priest was calling to him, but he could not hear the words.

Durmast was sleeping beneath the lead wagon when the dream came to him. He saw a man in silver armour: a handsome young man, clean-cut and strong. Durmast was dreaming of a woman with hair of shining chestnut brown – and of a child, sturdy and strong. He pushed away the image of the warrior, but it returned again and again.

'What do you want?' shouted the giant, as the woman and the child shimmered and disappeared. 'Leave me!'

'Your profits are dust unless you wake,' said the warrior.

'Wake? I am awake.'

'You are dreaming. You are Durmast and you lead the wagons to Gulgothir.'

'Wagons?'

'Wake up, man! The hunters of the night are upon you!'

The giant groaned and rolled over; he sat up, rapping his head sharply against the base of the wagon, and cursed loudly. Rolling clear, he straightened – the dream had gone, but a lingering doubt remained.

Taking up a short double-headed axe, he moved towards the west.

Danyal awoke with a start. The dream had been powerful and in it Dardalion had urged her to seek Waylander. Easing herself past the sleeping baker and his family, she slid the sabre clear of its scabbard and leapt forward from the tailboard.

Durmast swung round as she appeared beside him.

'Don't do that!' he snapped. 'I might have taken your head off.'

Then he noticed the sword. 'Where do you think you are going with that?'

'I had a dream,' answered Danyal lamely.

'Stay close to me,' he ordered, moving away from the wagons.

The night was clear, but clouds drifted across the moon and Durmast spat out an oath as he strained to see into the darkness. A hint of movement to the left! His arm swept out, knocking Danyal from her feet. Arrows hissed by him as he dived for the ground. Then a dark shadow lunged at him and the axe swept up to cleave into the man's side, smashing his ribs to shards before exiting in a bloody swathe. Danyal rolled to her feet as the clouds suddenly cleared to show two men in black armour running towards her with swords raised. She dived forward, rolling on her shoulder, and the men cannoned into her and fell headlong into the dust. Danyal came up, fast spearing the point of the sabre into the back of one man's neck; the second man swung round and lunged at her, but Durmast's axe buried itself in his back. His eyes opened wide, but he was dead before a scream could sound.

'Waylander!' bellowed Durmast as more black shapes came from the darkness.

At the boulder Waylander stirred, his eyes drifting open but his body heavy with deep sleep. Above him a man crouched, a wickedly curved blade in his hand.

'Now you die,' said the man and Waylander was powerless to stop him. But suddenly the man froze and his jaw dropped. Sleep fell from the assassin and his hand whipped out to punch his assailant from his feet. As he fell, Waylander saw that a long goose-feathered shaft had pierced the base of his skull.

Rolling to his left, Waylander lunged upright with knives in his hands as a dark figure leapt at him, He blocked the downward sweep of the sword, catching it on the hilt-guard of his left-hand knife. Dropping his shoulder, he stabbed his attacker low in the groin; the man twisted as he fell, tearing the knife from Waylander's hand.

The clouds closed in once more and Waylander threw himself to the ground, rolled several yards and lay still.

There was no movement around him.

For several minutes he strained to hear, closing his eyes and calming his mind.

Satisfied that his attackers had fled, he slowly raised himself to his feet. The clouds cleared . . .

Waylander spun on his heel, his hand whipping out. The black-bladed knife thudded into the shoulder of a kneeling archer. Waylander ran forward as the man lunged to his feet, but his opponent side-stepped and ran off into the darkness.

Weaponless, Waylander dropped to one knee and waited.

A scream sounded from the direction the wounded man had taken. Then a voice drifted to the kneeling assassin:

'You had best be more careful, Waylander.' A dark object sailed into the air to land with a thud beside him. It was his knife.

'Why did you save me?'

'Because you are mine,' replied Cadoras.

'I will be ready.'

'I hope so.'

Durmast and Danyal ran to him.

'Who were you speaking to?' asked the giant.

'Cadoras. But it doesn't matter – let's go back to the wagons.'

Together the trio moved back into the relative sanctuary of the camp, where Durmast stoked a dying fire to life and then cleaned the blood from his axe.

'That is some woman you have there,' he said. 'She killed three of the swine! And you had me thinking she was a casual bedmate! You are a subtle devil, Waylander.'

'They were Brotherhood warriors,' said the assassin, 'and they used some kind of sorcery to push me into sleep. I should have guessed.'

'Dardalion saved you,' said Danyal. 'He came to me in a dream.'

'A silver warrior with fair hair?' asked Durmast.

Danyal nodded.

'He came to me also. You have powerful friends – a she-devil and a sorcerer.'

'And a giant with a battleaxe,' said Danyal.

'Do not confuse business with friendship,' muttered Durmast. 'And now, if you'll excuse me, I have some sleep to catch up on.'

The old man gazed with weary eyes at the Vagrian warriors seated before him in what had once been the Palace of Purdol. Their faces shone with the arrogance born of victory, and he knew only too well how he appeared to them: old, tired and weak.

Gan Degas removed his helm and laid it on the table.

Stone-faced, Kaem sat opposite him.

'I take it you are ready to surrender,' said Kaem.

'Yes. If certain conditions are met.'

'Name them.'

'My men are not to be harmed – they are to be released to return to their homes.'

'Agreed . . . once they have laid down their weapons and the fortress is ours.'

'Many citizens fled to the fortress; they also must be allowed to go free and reclaim the homes your men took from them.'

'Petty bureaucracy,' said Kaem. 'It will cause us no problems.'

'What guarantees of faith can you give me?' asked Degas.

Kaem smiled. 'What guarantees can any man give? You have my word – that should be enough between generals. If it is not, you have only to keep the gates barred and fight on.'

Degas dropped his eyes. 'Very well. I have your word, then?'

'Of course, Degas.'

'The gates will be opened at dawn.'

The old warrior pushed himself to his feet and turned to leave.

'Do not forget your helm,' mocked Kaem.

Laughter echoed in the corridor as Degas was led from the hall, flanked by two men in black cloaks. Out in the night air he walked along the docks and up towards the eastern gate. There a rope was lowered from the gate tower; Degas looped his wrist around it and was hauled up into the fortress.

Back at the palace, Kaem silenced his officers and turned to Dalnor.

'There are some four thousand men in the fortress. Killing them all will take some planning – I don't want a mountain of rotting corpses spreading plague and disease. I suggest you split the prisoners into twenty groups, then take them down to the harbour group by group. There are a score of empty warehouses. Kill them and cart their bodies into the discharged grain ships. Then they can be dumped at sea.

'Yes, my lord. It will take some time.'

'We *have* time. We will leave a thousand men to man the fortress and push west into Skultik. The war is almost over, Dalnor.'

'Indeed it is – thanks to you, my lord.'

Kaem swung round to a dark-bearded officer on his right.

'What news of Waylander?'

'He still lives, Lord Kaem. Last night he and his friends fought off an attack by my Brothers. But more are on their way.'

'I must have the Armour.'

'You will have it, my lord. The Emperor has commissioned the assassin Cadoras to hunt Waylander. And twenty of my Brothers are closing in. Added to this, we have received word from the

213

robber Durmast; he asks 20,000 silver pieces for the Armour.'

'Of course you agreed?'

'No, my lord, we beat him down to 15,000. He would have been suspicious had we met his original request without argument. Now we have his trust.'

'Be careful of Durmast,' warned Kaem. 'He is like a rogue lion – he will turn on anyone.'

'Several of his men are in our employ, my lord; we have anticipated all eventualities. The Armour is ours. Waylander is ours – just as the Drenai are ours.'

'Beware of over-confidence, Nemodes. Do not count the lion's teeth until you see flies on his tongue.'

'But surely, my lord, the issue is no longer in doubt?'

'I had a horse once, the fastest beast I ever owned. It could not lose and I wagered a fortune on it. But a bee stung it in the eye just before the start. The issue is always in doubt.'

'Yet you said the war was almost over,' protested Nemodes.

'So it is. And until it is, we will remain wary.'

'Yes, my lord.'

'There are three men who must die. Karnak is one. Egel is the second. But most of all I want to see Waylander's head on a lance.'

'Why Karnak?' asked Dalnor. 'One battle is not sufficient to judge him dangerous.'

'Because he is reckless and ambitious. We cannot plan for him,' answered Kaem.

'There are some men who are good swordsmen, archers or strategists. There are others, seemingly gifted by the Gods, who are masters of all they touch. Karnak is one of these – I cannot read him and that disturbs me.'

'He is said to be in Skarta, serving under Egel,' said Dalnor. 'We will have him soon.'

'Perhaps,' said Kaem doubtfully.

Kaem fought to control his tension as he stood at the head of the Second Legion in the shadow of the eastern gate. Dawn was now minutes old, but still there was no movement from beyond the gates. He was acutely aware of the hostile stares from the archers on the battlements of the gate tower as he stood in full red and bronze battle gear with the sweat trickling between his shoulder-blades.

Dalnor stood behind him, flanked by swordsmen: dark-eyed warriors of the First Elite, the most deadly fighting men of the Second Legion of the Hounds of Chaos.

The sound of tightening ropes and the groaning of rusty ratchets ended Kaem's tension – beyond the gates of oak and iron, the huge bronze reinforced bar was being lifted. Minutes passed and then the gates creaked open. A swelling sense of triumph grew within Kaem, but he swallowed it back, angry at the power of his emotions.

Behind him men began shuffling their feet, anxious to end the long siege and enter the hated fortress.

The gates widened.

Kaem walked into the shadows of the portcullis and out into the bright sunlight of the courtyard . . .

And there stopped so suddenly that Dalnor walked into him knocking him forward; his helmet tipped over his eyes and he straightened it. The courtyard was ringed with fighting men, swords

215

drawn. At the centre, leaning on a double-headed battleaxe, stood a huge warrior, barbarously ill-clad. The man handed the axe to a companion and strolled forward.

'Who is that fat clown?' whispered Dalnor.

'Be silent!' ordered Kaem, his brain working at furious pace.

'Welcome to Dros Purdol,' said the man, smiling.

'Who are you, and where is Gan Degas?'

'The Gan is resting. He asked me to discuss your surrender.'

'What nonsense is this?'

'Nonsense, my dear general?' What can you mean?'

'Gan Degas agreed to surrender to me today after his conditions were met.' Kaem licked his lips nervously as the huge warrior grinned down at him.

'Ah, the conditions,' he said. 'I think there was a misunderstanding. When Gan Degas asked for safety for his men, he didn't quite mean taking them in groups of twenty to the warehouse dock and killing them.' The man's eyes narrowed and the humour vanished from his smile. 'I opened the gates to you, Kaem, so that you could see me. Know me . . . Understand me. There will be no surrender. I have brought with me three thousand men,' lied Karnak, 'and I command this fortress.'

'Who are you?'

'Karnak. Bear the name in mind, Vagrian, for it will be the death of you.'

'You make loud noises, Karnak, but few men fear a yapping dog.'

'True, but you fear me, little man,' said Karnak equably. 'Now – you have twenty seconds to clear your men from the gate. After that the air will be thick with arrows and death. *Go!'*

Kaem turned on his heel to find himself staring at several hundred warriors – the cream of his force – and the full humiliation struck him like a blow. He was inside the fortress with the gates open, yet he could not order the attack for every archer had his bow bent and the shaft aimed at himself. And to save himself – and save himself he must – he had to order them to withdraw. His stock would sink among the men and morale would be severely dented.

He swung back, his face purple with fury. 'Enjoy your moment, Drenai! There will be few such highlights from now on.'

'Fifteen seconds,' said Karnak.

'Back!' shouted Kaem. 'Back through the gates.'

The sound of mocking laughter followed the Vagrian general as he shouldered his way through his troops.

'Close the gates,' yelled Karnak, 'and then get ready for the whoresons!'

Gellan moved alongside Karnak. 'What did you mean about warehouses and killing?'

'Dardalion told me that was the plan. Kaem had promised Degas that the men would be unharmed; it was a foul lie and exactly what you would expect from Kaem, but Degas was too weary to see it.'

'Speaking of weariness,' said Gellan, 'having spent more than ten hours burrowing through rock below the dungeons, I am feeling a little weary myself.'

Karnak thumped him hard between the shoulder-blades. 'Your men worked well, Gellan. The Gods only know what would have happened had we arrived an hour later. Still, it is good to know we are riding a lucky horse, eh?'

'Lucky, general? We have burrowed our way into a besieged fortress and have angered the most powerful general on the continent. Tell me what's lucky.'

Karnak chuckled. 'He *was* the most powerful general on the continent, but he suffered today. He was humiliated. That won't help him; it will open a little tear in his cloak of invincibility.'

Jonat stalked the wall shouting at the fifty men under his command. They had been disgraced that morning, breaking in panic as the Vagrians cleared the wall beside the gate tower. With ten swordsmen, Jonat had rushed in to plug the gap and by some miracle the rangy, black-bearded Legion rider had escaped injury though six of his comrades had died beside him. Karnak had seen the danger and run to Jonat's aid, swinging a huge double-headed battle-axe, followed by a hundred fighting men. The battle by the gate tower was brief and bloody, and by the end of it the men of Jonat's section had returned to the fighting.

Now, with dusk upon them and the sun sinking in fire, Jonat lashed them with his tongue. Beyond his anger the tall warrior knew the cause of their panic, even understood it. Half the men were Legion warriors, half were conscripted farmers and merchants. The warriors did not trust the farmers to stand firm, while the farmers felt out of their depth and lost within the mad hell of slashing swords and frenzied screams.

What was worse, it had been the warriors who had broken.

'Look around you,' shouted Jonat, aware that other soldiers were watching the scene. 'What do you see? A fortress of stone? It is not as it appears – it is a castle built of sand and the Vagrians lash at it like an angry sea. It stands only so long as the sand binds together. You understand that, you dolts? Today you fled in terror and the Vagrians breached the wall. Had it not been retaken swiftly they would have flowed into the courtyard behind the gates and the fortress would have become a giant tomb.

'Can you not get it through your heads that there is nowhere to run? We fight or we die.

'Six men died beside me today. Good men – better men than you. You think of them tomorrow when you want to run.'

One of the men, a young merchant, hawked and spat. 'I did not ask to be here,' he said bitterly.

'Did you say something, rabbit?' hissed Jonat.

'You heard me.'

'Yes, I heard you. And I watched you today, sprinting away from the wall like your backside was on fire.'

'I was trying to catch up with your Legion soldiers,' snapped the man. 'They were leading the retreat.' An angry murmur greeted his words, but this fell to silence as a tall man moved along the battlements. He placed his hand on Jonat's shoulder and smiled apologetically.

'May I say a few words, Jonat?'

'Of course, sir.'

The officer squatted down amongst the men and removed his helm. His eyes were grey-blue and showed the weariness of six days and nights of bitter struggle. He rubbed at them wearily, then looked up at the young merchant.

'What is your name, my friend?'

'Andric,' replied the man suspiciously.

'I am Gellan. What Jonat said about a castle of sand was a truth to remember and was well put. Each one of you here is vital. Panic is a plague which can turn a battle, but so is courage. When Jonat led that suicidal counter-charge with only ten men, you all responded. You came back – I think you are the stronger for it. Beyond these walls is an enemy of true malevolence, who has butchered his way across Drenai lands slaying men, women and children. He is like rabid animal. But he stops here, for Dros Purdol is the leash around the mad dog's neck and Egel will be the lance that destroys him. Now I am not one for speeches, as Jonat here will testify, but I would like us all to be brothers here, for we are all Drenai and, in reality, we are the last hope of the Drenai race. If we cannot stand together on these walls, then we do not deserve to survive.

'Now look around you and if you see a face you do not recognise, ask a name. You have a few hours before the next attack. Use them to get to know your brothers.'

Gellan pushed himself to his feet, replaced his helm and moved away into the gathering darkness, taking Jonat with him.

'That there is a gentleman,' said Vanek, leaning his back to the wall and loosening the chin-strap of his helm. One of the ten to fight beside Jonat, he too had come through without a scratch, though his helm had been dented in two places and now sat awkwardly on his head. 'You listen to what he said – you take it in like it was written on tablets of stone. For those of you "brothers" who don't know me – my name is Vanek. Now I am a lucky bastard and anyone who feels like living ought to stay close to

220

me. Anyone who feels like running tomorrow can run in my direction, because I am not going through those two speeches again.'

'You think we can really hold this place, Vanek?' asked Andric, moving over to sit beside him. 'All day ships have been arriving, bringing more Vagrians, and now they're building a siege tower.'

'I suppose it keeps them busy,' answered Vanek. 'As for the men, where do you think they are coming from? The more we face here, the less there are of them elsewhere. In short, brother Andric, we are bringing them together like pus in a boil. You think Karnak would have come here if he thought we could lose? The man's a political whoreson. Purdol is a stepping-stone to glory.'

'That's a little unfair,' said a lantern-jawed soldier with deep-set eyes.

'Maybe it is, brother Dagon, but I speak as I see. Do not misunderstand me – I respect the man, I'd even vote for him. But he's not like us; he has the mark of greatness on him and he put it there himself, if you understand me.'

'I don't,' said Dagon. 'As far as I can see he's a great warrior and he's fighting for the Drenai same as me.'

'Then let's leave it at that,' said Vanek, smiling. 'We both agree he's a great warrior, and brothers like us shouldn't quarrel.'

Above them in the gate tower Karnak, Dundas and Gellan sat under the new stars and listened to the conversation. Karnak was grinning broadly as he signalled Gellan to the other side of the ramparts where their talk could not be overheard.

'Intelligent man, that Vanek,' said Karnak softly, his eyes locked on Gellan's face.

221

Gellan grinned. 'Yes, he is, sir. Except for women!'

'There isn't a man alive who knows how to deal with women,' said Karnak. 'I should know – I have been married three times and never learned a damned thing.'

'Does Vanek worry you, sir?'

Karnak's eyes narrowed, but there was a glint of humour in them. 'And if he does?'

'If he did, you wouldn't be a man I follow.'

'Well put. I like a man who stands by his own. Do you share his views?'

'Of course, but then so do you. There are no saga-poet heroes. Each man has his own reason for being prepared to die, and most of the reasons are selfish – like protecting wife, home or self. You have bigger dreams than most men, general; there's no harm in that.'

'I am glad you think so,' said Karnak, an edge of sarcasm in his voice.

'When you do not want to hear the truth, sir, let me know. I can lie as glibly as any man.'

'The truth is a dangerous weapon, Gellan. For some it is like sweet wine, for others it is poison, yet it remains the same. Go and get some sleep – you look exhausted, man.'

'What was all that about?' asked Dundas as Gellan moved into the torch-lit stairwell.

Karnak shrugged and walked to the ramparts, gazing out over the camp-fires of the Vagrian army around the harbour. Two ships were gliding on a jet-black sea towards the dock, their decks lined with men.

'Gellan worries me,' said Karnak.

222

'In what way? He's a good officer – you've said that yourself.'

'He gets too close to his men. He thinks he is cynic, but in fact he's a romantic – searching for heroes in a world that has no use for them. What makes a man like that?'

'Most men think you are a hero, sir.'

'But Gellan does not want a pretend hero, Dundas. What was it Vanek called me? A political whoreson? Is it a crime to want a strong land, where savage armies cannot enter??'

'No, sir, but then you are not a pretend hero. You are a hero who pretends to be otherwise.'

But Karnak appeared not to have heard. He was staring out over the harbour as three more ships ghosted in towards the jetty.

Dardalion touched the wounded soldier's forehead and the man's eyes closed, the lines of pain disappearing from his face. He was young and had not yet found need of a razor. Yet his right arm was hanging from a thread of muscle and his torn stomach was held in place by a broad leather belt.

'There is no hope for this one,' Astila's mind pulsed.

'I know,' answered Dardalion. 'He sleeps now . . . the sleep of death.'

The makeshift hospital was packed with beds, pallets and stretchers. Several women moved among the injured men – changing bandages, mopping brows, talking to the wounded in soft compassionate voices. Karnak had asked the women to help and their presence aided the men beyond even the skill of the surgeons, for no man likes to appear weak before a woman and so the injured gritted their teeth and made light of their wounds.

The chief surgeon – a spare slight man named Evris – approached Dardalion. The two had struck up an instant friendship and the surgeon had been overwhelmingly relieved when the priests augmented his tiny force.

'We need more room,' said Evris, wiping his sweating brow with a bloody cloth.

'It is too hot in here,' said Dardalion. 'I can smell disease in the air.'

'What you can smell is the corpses below. Gan Degas had nowhere to bury them.'

'Then they must be burnt.'

'I agree, but think of the effect on morale. To see your friends cut down is one thing, to see them tossed on a raging fire is another.'

'I'll talk to Karnak.'

'Have you seen anything of Gan Degas?' asked Evris.

'No. Not for several days in fact.'

'He's a proud man.'

'Most warriors are. Without that pride there would be no wars.'

'Karnak used hard words on him – called him a coward and a defeatist. Neither was true. A braver, stronger man never lived. He was trying to do what was best for his men and had he known Egel still fought, he would never have thought of surrender.'

'What do you want from me, Evris?'

'Talk to Karnak – persuade him to apologise, to spare the old man's feelings. It would cost Karnak nothing, but it would save Degas from despair.'

'You are a good man, surgeon, to think of such a

thing when you are exhausted from your labours among the wounded. I will do as you bid.'

'And then get some sleep. You look ten years older than when you arrived six days ago.'

'That is because we work during the day and we guard the fortress by night. But you are right again. It is arrogant of me to believe I can go on like this for ever. I will rest soon, I promise you.'

Dardalion walked from the ward to a small side-room and stripped off his bloodied apron. He washed swiftly, pouring fresh water from a wooden bucket into an enamelled bowl; then he dressed. He started to buckle on his breastplate, but the weight bore him down and he left his armour on the narrow pallet bed and wandered along the cool corridor. As he reached the open doors to the courtyard the sounds of battle rushed upon him – clashing swords and bestial screams, shouted orders and the anguished wails of the dying.

Slowly he climbed the worn stone steps into the Keep, leaving the dread clamour behind him. Degas' rooms were at the top of the Keep and there Dardalion tapped at the door and waited, but there was no answer. He opened the door and stepped inside. The main room was neat and spartanly furnished with a carved wooden table and seven chairs. Rugs were laid before a wide hearth and a cabinet stood by the window. Dardalion sighed deeply and strode to the cabinet. Inside were campaign medals ranging over forty years, and some mementoes – a carved shield presented to Dun Degas to celebrate a cavalry charge, a dagger of solid gold, a long silver sabre with the words FOR THE ONE etched in acid on the blade.

Dardalion sat down and opened the cabinet. On

the bottom shelf were the diaries of Degas, one for every year of his military service. Dardalion opened them at random. The writing was perfectly rounded and showed a disciplined hand, while the words themselves gave evidence of the military mind.

One ten-year-old entry read:

Sathuli raiding party struck at Skarta outskirts on the eleventh. Two forces of Fifty sent to engage and destroy. Albar led the First, I the Second. My force trapped them on the slopes beyond Ekarlas. Frontal charge hazardous as they were well protected by boulders. I split the force into three sections and we climbed around and above them, dislodging them with arrows. They tried to break out at dusk, but by then I had deployed Albar's men in the arroyo below and all the raiders were slain. Regret to report we lost two men, Esdric and Garlan, both fine riders. Eighteen raiders were despatched.

Dardalion carefully replaced the diary, seeking the most recent.

The writing was more shaky now:

We enter the second month of siege and I see no hope of success. I am not able to sleep as I used. Dreams. Bad dreams fill my night hours.

And then:

Hundreds dying. I have started to experience the strangest visions. I feel that I am flying in the night sky, and I can see the lands of the Drenai below me. Nothing but corpses. Niallad dead. Egel dead.

All the world is dead, and only we mock the world of ghosts.

Ten days earlier Degas had written:

My son Elnar died today, defending the gate tower. He was twenty-six and strong as a bull, but an arrow cut him down and he fell out over the wall and on to the enemy. He was a good man and his mother, bless her soul, would have been proud of him. I am now convinced that we stand alone against Vagria and know we cannot hold for long. Kaem has promised to crucify every man, woman and child in Purdol unless we surrender. And the dreams have begun once more, whispering demons in my head. It is getting so hard to think clearly.

Dardalion flipped the pages.

Karnak arrived today with a thousand men. My heart soared when he told me Egel still fought, but then I realised how close I came to betraying everything I have given my life to protect. Kaem would have slain my men and the Drenai would have been doomed. Harsh words I heard from young Karnak, but richly deserved they were. I have failed.

And the last page:

The dreams have gone and I am at peace. It occurs to me now that through all my married life I never spoke to Rula of love. I never kissed her hand, as courtiers do, nor brought her flowers. So strange. Yet all men knew I loved her, for I bragged about her constantly. I once carved her a chair that had flowers upon it. It took me a month and she loved the chair. I have it still.

Dardalion closed the book and leaned back in the chair, gazing down on the lovingly carved and polished wood. It was a work of some artistry. Pushing himself to his feet, he walked to the bedroom where Degas lay on blood-soaked sheets, his knife still in his hand. His eyes were open and Dardalion gently closed the lids before covering the old man's face with a sheet.

'Lord of All Things,' said Dardalion, 'lead this man home.'

15

Cadoras watched as Waylander rode from the wagons, heading away to the north towards a range of low hills. The hunter lay flat on his belly, his chin in his hands; behind him, on the far side of the hill, his horse was tethered. He eased his way back from the hill-top, walked slowly to the steel-grey gelding and unbuckled the thick saddle roll, opening it out on the ground. Within the canvas wrapping was an assortment of weapons ranging from a dismantled crossbow to a set of ivory-handled throwing knives. Cadoras assembled the crossbow and selected ten bolts which he placed in a doeskin quiver at his belt. Then he carefully slid two throwing knives into each of his calf-length riding boots, and two more into sheaths at his side. His sword was strapped to his saddle, along with a Vagrian cavalry bow tipped with gold; the quiver for this hung on his saddle horn. Fully equipped, Cadoras returned the saddle roll to its place and buckled the straps. Then he took some dried meat from his saddlebags and sat back on the grass and stared at the sky, watching the gathering storm clouds drifting in from the east.

It was time for the kill.

There had been little joy in the hunting. He could have killed Waylander on a dozen occasions – but then it took two to play the game, and Waylander had refused to take part. At first this had irritated

Cadoras, making him feel slightly as if his victim had held him in contempt. But as the days passed he had realised that Waylander simply did not care. And so Cadoras had not loosed the fatal shaft.

He wanted to know *why*. He was filled with an urge to ride in to the wagons and sit opposite Waylander, to ask him . . .

Cadoras had been a hunter for more than a decade and he knew the role better than any man alive. In the deadliest game of all he was a master – understanding every facet, every iron rule: the hunter stalked, the prey evaded or ran, or turned and fought back. But the prey *never* ignored.

Why?

Cadoras had expected Waylander to hunt him, had even set elaborate traps around his camp-site. Night after night he had hidden in trees, his bow slung, while his blankets lay by warm fires covering only rocks and branches.

Today would end the burning questions. He would kill Waylander and go home.

Home?

High walls and soul-less rooms, and cold-eyed messengers with offers of gold for death. Like a tomb with windows.

'Curse you, Waylander! Why did you make it so easy?'

'It was the only defence,' answered Waylander and Cadoras spun round as a sword of shining steel rested on his back. He froze and then relaxed, his right hand inching, towards the hidden knives in his boot. 'Don't be foolish,' said Waylander. 'I can open your throat before you blink.'

'What now, Waylander?'

'I have not yet decided.'

'I should have killed you.'

'Yes, but then life is full of "should haves". Take off your boots . . . slowly.' Cadoras did as he was bid. 'Now your belt and jerkin.' Waylander moved the weapons and hurled them on to the grass.

'You planned this?' asked Cadoras, sitting back and resting on his elbows. Waylander nodded and sheathed his sword, sitting some ten feet from the hunter. 'You want some dried meat?' Cadoras enquired. Waylander shook his head and drew a throwing knife, balancing the blade in his right hand.

'Before you kill me, may I ask a question?'

'Of course.'

'How did you know I would wait this long?'

'I didn't, I merely hoped. You should know better than any man that the hunter has all the advantages. No man is safe from the assassin, be he king or peasant. But you had something to prove, Cadoras – and that made you an easy prey.'

'I had nothing to prove.'

'Truly? Not even to yourself?'

'Like what?'

'That you were the better man, the greatest hunter?'

Cadoras leaned back and stared at the sky. 'Pride,' he said. 'Vanity. It makes fools of us all.'

'We are all fools regardless – otherwise we would be farmers, watching our sons grow.'

Cadoras rolled to one elbow and grinned. 'Is that why you've decided to be a hero?'

'Perhaps,' admitted Waylander.

'Does it pay well?'

'I don't know. I haven't been one very long.'

'You know the Brotherhood will be back?'

'Yes.'

'You can't survive.'

'I know that too.'

'Then why do it? I've seen you with the woman – why don't you take her to Gulgothir and head east to Ventria?'

'You think it would be safe there?'

Cadoras shook his head. 'You have a point. But then at least you'd have a chance – on this quest you have none.'

'I am touched by your concern.'

'You may not believe it, but it is genuine. I respect you, Waylander, but I feel sorry for you. You are doomed . . . and by your own hand.'

'Why by mine?'

'Because the skills that are yours are now shackled. I do not know what has happened to you, but you are no longer Waylander the Slayer. If you were, I would now be dead. The Slayer would not have stopped to talk.'

'I cannot argue with that, but then the Cadoras of old would not have waited before loosing an arrow.'

'Maybe we are both getting old.'

'Collect your weapons and ride,' said Waylander, sheathing his knife and rising smoothly to his feet.

'I make no promises,' stated Cadoras. 'Why are you doing this?'

'Just ride.'

'Why not merely give me your knife and offer me your throat?' snapped Cadoras.

'Are you angry because I haven't killed you?'

'Think back to what you were, Waylander, then you'll know why I'm angry.' Cadoras strode to his weapons and retrieved them. Then he pulled on his boots, tightened his saddle cinch and mounted.

Waylander watched as the assassin rode south,

then he wandered back over the hill-top to his own horse and stepped into the saddle. The wagons were lost in the heat haze to the north, but Waylander had no wish to catch up with them before nightfall.

He spent the day scouting the wooded hills, sleeping for two hours beside a rock pool shaded by spruce trees. Towards dusk he saw smoke curling into the sky in the north and a cold dread settled on him. Swiftly he saddled the gelding and raced for the trees, lashing the beast into a furious gallop. For almost a mile he pushed the pace, then sanity returned and he slowed the horse to a canter. His mind was numb and he knew what he would find before he crested the last hill. The smoke had been too great for a mere camp-fire, or even ten camp-fires. Sitting his horse atop the hill, he gazed down on the burnt-out wagons. They had been drawn into a rough semi-circle, as if the drivers had seen the danger with only seconds to spare and had tried to form a fighting circle. Bodies littered the ground and vultures had gathered in squabbling packs.

Waylander rode slowly down the hillside. Many of those now dead had been taken alive and cut to pieces – there had been, then, no prisoners. A child had been nailed to a tree and several women had been staked out with fires built on their chests. A little to the north Durmast's men lay in a rough circle, ringed by dead Nadir warriors. Already the vultures had begun their work and Waylander could not bear to search for Danyal's body. He turned his horse to the west.

The trail was not hard to follow, even under moonlight, and as he rode Waylander assembled his crossbow.

Images flickered in his mind and Danyal's face appeared . . .

Waylander blinked as tears stung his eyes. He swallowed back the sobs pushing at his throat, and something in him died. His back straightened as if a weight had been lifted from him and the recent past floated across his mind's eye like the dreams of another man. He saw the rescue of the priest, the saving of Danyal and the children, the battle at Masin and the promise made to Orien. He watched in astonishment as Cadoras was freed to strike again. Hearing himself talking to Cadoras about heroes, a dry chuckle escaped him. What a fool he must have sounded!

Hewla had been right – love was very nearly the downfall. But now the Nadir had killed Danyal and for that they would suffer. No matter that there were hundreds of them. No matter that he could not win.

Only one truth was of importance.

Waylander the Slayer was back.

Danyal knelt beside Durmast on the slopes of a hill overlooking a riverside town of rambling wooden buildings. The hill was thickly wooded and their horses were hidden in a hollow some sixty paces to the south.

She was tired. The previous day they had escaped from the Nadir raiders with seconds to spare and she had felt a deep sense of shame at their flight. Durmast had been scouting to the west and she had seen him galloping ahead of a Nadir war party, his axe in his hand. Arrows flashed by him as he thundered his bay gelding into line with the wagons, hauled on the reins alongside the baker's wagon and shouted for Danyal. Without thinking she had climbed alongside

234

him and he had spurred his mount for the hills. She would be lying to herself if she claimed she had not known he was taking her to safety while those around her were doomed to savage and cruel deaths. And she hated herself for her weakness.

Four Nadir riders had pursued them into the hills. Once into the woods Durmast had dumped her from the saddle and swung his horse to meet their charge. The first had died as Durmast's axe smashed his rib-cage. The second had thrust out a lance which the giant brushed aside before slashing the man's head from his shoulders. The rest of the vicious action had been so swift and chaotic that Danyal could not take it in. Durmast had charged the remaining riders and the horses had gone down in a welter of flailing hooves. He had risen first, looming like a god of war with his silver axe flashing in the sunlight. With the four men dead, he had looted their saddlebags for food and water and without a word brought her a Nadir pony. Together they had headed north into the trees.

That night, with the temperature falling, they had slept under a single blanket and Durmast, still without a word, had removed his clothes and reached for her.

Turning into him she smiled sweetly, but his eyes widened as he felt the touch of cold steel at his loins.

'The knife is very sharp, Durmast. I would suggest you calm yourself – and sleep.'

'A simple "No" would have been sufficient, woman,' he said, his blue eyes cold with anger.

'Then I shall say "No". Do you give your word not to touch me?'

'Of course.'

'Since I know your word is as strong as a withered

stick, let me tell you this: If you rape me, I shall do my best to kill you.'

'I am not a rapist, woman. Nor have I ever been.'

'The name is Danyal.' She withdrew the knife and turned her back to him.

He sat up and scratched his beard. 'You do not think highly of me, Danyal. Why?'

'Go to sleep, Durmast.'

'Answer me.'

'What a question! You led those people to slaughter and then fled without a backward glance. You are an animal – your own men stayed behind and died, but you just ran.'

'*We* just ran,' he pointed out.

'Yes – and don't think I don't hate myself for it.'

'What did you expect me to do, Danyal? Had I stayed I would have killed maybe six or seven Nadir, and then I would have died with the rest. There was no point.'

'You betrayed them all.'

'Yes, but then I was betrayed – I had an arrangement with the Nadir chieftan, Butaso.'

'You amaze me. The traveller paid you and had a right to expect loyalty – instead you sold them to the Nadir.'

'You have to pay a bounty to cross Nadir lands in safety.'

'Tell that to the dead.'

'The dead don't hear so well.'

She sat up and moved away from him, taking the blanket and wrapping it round her shoulders.

'They don't touch you, do they? The deaths?'

'Why should they? I lost no friends. All things die and their time had come.'

236

'They were people, families. They had put their lives in your hands.'

'What are you, my conscience?'

'You have one?'

'Your tongue is as sharp as your dagger. They paid me to guide them – am I responsible because some Nadir dog-eater breaks his word?'

'Why did you bother to rescue me?'

'Because I wanted to sleep with you. Is that a crime also?'

'No, it's just not a very attractive compliment.'

'Gods, woman, Waylander is welcome to you! No wonder he's changed – you're like acid on the soul. Now, can we share the blanket?'

The following day they had travelled in silence until they reached the last line of hills before the river. Halting the horses, Durmast had pointed to the distant blue mountains of the north-west.

'The tallest peak is Raboas, the Sacred Giant, and the river runs from that range and continues to the sea a hundred miles north of Purdol. It is called the Rostrias, the River of the Dead.'

'What are you planning?'

'There is a town yonder. There I shall book passage on a boat and head for Raboas.'

'What about Waylander?'

'If he is alive, we will see him there.'

'Why not wait in the town for him?'

'He won't come here – he'll strike north-west. We've moved north-east to avoid pursuit. Butaso is a Spear, a western tribe; this is Wolfshead land.'

'I thought you were travelling only as far as Gulgothir.'

'I've changed my mind.'

'Why?'

'Because I am a Drenai. Why should I not want to help Waylander regain the Armour of Bronze?'

'Because there's no profit in it for you.'

'Let's go,' he snapped, spurring his horse forward into the trees.

Hiding the horses in a hollow, Durmast crept to the crest of the hills overlooking the town. There were some twenty houses and seven warehouses built alongside a thick wooden jetty. Behind the warehouses was a long flat building with a shaded porch.

'That's the inn,' said Durmast, 'but it doubles as the main supply store. There don't seem to be any Nadir riders around.'

'Aren't those people Nadir?' asked Danyal, pointing to a group of men sitting beside the jetty.

'No. They are Notas – no tribe. Outcasts originally, now they farm and ply the river for trade and the Nadir come to them for iron tools and weapons, blankets and the like.'

'Are you known here?'

'I am known in most places, Danyal.'

Together they rode into the town, where they tied their horses to a hitching rail outside the inn. The inside was dimly lit and smelled of sweat, stale beer and food swimming in grease. Danyal moved to a table by a shuttered window; lifting the bar, she pushed the shutters open, rapping them firmly into the back of a man standing outside.

'You clumsy cow!' he shouted. Danyal turned away from him and sat down, but when he stormed into the inn, still shouting, she stood and drew her sword. The man stopped in his tracks as she advanced on him. He was stocky and dressed in a fur jacket with a thick black belt from which hung two long knives.

'Go away or I'll kill you,' snarled Danyal.

Durmast appeared behind the man and, grabbing his belt from the back, lifted him from his feet and carried him past Danyal.

'You heard the lady,' said Durmast. 'Go away!' Twisting, he hurled the man through the open window, watching in satisfaction as he crashed into the dust several feet beyond the wooden walkway. Then he turned to Danyal with a broad grin on his wide face.

'I see you are maintaining your reputation for sweetness.'

'I didn't need your help.'

'I am aware of that. I was doing him a favour. If he was lucky you would merely have stabbed him, but you might have lost your temper and used your acid tongue and he would never have recovered from that.'

'That's not very funny.'

'It depends on your standpoint. I have booked us passage on a sailing-boat which leaves tomorrow at mid-morning. I have also booked us a room . . . with *two* beds,' he added pointedly.

16

Butaso sat within his tent, gazing sullenly at the ancient shaman squatting before him. The old man spread out a section of tanned goatskin on the earth and casually tossed a dozen knuckle bones on to it. The bones had been shaped into rough cubes and strange symbols had been etched on each side. For a while the shaman stared at the bones – then he looked up, his dark slanted eyes burning with malicious humour.

'Your treachery has killed you, Butaso,' he said.

'Speak plainly.'

'Is that not plain enough? You are doomed. Even now a dark shadow hovers over your soul.'

'I am as strong as ever,' said Butaso, lurching to his feet. 'Nothing can harm me.'

'Why did you break your word to Ice-eyes?'

'I had a vision. I have many visions. The Chaos Spirit is with me – he guides me.'

'The Spirit of Dark Deeds is his Nadir name, Butaso. Why do you not use it? He is a deceiver.'

'So you say, old man. But he has brought me power and wealth, and many wives.'

'He has brought you death. What did he require of you?'

'To destroy the wagons of Ice-eyes.'

'Yet Ice-eyes lives. As does his friend, the Soul Stealer.'

'What is that to me?'

'Think you that I have no powers? Foolish mortal! Since the Soul Stealer filled your heart with fear that day, giving you your life, you have burned with the desire for vengeance. Now you have killed his friends and he hunts you. Do you not understand?'

'I understand that I have a hundred men scouring the Steppes for him. They will bring me his head by dawn.'

'This man is the prince of killers. He will evade your hunters.'

'That would please you, would it not, Kesa Khan? You have always hated me.'

'Your ego is bloated, Butaso. I do not hate you, I despise you – but that is neither here nor there This man must be stopped.'

'You would help me?'

'He is a danger to future Nadir generations. He seeks the Armour of Bronze, the Nadir Bane; he must not live to fulfil his quest.'

'Use the Shapeshifters then – hunt him down.'

'They are a last resort,' snapped Kesa Khan, rising to his feet. 'I must think.' Replacing the knuckle bones in a goatskin sack, he moved outside the tent and stared up at the stars. Around him there was little movement, except among the sentries guarding Butaso; eight men ringed his tent with swords in hand, facing outwards silently, occasionally stamping their feet against the cold.

Kesa Khan walked to his own tent, where the slave girl Voltis had prepared a brazier of burning coals to warm the air. She had also poured a bowl of Lyrrd and placed three warmed rocks in his bed. He smiled at her and drank the Lyrrd in a single swallow, feeling the alcohol pouring fire into his veins.

'You are a fine girl, Voltis. I do not deserve you.'

'You have been kind,' she said, bowing.

'Would you like to return home?'

'No, Lord. I wish to serve you.' He was touched by her sincerity and leaning forward he lifted her chin . . . then froze.

Eight!

The guard on Butaso's tent was normally seven!

Butaso turned as the guard entered. 'What do you want?'

'The return of my gift,' said Waylander. Butaso spun on his heel, a scream beginning in his throat – a scream cut off by six inches of shimmering steel hammering into his neck. His fingers scrambled for the blade, and his eyes widened in agony; then he fell to his knees, his gaze fixed on the tall figure standing impassively before him.

The last thing he heard as his eyes closed was the clash of steel as his guards rushed into the tent.

Waylander turned, his sword blocking a wild cut. Twisting his wrist, he sent his opponent's blade flying through the air. The guard wrenched a knife from its scabbard, but died as Waylander's sword lanced his ribs. More guards pushed forward, forcing the assassin back to the centre of the tent.

'Put down your sword,' hissed Kesa Khan from the entrance. Waylander gazed coolly at the ring of steel closing in on him.

'Come and take it,' he said.

As the Nadir surged forward, Waylander's sword flickered out and a man fell screaming. Then a blade crashed side on against his head and he fell. He struggled to rise, but pounding fists pushed him down and a sea of darkness washed over him . . .

Pain woke him – deep throbbing, insistent pain. His fingers were swollen and the sun beat mercilessly down on his naked body. He was hanging by his wrists from a pole at the centre of the Nadir camp; they had stripped him of his Nadir clothes and strung him in the sun, and already he could feel the burning of his marble-white skin. His face and arms were in no danger, burnt as they were to the colour of leather, but his body had never been exposed to harsh sunlight and already his chest and shoulders felt as if on fire. He tried to open his eyes, but only the left would function; the right was swollen shut. His mouth was dry, his tongue a stick.

His hands were throbbing and almost purple. Getting his feet under him he pushed himself upright, taking pressure from his swollen wrists. Immediately a fist lashed into his stomach and he winced and bit his swollen lip so hard that blood flowed to his chin.

'We have fine things in store for you, you round-eyed son of a slut,' said a voice. Waylander tilted his head to see before him a young man of middle height – his greasy black hair tied in a pony tail, his features obscured by the ash of mourning.

Waylander looked away and the man struck him again.

'Leave him!' ordered Kesa Khan.

'He is mine.'

'Obey me, Gorkai,' ordered the old man.

'He must die hard, and then serve my father in the Void.'

The young man walked away and Waylander looked at the old man.

'You did well, Soul Stealer, you took the life of a fool who would have led us to ruin.'

Waylander said nothing. His mouth was full of blood which moistened his dry tongue and eased his throat.

Kesa Khan smiled.

'Blood will not sustain you. Today we take you to the desert, where we will watch your soul drawn out by the burning sand.'

The long day wore on and the pain grew. Waylander closed his mind against the burning of his flesh and fought to stay calm, breathing slowly and deeply, conserving what energy he could against the moment when the nadir released him. If they were to take him to the desert, then they must first cut him loose from the pole – at that moment he would attack and force them to kill him.

His mind drifted, flowing back over the years. He saw again the young, idealistic Dakeyras: the child who yearned to be a soldier, to serve in the army of Orien, the Warrior King of Bronze. He recalled the day when Orien had led his victorious force through the streets of Drenan, how the crowds had cheered and thrown flowers. The King had seemed like a giant to the ten-year-old Dakeyras as his armour blazed in the noon sun. Orien had carried his three-year-old son before him and the child, dismayed by the noise of the crowd, had burst into tears. Then the King had lifted him high and kissed him gently. Dakeyras had enjoyed that moment of warmth.

His mind tore his memory from the scene, and pictured once more the moment King Niallad fell with Waylander's bolt jutting from his back. The sight dragged him back to the present and the agony returned. How had the noble young child become the soulless slayer? His wrists ached and he realised that his legs had given way once more; he forced himself upright and opened his good eye. A group of Nadir children squatted before him and one of them lashed at his leg with a stick.

A Nadir warrior stepped forward and sent the boy sprawling with a well-aimed kick.

Waylander drifted once more, his eyes closed. His heart sank as the vision returned of the child held high by the adoring father. With the kiss the boy had been comforted and had started to laugh, copying the King as he waved to the crowd. Tiny Niallad, the hope for tomorrow. One day, thought Dakeyras then, I will serve him as my father serves Orien.

'Waylander,' called a voice and he opened his eye. There was no one close, but the voice came again, deep in his mind. 'Close your eyes and relax.' Waylander did as he was bid, and his pain vanished as he sank into a deep sleep. He found himself standing on a bleak hillside under alien stars, bright and close and perfectly round. Two moons hung in the sky – one silver, one shot with blue and green like stained marble. On the hillside sat Orien, younger now and more like the king of Waylander's memory.

'Come, sit with me.'

'Have I died?'

'Not yet, though it is close.'

'I failed you.'

'You tried – a man can ask for no more.'

'They killed the woman I loved.'

'And you took your revenge. Was it sweet?'

'No, I felt nothing.'

'That is a truth you should have realised many years ago when you hunted down the men who slew

245

your family. You are a weak man, Waylander, to be so manipulated by events. But you are not evil.'

'I killed your son. For money.'

'Yes. I had not forgotten.'

'It seems so futile to say that I am sorry, yet I am.'

'It is never futile. Evil is not like a rock, static and immobile – it is a cancer that builds on itself. Ask any soldier who has been to war. You never forget the first man you kill, but not all the gold in the world could get you to remember the tenth.'

'I can remember the tenth,' said Waylander. 'He was a raider named Kityan, a half-breed Nadir. I followed him to a small town east of Skeln . . .'

'And you killed him with your hands after putting out his eyes with your thumbs.'

'Yes. He was one of those who slew my wife and children.'

'Tell me, why did you not search for Danyal among the dead?'

Waylander turned away and swallowed hard. 'I have seen one woman I loved after the killers left her. I could not witness another such scene.'

'Had you found the strength to search, you would not now be tied to a Nadir pole. She lives, for Durmast rescued her.'

'No?'

'Would I lie, Waylander?'

'Can you help me escape?'

'No.'

'Then I will die.'

'Yes,' said Orien sadly, 'You are dying. But it is happening painlessly.'

Waylander nodded, then his head jerked round. 'You mean now?'

246

'Of course.'

'Return me, damn you!'

'You wish to return to agony and death?'

'It is my life, Orien. *Mine*! I have known pain and I can stand it, but until the moment of death I will not surrender. Not to you, not to the Nadir, not to anyone. Return me!'

'Close your eyes, Waylander, and prepare yourself for pain.'

Waylander groaned as the agony touched him, the sound tearing his dry, swollen throat. He heard a man laugh and opened his eyes to find a crowd had formed about him.

The young man, Gorkai, was grinning widely. 'I told you he was alive. Good! Give him a drink – I want him to feel every cut.' A squat warrior forced Waylander's head back, pouring water from a stone jug to his cracked lips. He could not swallow at first, but allowed the liquid to trickle into his dry throat.

'That's enough!' said Gorkai. 'Know this, assassin: we are going to cut your body very lightly and then smear you with honey. After that we bury you beside an ant's nest. You understand?' Waylander said nothing. His mouth was full of water and every few seconds he allowed a small amount to ease his throat.

Gorkai drew a curved knife and was moving forward when the sound of galloping hooves stopped him, causing him to turn. The crowd parted as a rider thundered into the camp and Waylander looked up, but the sun was directly behind the horseman.

The Nadir scattered as the rider approached and Gorkai, shading his eyes against the sun, screamed, 'Kill him!' The Nadir ran for their weapons; Gorkai gripped his knife tightly and turned on Waylander.

The blade rose . . . But a crossbow shaft punched through his temple and he pitched to the earth. The horseman dragged on the reins beside the pole and a sword slashed through the ropes above Waylander's wrists. He slumped forward, recovered and staggered for the horse as two Nadir ran forward with blades in hand. Dropping his crossbow, the horseman hauled Waylander across his saddle; then he lashed out with his sword and the Nadir leapt back. Arrows flashed by the rider and he kicked his mount into a canter.

The pommel of the saddle cut into Waylander's side and he almost fell as the horse galloped towards the hills. He watched the tents flash by and twice saw Nadir archers bend their bows. The animal was breathing hard as they reached the trees. Behind them Waylander could hear the thunder of hooves and the furious screams of the pursuers. The rider dragged his mount to a stop in a hollow, then threw Waylander to the ground. He landed hard, then came to his knees; his hands were still tied.

Caporas leaned over him as Waylander pushed out his arms; his sword sliced down and the ropes parted. Waylander glanced round, seeing that his own horse was tethered to a bush, his clothes and weapons tied to the saddle. By the trees was the naked corpse of the nadir warrior he had slain the night before. He stumbled to his horse, pulled clear the reins and, with an effort, climbed into the saddle. Then they were off, hugging the tree-lined narrow trail.

Behind them the Nadir were closing and arrows flashed perilously close to the fugitives. then the two men were out of the trees and found themselves riding across open ground.

'I hope your horse can jump,' yelled Cadoras.

Waylander strained to see ahead, fear rising in him as he saw the trail end in a sudden drop. Cadoras spurred on. 'Follow me!' he shouted.

His huge grey gelding sailed over the chasm and Waylander dug his heels into his mount's flanks and followed. The jump was less than ten feet. Far below them a river rushed over white rocks. Cadoras' horse landed well, slithering on the scree; Waylander almost fell as his own mount leapt, but hung on grimly. The horse stumbled on the far side, but found its feet and carried its rider out of bowshot. Waylander swung in the saddle to see the nadir riders lining the chasm; the jump was too great for their ponies.

The two men headed deeper into the mountains, riding over rocks and through streams. Waylander swayed in the saddle, then lifted the canteen from the pommel and drank deeply. Turning, he pulled his cloak clear of the saddle rolls and swung it over his burning shoulders. Towards dusk, as they entered a thicker grove of trees, Cadoras suddenly pitched from his saddle. Waylander dismounted, tethered his horse and knelt by the fallen man. Only then did he see the three arrows that jutted from Cadoras' back. The man's cloak was drenched with blood. Gently Waylander eased him into a sitting position and Cadoras' head fell back against Waylander's chest. Glancing down, Waylander saw a fourth shaft deep in the man's left side.

Cadoras opened his eyes. 'Seems like a good place to camp,' he whispered.

'Why did you come back for me?'

'Who knows? Get me a drink.' With care Waylander eased the dying man against a tree before fetching a canteen. Cadoras drank deeply. 'I followed you. Found the Nadir you'd killed and saw that you had taken his clothes. I guessed then that you were engaged in some senseless act of folly.'

'You mean as senseless as attacking a Nadir camp singlehanded?'

Cadoras chuckled, then winced. 'Foolish, was it not? But then I've never been a hero. Thought I would try it just once – I don't think I'll ever do it again.'

'You want me to get those arrows out?'

'What would be the point? You'd rip me to pieces. Do you know . . . I have only been injured once in all these years, and that was merely a surface cut to the face which gave me this loathsome scar. Strange, is it not? I spend my life committing dark deeds, and the one time I try to do good I get killed. There's no justice!'

'Why did you do it? Truly, now?'

Cadoras leaned his head back and closed his eyes. 'I wish I knew. Do you think there's a heaven?'

'Yes,' lied Waylander.

'Do you think that one act can wipe out a lifetime of evil?'

'I don't know. I hope so.'

'Probably not. You know I never married? Never met anyone who liked me. Hardly surprising – I never liked myself much. Listen – don't trust Durmast, he sold you out. He's taken a commission from Kaem to fetch the Armour.'

'I know.'

'You know? And yet you ride with him?'

'Life's a puzzle,' said Waylander. 'How do you feel?'

'That's a ridiculous question. I can't feel my legs

250

and my back is burning like the devil. Have you ever had friends, Waylander?'

'Yes. Way back.'

'Was it a good feeling?'

'Yes.'

'I can imagine. I think you should go now. The Nadir will be here soon.'

'I'll stay awhile.'

'Don't be noble,' snapped Cadoras. 'Go and get that Armour! I would hate to think I was dying in vain. And take my horse with you – I don't want some dog-eating tribesman to have him. But watch out for him, he's a hateful beast; he'll take your hand off if he can.'

'I'll be careful.' Waylander lifted Cadoras' hand and squeezed it. 'Thank you, my friend.'

'Go away now. I want to die alone.'

17

The Drenai officer, Sarvaj, slept fitfully. He was huddled in the lee of the battlements with a thick blanket wrapped around him, his head resting on a ripped saddlebag he had found near the stables. He was cold and could feel each ring of his mailshirt, even through the leather backing and the woollen undershirt. Sleeping in armour was never comfortable, but add wind and rain and it becomes unbearable. Sarvaj turned over, catching his ear on a bronze buckle; he cursed and sat up, drawing his knife. After some minutes he sawed through the wet leather and hurled the offending metal out over the battlements.

Overhead thunder rolled impressively, and a fresh downpour lashed the grey stone walls. Sarvaj wished he had a rain cape of oiled leather, but even that would not have kept him dry in this storm. Beside him Vanek and Jonat slept on, blissfully unaware of the weather. In fact they had welcomed it, for it put a stop to the night attacks which wore down the spirit of the defenders.

Lightning speared the sky, illuminating the Keep which reared from the grey granite mountains like a broken tooth. Sarvaj stood and stretched. Turning, he gazed out over the harbour and the bay beyond. Vagrian triremes bobbed and swung on their anchors as the storm winds buffeted the bay. More than forty ships were now anchored at Purdol and Kaem's army had swelled to almost 60,000 fighting men – a sign, so Karnak assured the defenders, of growing desperation among the Vagrians.

Sarvaj was not so sure. Nearly a thousand men had died during the last fourteen bloody days, with almost the same number removed from the fighting by grievous wounds. When the wind changed you could hear the screams from the hospital.

Elban, a fine rider, had his leg amputated after gangrene set in, only to die during the ghastly operation. Sidrik, the jester of the regiment, took an arrow through the throat. The names spilled over in Sarvaj's mind, a rush of faces and jagged memories.

And Gellan seemed so tired. His hair shone with streaks of silver and his eyes were sunken and ringed with purple. Only Karnak seemed unchanged. Some of his fat had disappeared, yet he was still an awesome size. During a lull in the fighting the previous day he had wandered to Sarvaj's section.

'Another day closer to victory,' Karnak had said, a wide grin making him seem boyish in the dusk light.

'I hope so,' said Sarvaj, wiping his sword clean of blood and replacing it in its scabbard. 'You're losing weight, general.'

'I'll let you into a secret: a thin man couldn't keep up this pace! My father was twice my size and he lived to be over ninety.'

'That would be nice,' said Sarvaj, grinning. '*I'd* like to live to be twenty-five.'

'They won't beat us, they haven't the guts for it.'

It had seemed politic to agree and Karnak had walked off in search of Gellan.

Now Sarvaj listened to the thunder; it seemed to

be moving towards the east. Stepping over the sleeping soldiers, he picked his way to the eastern gate tower and climbed the winding stair. Even here men slept, choosing to keep dry. He trod on someone's leg, but the man merely grunted and did not wake.

Walking out on to the high battlements, Sarvaj saw Gellan sitting on a stone seat staring out over the bay. The rain was now easing to a fine drizzle, as if some dark god had realised that dawn was but an hour away and the Vagrians needed good weather to scale the walls.

'Do you never sleep?' asked Sarvaj.

Gellan smiled. 'I do not seem to have the need of it. I doze now and then.'

'Karnak says we are winning.'

'Fine. I'll start to pack.'

Sarvaj slumped down beside him. 'It seems as if we've been here forever – as if all that's gone before is just a dream.'

'I know the feeling,' said Gellan.

'Two men ran at me yesterday, and I killed them both while thinking about a dance in Drenan last year. It was a weird experience, as if my body had taken over and my mind was free to wander.'

'Do not let it wander too far, my friend. We are none of us invulnerable.'

For a while they sat in silence and Gellan leaned his head back on the stone and dozed. Then Sarvaj spoke again.

'Wouldn't it be nice to wake up in Drenan?'

'Farewell to the bad dream?'

'Yes . . . Sidrik died today.'

'I hadn't heard.'

'Arrow through the throat.'

'Swift, then?'

'Yes, I hope I go as swiftly.'

'You die on me and I'll stop your pay,' said Gellan.

'I remember pay,' mused Sarvaj. 'Wasn't that something we used to get way back when the world was sane?'

'Just think how much you'll be worth when it's over!'

'Over?' muttered Sarvaj, his humour disappearing as swiftly as the storm. 'It will never be over. Even if we win, can you see us forgiving the Vagrians? We'll turn their land into a charnel-house and see how they stomach it.'

'Is that what you want?'

'Right now? Yes. Tomorrow . . . probably not. What would it achieve? I wonder how Egel is faring?'

'Dardalion says he is only a month from attempting a breakout. And the Lentrians have smashed the Vagrian army and advanced into the Drenai lands. You remember old Ironlatch?'

'The old man at the banquet?'

'Yes.'

'The one with no teeth who had to eat soup and soft bread?'

'The very same. Well, now he leads the Lentrian army.'

'I cannot believe it. We all laughed at him.'

'Laughter or not, he is pushing them back.'

'That must be hard for them to take. They're not used to losing.'

'That's their weakness,' said Gellan. 'A man or an army need to lose once in a while. It's like putting steel through fire – if it doesn't break it comes out stronger.'

'Karnak has never lost.'

'I know.'

'So does your philosophy hold true with him?'

'You always manage to find the difficult questions. But yes, I think it does. When Karnak talks of the inevitability of victory he genuinely believes it.'

'And what about you?'

'You are my friend, Sarvaj, and I will not talk down to you. We have a chance – no more than that.'

'You are telling me no more than I know. What I want to know is: do you think we'll win?'

'Why should I be any more reliable in predictions than Karnak?'

'Because I trust you.'

'And I value that trust, but I can't answer you.'

'I think you already have.'

High in the Keep, Karnak was beginning to lose patience with the surgeon, Evris. Fighting to hold his temper, he cut across the man's argument by crashing his fist on the table.

'I will not have the wounded brought to the Keep! You understand? What do I need to say to you, Evris? Is my language not plain enough?'

'Oh, it is plain enough, general. I tell you that men are dying in their scores unnecessarily – and you do not care.'

'Care? Of course I care,' thundered Karnak. 'You impudent wretch! The audience is ended. Get out!'

'Audience, general? I thought one held those with kings. Not butchers!' In two strides Karnak rounded the table and grabbed the slightly-built surgeon by his blood covered apron. Evris was hauled from his feet to dangle before the furious warrior.

Karnak held him high for several seconds and then hurled him against the far door. Evris hit hard and slid to the floor.

'Get out before I kill you,' hissed Karnak. Dundas, who had been watching the scene in silence, moved to his feet and assisted the surgeon, helping him out into the corridor.

'You went too far, surgeon,' said Dundas softly. 'Are you hurt?'

Evris wrenched himself clear of Dundas' supporting arms. 'No, I'm not hurt, Dundas. I don't have gangrene spreading through my limbs. I don't have maggots breeding in my wounds.'

'Try to understand the wider view,' urged Dundas. 'We face many enemies, not least of which is the threat of plague. We cannot take the wounded into the Keep.'

'You think me so lacking in understanding of strategy that you must feed me the same simple line as your leader? I know what he is thinking and I would have respected him far more had he admitted it. We cannot hold the walls for much longer. Then the soldiers will retreat to the Keep. Karnak wants only fighting men there – he doesn't need a thousand or more wounded men clogging the space, needing to be fed . . . watered . . . cleansed and healed.'

Dundas said nothing and Evris smiled. 'Thank you for not disagreeing. When the retreat comes the Vagrians will kill every wounded man – butcher them in their beds.'

'Karnak has no choice.'

'I know that, damn you.'

'Then why did you rail against him?'

'Because he is there! It is his responsibility; it comes with power. And also because I detest him.'

257

'How can you say that when he is fighting to defend everything you have lived for?'

'Defending? You cannot defend what I have lived for with a sword. You cannot see it, can you, Dundas? There is no real difference between Karnak and Kaem. They are brothers of the Soul. But I cannot stand here talking to you when men are dying.' He stumbled away, then turned by the stairs.

'This morning I found three men dead in the stable cellar, where I had been forced to place them. Rats had eaten them alive.'

Then he was gone and Dundas sighed and returned to the general's rooms. He took a deep breath as he opened the door. Karnak was sitting at the table. his fury still present.

'Insipid worm!' he declared as Dundas entered. 'How dare he say that to me? When this is over, there will be a reckoning.'

'No, there won't, general,' said Dundas. 'You will honour him with medals and apologise.'

'Never! He accused me of forcing Degas to suicide – of not caring about my men.'

'He is a good surgeon and a caring man. And he knows why you will not allow the wounded into the Keep.'

'How? How does he know?'

'Because he is also a soldier.'

'If he knows, why in Hell's name did he attack me?'

'I don't know, general.'

Karnak grinned, and his anger passed. 'For a small man he certainly stood up to me.'

'He did that well enough.'

'I'll only give him a *small* medal – and no apology,'

said Karnak. 'Now tell me, how is the water situation?'

'We've moved six hundred barrels into the Keep. That's the limit.'

'How long will that last?'

'It depends how many men we have left.'

'Say two thousand when the retreat comes?'

'Roughly six weeks, then.'

'It's not enough, not nearly enough. Why the Hell doesn't Egel break out?'

'It's not time; he's not ready.'

'He's too cautious.'

'He knows what he's doing, sir. He's a canny thinker.'

'He lacks flair.'

'You mean he isn't reckless?'

'Don't tell me what I mean,' snapped Karnak. 'Go away and get some rest.'

Dundas returned to his quarters and lay back on the narrow bed. There was no point in removing his armour; dawn was less than an hour away.

As he drifted towards sleep, images of Karnak and Egel floated in his mind. Both were men of awesome power. Karnak was like a storm, dramatic and inspiring, while Egel was more like an angry sea – deep, dark and deadly. They would never be friends. *Could* never be friends.

The images shifted and Dundas saw a tiger and a bear surrounded by snarling wolves. While the common enemy was close, the two animals would fight side by side.

But what would happen when the wolves departed?

Sarvaj buckled the chin-strap of his helmet and

sharpened his sword with a black whetstone. Beside him Jonat was silent as the enemy raced forward carrying their ladders and coiled ropes. There were few archers now on the walls, the supply of arrows having been virtually drained three days before.

'What I'd give to be astride a horse with five thousand Legion riders,' muttered Vanek, staring down at the massed ranks of the infantry as they surged towards the fortress.

Sarvaj nodded. A cavalry charge would cut them apart like a lance slicing through pork fat. The first of the Vagrians reached the wall and the defenders took several paces back as the heavy grappling irons sailed over the ramparts, snagging tight.

'Another day begins,' said Vanek. 'You'd think they would be tired of it by now.'

Sarvaj found his mind wandering as he waited for the first enemy soldier to appear. Why would anyone want to be first? They always died. He wondered how he would feel as an attacker standing at the foot of the ladder. What did they think as they climbed towards death?

A hand reached over the ramparts, broad fingers clamping to the stone. Vanek's sword slashed down and the hand fell at Sarvaj's feet, fingers twitching. Scooping it up, he threw it over the ramparts. More warriors appeared and Sarvaj stabbed out, his blade thrusting between a man's teeth and through the back of his neck. Dragging the blade clear, he back-handed it across the throat of another climber. Already his arm was weary and the battle proper had yet to begin.

For an hour the enemy were unable to get a foothold on the ramparts; then a huge warrior forced his way to the wall west of the gate tower, opening a gap behind him. Climbers surged over the ramparts and soon a fighting wedge had formed. Gellan saw the danger and took five men from the tower to launch a blistering attack to their flank. The massive Vagrian turned and aimed a slashing blow at the tall Drenai. Gellan ducked and lunged and his blade slid into the man's side. The Vagrian grunted, but was far from finished. His blade whistled down but Gellan blocked and moved.

'I'll kill you!' screamed the Vagrian. Gellan said nothing. The man lunged but Gellan sidestepped the blade and countered with a thrust to the throat. Choking on his blood, the warrior fell, but even as he died he lashed out, though his blade cut into the leg of the man beside Gellan. The Vagrian's wedge was collapsing in on itself and Gellan forced his way closer, drawing his dagger and stabbing an enemy soldier who had just climbed into view. The man fell back to be dashed on the rocks below. From the other side of the wedge Gellan could could hear Sarvaj shouting orders for the men to close in. Slowly the Vagrians were forced back and the wall cleared – only for a new wedge to open up thirty paces to the right.

This time Karnak led to the counter-charge, swinging a double-headed battleaxe that smashed through armour, snapping ribs and disembowelling his assailants.

Sarvaj tripped over a body and fell heavily, rapping his head against the rampart steps. Rolling on to his back, he saw a sword-blade flash towards his face.

A second sword blocked the cut, deflecting the blade to strike the stone beside Sarvaj's head. Sarvaj rolled to his feet as Vanek killed the attacker, but there was no time for thanks as they hurled themselves once more into the fray.

A steady thudding boom rose above the noise of clashing steel and Sarvaj knew that the battering ram was once more in place, its bronze head crashing against the reinforced oak of the gates. The sun blazed down from a clear sky and he could feel the salt of his sweat stinging his eyes.

At noon the attack ceased and the Vagrians drew back, carrying their wounded with them, while the Drenai stretcher-bearers gathered the injured in the courtyard below. There was no longer room to carry them inside.

Other soldiers were toiling along the ramparts carrying buckets of water from which the defenders filled their canteens. Still others were washing the blood from the ramparts and spreading sawdust on the stone.

Sarvaj sent three men to fetch bread and cheese for the section, then sat down and removed his helmet. He remembered Vanek saving his life and looked round for the man, seeing him sitting by the wall of the gate tower. Pushing himself wearily to his feet he joined him.

'A tough morning,' he said.

Vanek smiled wearily. 'It will get tougher yet,' he responded.

'Thank you for saving me.'

'No problem. I wish someone had done the same for me.'

Sarvaj saw that Vanek's face was grey with pain and that he was sitting in a pool of blood with one hand clenched to his side.

'I'll get the stretcher-bearers,' said Sarvaj, half-rising.

'No . . . no point. Anyway, I don't want to be eaten by rats in the night. It doesn't matter – there's no pain, which I'm told is not a good sign.'

'I don't know what to say.'

'Don't worry about it. Did you hear that I left my wife?'

'Yes.'

'Stupid. I loved her too much to bear the sight of watching her grow old. You know? I took up with a young woman. Beautiful girl. She robbed me blind and had a young lover on the side. Why do we have to grow old?'

Sarvaj said nothing, but he drew closer for Vanek's voice was fading to a whisper.

'A year ago I would have seen that cut coming. Too slow . . . killed the bastard, though. Twisted my body to trap his blade, than cut his cursed throat. I think it was the twist that killed me. You know? Gods, I wish my wife was here! Isn't that stupid? Wanting to bring her here with all the bloodshed and death? Tell her for me, Sarvaj – tell her I was thinking about her. She was so beautiful once. People are like flowers . . . Gods! Look at that!'

Sarvaj swung round, but there was nothing to be seen.

'What is it?'

But Vanek was dead.

'They're coming back!' yelled Jonat.

18

Waylander had known much pain in his life and had always considered himself capable of withstanding any torment the world could inflict. Now he knew better. His blistered skin felt as if a thousand bees swarmed upon it, stabbing and stinging, while his head throbbed to the rhythms of the waves of nausea racking his body.

At first, as he rode away from the clearing and the dying Cadoras, the pain had been bearable but now, with the coming of night, it was insufferable. A fresh flood of agony struck him and he groaned, cursing himself for his weakness. He sat up, shivering, and moved deeper into the cave, where with trembling hands he shredded some bark for tinder and lit a small fire. His horses, tethered at the rear of the cave, whinnied and the sound ripped through him. He stood, staggered and then recovered his balance, moving to the beasts and patting their necks. Loosening the saddle cinch of his own mount, he spread a blanket over the beast's back before returning to the fire.

Adding thicker sticks to the blaze, he felt the warmth spread through him and slowly removed his shirt, wincing as the wool pulled clear of the blisters on his shoulders. Then he opened a leather pouch at his belt and drew out the long green leaves he had picked before dusk. There was danger in using

Lorassium. In small quantities it eased pain and gave rise to colourful dreams; in large quantities it killed. And Waylander had no idea how much or how little to take – or how to prepare it. He crushed a leaf in his hand and smelled it, then placed it in his mouth and chewed slowly. It was bitter and he gagged. Anger rose in him, making his head pound, and he chewed faster. When after ten minutes there was no relief, and he ate a second leaf.

Now flame dancers leapt above the tiny blaze, twisting and pirouetting, flinging their arms high with sparks streaming from their tiny fingers. the walls of the cave creaked and swelled and Waylander chuckled as his horse grew wings and horns. The chuckle faded as he saw his own hands had become scaled and taloned. Now the fire reshaped itself into a face, broad and handsome with flaming hair.

'Why do you seek to thwart me, man?' asked the fire.

'Who are you?'

'I am the Morning Star, the Lord of Dark Light.'

Waylander leaned back and threw a stick at the face. Fire leapt from its mouth and devoured the stick; the tongue of flame, Waylander noticed, was forked.

'I know you,' said the assassin.

'So you should, child, you have served me for many years. I am filled with sadness that you should betray me now.'

'I never served you. I have always been my own man.'

'Think you so? Then we will leave it at that.'

'No – tell me.'

'What is there to tell, Waylander? You have hunted and killed for many years. Do you think your

265

actions aided the Source? They served the cause of Chaos. *My* cause! You are mine, Waylander – you have always been mine. And in my way I have protected you from harm, turned aside the daggers in the night. Even now I protect you from the Nadir huntsmen who have sworn to eat your heart.'

'Why would you do this for me?'

'I am a good friend to those who serve me. Did I not send Cadoras to you in your need?'

'I don't know. Yet I do know you are the Prince of Deceivers, so I doubt it.'

'Harsh words, mortal. Words of death, if I so choose.'

'What do you want from me?'

'I want to rid you of your taint. You are less of a man since Dardalion touched you with his weakness. I can remove it – I almost did when you went hunting Butaso – but now I see it reaffirming itself like a cancer in your heart.'

'How will you rid me of this taint?'

'Merely say that you desire it and it will be gone.'

'I do not desire it.'

'You think the Source will take you? You are defiled by the blood of the innocents you have slain. Why risk death for a God who despises you?'

'It is not for any God, it is for myself.'

'Death is not the end, Waylander – not for such as you. Your soul will enter the Void, be lost in the darkness, but I will find it and lash it with tongues of flame for eternity. Can you understand what you are risking?'

'I find your threats more acceptable than your promises. They are more in keeping with your reputation. Now leave me.'

'Very well, but know this: I am not an enemy you

should desire, assassin. My reach is long and my talons deadly. Your death is already set; the scenario is written in the Book of Souls and I have read it with pleasure. But there is someone you should consider – Danyal. She travels with another whose soul is mine.'

'Durmast will not harm her,' said Waylander, though his words were empty and filled more with hope than conviction.

'We shall see.'

'Leave me, demon!'

'One last gift before I go. Watch and learn!' The face shimmered and shrank, the flames surged anew and within the blaze Waylander saw Durmast chasing Danyal through a dark wood. He caught her by the banks of a river and swung her round. She lashed at his face, but he parried the blow. Then he struck her and she fell; his hands ripped away her tunic . . .

Waylander watched the scene that followed, screaming only when Durmast drew his knife across her throat. Then he passed out.

And the pain ceased.

Dardalion and The Thirty knelt in the open courtyard by the stables, their minds joined, their concentration honed, their spirits seeping through the timbers and gullies below the stable.

The first rat was asleep, but its button eyes opened in alarm and it scurried away as it felt the presence of Man. Its nostrils quivered, but no scent of the enemy could be found in the dank air. It turned, filled with a terrible terror, squealed and ran for the open. More and more of its fellows joined it in the panic race for life. From gullies and drains and forgotten sewers the rats poured out into the courtyard, drawn to the circle of priests. The first rat ran to lie beside Astila, knowing only that here in the courtyard was an end to fear. Nothing could harm it while it lay thus, in the moon shadow of the Man. Others followed it and a great circle formed about the priests.

From the ramparts above Karnak watched in fascination, while around him officers and men made the sign of the Protective Horn.

Hundreds of rats clustered about the priests, clambering over their robes and on their shoulders. Sarvaj swallowed hard and looked away. Gellan shook his head and scratched his arm.

Dardalion slowly raised his arm and Gellan caught the movement.

'Open the gates. Gently now, only a foot or so!' Gellan glanced up at the soldier on the gate tower. 'What can you see?'

'No movement from the enemy, sir.'

As silently as they could, the soldiers by the gate removed the bronze reinforced bars from the gates and pulled them open.

The first rat blinked and shivered as the comforting blanket of safety slipped away from him. He scampered towards the gates and the horde followed.

The night air was cool as the black mass moved down the hill and into the silent streets of Purdol town, then on to the market squares and the pitched tents of the Vagrian army. On flowed the rats, over cobbled streets and into the tents.

One man awoke as a black rat scampered across his face; he sat up screaming and lashing out. Then a second one fell from his shoulder, landing in his lap with its teeth plunging into his thigh. Other screams filled the night as the rats moved on. Lunging men snapped tent poles and the white canvas billowed around them; others ran from the streets to hurl themselves into the sea. A burning brazier fell and flames licked at dry canvas, while the eastern breeze fanned the blaze and sent it leaping from tent to tent.

High on the Purdol walls Karnak's laughter echoed in the mountains, as the sounds of panic rose from the city below.

'It's not often that visiting relatives are greeted with such a display,' said Sarvaj. Jonat chuckled.

'Gods, what pandemonium,' said Gellan. 'Dardalion!' he called. 'Come up and view your handiwork.'

The priest in silver armour shook his head and led The Thirty back into the hospital building, where Evris was waiting.

'Mighty fine, young man,' he said, grasping Dardalion's hand. 'Mighty fine indeed. What can you do with cockroaches?'

Dardalion grinned. 'I think I'll leave that for another day, Evris, if you don't mind—'

Astila, alert as always, caught Dardalion as he fell.

'Carry him in here,' said Evris, pushing open the door to his own room. Astila laid Dardalion on the narrow bed and removed the silver armour, while Evris lifted Dardalion's wrist. 'The pulse is strong. I think he's just exhausted – how long since he slept?'

Astila shrugged. 'I don't know, surgeon. But I have only had three hours in the last eighty. There is so much to do – so many wounded and dying. And then at night . . .'

'I know. The Brotherhood stalks the darkness.'

'We will not hold them much longer. Soon we will die.'

'How many of them are there?'

'Who knows?' answered Astila wearily. 'They have been reinforced. Last night we almost lost Baynha and Epway. Tonight . . . ?'

'Get some rest. You are taking on too much.'

'It is the price of guilt, Evris.'

'You have nothing to feel guilty about, surely?'

Astila placed his hands on the surgeon's shoulders. 'It is all relative, my friend. We are taught that life is sacred. *All* life. I once got out of bed and trod on a beetle – I felt somehow defiled. How do you think I feel tonight, with scores of men dying in the town below? How do you think we all feel? There is no joy for us here, and the absence of joy is despair.'

Six men knelt before the shaman, six warriors with shining eyes and grim faces: Bodai, who had lost his right arm two years before; Askadi, whose spine was twisted following a fall from a cliff; Nenta, once a fine swordsman, now crippled with arthritis; Belikai the blind; Nontung the leper, fetched from the caves of Mithega; Lenlai the possessed, whose fits grew more frequent and who had bitten off his own tongue in a terrible spasm.

Kesa Khan, dressed now in a robe of human scalps, gave each man a draught of Lyrrd, spiced with the herbs of the mountains. He watched their eyes as they drank, noting the swelling of the pupils and the dawning of incomprehension.

'My children,' he said slowly, 'you are the Chosen. You whom life has robbed, you will be strong again. Sleek and strong. Power will flow in your veins. And then having tasted the strength you will die, and

270

your souls will flow to the Void on a sea of joy. For you will have served the blood of your blood and fulfilled a Nadir destiny.' They sat still, their eyes fixed on his. Not a movement came from them – not a blink, seemingly not a breath. Satisfied, Kesa Khan, clapped his hands lightly and six acolytes entered the cave, leading six grey timber wolves, muzzled and wary.

One by one, Kesa Khan approached the wolves, removing first the leash and then the muzzle. He laid his bony fingers across their eyes and each sat obediently where he led them, until at last all six were squatting before the crippled warriors. The acolytes withdrew.

Kesa Khan closed his eyes, allowing his mind to flow around the cave and out into the darkness of the Nadir night, feeling the pulse of the land and tuning it to his own. He felt the vast elemental power of the mountains rushing into his mind, swelling within him, seeking to explode the frail man-shell that held it. The shaman opened his eyes, stilling the adrenal surge within his veins.

'In this cave the assassin rested. His scent is upon the rocks. Your last memory must be of this man: this tall, round-eyed Drenai who seeks to thwart the destiny of our race. Burn his image into your minds, even as the wolves feel the searing hatred of his scent in their nostrils, Waylander the Slayer. The Soul Stealer in the shadows. He is a strong man, this one – but not as strong as you will be. He is fast and deadly – but not as fast as you, my children.

'His flesh will be sweet, his blood like the wine of the mountains. No other flesh can sustain you. All other food will be poison to you. He alone is your life.'

Kesa Khan took a deep breath and stood, moving along the squatting wolves to touch each gently on the neck. As he touched them they tensed and growled, their eyes fixed on the silent men.

Suddenly the shaman screamed and the wolves leapt, their great fangs fastening on the throats before them. The men made no move as the fangs sliced through flesh and bone.

The wolves shuddered.

And swelled . . .

While the men shrank, their skin hanging in flapping folds, the wolves stretched, paws swelling into fur-covered fingers, nails darkening and curving into talons. Rib-cages expanded, bloated with new muscle; shoulders formed and the creatures loomed upright, dropping to the ground what appeared to be wizened sacks of old bones.

'Turn to me, my children,' said Kesa Khan. The six beasts obeyed him and he felt the power of their blood-red eyes upon him, felt the full savagery of their stares.

'Go forth and kill,' he whispered.

And six beasts padded into the night.

After a while the acolytes returned.

'Remove the bodies,' said the shaman.

'Can we call these things bodies?' asked a young man, his face ashen.

'Call them what you will, boy, but remove them.'

Kesa Khan watched them depart, then built a fire and wrapped himself in a goatskin robe. The ritual had drained him and he felt very old and very tired. There had been a day when only the strongest of warriors had been used, but that offended Kesa Khan. This way was better, for it gave a last glimpse of true life to men bowed by disaster.

They would hunt Waylander and devour him. Then they would die. If they drank water, it would choke them. If they ate meat, it would poison them. Within a month they would starve to death.

But they would have one last fine meal, as their great jaws closed upon the flesh of Waylander.

Kaem sat silently listening to the reports: sixty-eight men dead; forty-seven injured. Four hundred tents had been destroyed and two warehouses burnt to the ground, both containing meat and grain. One ship moored to the jetty had lost its sails in the blaze, but had otherwise survived intact. The rats, however, had infiltrated the remaining food stores and were overrunning the warehouses. Kaem dismissed the officers and turned to the black-coated figure beside him.

'Restore my good humour, Nemodes. Tell me once more how the Brotherhood is in sight of victory against the priests.'

Nemodes shrugged, his heavy-lidded eyes avoiding the general's gaze. The Brotherhood leader was a small, emaciated man with a thick fleshy nose which seemed out of place on his thin features. His mouth was lipless, his teeth like tombstones.

'Three of them died last night. The end is near,' he whispered.

'Three? I lost forty-eight.'

'The three are worth more than your scum,' snapped Nemodes. 'Soon they will lose the strength to keep us out and then we will work on Karnak as we destroyed Degas.'

'Your promises are as pig-wind,' said Kaem. 'Strong, but not lasting. Do you know how badly I need this fortress? Ironlatch has smashed our armies in the south and is advancing on Drenan. I cannot release men to stop him because Egel is still at large in Skultik and Karnak holds this last fortress. I cannot lose . . . and yet I cannot win.'

'We will kill the renegade priests,' Nemodes assured him.

'I don't want them dying of old age, Nemodes! You promised me the fortress would fall. It did not. You promised me the priests would be dead. They live. You promised me Waylander. What bad news have you on this front?'

'Cadoras betrayed us. He rescued the assassin from a Nadir village where his death would have been certain.'

'Why? Why would Cadoras do such a thing?'

Nemodes shrugged. 'It is beyond me. In all his life Cadoras never acted without self-interest. Perhaps he and Waylander struck a bargain. It matters not, for Cadoras is dead. However, nine of my brethren are currently approaching Raboas; they are the best warriors of my Order, and that means the best on the continent. And always we have Durmast.'

'I don't trust him.'

'That's why he *can* be trusted. Greed is the spur and that one will always sell to the highest bidder.'

'You depress me, Nemodes.'

'I do have some good news for you, general.'

'I can scarce believe that.'

'We have found the mountain entrance to the fortress – the route by which Karnak entered.'

Kaem took a deep breath and smiled. 'I want a thousand men ready to march in two hours.'

'I shall see that it is done,' promised Nemodes.

19

The wood was not large, but within it was a hollow where Waylander could build a fire. He was cold through, and though recovering fast from his ordeal still felt the effects of the fever caused by his tortured skin. For three days he had rested within the cave; then he had journeyed north, meeting a small group of Notas who sold him some foul-smelling salve which he smeared across his shoulders and upper back. While he was with them, a young woman had tended to the wound at his temple and the old Notas leader had given him a new name: Oxskull. Using a bronze mirror, Waylander had examined the wound. It was a swelling, purple and gross, the skin split across it in a jagged line. He remembered the sword-blade crashing against his head, and realised that it must have turned and struck him semi-flat. The swelling in his eye had reduced considerably, but he still found his vision troubled by harsh sunlight, which caused the eye to water heavily.

The Notas leader – a wizened, jovial ancient – examined his head, pressing and pushing.

'No crack, Oxskull. You live.'

'How far to Raboas?'

Five days if you travel without care. Seven if your eyes are open.'

The girl moved forward with a pitcher of stone-cooled water and bathed Waylander's head. She was petite and pretty, her hands gentle.

'My youngest wife,' said the old man. 'Good, yes?'

'Good,' agreed Waylander.

'You carry many weapons, Oxskull. You are fighting a war?'

Waylander nodded. 'It would displease me to think I will leave here with less than I arrived.'

'Your black horse is ferocious,' countered the ancient leader. 'He bit my eldest son in the shoulder.'

'He is of uncertain temper. When your people gather my possessions back into one place, I will put them in my blanket roll. The horse will not bite me.'

The old man chortled and dismissed the girl, but his face lost its smile as the tent-flap settled back into place and he and the stranger were alone.

'You are a hunted man, Oxskull. Many, many riders seek you.'

'I know this.'

'Some Nadir. Some Southriders.'

'I know this also.'

'The Southriders wear black cloaks and their eyes are cold. They are like a cloud across the sun and our children fear them – the young are so perceptive.'

'They are evil men,' said Waylander. 'Their promises are dust, but their threats are sworn in blood.'

'This I know,' said the Notas leader. 'They promised gold for knowledge and death for silence.'

'When they return, tell them I was here.'

'This I would have done anyway. Why do they seek you? Are you a king in exile?'

'No.'

'What then?'

Waylander spread his hands. 'A man makes many enemies.'

The old man nodded grimly, his dark eyes fixed on the assassin.

'You know why I have lived this long?' he asked, leaning sideways and pouring a goblet of Lyrrd for his guest.

Waylander shrugged, accepting the goblet and drank deeply.

'Because I am blessed. I see things within the mist of minds. I walk the spirit roads and view the births of mountains. Nothing is hidden from me. The Southriders worship the darkness and feed on the hearts of babes. They swallow the long green leaf and soar on the night winds. But you they cannot find. These men, who could hunt the smallest bat within a night-dark cavern, cannot find a rider on an arid plain. When I close my eyes I can see all things – the children playing beyond the tent, your horses cropping the grass, my youngest wife telling my oldest that she fears my touch for it reminds her of death. And yet I cannot see you, Oxskull. Why is that?'

'I don't know.'

'You speak the truth. *But I know*. Somewhere you have a friend – a friend of great power who has laid a charm over your spirit. Only with true eyes can you be seen.'

'I have such a friend.'

'Does he sit in a fortress under siege?'

'He may. I do not know.'

'He is in great danger.'

'I cannot help him.'

'You are the key, I think.'

'We shall see. How long ago did these riders come?'

'Did they say they would return?'

'They did not say . . . but I know. They will ride into my camp at sunset.'

'From which direction?'

'From the east. Your journey to the north will avoid them – but only for now. Your paths will cross and nothing can change that. You need more friends, Oxskull – alone, you are lost.' The old Notas closed his eyes and shivered. When a sudden cool breeze sprang up within the tent, guttering the candles, he shook and trembled, his eyes flaring open.

'You must go from here and I must move camp,' he said, fear shining in his dark slanted eyes.

'What do you see?'

'Your enemies are powerful indeed. They have opened the ninth gate of Hell and the Shapeshifters are unleashed. You must ride far and fast, Oxskull.'

'What are the Shapeshifters?'

'I can tell you nothing more. Time is gone and every heartbeat brings us closer to destruction. Bear this in your soul: Do not try to fight them. Run! They are power and they are death. Run!'

The old man sprang to his feet and raced from the tent. Waylander could hear his shouted orders and the edge of panic in his voice. Finding that his possessions had been placed in a neat pile beside his horse, he packed them swiftly and rode from the camp, leaving Cadoras' mount in payment for the aid they had given him.

Now, camped some eight miles away, he pondered the old man's words: 'Do not fight. Run.'

But what were they, these Shapeshifters? Why

278

could he not kill them? Did they lack a beating heart? What manner of thing could survive an encounter with Waylander the Slayer?

The old man was no coward. He had sensed the evil of the Brotherhood riders, but was not cowed by them. Yet this new threat had all but unmanned him. Why move his camp? Waylander added sticks to the blaze and warmed his hands. The night breeze rustled the branches of the trees, while in the distance a wolf howled.

The assassin looked to his weapons, honing the blades of his throwing knives. Then he checked his crossbow, a beautiful weapon designed to his specifications and fashioned by a Ventrian armourer. The stock was polished ebony and the two triggers were dulled bronze. The crafting of the weapon was beyond compare, and Waylander had paid the man a fortune in opals. That they were stolen gems took nothing from the gift and the armourer had blinked in astonishment when Waylander poured them into his outstretched hands.

'You are an artist, Arles, and this is a masterpiece.'

Suddenly Waylander's horse whinnied in terror and the assassin came smoothly to his feet, stringing the crossbow swiftly and slipping two bolts in place. The animal was tugging at the reins, seeking to pull them clear of the low-hanging branch to which they were tied. Its ears were flat to its skull and its eyes wide with fear.

'*Do not fight. Run!*' The old man's words hammered at him.

Scooping his blanket from beside the fire, Waylander rolled it and ran to his horse. It took some seconds to tighten the saddle cinch and settle the blanket in place, then he tugged the reins loose and vaulted into the saddle. He was almost thrown as the horse sprang to a gallop, then they were clear of the wood and racing north.

Waylander swivelled in the saddle – behind him several dark shapes had emerged from the wood. He blinked, but a cloud obscured the moon and they faded into darkness. He fought to control the mad gallop, hauling on the reins. It was madness to race across the Steppes in darkness. A pothole, a rabbit's burrow, a large rock – all could bring down his horse with a broken leg.

After about a mile the horse began to lose his wind and Waylander dragged him to a halt, then walked him gently. The beast's sides were lathered, his breathing ragged. Waylander stroked the long neck and whispered soothing words. He glanced back, but could see nothing. He had caught only a brief glimpse of his pursuers, but his memory was of huge men in wolfskin cloaks, running bent double. He shook his head – it must have been a trick of the light, for their speed was awesome. Now travelling at a more sedate pace, he stripped the bolts from the crossbow and loosed the strings.

Whatever men were behind him, they were on foot and would not catch him this night.

He dismounted and led his horse on towards the north, pausing only to wipe him clear of lather. 'I think you saved my life,' he whispered, stroking the velvet neck.

The clouds cleared and the moon shone silver above the distant mountains as Waylander walked the horse for about a mile before stepping into the saddle once more.

He rubbed his eyes and yawned, drawing his cloak

tightly about him. The need to sleep rose in him like a warm blanket around his mind.

A night owl swooped overhead, then dropped like a stone with talons outstretched . . . a tiny rodent squealed as the owl struck.

A dark shadow moved to Waylander's right and he swung in the saddle, yet saw nothing but a screen of low bushes. Instantly alert, he glanced left to see two dark shapes emerging from the long grass at terrifying speed. His horse reared and came down running as Waylander's boots hammered into its side. Then it sprinted away with Waylander leaning low in the saddle.

A figure loomed ahead and the horse swerved. When the figure leapt, Waylander's blood chilled as he saw the demonic face, fangs bared, hurtling towards him. The assassin's fist lashed out to catch the creature on the side of the head; the horse's shoulder cannoned into the beast, sending it sprawling. This time Waylander made no effort to check its mad rush into the night. His own fear was as great, his mind filled with the image of those terrible red eyes and the dripping fangs. His heart was drumming against his chest as he rode. No wonder the old man was so desperate to move his camp – he was taking it away from Waylander's scent.

Three miles further on, Waylander regained control of himself. The horse had begun to tire badly and was now barely cantering. He slowed it and glanced back.

There was nothing to be seen, but he knew they were there; loping along his trail, smelling his fear. He searched the horizon for some hiding-place, but none was in sight. So he pushed on, knowing the beasts would run him down, for his horse was weary and, though faster on the short sprint, could not stay ahead on a long chase.

How many of the beasts were there? He had seen at least three. Three was not so terrible – surely he could handle three? He doubted it.

Anger flared in him. Dardalion had told him he was serving the Source, but what kind of a god left a man in such peril? Why did all the strength remain with the enemy?

'What do you want from me?' he shouted, staring up at the sky.

Ahead, a low line of hills rose gently from the plain; there were no trees and little cover in sight. Slowly his horse plodded up the slope and at the top Waylander pulled on the reins and studied his back trail. At first he could see nothing, then in the distance he glimpsed them – six dark shapes running together, hugging his trail. Only minutes separated them now.

Waylander strung his crossbow, slipping the bolts into place. Two of the beasts he could take swiftly, maybe a third with his sword.

He glanced over the brow of the hill and saw the river below, winding towards the mountains like a silver ribbon. At the foot of the hills was a shack and beyond it a small ferry. Hope rose within him and he urged the horse onward.

Halfway down the hill he began to shout for the ferryman.

A lantern flared in the window of the shack and a tall man walked out into the night.

'Take me across the river,' said Waylander.

'I'll take you in the morning,' replied the man. 'You can bed down in the house.'

'In the morning we'll be dead. There are six beasts

282

from Hell just behind me. If you have family in the house, get them on the ferry.'

The man held up his lantern. He was tall, with wide shoulders and a thick black beard; his eyes, though slanted, gave evidence of his mixed blood. 'You'd better explain,' he said.

'Believe me, there is no time. I will give you twenty silver pieces for the crossing, but if you don't move fast I'll make a try at swimming the river.'

'You won't make it – the current is too strong. Wait here.'

The man walked back into the house and Waylander swore at his lack of speed. Several minutes later he emerged leading three children; one held a rag-doll clutched to her face. He led them to the ferry, lifting the bar to allow Waylander's horse to scramble aboard. The assassin dismounted and locked the bar in place, then unhooked the ropes from the jetty as the ferryman moved to the front, took a firm hold on the lead rope and pulled. The ferry inched forward and the man leaned harder into the rope as Waylander stood at the stern, watching the hillside.

The creatures came into sight and burst into a run.

The ferry was still only yards from the jetty.

'By all the Gods, what are they?' shouted the ferryman, letting go of the rope.

'Pull if you want to live!' screamed Waylander and the man seized the rope, throwing his full weight against it. The creatures plunged down the slope and on to the jetty, in the lead a giant with glittering eyes. Talons outstretched, it reached reached the end of the jetty and sprang. Waylander tugged on the first trigger and the crossbow bolt flew into the beast's mouth, punching through the bone above the

283

throat and skewering the brain. The creature crashed against the bar, snapping it in two. Waylander's horse reared and whinnied in terror as a second beast leapt. A second bolt bounced from its skull and it hit the ferry and staggered. Waylander ran forward and leapt feet-first, his boots hammering into its chest so that it catapulted from the ferry into the swirling water of the river.

The other beasts howled in rage as Waylander came to his feet and snapped two bolts into place. He loosed one across the twenty-foot gap, watching it thud home in a fur-covered chest. The creature roared in anger, then plucked the bolt free and hurled it into the river.

A taloned hand fastened on Waylander's ankle. Dropping the crossbow, he dragged his sword from its scabbard and sliced downwards with all his strength. The blade bit deep into the creature's arm, but did not break the bone. Three times more Waylander hacked at the limb, until at last the talons loosened. Dragging his foot clear, he jumped back.

The creature rolled to its back, the crossbow bolt jutting from its mouth and blood pumping from its mutilated arm. It was lying on the edge of the ferry and Waylander ran forward and kicked it clear; the body sank like a stone.

'Where else can they cross?' asked Waylander

'About twenty miles upstream, fifteen down. What *were* they?'

'I don't know. I don't want to know.'

The children were huddled in the far corner of the ferry, too frightened for tears.

'You had better see to them,' said Waylander. 'I'll pull for a while.' The man left the rope and knelt by his children, talking to them in a low voice, taking them into his arms. Opening a chest fixed near the front of the ferry, he removed blankets and the children lay down on the deck, cuddled together.

It took just over an hour to cross the river, and Waylander was deeply grateful that he had not been forced to swim it. Out in the centre the current was too powerful for human endeavour.

The ferryman moved to the front, lifting a mooring rope as the jetty loomed. A second shack was built beyond the jetty and he and Waylander carried the now sleeping children inside, laying them on two beds pushed together by the far wall. The man prepared a fire and the two of them sat together as the blaze crackled to life.

'It's bad enough with the tribes,' said the ferryman suddenly, 'but now I think I'll move.'

'The beasts are hunting me. I do not think they will return to trouble you.'

'All the same, I have the children to think of – this is no place for them.'

'How long have you been here?'

'Three years. We moved when my wife died. I had a farm near Purdol, but raiders wiped me out – took all my seed-corn and the winter food store. So I set up here, helping an old Notas. He died last year, fell overboard.'

'The tribes don't bother you?'

'Not as long as I keep the ferry operating. But they don't like me. Mixed blood!'

'You are taller than most Nadir,' Waylander observed.

'My mother was a Vagrian woman. My father was Notas, so at least I'm in blood feud with no one. I hear there's a war in the south?'

'Yes.'

'And you are Waylander.'

'The riders have been, then. Which were they, Nadir or Vagrian?'

'Both,' said the man. 'But I won't betray you; I owe you four lives.'

'You owe me nothing – in fact the reverse. I led the creatures to you. When the riders come back, tell them what happened. Tell them I rode north.'

'Why should I do that?'

'Two reasons. First it is the truth, and second they know already where I am heading.'

The man nodded and stirred the blaze to fresh life before adding more fuel.

'If they know, why do you travel there? They will be waiting.'

'Because I have no choice.'

'That is nonsense. Life is all about choice. From here you can ride in any direction.

'I gave my word.'

The ferryman smiled in understanding. 'That I cannot argue with. Nor would I try. But I am intrigued by it – what could make a man give such an oath?'

'Stupidity cannot be ruled out,' said Waylander.

'But you are not stupid.'

'All men are stupid. We plan as if we will live for ever. We think our efforts can match the mountains. But we fool ourselves – we count for nothing and the world never changes.'

'I detect bitterness, Waylander. But your deeds do not match your words. Whatever quest you are engaged upon must count. Else why risk your life?'

'Whether I succeed or fail, within a hundred years – maybe less – no one will remember the deed. No one will care. I can bring an hour's sunshine to a mountain-side; if I fail, it will bring an hour's rain. Does the mountain care?'

'Perhaps not,' said the ferryman, 'but *you* care. And that is enough. There is too little caring in the world – too much greed and violence. I like to see things grow. I like to hear laughter.'

'You are a romantic, ferryman.'

'My name is Gurion,' said the man, extending his hand.

Waylander took it and grinned. 'And I was once called Dakeyras.'

'You too are a romantic, Dakeyras, because only romantics stay true to their word despite the world. It ought to make us stronger, but it does not. Honour is a weighty chain that slows us down.'

'A philosopher *and* a romantic, Gurion? You should be a teacher, not a ferryman.'

'What is your quest, Dakeyras?'

'I seek the Armour of Bronze.'

'For what purpose?'

'There is a Drenai general named Egal and I am to deliver it to him. It will aid him in his war.'

'I have seen it.'

'You have been to Raboas?'

'Once, many years ago. It is a chamber deep in the caves. But it is guarded.'

'By the Nadir?'

'No, by creatures far worse – werebeasts that live in darkness at the centre of the mountain.

'How then did you see it?'

'I was with my wife's people, the Wolfshead; there were fifty of us. It was a marriage ceremony: the Khan's youngest son. He wanted to see the legendary Armour.'

'I am surprised the Nadir did not remove it.'

'They could not,' said Gurion. 'Did you know? It does not exist.'

'Speak plainly, man.'

'The Armour is an image; you can pass your hands through it. The real Armour is said to be hidden somewhere in the mountain, but no man knows where. All that can be seen is a ghostly, shimmering vision and that is why it is worshipped.'

Waylander said nothing. He stared into the fire, lost in thought.

'I thought you knew where the real Armour was hidden,' said Gurion.

Waylander chuckled and shook his head, then he began to laugh. Gurion turned away as the sadness touched him.

'Curse all romantics,' said Waylander as the laughter left him. 'May they rot in seven hells!'

'You don't mean that,' said Gurion.

Waylander swept his fingers through his hair and stood.

'I cannot begin to tell you how tired I am. I feel I am drowning in a sea of quicksand, and my friends are helping me by tying rocks to my legs. You understand? I am a killer, who kills for money. Does that sound romantic? I am a hunter of men. Yet here I am being hunted . . . by men and beasts, and spirits of the dark. According to my friend Dardalion, my quest serves the Source. You have heard of the Source?' Gurion nodded. 'Well, let me tell you, my friend, that serving the Source is not easy. You cannot see him or hear him, and certainly he offers no help in his own cause.'

'He led you to my ferry,' offered Gurion.

Waylander chuckled. 'My enemies can soar into the night like invisible demons, conjure wolf-crea-

288

tures from Hell and read minds. On our side is a
God that can lead a man to a ferry!'

'And yet you still live.'

'For now, Gurion. Tomorrow is another day.'

20

Dardalion turned away from Astila and leaned on the broad-silled window. Like all the windows of the Keep it tapered from a broad base to a narrow slit, built for defence rather than for view or light. An archer could loose a shaft to the left, right or centre, covering a wide angle of attack; whereas the attackers could gain no access to the Keep through it nor, unless by a freak of chance, loose their arrows past the crack. Dardalion leaned on his elbows and stared at the ramparts below.

Once more blood and death stalked the walls, but the defenders were holding. Beyond the wall lay the charred remains of two Vagrian siege towers, blackened corpses scattered about them. A third siege tower was being hauled slowly towards the ramparts, and the defenders waited with oil and fire. Beyond the towers a second Vagrian army sat and waited the command to attack. Dardalion blinked and transferred his gaze to the grey stone of the window.

'Why will you not hear me, Dardalion?' asked Astila.

Dardalion turned. 'I hear you, my brother, but I cannot help you.'

'We need you here. We are dying. Seven now have gone to the Source and we need your strength.'

'Waylander also needs me. I cannot desert him.'

'We are losing heart, Dardalion.' Astila slumped to the narrow bed and sat with his head in his hands. For the first time Dardalion noticed the fatigue in the blond priest: the bowed shoulders, the purple smears under the once bright eyes. He left the window and sat beside Astila.

'I can only do so much, and there is so much to do. I truly believe that Waylander's quest is the answer for the Drenai. I cannot explain why. But through all my prayers the Armour returns to haunt me and night after night I see it shining in that dark cave. Yet despite its importance we have only one man seeking it for us. One man, Astila! And ranged against him are the Brotherhood, the Nadir, and now unholy creatures . . . He has no chance without me. Try to understand. Please try.'

Astila said nothing for a moment, then looked up and met Dardalion's gaze. His bright blue eyes were red-rimmed and hollow.

'You are the leader and I will follow you to death and beyond. But I tell you the end is very close. I say this without arrogance, but I am the strongest of the brothers and yet I am finished. If I travel the night, I shall not return. If that is your wish, so be it. But believe me, Dardalion, it is The Thirty or Waylander. I stand by your judgement.'

Dardalion laid his arm on Astila's shoulder. 'I also am at the limits of my power. It costs me greatly to hold the shield over Waylander. And I cannot break it, not even for you.'

'I understand,' said Astila dully. 'I will go and prepare for the night.'

'No. We must accept that we have lost the greater battle – merely put a shield on Karnak and those of his officers we can cover.'

'The Brotherhood will have the run of the fortress.'

'So be it. These are strong men, Astila. Good men. They will stand, even against the despair-clouds.'

'You believe that? Truly?'

'What else is there to believe when we are bereft of choice? Some will falter, some will die. Others will fight back. I cannot believe that evil will triumph. I cannot.'

'It has triumphed elsewhere and now the land is in ruins.'

'It has not triumphed here, Astila.'

'The war is not yet over, Dardalion.'

Jonat's sleep was plagued with bad dreams and he awoke with a start. He had seen his dead father dance as they cut him down from the gallows tree, his face purple, his tongue distended. Yet still he danced as the nobles laughed and threw copper coins – the nobles, dining on larks' tongues while his father begged for bread; paying more for a goblet of wine than his family saw in a month. Jeering, mocking.

He sat up, shivering. High on the walls Karnak walked with Gellan and Dundas. Jonat spat.

If only they had listened to him a year ago, the Vagrians would never have invaded. But the nobles thought differently. Cut down the Legion. Throw soldiers out of honest work. Let them starve, for the farms could not support them all. And who cared about the common soldier? No one. Least of all silk-robed noblemen with their gem-encrusted swords. What would they do if all the common soldiers went home? Both Vagrian and Drenai? Would the nobles fight among themselves? No. The game would be over, the fun spoiled.

He was jerked from his thoughts by Gellan's arrival. The officer sat down beside him.

'I saw you were awake. Mind if I join you?'

'Why not?'

'How are you faring?'

'Well enough.'

'I wish I was. I don't think I can handle too many days like today. You ever feel like that?'

'Sometimes. It'll pass, sir – when the first attack comes tomorrow.'

'I hope so. You did well today, Jonat; you held them together when all seemed lost. Not many men could have done that. It's a gift and I saw it in you from the first. I'm proud of you – I mean that. That's why I promoted you.'

'Not because I was a rabble-rouser?' snapped Jonat.

'No. You were what you were because you cared. You cared about the Legion, the real Legion, the men. And you had drive and energy and you commanded respect. An officer needs respect. The title is nothing unless the man is right. You were right. You *are* right.'

'But not right by birth,' said Jonat.

'I neither know nor care about your ancestry, but if it matters to you then let me tell you that my father was a fishmonger. No more than that. And I am proud of him, because he slaved to give me an education.'

'My father was a drunk – he was hung for riding a nobleman's horse.'

'You are not your father.'

293

'Damned right I am not! And I tell you this: I'll never serve another king.'

'Nor I. But that's a battle for another day. Now I am going to get some sleep.'

As Gellan stood, Jonat grinned. 'Was your father really a fishmonger?'

'No, he was an earl. I just said it to annoy you.'

'I would sooner believe that.'

'So would I. Good night, Jonat.'

'Good night, sir.'

'By the way, Dardalion says the priests can no longer hold back the power of the Brotherhood. He says to watch out for signs of despair among the men – the enemy will work on the weak. So keep an eye out.'

'I will.'

'I know. I have no worries about your section.'

Gellan moved away into the darkness and chuckled softly. His father had owned five fishing fleets and Gellan wondered how the earl would have relished the title of fishmonger.

Waylander slept for an hour, then saddled his horse and bade farewell to the ferryman. The night was clear and the distant mountains loomed like the wall at the end of the world.

'Take care,' offered Gurion, extending his hand.

'And you, my friend. Were I you, I'd head back across the river. Those beasts are hunting me – they'll not be back to trouble you.'

For three days he rode warily, covering his tracks as best he could, angling along swift-moving streams and over rocky slopes, disguising both his scent and his spoor. But he doubted his efforts would do more than delay his demonic pursuers. Added to this, he had to watch out for human foes.

Twice he stopped at Notas camps and once shared a meal with a small group of hunters. The four men had greeted him coolly and considered robbing him. But there was something about the tall southlander which kept them at bay – not his bow, his knives or his sword, more a calculating look in his eyes and a subtle confidence in his stance. So they had fed him and watched him depart with evident relief.

At nightfall a larger band of Nadir descended on the hunters, questioning them at length before killing them horribly.

The bodies were discovered the following day by nine Brotherhood warriors whose arrival disturbed the vultures. The riders did not stay long.

Towards dusk the first of the Shapeshifters came upon the scene, drawn by the scent of blood. Saliva dripped from its maw and its red eyes gleamed. The vultures scattered as it approached, their great wings flapping to lift their bloated bodies from the ground. Through superhuman efforts they made their way to the branches of surrounding trees, where they glowered down at the new invaders.

The other wolf-beasts emerged from the undergrowth and approached the remains. One pushed its snout into the bloody carcasses and, overcome by hunger, closed its jaws upon a piece of meat and bone. Then it coughed and spat the flesh from its mouth. Its howl rent the air.

And the four beasts loped towards the north.

Forty miles on, Waylander was close to the southern edge of the mountain range. Here the Steppes were jagged, deep canyons appearing and slashing across the land like a gigantic knife-cut. Trees and streams abounded within the canyons and, here and there, deserted huts and houses dotted the landscape. Wild sheep and goats grazed on the slopes, while to the north-east Waylander saw a herd of wild horses cropping grass beside a waterfall.

Urging his mount onward, he descended the slope into a shaded wood.

The land here was good, richer than the arid Steppes, the thick, black earth as fertile as any on the Sentran Plain. Yet there were no farms. No grain or wheat, nor fruit trees, nor golden corn.

For the Nadir were a nomadic race: hunters, warriors and killers who built nothing, caring little for the bleakness of their future. 'Conquer or die' was the most common phrase among the tribes. Though ultimately, Waylander realised, the phrase should have been conquer *and* die.

What future could there be for a people of no foundation?

Where were the books, the poems, the architecture, the philosophy? All the vast panoply of civilisation?

The Nadir were doomed – the future dust of history, bonded by blood and war and skimming across the surface of the planet like a vicious storm.

What purpose did they serve, he wondered? Scattered tribes full of hate, warring one upon the other, they could never be welded into one people.

That, at least, was a small blessing, for it meant that never would the tribesmen trouble the peoples of the south. But then they had troubles enough of their own.

Waylander made a brief camp in a cave at the far side of the canyon. Taking a stiff brush from his saddlebag, he worked to ease the burrs from his horse's back and then led him to water. He prepared a small fire and made some broth from his dried meat before snatching two hours' sleep. Back in the saddle, he started on the long climb out of the canyon. He studied his back trail often and now, for the first time since leaving the ferry, he saw his pursuers. As he crested the skyline to the north, they were entering the canyon from the south.

There appeared to be about twenty Nadir riders.

Waylander rode on. They were some four hours behind him, but he would increase that distance during the night.

He did not fear the pursuit, but ahead of him towered Raboas, the Sacred Giant, and here was the end of the journey where hunter and hunted were destined to meet.

His thoughts swung to Cadoras. Why had the assassin thrown his life away to rescue a man he hardly knew, a man he was pledged to kill? What had prompted an ice-cool killer to act in such a way?

Then he chuckled.

What had prompted Waylander to rescue Dardalion? Why had he fought so hard to protect Danyal and the children? Why was he now riding towards the certainty of the grave in such a foolhardy and impossible quest?

Danyal's face floated before his eyes, to be replaced in an instant by the bearded, heavy features of Durmast. He remembered once more the vision in the fire, but could not bring himself to believe it. Yet had not Durmast killed women? Children?

The horse plodded on and the sun sank beyond the western horizon. The night air was chill and Waylander pulled his cloak from his saddle roll and swept it over his shoulders. With the coming of

297

night, his fear of the wolfbeasts grew. Where were they now?

His eyes flicked from left to right, and he swung in the saddle to study his back trail in the fast fading light. Hefting his crossbow, he resisted the temptation to load it. Lengthy stress on the metal arms would weaken the weapon, and for these beasts he needed it at full strength.

The moon blazed her white light as the clouds cleared, illuminating a thickly wooded hillside. Waylander had no wish to enter the trees during dark, but the tree-line stretched on far to the west and east. With a whispered curse, he flicked the reins and rode on.

Once inside the wood, he found his heart beating faster and his breathing increasing in speed as panic struggled to overcome him. Moonlight blazed ahead, silver shafts shining through the breaks in overhead branches. His horse's hooves thudded dully on the soft loam, and to the left a badger broke through the undergrowth and ambled across his trail, its fur bathed in light which turned it to silver armour. Waylander swore and gave in to the temptation to load his crossbow.

Suddenly a wolf's howl shattered the silence of the night. Waylander jerked and one of his bolts flew from the crossbow, slicing up through the branches overhead.

'You dolt!' he told himself. 'Get a grip, man!'

Slipping a second bolt home, he re-strung the bow. The howling came from some distance to the east, and from the sound Waylander guessed that a wolf-pack had cornered its quarry – possibly a stag – and the last battle was under way. The wolves would have chased the beast for many miles, tiring it and sapping the strength from its great muscles. Now it was at bay.

Waylander rode on, but the wolves fell silent and the assassin knew that the prey had eluded them once more. He dragged on the reins, not wishing to cross the line of the chase. His horse whinnied and tried to turn, but Waylander hauled him back.

A running figure emerged from the trees some thirty paces ahead. He was wounded, and dragged his left foot; in his hands was a huge wooden club. A wolf burst into view and leapt. The man turned, the club flashing in the moonlight to crunch against the wolf's ribs, stoving them in. It landed with a thud ten feet away from him.

He was big, bigger than any man Waylander had ever seen, and he appeared to be wearing a gruesome mask decorated with a white sphere at the forehead. The lower part of the mask had a lipless mouth, lined with fangs. Waylander could not see him clearly, but he did not look like a Nadir.

More wolves came into sight and the man bellowed his fury and frustration, then limped to a tree and turned to face the pack. They spread out in a cautious semi-circle and crept in upon him. Suddenly one darted from the right and he turned to meet it. Immediately another beast sprinted from the left and leapt. The man fell back as the jaws snapped shut just short of his throat. He lashed out with his club, but a third wolf ran forward.

A crossbow bolt flashed through its neck, and it slumped to the ground.

Waylander yelled at the top of his voice and spurred the horse into a gallop. The wolves scattered, but not before a second beast died with a bolt through its brain.

The man at the tree sagged and fell forward. Waylander sprang from the saddle and tied the reins to a stout bush. He reloaded the crossbow and scanned the undergrowth. The wolves were gone . . . for now.

He moved to the man, who was now kneeling, his hand clamped to a badly bleeding wound on his upper arm.

'You are lucky, my friend,' said Waylander.

The man looked up . . . and Waylander blanched.

He was wearing no mask. He had but a single eye at the centre of his forehead, wherein were two pupils each rimmed with gold iris. His nose was missing; two membrane-covered slits stretched beneath his eye. And his mouth was nightmare.

Shaped like an upturned V, it was lined with fangs sharp as arrow points. Once Waylander had seen a huge white fish with a mouth such as this, and he had never forgotten it. It had filled him with fear at the time, and made him vow never to enter the sea.

But *this?*

His crossbow was ready and he contemplated stepping back and loosing both bolts into the man-creature before it could attack him. But his great round eye closed and he slid to the ground.

It was almost too good an opportunity to miss and Waylander backed to his horse, ready to ride away. But he could not. Some contrariness in his nature made him stop and return to the wounded thing.

As he had with Dardalion so long before, Waylander stitched the wounds to the creature's arm and leg and then bandaged them as best he could. He was naked, but for a moth-eaten loincloth of old fur, and Waylander wrapped him in a blanket and prepared a fire.

After an hour the creature's eyes opened and he sat up. Waylander offered him some dry meat and he took it without a word. The fangs closed on it and it disappeared.

'Can you talk?' asked Waylander.

The great eye merely looked at him. Waylander shrugged and passed more jerked beef which vanished instantly into the cavernous mouth.

'Can you understand me?'

The creature nodded.

'I cannot stay to help you. I am being hunted. Beasts and men. You understand?'

The creature lifted his hand and pointed south.

'That's right, they are coming from the south. I must go, but I will leave you food.'

Waylander walked to his horse, stood for a moment and then unpacked his blanket roll, removed two long hunting knives which were bone-handled and razor-sharp. He took them back to the fire. 'Here. You may need these.' The man-creature reached out. His fingers were incredibly long, the nails curved into dark talons which curled around the bone hilts as he raised the knives to his eye. His reflection came back at him and he blinked and looked away; then he nodded and pushed himself to his feet, towering over Waylander.

The assassin swallowed hard. It was difficult to read the expression on the monster's face, but Waylander was uncomfortably aware of the two knives in his hands.

'Goodbye, my friend,' he said, forcing a smile.

He went to his horse and stepped into the saddle, wrenching the reins clear of the bush. The creature moved forward, its jaws moving and a low grunting noise issuing forth which caused Waylander's mount to back away. The creature's head tilted to one side with the effort he was making.

'Udai rend,' he said. Not understanding, Waylander nodded and moved away.

'Urbye vrend.'

Understanding at last, Waylander turned in the saddle and waved.

'Goodbye, friend,' he called and rode into the darkness.

21

On the mountain pass east of Purdol, two young men ate a breakfast of cheese and bread while swapping tall stories concerning the legendary whores of Purdol Docks. The sun was shining and the taller of the two – a five-year soldier named Tarvic – stood up and walked to the edge of the cliff path, staring out over the desert to the north. He had been pleased to get this assignment; watching a cliff path was a lot less dangerous than defending a rampart.

He was still grinning when an arrow entered his throat and punched up through the roof of his mouth and into his brain.

The second soldier looked round as he staggered back, his hands twitching.

'What's wrong, Tarvic?' called Milis. As Tarvic fell back, his head bouncing from a jagged white rock, Milis saw the arrow and his mouth dropped open. The fear surged through him and he began to run. An arrow chipped him from the rock to his right and flashed by his face. Legs pumping hard, Milis sprinted towards the cave. Something hit him hard in the back, but it did not slow him.

The cave entrance loomed and twice more he was struck from behind, but there was no pain and he made his way into the security of the tunnel. Safe at last, he slowed his pace.

His face crashed into the rocky floor as the ground

leapt up at him. He tried to rise, but his arms had no strength. He began to crawl, but hands pulled at him, turning him over.

'The Vagrians are coming,' he said.

'I know,' said the Vagrian, drawing his knife across Milis' throat.

He was alone, as he had always been alone. He sat by the murky waters of a lily-covered pond and stared at his reflection in the silver steel blade of the hunting knife. He knew he was a monster; the word had been hurled at him since the beginning – along with stones, spears and arrows. He had been hunted by horsemen carrying lances, by wolves with sharp fangs and cunning minds, and by the long-toothed snow tigers which came down from the mountains with the winter ice.

But he had never been caught. For his speed was legend and his strength terrifying.

He pushed his broad back against the bole of a willow and lifted his great head at stare at the twin moons high above the trees. He knew by now there was only one moon, but the pupils of his huge eye could never focus as true eyes. He had learned to live with that, as he had learned to live with the other savage gifts nature had bestowed on him.

For some reason his memory was sharper than most, although he did not realise it. He could remember vividly the moment of his birth, and the face of the old woman who guided him into the world from the black-red tunnel of the Void. She had screamed and let him fall and he had hurt himself, twisting his arm under his body and hitting the edge of a wooden bed.

A man entered then and picked him from the

floor. He had taken a knife, but another woman's scream had stopped him dead.

For a little while he remembered feeding at the breast of a dark-haired, sad-eyed young girl. But then his teeth grew, pointed and sharp – red blood had mixed with the milk and the girl had cried as she fed him.

It was not long before he was carried out into the night and left under the stars, listening to the sound of hoofbeats fading into the distance. Fading, dying . . .

Still the sound of hooves on dry earth filled him with sadness.

He had no name and no future.

Yet something had come from the mountains and drawn him into the darkness . . .

There were many of them, skittering and screeching, touching and pinching, and he had grown among them through the Darkness years, rarely seeing the light of day.

And then, on a summer morning, he heard a lilting cry from Outside echoing down a crack in the rocks and reverberating in the tunnels of the mountain heart. He was lured by the sound and he climbed out into the light. High overhead, great white birds were wheeling and diving, and in their cries he felt his life encapsulated. From that moment he saw himself as Kai and he spent many hours each day lying on the high rocks watching for the white birds, waiting for them to call his name.

Then began the Long years as his strength grew. Nadir tribes would gather near the mountains and pass on to greener meadows and deeper streams. But while they camped he watched them, seeing the children at play, the women arm-in-arm and laughing as they strolled.

Sometimes he strayed too close and the laughter would become familiar screams and the hunters would ride. Kai would run, and then turn, and rend and tear until he was alone once more.

How many years, he wondered, had he lived thus?

The forest in which he now sat had been a small wood of slender trees. Was that a long time? He had no terms of reference. One tribe had camped for longer than most and he had watched one young girl as she grew to womanhood, her hair turning grey and her back becoming bent. They lived such short lives, these Nadir.

Kai stared at his hands. Special hands these, he knew. Slowly he unwrapped the bandage from his arm and plucked out the stitches Waylander had placed there. Blood eased from the wound, then ran freely. Kai covered the gash with his hand and concentrated deeply. A strong sense of heat grew over the area, like a thousand tiny needles probing the flesh. After several minutes he removed his hand . . . And the gash was gone, the skin supple and unblemished by scab or scar. Removing the bandage and stitches from his leg, he repeated the process.

Strong again, he rose smoothly to his feet and breathed deeply. He could have killed the wolves eventually, but the man had helped him, and given him the knives.

Kai had no need of knives. He could run down an antelope and destroy it with his hands and tear its warm flesh with his fangs. What need of shiny metal?

But they were gifts, the first he had ever received, and the handles were pretty and handsomely carved.

He had owned a knife once, but within a short time it had turned from shining grey to red-brown and had become brittle and useless.

He thought of the giver – the short, small man on the horse. Why had he not screamed and attacked? Why had he killed the wolves? Why had he bandaged the wounds? Why had he given him the knives?

All were mysteries.

Goodbye friend. What did it mean?

Over the years Kai had learned the language of men, piercing the jumble of sounds into linked sentences. He could not speak, for there was no one to listen, but he could understand. The man had said that he was hunted. Kai could understand that.

By beasts and men? Kai wondered why he had made the distinction.

He shrugged and sighed. Strangely he felt more alone today than yesterday.

He missed the small man.

Karnak was asleep on the floor of the great hall, a single blanket pulled across his massive frame. The log fire in the wide hearth had shrivelled to glowing cinders as the Drenai general lay on a goatskin rug, lost in dreams of childhood and the birth of ambition.

Despite their riches Karnak's family retained a puritan streak and early in their lives the children were taught of the necessity for self-sufficiency. Young Karnak had been apprenticed to a shepherd to the north of the family estates and one night, while camped high in the wooded hills, a great grey wolf had stalked the flock. Karnak, at the age of seven, took a stout staff of unshaped wood and walked towards the beast. For several seconds it stood its ground, yellow eyes fixed on the advancing child. then it had backed away and run into the darkness.

When Karnak returned home he told the tale to his father with great pride.

'I knew of it,' said his father coldly. 'But you have lessened the deed by bragging of it.'

For some reason he never forgot his father's dismissal and the scene returned time and time again to haunt his dreams. Sometimes he dreamt he fought off a dozen tigers, and crawled to his father dying of his wounds.

Always the old man responded with icy indifference.

'Why are you not dressed for dinner?' he would ask the blood-covered boy.

'I have been hurt by tigers, father.'

'Still bragging, Karnak?'

The sleeping man groaned and opened his eyes. The hall was silent, yet some sound had disturbed his slumber and now a faint drumming noise came to him. Karnak lay down, pressing his ear to the rug. Then he pulled the goatskin aside and pushed his ear to the stone.

Men were moving below ground . . . a lot of men.

Karnak swore and ran from the hall, snatching his axe from the great table of oak. In the corridor, several soldiers were rolling dice. And he called them to him and ran on towards the dungeon stairwell. A young warrior with a bandaged arm was just coming up the stairs and Karnak stopped him.

'Find Gellan and get him to bring a hundred men to the dungeons *now*. You understand? Now!'

With that the general hurled the man from him

and raced down the stairs. Twice he almost slipped on the slime-covered stone and then he was into the narrow prison row. The door at the end of the row led to a wide chamber and from the back of this room Karnak could see the rough-hewed entrance to the mountain tunnel. Wiping his sweating palms on his green tunic, Karnak hefted his axe and ran through the torch-lit chamber and into the tunnel. The air was cold here and water glistened on the dark jagged walls. The tunnel was narrow; only three men could walk abreast. Karnak stopped to listen and a soldier walked into him from behind and cursed.

'Be silent!' hissed the general.

From some way ahead they could hear the whispering sound of stealthy footfalls on the rocky floor. Dancing torch shadows leapt from the far walls where the tunnel curved to the left.

Karnak lifted his axe and slowly, reverently, kissed both blades.

The Vagrians rounded the corner – to be met by an ear-piercing scream and a flashing axe of silver steel that smashed the ribs of the leading warrior. Torches were dropped as men scrambled for their swords, then more screams filled the tunnel as the axe swept and scythed the milling men. Booted feet trampled the torches to extinction and in the darkness terror grew. For Karnak the way was easy – he had fought his way in alone among the enemy, and anything he struck was likely to be hostile flesh. For the Vagrians it was a nightmare in which men stabbed comrades, or felt their swords clattering from stone walls. Confusion became chaos and the invaders fled.

Suddenly a short blade stabbed into Karnak's face,

bouncing from his left cheekbone and lancing into his eye. He staggered back. The hurled knife fell to the floor and he clasped his hand to his face, where blood gushed from the eye-socket. With a curse he stumbled on after the Vagrians, screaming and yelling, the noise echoing ahead like the rage of an angry giant.

The pain of his ruined eye was intense and the darkness almost total, but still he ran, his axe held high. Ahead the tunnel widened and the darkness lifted slightly.

Three Vagrians, left as a rearguard, ran at him. The first died with his skull split in two. the second followed as the blade reversed and clove his ribs. The third dived at the general, who sidestepped and then whipped up his knee into the diving man's face; his head snapped back and he hit the floor unconscious. Karnak's axe hammered into his back.

He ran on, scanning the rocks for the support ropes and praying the Vagrians had not discovered them.

At the widest part of the tunnel he saw them, looped and partly hidden behind a jutting section of black rock. Moving to his left he lifted the rope and took in the slack. He began to play out the rope as he backed down the tunnel, but the Vagrians had seen at last that only one man faced them and now they came at him with a rush.

Karnak knew he was finished and a terrible anger welled in him. Dropping his axe, he took the rope in both hands and pulled with all his strength. A creaking sound from above gave evidence that the pulleys and winches were transmitting the power.

The Vagrians were now only twenty paces from the straining figure, their yells of rage deafening in the enclosed tunnel. Karnak pushed his right foot against the tunnel wall and tugged hard. A tortured groan came from the roof and a huge boulder toppled above the running soldiers. Then the entire roof gave way and a great crack sliced along the granite wall.

Karnak saw the Vagrians buried screaming under tons of rock and earth. Then he turned and began to run.

Rocks and boulders tumbled about him as he ran on into the dark, then he tripped and fell and something sharp and heavy hit his ribs. He rolled and coughed as swirling dust caught in his throat. It seemed alien and stupid to run into darkness and death, but still he forced himself on. The rock above him exploded and he was swept from his feet, his legs partially buried by rubble. Pulling himself clear, he staggered on until the ground tilted under him and he fell forward.

'Gellan!' he screamed, as the walls closed in and engulfed him. A rock struck his head . . . more covered his legs and waist. He threw his arms over his face and tried to move. Then something slammed into his forehead and his movements ceased.

For more than a full day and night Gellan had men toiling at the rocks, moving forward inch by dangerous inch, while outside on the walls the battle raged endlessly. Many of the officers were now dead and Gellan had promoted Sarvaj and Jonat to commands of 500 men apiece. The number of wounded had swelled to awesome proportions, and now fewer than 2,000 fighting men held the might of the Vagrian army at bay.

But Gellan himself remained in the treacherous

tunnel, angrily shaking off the protest from brother officers.

'He's dead – what is the point?' argued one.

'We need him,' said Gellan.

'The roof has gone, man! Every foot we move forward only increases the risk of a further fall. It's madness!'

But he ignored them, refusing to allow their arguments to lodge in his mind where he knew he would be forced to accept their logic. It was a kind of madness, he knew. But he would not stop. Nor would the men. They worked tirelessly, pushing their frail bodies into the blackness, ton upon ton of delicately balanced rock above and around them.

'How the hell will you find him? The men originally with him say he ran ahead. It would take years to dig your way through to the far side – and the ropes were a hundred paces from the first corner.'

'Get out and leave us alone.'

'You are insane, Gellan.'

'Leave or I'll kill you.'

By the second day even the most tireless of the workers had given up hope, but still they toiled on.

'We need you on the walls, Gellan. Despair is growing.'

This time the words got through, lodging where Gellan had no defence.

'One more hour,' he said, hope draining from him. 'I'll be there with you in one hour.'

The pain from his eye woke Karnak and he tried to move, panic welling in him as realisation struck home that he was trapped . . . buried alive. Madness surged in him and he struggled maniacally, stopping only when he felt the rocks move above him. He breathed slowly and deeply, fighting for calm.

'Why are you not dressed for dinner, Karnak?'

'A mountain fell on me, father.'

Manic laughter bubbled from his throat, but he fought it down and began to weep.

Stop it! You are Karnak, his strength told him.

I am a piece of flesh trapped in a tomb of rock, his weakness screamed.

All his plans were finished now and perhaps it was just as well, he thought. In his arrogance he had believed he could defeat the Vagrians, push them from the lands of the Drenai. His new-found heroic status would have guaranteed him leadership of the people. Egel could never have stood against him. Egel had no way with the mob – no charisma. And there were other ways to dispose of political enemies.

Waylander, and men like him, were easy to find.

But now there would be nothing. No purple robes. No public acclaim.

Why, he wondered, had he taken on the enemy single-handed?

Because he had not stopped to think. Dundas had seen through him: a hero who pretended to be otherwise.

Not exactly the death you would have chosen for yourself, Karnak, said his strength. Where was the drama? Where were the adoring crowds?

If a tree falls in the forest and no one hears, does it make a sound?

If a man dies unobserved, how will his death be chronicled?

'Damn you, father,' whispered Karnak. 'Damn you!'

Laughter shook him. Tears followed. 'Damn you!' he bellowed.

The rock beside him shifted and Karnak froze, waiting for the crushing death. Light fell on his face and a ragged cheer went up from the men. Karnak squinted against the torchlight, then forced a grin.

'You took your time, Gellan,' he whispered. 'I thought I'd have to dig myself out!'

22

Danyal lay back on the aft deck of the river barge, listening to the gentle lap of the waves against the hull. Some few paces to her left Durmast leaned on the rail, eyes scanning the river bank.

For some time she watched him, closing her eyes every time his shaggy head turned in her direction. For the last three days he had been either silent or surly, and whenever she glanced at him she found his glittering eyes focused on her. At first she had been irritated, but that had grown into fear, for Durmast was no ordinary man. Everything about him radiated power. In him was raw strength, and an innate savagery held in check by gossamer threads of reason and logic. All his life, she sensed, he had gained everything he desired by strength, or cunning, or calculated ruthlessness.

And he wanted her.

Danyal knew it – it was in his eyes, his movements, his lack of words.

There was little she could to to make herself less attractive. She had but the one tunic and that disguised her not at all.

Now he turned from the rail and approached her, looming in the darkness like a giant.

'What do you want?' she asked, sitting up.

He squatted beside her. 'I knew you weren't asleep.'

'You want to talk?'

'No . . . yes.'

'Then talk. I'm not going anywhere.'

'What does that mean?'

'It means I'm a captive listener.'

'You are not my captive. You can go or stay as you choose.'

He sat back and scratched his beard. 'Why do you twist everything into confrontation?'

'You bring out the worst in me, Durmast – put it down to that. How long before we disembark?'

'Tomorrow. We'll buy horses and be camped at Raboas by nightfall.'

'And then?'

'We'll wait for Waylander – if he is not already there.'

'I wish I could believe you,' she said bitterly.

'Why should you not?'

She laughed then and his hand shot out to grab her arm, dragging her to him. 'You bitch!' he hissed. In his eyes she saw insanity, the deadly madness of the beserker.

'Take your hand off me,' she said, fighting for calm.

'Why? I like to smell your fear.' He crushed her to him, holding her arms tight against her side. His face pushed against hers and she felt his breath against her cheek.

'I thought you said you were no rapist,' she whispered.

He groaned as he released her, pushing her from him.

'You make my head swim, woman. Your every movement, every look, urges me to take you – you want me, I know you do.'

'You misread me, Durmast. I want nothing to do with you.'

'Don't give me that! Women like you don't stay long without a man. I know what you need.'

'You know nothing; you are an animal.'

'You think Waylander is different? He and I are two sides of the same coin. We are killers. Why should you lust for one and not the other?'

'Lust?' she sneered. 'That's what you'll never understand. Lust has little to do with it. I love him as a man and I want to be with him. I want to talk to him, to touch him.'

'But not me?'

'Who could love you, Durmast?' she snapped. 'You are obsessed with yourself. You think you fooled me with your talk of helping Waylander? You want the Armour yourself and you'll sell it to the highest bidder.'

'So sure, are you?'

'Of course I am sure, I know you – you are physically strong, but morally you're less than a sewer rat.'

He moved towards her and she froze, realising she had gone too far, said too much. But he laid no hand upon her. Instead he smiled and his eyes cleared, humour replacing the malicious glint.

'Very well, Danyal, I'll admit to you: I do intend to sell the Armour to the highest bidder. And that will be Kaem and the Vagrians. I also intend to kill Waylander and collect the bounty. Now what will *you* do?'

Her hand flashed towards his face, the silver steel dagger clenched in her fist, but his arm snaked out to rap her wrist. The knife flew from her fingers.

'You can't kill me, Danyal,' he whispered. 'Way-

317

lander himself would find that difficult – and you are but an able student. You'll have to find another way.'

'To do what?' she asked, rubbing her numbed wrist.

'To outbid Kaem.'

Understanding struck her like a blow. 'You despicable swine. You wretch!'

He nodded. 'What is your offer?'

'You want me that badly?'

'Yes, I want you, woman. I always have, ever since watching you and Waylander make love in the hills above Delnoch.'

'And what will you give me, Durmast?'

'I'll let Waylander keep the Armour. And I won't try to kill him.'

'I agree,' she said softly.

'I thought you would,' he replied, reaching for her.

'Wait!' she commanded and this time he froze, for there was in her eyes a look of triumph. 'I agree to your terms, and I will pay you when Waylander rides away with the Armour. You and I will remain at Raboas.'

'You are asking for a lot of trust, Danyal.'

'Well, unlike you, Durmast, I can be trusted.'

He nodded. 'I think you can,' he asserted and moved away into the darkness.

Alone at last, the enormity of her promise swept over her.

Dundas, Gellan and Dardalion waited in the outer sitting-room while the surgeon, Evris, tended the now unconscious Karnak.

Gellan, still filthy from his days in the tunnel, sat

slumped in a wide leather chair, seeming frail without his armour. Dundas paced the room from window to bedchamber door, occasionally stopping to listen as if to hear the surgeon's work. Dardalion sat silently, fighting off the urge to sleep; he could feel the tension in the two men and he relaxed his mind to flow with theirs.

He merged with Gellan, feeling first the man's inner strength – a power stretched to its limits and threatened by doubt. This was a good man, Dardalion knew, and the suffering among the men hurt him cruelly. He was thinking of Karnak and praying for his recovery, fearing some internal injury that would yet rob the Drenai of hope. He was thinking also of the wall and the dreadful toll it took daily.

Then Dardalion withdrew from Gellan and merged with the tall, blond Dundas. He too was praying for Karnak, but not only for friendship. The weight of responsibility towered over Dundas like a mountain. If Karnak should die he would lose not only his greatest friend, but would have to bear the full awesome responsibility for the defence. And here was a terrible quandary. The wall could not be held, but to retreat meant to doom a thousand wounded men. Dundas could picture the scene: the defenders watching from the transient safety of the Keep as the wounded were dragged out and slain before their eyes. Dundas was a soldier, and a good one, but he was also revered by the men for his natural kindness and understanding. As a man, these were qualities to be admired. As a warrior, they were weaknesses to be exploited.

Dardalion fell back on his own thoughts. He was no military man, no planner. What would he do, assuming the choice was laid at his door?

Fall back?

Hold?

He shook his head, as if to push the thoughts from him. He was tired and the effort of holding the shield over Waylander sapped him more by the hour. He closed his eyes and reached out, tasting the despair that permeated the fortress. The Brotherhood were everywhere: four men so far had committed suicide, while two others had been caught trying to open a blocked postern gate high on the north wall.

The bedchamber door opened and Evris came out, wiping his hands on a linen towel. Gellan surged to his feet, but the surgeon lifted his hands and said quietly, 'It's all right. He is resting.'

'What of his injuries?' asked Gellan.

'As far as I can tell, he has lost the sight of his left eye. But nothing more. Heavy bruising, maybe a cracked rib or two. He is passing no blood. His bulk saved him.'

Evris left the room to tend the other wounded and Dundas sank into a chair by an oval writing table.

'One bright ray of hope,' he said. 'Now if Egel were to arrive tomorrow with fifty thousand men, I would believe in miracles.'

'One miracle at a time suits me,' said Gellan. 'But we must make a decision – the wall cannot hold.'

'You think we should pull back?' asked Dundas.

'I think we must.'

'But the wounded . . .'

'I know.'

Dundas swore bitterly, then chuckled without humour. 'You know, I always wanted to be a general – a First Gan with a cavalry wing under my command. You know why? So that I could have a white horse and a red velvet cloak. Gods, I think I know how poor Degas felt!'

Gellan leaned back and closed his eyes. Dardalion watched the two men for a moment, then spoke. '-Wait for Karnak – let him make the decision,' he advised softly.

Gellan's eyes snapped open. 'Wouldn't that be easy? Hard decisions to make, so load them on the broadest shoulders. We are running short on arrows – if they're not flown already. There is no meat, the bread is maggoty, the cheese green with mould. The men are exhausted and some of them are fighting in a trance.'

'It is almost as hard for the Vagrians, Gellan,' said Dardalion. 'They may have the strength, but they are running short of food and disease is in their camp. They may have stopped Ironlatch in the south, but at great cost. They are stretched thin, and only two months from winter.'

'We do not have two months,' said Dundas. 'Once they take Purdol, they can sweep along the Delnoch range and down through Skoda to circle Ironlatch. Winter won't mean a damn then.'

'I have walked these walls,' said Dardalion, 'but not in the way you have. You see men at war. But I have walked the walls in spirit and I have felt the strength there. Do not be too sure of failure.'

'As you said, Dardalion,' snapped Gellan, 'you have not walked the walls as we have.'

'Forgive me, Gellan, I did not mean to be condescending.'

Gellan shook his head. 'Do not mind me, young priest. I know my men. They are stronger even than they believe and they have already performed miracles. No one could have expected them to last this long. I just wonder how much longer they can stand.'

'I agree with Gellan,' said Dundas. 'The decision is one we may rue for the rest of our lives, but it must be made. We must pull back.'

'You are the military men,' agreed Dardalion, 'and I am not trying to sway you. But the men are fighting like demons and there is no give in them. This morning, I am told, a man with his arm hacked off killed three Vagrians before pitching from the battlements. And when he fell, he dragged another enemy soldier with him. That does not sound like the attitude of defeat.'

'I saw that from the gate tower,' said Dundas. 'The man was a farmer, I spoke to him once – he'd lost his entire family to mercenaries.'

'One man doesn't alter the situation,' said Gellan. 'What we are asking of the men is inhuman and sooner or later they must crack.'

The door to the bedchamber swung open and the three men turned to see Karnak looming in the doorway, one huge hand steadying himself on the wooden frame.

'They won't crack, Gellan,' he said. Blood was seeping through the bandage over his eye and his face was ashen, but the power of the man dominated the scene.

'You should be resting, general,' said Dardalion.

'I had a rest in the tunnel. You've no idea what a rest it was, old lad! But I am back now. I've listened to all of you for some time, and there's something to be said for each argument. But my decision is the final one and it is this: We hold the wall. There will be no retreat to the Keep.

'Those men out there have been magnificent –

322

they will continue to be so. But if we withdraw them to see their comrades butchered, they will lose that iron edge. Then the Keep would fall within days.'

He moved forward and slumped into a wide chair. 'Dundas get some clothes for me – garish clothes. And find me a leather patch to wear over this bandage. And fetch me another axe. I'm going out on to the ramparts.'

'That is insane, sir,' said Gellan. 'You are in no condition to fight.'

'Fight? I am not going to fight, Gellan. I'm going to be *seen*. There's Karnak, they'll say. A mountain fell on him and he's back! Now get me the clothes!' He turned to Dardalion. 'One of your priests told me days ago that your powers to push back the Brotherhood have been cut so that you can hold some sort of magic shield over Waylander. Is that true?'

'It is, sir.'

'Where is Waylander now?'

'Close to the mountain.'

'Then lift the shield.'

'I cannot.'

'Listen to me, Dardalion, you believe in the power of the Source against all the forces of Chaos, and you have fought steadfastly in that belief.

'But now I think you are guilty of arrogance. I don't say that lightly, or even critically. I am an arrogant man myself. But you have decided that Waylander is more important to the Drenai than Purdol. Maybe you are right. But he is now close to the Armour and you have got him there. Let the Source bring him home.'

Dardalion looked up and met Karnak's stare. 'You must understand, sir, that the enemies Way-

323

lander faces are not all human. The Nadir and the Brotherhood trail him, yes, but there are others – beasts from the pit. If I lift the shield he will be alone.'

'Understand this: If he is alone it means only that there is no Source. You follow the reasoning?'

'I believe so, though I fear it is specious.'

'And that is your arrogance speaking. The Source existed before you were born and will continue to exist after you are dead. You are not the only weapon he has.'

'But if you are wrong!'

'Then he dies, Dardalion. But trees will grow, streams will run to the seas and the sun will shine. Lift the damned shield!'

The priest pushed himself to his feet and moved towards the door.

'Will you do it?' said Karnak.

'It is done,' said Dardalion.

'Good! Now push the Brotherhood from Purdol!'

It was close to midnight and the last of the Vagrians limped back to their camp-fires. Jonat leapt to the ramparts and bellowed after them: 'Come back, you bastards, we're not finished with you yet.'

Along the wall stretcher-bearers carried away the wounded, while the dead were thrown from the battlements. Jonat sent a dozen men to fetch food and water before patrolling his section, checking casualties. For days now he had felt the burden of his new responsibilities weighing him down, and his own deep well of bitterness had brought him close to despair. The knowledge that the Brotherhood were at work had helped him a little, but tonight he felt free. The stars shone, the breeze from the sea was fresh and clean and the enemy were scurrying to their tents like whipped dogs. Jonat felt stronger than at any time in his life, and his grin was wide as he swapped jests with the soldiers around him. He even waved to Sarvaj at the gate tower, his intense dislike of the man submerged in his new-found good humour.

Suddenly a ragged cheer went up from the right and Jonat turned to see Karnak striding up the battlement steps. Behind him were four soldiers bearing flagons of wine.

'I see you, Jonat, you rascal,' roared Karnak. Jonat chuckled and caught the bottle Karnak lobbed in his direction. 'I take it you'll drink with me?'

'Why not, general?'

Karnak sat down and called the men to him. 'You've probably heard that I had to close the tunnel,' he said, grinning. 'It means the only way out is through the main gates. How do you feel about that?'

'Just let us know when you're ready to leave, general!' called a man at the back.

'Well, I would have said tonight, but the enemy seems downhearted enough,' said Karnak. 'After all, we don't want to rub their noses in it.'

'Is it true you caved in the mountain?' asked another man.

'I'm afraid so, old lad. My engineers left winches and pulleys in the tunnels and an elaborate set-up by one of the main beams. After all, you can't have an open road into a fortress.'

'We heard you were dead,' said Jonat.

'Good Gods, man, you think a mere mountain could kill me? What little faith you have! Anyway, how are you all faring?'

For some minutes Karnak sat and chatted with them, before moving further down the line. Two hours later he returned to his room, his eye a blistering agony, his strength all but gone. He lowered his body to the bed, rolled on to his back and groaned.

In the hall below Dardalion opened his eyes and looked about him. eight priests met his gaze and nine more were stirring, but six lifeless bodies were slumped across the table.

'The Brotherhood are no longer a threat,' said Astila, 'but the price of victory is high.'

'The price is always high,' said Dardalion. 'Let us pray.'

'For what should we pray, Dardalion?' asked the young priest named Baynha. 'That we kill more enemies? More than sixty of the Brotherhood died tonight. I cannot take much more of this endless slaying.'

'You think we are wrong, Baynha?' questioned Dardalion gently.

'It is more a question of not knowing if we are right.'

'May I speak, Dardalion?' asked Astila and Dardalion nodded.

'I am not as intellectually gifted as some of our Order,' Astila began, 'but bear with me, brothers. I recall a phrase the Abbot used when I was a novitiate. He said: "When a fool sees himself as he is, then he is a fool no longer; and when a wise man learns of his own wisdom, then he becomes a fool." This caused me great trouble, for it seemed mere word play. But after many years I have come to this conclusion: that only in certainty is there moral danger. Doubt is the gift we must cherish, for it forces us to question our motives constantly. It

326

guides us to truth. I do not know if we chose wisely the path we now walk. I do not know if we are right in what we do. But we walk it in faith.

'I despise the slaying, but I will continue to fight the Brotherhood with all the powers the Source has allowed me. But if you, Baynha, believe it is wrong, you should fight no longer.'

Baynha bowed his head briefly, then smiled.

'I am not wise, Astila. Does knowing this make me wise?'

'It makes you human, my brother, and I for one am glad of it. My biggest fear was that we would grow to love the battle.'

'I will fight on,' said Baynha, 'and on your advice will cherish my doubts. Yet I wonder what the future holds for us all. What happens if we win? Do we form a temple of warrior priests? Do we return to our former lives? We have begun something here which is new to the world. What is our purpose?'

Dardalion lifted his hand and they turned to him.

'My friends, these are great questions. But we should not attempt to answer them now. Those of us who survive must decide our future. Yet I must say now that I have had many dreams these past days, terror-filled dreams. But each has ended in the same way. I see a desert of broken souls and undead beasts. At the centre of this desert is an oasis – and beside it a tree. Beneath its branches men gather for shade, and rest, and peace. Not one of the undead beasts can gather near the tree, nor any creature of evil approach it.'

'And what does it mean, do you think?' asked Astila.

'The tree has Thirty branches,' said Dardalion.

23

Waylander slept and in his dreams he found himself once more upon the lonely hillside with the blind King Orien. He opened his eyes and gazed at the sky and the unfamiliar stars.

'Welcome!' said Orien.

Waylander sat up and the old man took his hand and patted it paternally.

'You have pleased me, Waylander. Restored my faith to full vigour. Your courage is great and you have proved to be a man of honour.'

'I am uncomfortable with compliments,' said Waylander, turning away and pulling free his hand.

Orien nodded. 'Then ask that which you fear.'

'Where is the Armour?'

'You will find it. Tomorrow, if the Source blesses you, you will ride upon the flanks of Raboas. There you will find a narrow path which winds to a cave. The cave is on a ledge, and there you will find a second path. These two roads are the only route to the mountain's heart. Enter the cave and you will see three tunnels. Take the right-hand entrance and journey on until you come to a wide, arching chamber. There is the Armour for all to see.'

'It is an image which cannot be taken,' said Waylander.

'It is real, but only the Chosen One can lift it.'

'And I am the Chosen One?'

'That you will know tomorrow.'

'Is Danyal safe?'

'I cannot say, for I do not know. I am not a God, Waylander.'

'Then what are you?'

'I am nothing but an image in your dreams.'

'You must be more than that.'

'Then think of me as the spirit of Orien, the last flickering evidence of the once-King. When you take the Armour I shall be gone, never to return.'

'Where will you go? Is paradise a reality? Does the Source exist?'

'I cannot answer your questions. Only you can decide. But you must go now, for your danger is great. Dardalion no longer shields you from the Brotherhood. Go now!'

Waylander opened his eyes a second time and jerked upright. He was back in his blankets at the foot of Raboas.

And his horse was gone.

He rolled to his feet and saw that the bush where his mount had been tethered had been uprooted. The beast must have been terrified. But by what?

Waylander strung his crossbow and scanned the undergrowth.

He could see nothing untoward, but closed his eyes and listened. From the right he heard a faint rustling.

He spun and loosed both bolts as the werewolf rose and charged. The bolts thudded home, but the corded muscles of the beast's great chest prevented them reaching the heart and lungs and its advance continued unchecked.

Waylander dived to his right, and a second beast

reared above him. He rolled to his feet, his sword slicing out and bouncing from the creature's head.

He backed away as the four beasts advanced, their great jaws open, tongues lolling and red eyes fixed upon him. Gripping his sword two-handed, he raised it over his right shoulder, ready to take at least one of them with him.

A dark shadow reared up behind them and Waylander blinked as a massive hand grabbed a furry neck and squeezed. A terrible howl began and was cut short as the werewolf was lifted from the ground. A silver knife plunged between its ribs and the corpse was hurled ten feet into the bushes. The other beasts swung on the attacker, but with one bound he was among them and a second knife thudded home, disembowelling the creature which had been Lenlai the possessed. Fangs fastened on Kai's shoulder as a third beast leapt at him. He tore it loose, curling his huge hands around its throat and dangling it before him. Waylander winced as he heard the neck creak and snap, then Kai tossed the corpse aside.

The fourth werebeast had fled.

Waylander sheathed his sword and watched in grim fascination as the monster placed his hand over the gushing wound in his shoulder. Minutes later, when the hand was removed from the place, the wound had gone. Kai moved to the corpses, pulling clear the knives. His legs weak, Waylander sat down with his back to a tree. Kai approached him and squatted down, offering the knives hilt first. Waylander accepted them without comment.

Kai watched him for some seconds, then lifted his hand and tapped his enormous chest.

'Vrend,' he said.

'Friends,' agreed Waylander.

After a while Waylander moved to his pack, sharing out some jerked meat and dried fruit. The food disappeared swiftly, then Kai belched and tapped his chest once more.

'Kai,' he said, his head tilting with the effort of speech.

'Waylander.'

Kai nodded, then stretched himself out with head on arm and closed his great eye.

A noise in the undergrowth startled the assassin and he started to rise.

'Orsh,' said Kai, without moving.

Waylander's horse moved into the clearing. He patted its neck and fed it the last of the grain, before tethering it to a stout branch.

Taking his blanket, he lay down beside the man-monster and slept until dawn. When he awoke, he was alone. The bodies of the wolf-beasts had gone and so had Kai.

Waylander finished the last of his food, then saddled his horse. Moving from the clearing, he gazed up at the rearing bulk of Raboas.

The Sacred Giant.

A strange yet perfect sense of calm settled over Waylander as he guided his horse up the slopes of Raboas. The sun was shining through a latticework of cloud which gave incredible depth to the beauty of the sky, while overhead gulls swooped and dived like tiny living shreds of cloud. Waylander pulled on the reins and scanned the land about him. There was a beauty here he had never seen before: a savage elemental magnificence which spoke of the arrogance of eternity.

To his right a stream whispered across white rocks, gushing from a crack in the mountain. He dismounted and stripped his clothing; then he washed and shaved and combed his hair, tying it at the nape of the neck. The water was cold on his skin and he dressed again swiftly after shaking the dust of travel from his clothes. From his pack he took a shawl of black silk which he looped over his shoulders and head in the style of the Sathuli burnoose. Then he placed his mail-ringed shoulder-guard in place. From his pack he took two wrist-guards of silver which he buckled over his forearms, then a baldric carrying six sheathed throwing-knives. He sharpened his knives and his sword-blade and stood, facing the mountain.

Today he would die.

Today he would find peace.

In the distance he saw a dust-cloud heading towards Raboas. Many riders were galloping towards the mountain, but Waylander did not care.

This was his day. This glorious hour of beauty was his hour.

He stepped into the saddle and located the narrow path between the rocks, urging the horse onward.

All his life he had been heading for this path, he knew. Every experience of his existence had conspired to bring him here at this time.

From the moment he killed Niallad he had felt as if he had reached the peak of a mountain from which there was no return. All the paths had been closed to him, his only choice to step from the peak and fly!

Suddenly it did not matter whether he found the Armour, or indeed whether the Drenai won or died.

This was Waylander's hour.

For the first time in two decades he saw without anguish his beloved Tanya standing in the doorway of the farm and waving him home. He saw his son and his two daughters playing by the flower garden. He had loved them so much.

But to the raiders they had been no more than playthings. His wife they had raped and murdered; his children they had killed without thought or remorse. Their gain had been an hour of sated lust, several bags of grain and a handful of silver coin.

Their punishment had been death, hideous and vengeful – not one of them had died in less than an hour. For Dakeyras the farmer had died with his family. The raiders had created Waylander the Slayer.

But now the hatred was gone . . . vanished like smoke in the breeze. Waylander smiled as he remembered his first conversation with Dardalion.

'Once I was a lamb playing in a green field. Then the wolves came. Now I am an eagle and I fly in a different universe.'

'And now you kill the lambs?' Dardalion had accused.

'No, priest. No one pays for lambs.'

The path wound on and up, over jagged rocks between towering boulders.

Orien had said that werebeasts guarded the Armour, but Waylander did not care.

He would dismount and walk into the cave, fetch the Armour and wait for the enemy he could not slay.

His horse was breathing hard as they reached level ground. Ahead of him was a wide cave and before that a fire at which sat Durmast and Danyal.

'You took your time,' said the giant, grinning.

Waylander dismounted as Danyal ran to him, folding his arms around her he kissed her hair, closing his eyes to stem the tears. Durmast looked away.

'I love you,' said Waylander softly, his fingers touching the skin of her face. His words carried such overwhelming regret that Danyal pulled away from his arms.

'What is the matter?'

He shook his head. 'Nothing. You are well?'

'Yes. You?'

'Never better.' Taking her by the hand, he walked back to Durmast. The giant pushed himself to his feet, eyes flicking from one to the other.

'It is good to see you,' said Waylander. 'But I knew you would make it.'

'You too. Is everything all right with you?'

'Of course.'

'You seem strangely distant.'

'It has been a long journey and I am tired. you saw the dust-cloud?'

'Yes. We have less than an hour.'

Waylander nodded agreement.

Hobbling the horses, the trio prepared torches and entered the cave. It was dark and foul-smelling and, as Orien had promised, split into three tunnels. Waylander led the way and they moved deeper into the gloom.

Shadows leapt and swayed on the damp granite walls and Danyal, sword in hand, stayed close to the warriors. At one point they walked into a deep chamber where the flickering torchlight failed to pierce the darkness. Danyal pulled at Waylander's cloak and turned.

'What is it?'

334

At the furthest edges of the torchlight were scores of glittering, feral eyes.

'Ignore them,' said Waylander.

Durmast swallowed hard and drew his battleaxe from its sheath.

They walked on and the eyes closed in around them.

At last they reached the chamber Orien had described.

Inside, along the walls, were placed torch brackets containing sticks soaked with pitch. One by one Waylander lit them all until the chamber was bathed in light.

At the far end, on a wooden frame, stood the Armour of Bronze: winged helm, ornate breastplate bearing an eagle with wings spread, bronze gauntlets and two swords of rare beauty.

The three travellers stood silently before the Armour.

'It makes you believe in magic,' whispered Durmast.

'Who could lose, wearing such as that?' asked Danyal.

Waylander walked forward and reached out his hands.

They passed through the armour and he reached again.

But the image remained.

'Well, get it, man!' said Durmast.

'I cannot. I am not the Chosen One.'

'*What?*' hissed Durmast. 'What are you talking about?'

Waylander chuckled, then sat down before the Armour.

'There is a spell on it, Durmast. The old King,

Orien, told me of it. Only the Chosen One can remove the Armour. It is a safeguard, I suppose – it is so vital to the Drenai that they could not risk it being taken by an enemy. But it does not matter.'

'Doesn't matter?' stormed Durmast. 'We've risked our lives to get this damned tin suit! Even now the Nadir are gathering – and I'm not too damned sure about those eyes out there. Of course it matters.'

'All that matters is that we tried,' said Waylander.

Durmast's response was short, vulgar and explosive. 'Horse dung! The world is full of sorry triers and I'll have no part of it. what do we do now? Wait for some golden-haired grinning Drenai hero who's been blessed in some magic fountain?'

Danyal approached the Armour and tried to touch it, but it remained ethereal.

'What do you think you're doing?' snapped Durmast.

'*You* try,' she said.

'What's the point? Do I look like a Drenai hero to you?'

'I *know* what you are, Durmast. Try anyway. What can you lose?'

The giant pushed himself upright and stalked to the Armour.

It looked so damned solid. He shrugged and his fingers snapped out . . .

And struck metal.

Danyal's jaw dropped. 'Gods! It *is* him!'

Durmast stood transfixed, then he swallowed hard and reached out once more. This time he lifted the helm and placed it reverently before Waylander. Then he stared at his hands -- Waylander saw they were shaking uncontrollably. Piece by piece Durmast lifted the Armour from the stand. Then he sat beside Waylander, saying nothing.

The torches were guttering now and Danyal tapped Waylander's arm. 'We should go.'

Waylander and Durmast gathered up the Armour and followed Danyal to the doorway. Outside a sea of eyes gazed in at them. Danyal froze, then she lifted her torch and the eyes withdrew into the shadows.

'It's going to be a long walk,' muttered Durmast.

He stepped forward and the torchlight fell on the Armour of Bronze. A sibilant whispering rose up from all around them, then subsided into silence. But the eyes fell back and Danyal led the way out into the light.

Once in the open, Durmast and Waylander strapped the Armour to the back of Durmast's pack pony and covered the shining metal with a grey blanket.

The sound of hooves on stone brought a curse from Durmast and sweeping up his bow, he ran to the sloping path. Waylander joined him, crossbow in hand.

Two Nadir warriors rode into sight, lances in their hands. They catapulted from the saddle, one with a bolt through the eye, the other with a long shaft through the ribs.

'They are merely the vanguard; I think we are in trouble,' said Durmast, pulling a second arrow from his quiver. 'Unfortunately, I think we're trapped up here.'

'The second path may be clear,' said Waylander. 'Take Danyal and run. I'll hold them here and join you later.'

'*You* take her and run,' said Durmast. 'I have had enough of her company.'

'Listen to me, my friend. The Brotherhood are seeking me with all their powers. Wherever I run, they will follow. If I stay here I'll draw them to me like a beacon, which will give you a chance to get the Armour to Egel. Now go – before it's too late.'

Durmast swore, then backed away to Danyal.

'Saddle your horse,' he said. 'We're leaving.'

'No.'

'It's his idea – and it's a damn good one. Go and say goodbye; I'll saddle your damned horse.'

Danyal ran to Waylander.

'Is it true?' she asked, tears in her eyes.

'Yes, you must go. I am sorry, Danyal – sorry that we never had a chance at life together. But I am the better man for knowing you. Whether I run or stay, I am doomed . . . so I'll stay. But it will make it easier knowing I am helping you to succeed.'

'Durmast will betray you.'

'If he does, so be it. I have played my part and I can do no more. Please go.'

She reached for him, but at that moment a Nadir warrior ran forward. Waylander brushed her aside and loosed a bolt which took the man high in the shoulder; he fell and scrambled back under cover.

'I love you, Dakeyras,' whispered Danyal.

'I know. Go now.'

Waylander listened as the horses rode away, but he neither turned to watch them leave, nor saw Danyal straining for one last glimpse of him.

The Nadir came in a rush and two went down instantly. Two more fell as Waylander swept up Durmast's bow. Then they were on him and with a terrifying scream he leapt forward, his sword cleaving among them. The path was narrow and they could not circle him. The sword scythed among them and they backed away from his rage.

Six were now dead.

Waylander staggered back to his crossbow and loaded it, blood running freely now from a wound in his leg. He wiped the sweat from his eyes and listened.

The faintest sound of cloth on rock came to him and he glanced up as a Nadir warrior leapt from the boulder with knife raised. Waylander threw himself back, his finger jerking on the bronze triggers of the crossbow. Both bolts hammered into the diving warrior, but as he landed on top of the assassin his knife buried itself in Waylander's shoulder. Waylander pushed the corpse clear and rolled to his feet. The Nadir knife jutted from his flesh, but he left it where it was – to tear it loose would be to bleed to death. With difficulty he strung the crossbow.

The sun was dropping in the sky and the shadows lengthened.

The Nadir would wait for night . . .

And Waylander could not stop them.

The fingers of his left hand felt numb and he clenched them into a weak fist. Pain swept up and around the Nadir knife in his shoulder and Waylander swore. As best he could, he bound the wound in his thigh, but it continued to ooze blood.

He felt cold and began to shiver. As he lifted his hand to wipe the sweat from his eyes a Nadir bowman leapt into view and an arrow flashed from his bow. Waylander lurched left and fired and the archer vanished from sight. As Waylander sank back against the wall of the path he glanced down and saw that the black-feathered shaft had struck him above the left hip and punched its way through the flesh and muscle. Gingerly he reached behind him. The point of the arrow had exited high under his ribs and with a groan he snapped the shaft.

The Nadir charged . . .

Two bolts punched home and the enemy dropped behind the rocks.

But they were closer now and knew he was badly wounded. He struggled to re-string the crossbow, but his fingers were slippery with sweat and the effort tore at his wounded side.

How many more of them were there?

He found he could not remember how many he had slain.

Licking his lips with a dry tongue, he leaned against the wall. About twelve paces ahead of him was a round boulder and behind it, he knew, crouched a Nadir warrior. The wall beyond had a curving jut. Waylander aimed the crossbow and loosed the bolt, which struck the wall and ricocheted right. A piercing scream rent the air and a warrior loomed into sight with blood streaming from a wound at his temple. Waylander's second bolt plunged between his shoulder-blades and he fell without a sound.

Once more the assassin strung the bow. His left arm was now all but useless.

A sudden terrible cry froze Waylander's blood. He risked a glance down the path and saw the last of the werewolves surrounded by Nadir warriors. They hacked and cut at the beast, but its talons flashed among them and its great jaws tore at their flesh.

Six were down, with at least three for sure – and two men only remained to fight the beast. It leapt upon the first, who bravely tried to thrust his sword into its belly; the blade entered the fur-covered flesh just as the beast's fangs closed over the head of the warrior and his face disappeared in a crimson spray. The last Nadir fled down the slope.

And the werebeast advanced on Waylander.

The assassin pushed himself to his feet, staggered and regained balance.

The beast came on, slowly, painfully, blood pouring from countless wounds. It looked pitifully thin and its tongue was swollen and black. The Nadir sword jutted from its belly.

Waylander lifted his crossbow and waited.

The beast loomed above him, red eyes glittering.

Waylander squeezed the triggers and two black bolts flew into the beast's mouth, skewering its brain. It arched back and rolled over as Waylander fell to his knees.

The beast reared up once more, its taloned claw raking at the sky.

Then its eyes glazed and it pitched back down the path.

'And now you will rot in Hell,' said a voice.

Waylander turned.

The nine warriors of the Brotherhood emerged from the left-hand path with dark swords in their hands, their black armour seemingly ablaze in the fading light of the dying day as they moved forward. Waylander struggled to rise, but fell back against the cold stone, groaning as the arrow-head gouged back into his flesh. The Brotherhood warriors loomed closer, black helms covering their faces, black cloaks billowing behind them as the breeze picked up. Waylander tugged a throwing knife from its baldric sheath and hurled it, but the blade was contemptuously batted aside by a black-gauntleted hand.

Fear struck the assassin, overwhelming even his pain.

He did not want to die. The peace he had felt earlier evaporated, leaving him lost and as frightened as a child in the dark.

He prayed for strength. For deliverance. For bolts of lightning from the heavens . . .

And the Brotherhood laughed.

A booted foot cracked against Waylander's face and he was hurled to the ground.

'Pestilential vermin, you have caused us great trouble.'

A warrior knelt before him and grasped the broken shaft of the arrow in Waylander's side, twisting it viciously. Despite himself the assassin screamed. A bronze-studded leather gauntlet cracked against his face and he heard his nose break. His eyes filled with tears of pain and he felt himself hauled into a sitting position. Then as his vision cleared, he found himself gazing into the dark eyes of madness beyond the slit on the face of the black helm.

'Yours is the madness,' said the man, 'for believing you could stand against the power of the Spirit. What has it cost you, Waylander? Your life certainly. Durmast has the Armour – and your woman. And he will use both. Abuse both.'

The man took hold of the knife-hilt jutting from Waylander's shoulder.

'Do you like pain, assassin?' Waylander groaned as the man slowly exerted pressure on the knife. '*I* like pain.'

He lost consciousness, drifting back into a dark

sea of tranquility. But they found him even there and his soul fled across a jet-black sky, pursued by beasts with tongues of fire. He awoke to their laughter and saw that the moon had climbed high above Raboas.

'Now you understand what pain is,' said the leader. 'While you live you will suffer, and when you die you will suffer. What will you give me to end your pain?'

Waylander said nothing.

'Now you are wondering if you have the strength to draw a knife and kill me. Try it, Waylander! Please try. Here, I will help you. He pulled a throwing knife from the assassin's baldric sheath and pushed it into his hand. 'Try to kill me.'

Waylander could not move his hand, though he strained until blood bubbled from the wound in his shoulder. He sagged back, his face ashen.

'There is worse to come, Waylander,' promised the leader. 'Now stab yourself in the leg.'

Waylander watched his hand lift and turn . . . and he screamed as the blade plunged down into his thigh.

'You are mine, assassin. Body and soul.'

Another man knelt beside the leader and spoke. 'Shall we pursue Durmast and the girl?'

'No. Durmast is ours. He will take the Armour to Kaem.'

'Then if you permit, I would enjoy a conversation with the assassin.'

'Of course, Enson. How selfish of me. Pray continue.'

The man knelt over Waylander. 'Pull the knife from your leg,' he ordered. Waylander felt himself on the verge of begging, but gritted his teeth. His hand came down and wrenched the blade cruelly, but it would not come loose.

'Keep calm, Enson,' said the leader. 'Your excitement is lessening your power.'

'My apologies, Tchard. May I try again?'

'Of course.'

Once more Waylander's hand pulled at the blade, and this time the knife tore free of the wound.

'Very good,' said Tchard. 'Now try something a little more delicate. Get him to slowly put out one of his eyes.'

'Gods, no!' whispered Waylander. But the knife rose slowly, its blood-covered point inching inexorably towards the assassin's face.

'You stinking whoresons!' bellowed Durmast, and Tchard twisted to see the bearded giant standing by the path with a double-headed battleaxe in his hands. Enson turned also, and Waylander felt the spell that held him fall away. He stared at the knife blade only inches from his eye, and anger rose in him, blanketing the pain.

'Enson!' he said softly. As the man's helm turned back towards him, Waylander stabbed the knife through the the eye-slit until the hilt slammed against the helm.

Tchard hammered a fist against Waylander's head and the assassin slumped to the ground beside the dead Enson.

Then the Brotherhood leader rose to his feet and faced Durmast.

'Why are you here?' he asked.

'I came for him.'

'There is no need, we have him. But if you are worried about the bounty, we will see that you get it.'

'I don't want the bounty. I want him . . . alive.'

'What is the matter with you, Durmast? This display is more than a little out of character.'

'Don't tell me about my character, you lump of chicken dung! Just move away from him.'

'Or else what?' snarled Tchard.

'Or else you die,' said Durmast.

'You think to kill eight members of the Brotherhood? Your wits are addled.'

'Try me,' urged Durmast, moving forward with axe raised.

Tchard moved to meet him, while the other seven warriors spread out in a semi-circle with swords drawn.

Suddenly Tchard pointed at Durmast. 'You cannot move!' he shouted and Durmast staggered and froze. Grim laughter came from Tchard as slowly he drew his sword and advanced.

'You great plodding fool! Of all the people unsuited to the part of hero, you take pride of place. You are like a great child among your elders and betters – and like all unruly children, you must be punished. I will listen to your song of pain for many, many hours.

'You don't say,' said Durmast as his axe smashed down through Tchard's shoulder, exploding his ribs and exiting through his smashed hip.

'Any other speeches?' asked Durmast. 'Any more mind games? No? Then let's start killing one another!'

With a terrible cry he ran at the warriors, the axe swinging in a murderous arc of flashing silver. They leapt back, one falling to roll clear but another going down as the axe-blade tore into his skull. Waylander fought his way to his knees, but could not rise.

Taking a throwing knife he waited, praying for the strength to aid the giant.

A sword slid into Durmast's back and he twisted, tearing the blade loose from the assailant's hand and backhanding the axe across his neck. Another sword lanced his chest, the wielder dying as Durmast hit him in the throat with his fist. The warriors closed in around the giant then, swords burying themselves deep in his huge body. But still the axe scythed into them. Only two of the Brotherhood were left now and these moved away from the wounded Durmast.

Waylander waited as they backed towards him. Wiping his fingers on his jerkin to free them of sweat and blood, he took the throwing knife in his fingers and hurled it. It thudded home under the helm of the warrior on the left, slicing down through the jugular. Blood pumped from the wound and the man lurched to the left, his hand clasped to his throat, seeking vainly to stem the red tide.

Durmast charged the only remaining warrior, who ducked under the sweeping axe to bury his blade in Durmast's belly. The giant dropped the axe and grabbed the warrior by the throat, snapping his neck with a surging twist of the wrists. Then he fell to his knees.

Waylander crawled agonisingly across the rocks to where the dying man knelt, his great hands closed around the sword-hilt protruding from his body.

'Durmast!'

The giant slid sideways to the ground beside Waylander. He smiled through bloody lips.

'Why?' whispered Durmast.

'What, my friend?'

'Why was *I* chosen?'

Waylander shook his head. Reaching out he took

Durmast's hand, gripping it firmly. The giant's body was seeping blood from a score of wounds.

Durmast swore softly, then he smiled. 'It's a beautiful night.'

'Yes.'

'I bet the bastard was surprised when I cut him in half.'

'How did you do it?'

'Damned if I know!' Durmast winced and his head sagged back.

'Durmast?'

'I'm here . . . for a while. Gods, the pain is terrible! You think his power could not work against me because I am the Chosen One?'

'I don't know. Probably.'

'It would be nice.'

'Why did you come back?'

Durmast chuckled, but a coughing spasm struck him and blood bubbled from his mouth. He choked and spat. 'I came to kill you for the bounty,' he said at last.

'I don't believe you.'

'I don't believe myself sometimes!'

For a while they lay in silence.

'You think this counts as a decent deed?' asked Durmast, his voice little more than a whisper.

'I would think so,' said Waylander, smiling.

'Don't tell anybody,' said Durmast. His head rolled and a grating whisper of breath rattled in his throat.

A scraping sound caused Waylander to turn.

From the cave came a score of beasts, twisted and deformed. They ran to the bodies of the slain, cackling their delight. Waylander watched the corpses being dragged into the blackness of the inner mountain.

'I won't tell anybody,' he whispered to the dead Durmast.

And the creatures loomed above him.

24

Below the ramparts Gellan, Jonat and one hundred warriors waited, listening to the sounds of battle from above. All were dressed in the black armour of the Vagrian Hounds, blue capes over gilded breastplates. Gellan alone wore the officer's helm with its white horsehair plume.

It was almost midnight and the attack wore on. Gellan swallowed hard and tightened the helm's chinstrap.

'I still say this is madness,' whispered Jonat.

'I know – at this moment I'm inclined to agree with you.'

'But we'll go anyway,' muttered Jonat. 'One of these days someone is going to listen to my advice and I'll probably die of the shock!'

A Drenai soldier ran down the battlement steps, a bloody sword in his hand.

'They're retreating,' he said. 'Get ready!'

The man crouched on the steps, watching the ramparts.

'Now!' he shouted. Gellan waved his arm and the hundred soldiers followed him up the steps and over the wall. Ladders and ropes were still in place and Gellan took hold of a wooden slat and glanced down. Three men were still on the ladder and almost at the foot of the wall. Swinging his leg over the ramparts, he began to descend. Behind him some of the soldiers were waving their swords, pretending combat to fool any watchers in the Vagrian camp; Gellan found it unconvincing. Swiftly he climbed to the ground and waited for his men to join him. They they began the long walk to the Vagrian camp.

Several enemy soldiers joined them, but there was no conversation. The men were bone-weary and demoralised following another grim, fruitless day.

Gellan flicked a glance at Jonat. The man was tense, yet his face was set and, as always, he had pushed his bitterness aside and was ready to give his all for the job in hand.

All around them men were sitting down by camp-fires, and to the right a unit of cooks were preparing a hot meal in three bubbling cauldrons.

The aroma swamped Gellan's sense and his dry mouth suddenly swam with saliva. No one at Purdol had eaten for three days.

The daring plan had been Karnak's. Masquerading as Vagrians, a party of Drenai warriors would raid the warehouse and carry back precious food to the starving defenders. It had sounded fine when sitting around the great table of the Purdol hall. But now walking through the enemy camp, it seemed suicidal.

An officer stepped out of the darkness.

'Where are you going?' he asked Gellan.

'None of your damned business,' he replied, recognising the rank of the man by the bronze bars on his epaulettes.

'Just a moment,' said the officer in a more conciliatory manner, 'but I have been told no one is to enter the eastern quarter without authorisation.

'Well, since we are due to be guarding the docks

I would appreciate you telling me how we can accomplish that without being there.'

'Third wing are on dock duty,' said the man. 'I have it written down.'

'Fine,' said Gellan. 'In that case I shall ignore the First General's instructions and take my men back for some rest. But in case he asks me why I did so what is your name?'

'Antasy, sixth wing,' replied the officer, snapping to attention, 'But I'm sure it won't be necessary to mention my name. Obviously there's been an error in the orders.'

'Obviously,' agreed Gellan, swinging away from him. 'Forward!'

As the men trooped wearily past the officer and on through the winding streets of the dockside, Jonat moved up alongside Gellan.

'Now comes the difficult part,' he said softly.

'Indeed it does.'

Ahead of them a party of six soldiers was stationed at the front of a wooden warehouse. Two were sitting on empty boxes while the other four were playing dice.

'On your feet!' bellowed Gellan. 'Who is in charge here?'

A red-faced young warrior ran forward, dropping the dice into a pouch at his side.

'I am, sir.'

'What is the meaning of this?'

'I'm sorry, sir. It was just . . . we were bored, sir.'

'Little chance of worrying about boredom with a hundred stripes on your back, boy!'

'No, sir.'

'You are not from my wing, and I do not intend getting involved with endless bickering and bureacracy. Therefore I shall overlook your negligence. Tell me, are your friends at the back also engaged in dice?'

'I don't know, sir.'

'How many men are there?'

'Ten, sir.'

'When are you due for relief?'

The man glanced at the sky. 'Two hours, sir.'

'Very well. Open the warehouse.'

'I beg your pardon, sir?'

'Are you hard of hearing as well as negligent?'

'No, sir. It is just that we have no key.'

'You mean the key has not been sent?'

'What do you mean, sir?'

'The First General,' said Gellan, slowly and with infinite patience, 'has ordered us to transfer certain goods from this warehouse to his quarters. Your second officer . . . what is his name?'

'Erthold, sir.'

'Yes – Erthold – was due to meet me here, or to leave the key. Where is he?'

'Well . . .'

'Well what?'

'He is asleep, sir.'

'Asleep,' said Gellan. 'Why did I not consider such a possibility? A group of men lounging while on duty. Playing dice, no less, so that a hundred armed men could march up without being seen. Where else would the officer be but asleep? Jonat!'

'Yes, sir.'

'Be so good as to break open the door.'

'Yes, sir,' said Jonat joyously as with two other soldiers he ran forward. Within seconds they had splintered the side door, entered the building, lifted the bar of the main doors and pushed them wide.

Gellan waved his troops forward and the men surged into the warehouse.

'Erthold will be furious, sir,' said the soldier. 'Should I send someone to wake him?'

'As you please,' replied Gellan, smiling. 'But he might ask who gave permission for the man to leave his post. Is that your role?

'You think it would be best not to disturb him?' asked the man.

'I leave that to you.'

'It would probably be best,' said the soldier, looking to Gellan for signs of approval. Gellan walked away from him, but turned as he heard the pounding of running feet. Ten men were sprinting from the rear of the warehouse with swords in hand.

They saw Gellan and halted. Three men saluted nervously and the others followed suit.

'Get back to your posts,' ordered Gellan.

The men glanced at their leader, who shrugged and waveed them away.

'I'm sorry about all this, sir,' he said, 'but I am grateful to you for not taking us to task over the dice.'

'I have played on duty myself from time to time,' said Gellan.

The Drenai, heavily laden, began to leave the warehouse. Jonat supervised the food-gathering, making sure that only dried food was taken: flour, dried fruit, jerked meat, oats and salt.

He had also found a small medical store at the back and had packed three pouches of herbs he felt sure Evris would find useful.

Closing the great doors and replacing the bar, he was the last to leave. The men were standing in marching file, bulging packs upon their shoulders.

Jonat approached the sentry leader.

'I don't want anyone entering the warehouse, despite the broken door. If one drop of that spirit is consumed, there'll be trouble!' He winked broadly.

The man saluted and Gellan led the men back towards the Vagrian camp.

The column wound through deserted streets, on past the tents and the sentries, and out on to the broken ground before the fortress. There, glancing to his right, Gellan saw a sight that froze his blood.

In a dip beyond a row of houses hidden from the fort, three great machines were under construction. He had seen them in use while on a visit to Ventria. They were ballistae, great catapults capable of hurling huge rocks against a castle wall. The carnage would be intolerable once these were completed. The parts must have been sent from Vagria, round the Lentrian Horn, to be assembled here. He tapped Jonat on the shoulder and pointed to the work being undertaken by lantern light.

Jonat swore, then looked into Gellan's face. 'You are not thinking . . . ?'

'Take the men back to Purdol, Jonat. I'll see you later.'

'You can't . . .'

'No arguments. Get moving!'

Dardalion returned to the fortress and his sleeping body. His eyes flickered open and he swung his legs from the bed. Sadness engulfed him and he covered his face with his hands and wept.

He had watched Waylander's dying body being hauled into the mountain and had sensed the hunger of the mountain dwellers.

Astila entered the room silently and sat beside the weeping priest.

'Waylander is dead,' Dardalion told him.

'He was your friend,' said Astila. 'I am so sorry.'

'I do not know how friendship is judged under such circumstances. We were comrades, I suppose. He gave me new life, new purpose. From his gift of blood came The Thirty.'

'Did he fail in his quest?'

'Not yet. The Armour is safe at present, but a lone woman is carrying it across Nadir lands. I must reach her.'

'It is impossible, Dardalion.'

The warrior priest smiled suddenly. 'Everything we have attempted so far has seemed impossible at the outset.'

Astila closed his eyes. 'The men are coming back with food,' he said. 'Baynha reports there are no losses, but the officer has not yet returned.'

'Good. What of the Brotherhood?'

'There has been no attack tonight.'

'Are they marshalling their forces, or have we beaten them, I wonder?'

'I do not think they are beaten, Dardalion.'

'No,' said Dardalion sadly. 'That would be too much to hope for.'

Sensing that his leader wished to be alone, Astila left the room and Dardalion wandered to the high window to gaze out at the distant stars.

He felt a sense of calm as he looked into eternity, and Durmast's face loomed in his mind. He shook his head, remembering his own sense of shock as he had sped to Raboas anxious to observe Waylander. He had arrived to see the assassin being tortured and the giant Durmast confronting the Brotherhood.

With all his power, Dardalion had focused a shield over Durmast, blocking the mind spell of the man Tchard. But he could not prevent the terrible swords from plunging into the giant. He had listened as Waylander and Durmast spoke, and a great sorrow touched him as the giant talked.

'Do you think his power could not work against me because I am the Chosen One?'

Dardalion wished with all his heart that it could have been true, that it was not simply a case of happenstance: one man, one spirit in the right place at the right time.

Somehow, he felt, Durmast deserved more than that.

Dardalion found himself wondering whether the Source would accept Durmast. Did a lifetime of petty evil weigh more than a moment of heroism? Somehow it should, and yet . . .

The priest closed his eyes and prayed for the souls of the two men. Then he smiled. But what would such men make of the peaceful paradise promised by the ancients? An eternity of song and praise! Would they not prefer an end to existence?

One of the old religions promised a hall of heroes, where strong men were welcomed by warrior maidens who sang songs of the deeds of the brave.

Durmast would probably prefer that.

Dardalion stared at the moon . . . and trembled.

A single question lanced through his mind.

What is a miracle?

The simplicity of the answer dazzled him, as it leapt from the depths of his intellect to cover the unbidden question.

A miracle is something that happens unexpectedly

at the moment it is needed. No more than that. No less.

His rescue of Durmast had been a miracle, for Durmast could never have expected such aid. And yet, why had Dardalion been on hand at just the right moment?

Because I chose to find Waylander, he told himself.

Why did you so choose?

The enormity of it all overcame the priest and he stepped back from the window and sat down on the bed.

Durmast had been chosen many years ago, even before his birth. But without Waylander, Durmast would have remained a killer and a thief. And without Dardalion, Waylander would have been nothing more than a hunted assassin.

It was all a pattern, created from an interweaving series of apparently random threads.

Dardalion fell to his knees, overcome with a terrible shame.

Gellan sat beyond the glare of the lanterns and watched the engineers constructing the ballistae. Some two hundred men were at work, hoisting the giant arms of the catapults into place and hammering home the wooden plugs against the resistance bar. At the top of each arm was a canvas pouch in which could be placed boulders weighing almost a quarter of a ton. Gellan had no real idea of the range of the Vagrian machines, but in Ventria he had seen rocks hurled hundreds of feet.

The ballistae were placed on wooden frames with two huge wheels at each corner. They would be hauled before the walls, probably in front of the gate tower.

The bronze-studded gates of oak had so far withstood all assaults. But they would not stand against these engines of destruction.

Gellan glanced at the fortress, silver-white now in the moonlight. The last of the men had been lifted to the ramparts; by now the food would be stored and bronze cauldrons would be sitting atop the cooking fires, bubbling with oats and meat.

Gellan wished he had said goodbye to Jonat. Somehow it seemed churlish to have sent him on his way without a word of farewell.

Pushing himself to his feet he walked boldly into the work area, stopping to study the constructions – peering into the massive joints and marvelling at the scale of the carpentry. He walked on, ignored by all, until he came to a storage hut. Stepping inside, he located the barrels of lantern oil and several buckets.

Removing his helm and breastplate, he filled the buckets with oil and carried them outside, placing them in front of the hut. When he had filled six buckets, he found an empty jar which he also filled with oil. Taking a lantern from a nearby post, he walked to the furthest of the siege engines and calmly poured oil into the wide joint that pinned the huge arm to the frame.

Then he moved to a second engine and emptied the jug over the wood. Pulling the glass from the lantern, Gellan held the flame to the saturated joint. Fire leapt from the frame.

'What are you doing?' screamed an engineer. Gellan ignored him and walked to the first engine, touching the flame to the oil.

The man grabbed him by the shoulder and spun him round, but Gellan's dagger slid between his ribs. Men were running now towards the engines.

'Quick!' shouted Gellan. 'Get water. Over there!'

Several men obeyed instantly, sweeping up the buckets Gellan had left by the hut.

A searing sheet of flame roared into the sky as the oil splashed on to the blaze. A second flare, though not quite as spectacular, streamed from the other machine.

With no time to destroy the third of the ballistae, Gellan backed away from the blazing engines, disbelieving his luck.

It had been so simple, but then he had moved about in an unhurried way and had thus escaped attention. Now he would make it to the fortress and enjoy a good meal.

He turned to run – and found himself facing a score of armed men, led by a dark-haired officer carrying a silver-steel sabre.

The officer walked forward, raising a hand to halt his soldiers. 'Gellan, isn't it?' he asked.'

Slowly Gellan drew his own sword. 'It is.'

'We met two years ago when I was the guest of honour at the Silver Swords tourney in Drenan. You won, I believe.'

Gellan recognised the man as Dalnor, a Vagrian swordsman and aide to the general Kaem.

'It's pleasant to see you again,' said Gellan.

'I take it that you are not considering surrender?'

'The thought had not occurred to me. Do *you* wish to surrender?'

Dalnor smiled. 'I watched you fence, Gellan. You were very good – but suspect, I thought. There are certain gaps in your defences. May I demonstrate?'

'Please do.'

Dalnor stepped forward and presented his sword. Gellan touched blades and the two men sprang back and began to circle one another. Dalnor's slender sabre flicked forward, to be parried instantly; he in turn swiftly countered the riposte and the two men stepped apart.

Behind them the engines blazed and the duel was fought in the giant shadows cast by the flames.

The sabres clashed and sang time and again, with no wounds apparent on the warriors. First Dalnor feinted left and with a flick of the wrist scythed his blade to the right. This move Gellan blocked and countered with a stabbing thrust to the belly. Dalnor sidestepped, pushing the sword clear, then backhanded a cut to Gellan's head. Gellan ducked.

Again the sabres crossed and this time Dalnor feinted high and plunged his blade through Gellan's side above the right hip. The sabre landed through flesh and muscle and slid clear in a fraction of a second.

'You see, Gellan?' said Dalnor. 'The gap is in your low defence – you are too tall.'

'Thank you for pointing it out. I will work on it.'

Dalnor chuckled. 'I like you, Gellan. I wish you were a Vagrian.'

Gellan was weary and lack of food had sapped his strength. He did not answer, but presented his blade once more and Dalnor's eyebrows rose.

'Another lesson?' He stepped forward and the blades came together. For several seconds the duel was even, then Gellan made a clumsy block and Dalnor's sword slid between his ribs. Instantly Gellan slammed his fist round the blade to trap it in his body, then his own sabre licked out, slicing across Dalnor's jugular.

Dalnor fell back, gripping his throat.

Gellan fell forward, dropping his sabre.

'I enjoyed the lesson, Vagrian,' he said.

A Vagrian ran forward, cleaving his sword through Gellan's neck. Dalnor raised a hand as if to stop him, but his lifeblood frothed and bubbled from his throat and he fell beside the dead Drenai swordsman.

Beyond the scene the ballistae burned, a black plume of smoke rising above the grey fortress and curling like a huge fist above the defenders.

Kaem surveyed the wreckage after dawn. Two engines were destroyed.

But one remained.

It would be enough, Kaem decided.

25

Karnak watched the flames rearing high above the ridge and scanned the broken ground beyond for sign of Gellan. He did not expect to see him, yet the hope remained.

In terms of the future – if there was to be a future – it was probably just as well that Gellan had died. He would never have made a good follower; he was too independent of mind to slavishly align himself to any leader. And yet Karnak knew he would miss him; he was the thorn in the rose which reminds a man the flesh is weak.

'It looks like two fires,' said Dundas, moving alongside the general.

'Yet. Jonat says there are three ballistae.'

'Still, two was a fine effort by a single man.'

'One man can do anything if he sets his heart on it,' said Karnak softly.

'We lost three hundred men today, general.'

Karnak nodded. 'Egel will be here soon.'

'You cannot believe that.'

'We will hold until he gets here, Dundas. We have no choice. Tell Jonat he must take Gellan's place.'

'Sarvaj is the senior man.'

'I know who the senior man is. Put Jonat in charge.'

'Yes, sir,' Dundas walked away, but Karnak stopped him.

'In peacetime I wouldn't put Jonat in charge of stable clearance. But this is a game of death.'

'Yes, sir.'

Karnak gazed from the gate tower ramparts, watching the men along the walls. Some were sitting and eating, others were spread out asleep; still more were sharpening sword-blades dulled by ceaseless combat.

Too few, he thought. He glanced back at the Keep.

Soon the hard decisions must be made.

On the wall below, Jonat sat with Sarvaj. For some while both men had watched for Gellan; now they knew he was either taken or slain.

'He was a good man,' said Sarvaj at last.

'He was a fool,' hissed Jonat. 'He didn't have to kill himself.'

'No,' agreed Sarvaj, 'but I shall miss him.'

'I won't! I couldn't care less how many officers die. I just wonder why I stay at this cursed fortress. I used to have a dream, an ambition if you like . . . Have you ever been up into the Skoda mountains?'

'No.'

'There are peaks there which have never been climbed; they are bathed in mist for nine months of the year. I wanted to build a home near one of those peaks – there is a glen, sheltered, where horses could be raised. I know about horses. I like horses.'

'I'm glad to hear there's something you like.'

'I like a lot of *things*, Sarvaj. But not many people.'

'Gellan liked you.'

'Stop it! I don't want to hear any more about Gellan. You understand?'

'I don't think that I do.'

'Because I care. Does that satisfy you? Is that what you wanted to hear? I am sorry that he's gone. There! And . . . I don't want to talk about it.'

Sarvaj removed his helmet and leaned back against the cold stone. 'I had a dream once too. There was a girl back in Drenan – bright, talented and available. Her father owned a fleet of traders which sailed from Mashrapur to the east. I was going to marry her and become a merchant.'

'What happened?'

'She married someone else.'

'Did she not love you?'

'She said she did.'

'You were better off without her.'

Sarvaj chuckled. 'Does this look like better off?'

'At least you are among friends,' said Jonat, extending his hand. Sarvaj took it.

'I always wanted to die among friends.'

'Well, that is one ambition you'll achieve.'

Danyal had been riding for four days across rough open country. In that time she had seen no one but now, as she rode through thick forest, she knew she was not alone. In the undergrowth to her right she had seen a dark shadow, moving from the thick cover and darting between the trees.

She had spurred her horse away, the pack pony following.

But still the shadower stayed in touch. She rarely caught more than a glimpse of him, but he moved with great speed and supernatural silence.

The light was fading and Danyal's fears grew. Her mouth was dry, but her hands were slick with sweat. She wished Waylander were here – or even Durmast.

Momentarily her fear eased as her last conversation with Durmast rose in her mind.

When they had travelled for some five miles, they had come across the party of warriors in black armour. Durmast had cursed and reached for his battleaxe, but they had ridden by with scarcely a glance at the two travellers.

Durmast's anger had been a sight to behold.

'They ignored me,' he had said.

'I'm glad,' she had told him. 'Did you want to fight them?'

'They were Brotherhood warriors seeking the Armour. They can read minds and they know we have it.'

'Then why did they not take it?'

He had dismounted and walked to a nearby rock where he sat and stared at the now distant mountain of Raboas.

Danyal joined him. 'We cannot stay here. Waylander is risking his life to give us time.'

'They knew,' said Durmast.

'Knew what?'

'They knew my thoughts.'

'I do not understand you.'

'You know what I am, Danyal . . . what I have been. There is no real strength in me except what I have in the muscles of this over-large body. I am a wretch, always have been. Take the Armour and go.'

'And what will you do?'

'I'll travel east – maybe go to Ventria. They say it is a rare experience to view the Opal Mountains in winter.'

'I cannot get through alone.'

'You don't understand, do you? I'll betray you, Danyal, and steal the Armour. It's worth a fortune.'

'You gave your word.'

'My word isn't worth pig-droppings.'

'You are going back to help Waylander.'

Durmast laughed. 'Do I look stupid? That would be the act of a madman. Go on. Ride! Go before I change my mind.'

As the days passed Danyal had hoped to see Waylander riding the back trail. She would not accept that he might be dead – could not accept it. He was strong. Invincible. No one could bring him down. She remembered the day when he had stood against the warriors in the forest. One man standing strong in the fading light, the red glow all around him. And he had won. He always won – he could not be dead.

She jerked back to the present as tears blurred her vision, blinking hard. The path was narrow and the darkness was gathering; she was loth to camp, but the horses were tired. Glancing to her right, she peered into the undergrowth, but there was no sign of the other traveller. Perhaps it had been a bear hunting for food. Perhaps her imagination had fuelled her fear.

Danyal rode on until she heard the sound of running water and then made camp by a shallow stream, determined to stay awake through the night, sword in hand.

She awoke with the dawn and stretched. Swiftly she washed in the icy stream, the water stinging the sleep from her. Then she tightened the saddle cinch of her mare and mounted. Durmast had told her to steer south-east until she reached the river. There was a ferry – cross that and head due south to Delnoch Pass.

The forest was silent as she rode and the day warm and close.

Four Nadir riders came into sight and Danyal jerked on the reins, her heart pounding as they came closer. One of them had a dead antelope roped across his saddle and the others carried bows. The lead rider halted before her.

'You are blocking the path,' he said.

Danyal steered the mare to the left and the men rode on.

That night she lit a small fire and fell asleep within seconds.

She awoke just after midnight to see a towering figure sitting by the fire, feeding branches to the flames. As silently as she could, she drew her dagger and pushed back the blanket. His back was to her, his naked skin shining in the moonlight – he was big, and would dwarf even Durmast. She moved to her feet. He turned . . .

And she found herself staring into a single dreadful eye about a slitted nose and a fang-rimmed slash of a mouth.

'Vrend,' grunted Kai, tapping chest. 'Vrend.'

Danyal's legs felt weak, but she took a deep breath and advanced with the knife outstretched. 'Go away,' she said.

Kai pushed out a taloned finger and began scratching at the earth. He was not looking at her. Tensing herself to spring and plunge the knife into him, she suddenly saw what he was doing: in the hard-baked clay, he had sketched a stick-figured man holding a small crossbow.

'Waylander,' said Danyal. 'You know Waylander?'

'Vrend,' said Kai, nodding. He pointed at her. 'Anyal.'

'Danyal. Yes, yes. I am Danyal. Is Waylander alive?'

'Vrend.' Kai curled his hand into a fist as if it held a dagger. Then he stabbed his shoulder and hip.

'He has been badly hurt? Is that what you are saying?'

The monster merely looked at her.

'The Brotherhood warriors. Did they find him? Tall men in black armour.'

'Dead,' said Kai, mimicking the actions of a sword or axe. Danyal sheathed her knife and sat beside Kai, reaching out and touching his arm. 'Listen to me. The man who killed them – is he alive?'

'Dead,' said Kai.

Danyal sat back and closed her eyes.

A few months ago she had been performing a dance in front of a king. Weeks later she had fallen in love with that king's assassin. Now she sat in a lonely forest with a monster who could not speak. She began to laugh at the lunacy of it all.

Kai listened to the laughter, heard it change and become weeping and watched the tears flow on her pretty cheeks. So pretty, he thought. Like the Nadir girl he had watched. So small, fragile and bird-boned.

Way back, Kai had wanted one of these soft beings as a friend. And he had seized a girl as she washed clothes by a stream, carrying her into the mountains where he had gathered fruit and pretty stones. But when they had arrived Kai had found her broken and lifeless, her ribs in shards where his arm had encircled her. Not all his healing power could help her.

He didn't touch them any more . . .

Six hundred men hauled the ballista into place some fifty paces from the gate. Then six carts came into view, pulled by teams of oxen, the Drenai watched as men milled around the carts, unyoking the beasts. Then a winch was set up behind the ballista.

Karnak called Dundas, Jonat and several other nearby officers to him.

'Get the majority of the men back into the Keep. Leave only a token force on the walls,' he instructed.

Within minutes the men had streamed back through the Keep gates, taking up positions on the battlements.

Karnak opened a leather pouch at his side and removed a hard cake of rolled oats and sugar. Tearing off a chunk, he chewed it thoughtfully as the preparations continued.

Several soldiers had manoeuvred a massive boulder to the rear of the cart and were tying ropes around it. At a signal, four soldiers winched it into place on the ballista. An officer raised an arm, a lever was swiftly pulled and the ballista arm shot forward.

Karnak watched the boulder soar through the air, seeming to grow as it approached. With a thundering crash it struck the wall beside the gate tower. Rocks exploded and an entire section of battlements crumbled under the impact.

The general finished his cake and walked to the rampart edge, stepping up on to the crenellated wall.

'Up here, you whoresons!' he bellowed. Then he stepped back and walked slowly down the stairwell to the main battlements.

'Get off the wall, you men,' he shouted. 'Back to the Keep!'

As a second section of wall exploded some thirty feet from the general, rocks and stones shrieked past his head. Two men were hurled from the battlements to smash against the cobbled courtyard.

Karnak cursed and ran down the steps to them. Both were dead.

A boulder struck the gate tower, sheering off to crash into the field hospital roof. Timbers cracked, but the boulder did not penetrate. Twice more the gate tower endured against the missiles, but on the third strike the entire structure shifted and sagged. With a creaking groan, the stone blocks gave way and the tower slid to the right to crash behind the gates.

In the hospital, Evris was completing the stitching of a stomach would in a young soldier. The boy had been lucky; no vital organs had been sliced by the thrusting sword and now all he had to fear was gangrene.

The wall came apart and Evris' last sight was of an immense black cloud engulfing the room. The slight surgeon was crushed against the far wall beside the body of his patient. Four more boulders struck the hospital and a fallen lantern spread fire through a linen basket. The flames licked out through a door frame, and up between the walls of the hospital. Soon the blaze grew into an inferno. Many of the wards had no windows and smoke killed hundreds of wounded men. Orderlies struggled at first to control the fire, and then to carry their patients to safety; they succeeded only in trapping themselves.

The gates splintered as a huge rock punched through the oak beams. A second missile finished the work and the massive bronze hinges buckled; the left-hand gate sagged and fell.

Karnak spat and cursed loudly. Then he walked to the Keep gates.

'It's all over, general,' said a soldier as the general entered.

'It's not looking too hopeful,' agreed Karnak. 'Shut the gates.'

'Someone may get out of the hospital,' protested the man.

'No one will live through that inferno. Shut the gates.'

Karnak made his way to the great hall where Dardalion and the surviving twelve priests of the The Thirty were deep in prayer.

'Dardalion!'

The priest opened his eyes. 'Yes, general?'

'Tell me that Egel is on his way.'

'I cannot. the Brotherhood are everywhere and we cannot break out.'

'Without Egel, we are doomed. Finished. It will all have been for nothing.'

'We will have done our best, general. No one can ask for more.'

'I damn well can. Trying is for losers – all that counts is winning.'

'Waylander is dead,' said Dardalion suddenly, 'but the Armour is on its way to Egel.'

'The Armour is too late for us now, it was to have been a rallying point. If Egel has not yet raised an army, it will matter not at all.'

'Not to us, general. But Egel could link with Ironlatch.'

Karnak said nothing. The logic was irresistible and perhaps that had been Egel's plan all along. He must have known Karnak was a potential enemy in the long term – what better way to handle him than to allow the Vagrians to end his ambitions? And a link with Ironlatch would drive a wedge through the Vagrian forces, freeing the capital.

Purdol would wait.

Egel would have it all: the Armour, the army and the nation.

'He will come if he can, general,' said Dardalion.

'Why should he?'

'Egel is a man of honour.'

'What does that mean?' snapped Karnak.

'I hope that it means Egel will do exactly what you would if you were in his place.'

Karnak laughed, his good humour restored. 'I do hope not, Dardalion. I am rather counting on him getting here!'

As she slept, Danyal became aware of a voice piercing her dreams, blending with her sleeping thoughts. The awareness grew and she recognised Dardalion; he seemed thinner now and older, bowed down by enormous pressures.

'Danyal, can you hear me?'

'Yes,' she said and smiled wearily.

'Are you well?'

'I am unhurt, no more than that.'

'Do you have the Armour still?'

'Yes.'

'Where are you?'

'Less than a day from the river and the ferry. There is someone with me – a monster creature. He saw Waylander die.'

'Open your eyes and show me,' he said and

372

Danyal sat up. Kai still sat by the fire, his great eye closed, his huge mouth hanging open.

'There is no evil in him,' said Dardalion. 'Now listen to me, Danyal – I am going to try to reach Egel and urge him to send a troop to escort you home. Wait at the ferry until you hear from me.'

'Where are you?'

'I am at Dros Purdol, but the situation here is desperate and we are mere days from destruction. There are fewer than six hundred men to hold the fortress and we have barricaded ourselves within the Keep. The food is almost gone and the water is stale.'

'What can I do?'

'Wait at the ferry. May the Source bless you, Danyal.'

'And you, priest.'

'Priest no longer. The war has come to me and I have killed.'

'We are all sullied, Dardalion.'

'Yes. But the end is very near – then I shall know.'

'What will you know?'

'Whether I was right. I must go now. Wait at the ferry!'

Danyal and Kai found the crossing at dusk the following day. There was no sign of life and the ferry itself was moored on the far side of the river. Danyal unsaddled her horse and Kai carried the bulging pack containing the Armour into a small hut. She prepared a fire and some food, averting her eyes as Kai ate, spooning the oats into his mouth with his fingers.

She slept in a narrow bed while the monster sat, cross-legged before the fire.

Just after dawn she awoke to find herself alone.

After a breakfast of dried fruit she wandered to the river and washed, removing her tunic and wading naked into the waist-deep water by the bank. The current was swift and she had difficulty in keeping her feet. After several minutes she returned to the shore and washed the tunic as best she could, beating it against a rock to dislodge the grit of travel.

Two men rose from the bushes to her left. Rolling to the right she scooped her sword into her hand, hurling aside the scabbard.

'She's feisty,' said the first man, a short stout warrior wearing a brown leather jerkin and carrying a curved dagger. As he grinned at her, she saw he had lost his front two teeth; he was unshaven and dirty, as was his companion – a thickset man with a drooping moustache.

'Will you look at her!' said the first man. 'The body of an angel.'

'I'm looking,' said the second, grinning.

'You geldings never seen a woman before?' asked Danyal.

'Geldings? We'll show you who's a gelding,' snarled the gap-toothed warrior.

'You gutless dung-eater! You'll show me nothing but your entrails.'

Her sword came up and the men backed away.

'Take her, Cael!' ordered Gap-tooth. 'Take the sword away.'

'You take it.'

'You frightened?'

'No more than you.'

As they argued the immense figure of Kai rose behind them, his hands reaching out. His palms slammed their heads together with a sickening crack and both men slid to the ground. Kai leaned over to grab Gap-tooth's belt and with a casual flick of his arm he hurled the unconscious man far out into the river. His companion followed and both sank from sight.

Kai ambled forward. 'Bad.' he said, shaking his head.

'Not any more,' said Danyal, 'but I could have handled it.'

That night as Danyal was carrying wood into the hut, her foot crashed through a rotted floorboard and the flesh of her leg was deeply gashed. Limping into the hut she began to bathe the wound, but Kai knelt by her and covered the place with his hand. Pain lanced her leg and she struggled to pull clear of his grasp. But the pain passed, and when he released her the wound had vanished.

'Gone!' he said, his head tilting to one side. Carefully she probed the leg; the skin was unbroken.

'How did you do that?'

He lifted his hand and pointed to the palm.

'Vrend,' he said. Then he tapped his shoulder and hip. 'Aynander.'

But she could not understand him.

A troop of Legion riders reached the opposite bank at noon the next day, and Danyal watched as they hauled the ferry across the river. She turned to Kai.

'You must go,' she said. 'They will not understand you.'

He reached out and lightly touched her arm. 'Urbye Anyal.'

'Goodbye, Kai. Thank you.'

He walked to the edge of the trees and turned as the ferry was docking, pointing north. 'Aynander,' he called and she waved and turned to the officer approaching her.

'You are Danyal?' he asked.

'Yes. The Armour is in the hut.'

'Who was the big man with the mask.'

'A friend, a good friend.'

'I wouldn't like anyone that big for an enemy.' He was a handsome young man with an easy smile and she followed him to the ferry. With the Armour aboard she sat back, relaxing for the first time in days. Then a sudden thought struck her and she ran to the rear of the ferry.

'Kai!' she shouted. 'Kai!'

But the forest was silent, the giant gone.

Aynander! Waylander.

The giant had cured him. That's what he had been trying to tell her.

Waylander was alive!

The Keep held the enemy at bay for five days before the bronze-headed battering ram finally cracked the timbers of the gates. Soldiers swarmed forward, tearing at the wood with axe and hook, ripping wide a gaping entrance to the Keep itself.

Beyond the gates, in the portcullis archway, Sarvaj waited with fifty swordsmen and a score of archers. The last of the arrows lay before the kneeling bowmen, and these they loosed as the gates opened and the Vagrians filled the breach. The enemy front line fell as the shafts sliced home, but more warriors pushed forward with shields held high. The bowmen retired and Sarvaj led his swordsmen in a wild charge, blades flashing in the light streaming from the ruined gates.

The two groups crashed together, shield on shield,

and for almost a minute the Vagrians gave way. Then their greater numbers began to push the Drenai back across the blood-covered cobblestones of the archway.

Sarvaj hacked and thrust his sword into the sea of bodies before him, his senses dulled by the screams and war-cries echoing alongside the clanging crash of sword and shield. A dagger rammed into his thigh and he chopped his sword across the neck of the wielder, watching him fall beneath the booted feet of his comrades. Sarvaj and a dozen others cut their way clear of the skirmish and tried to close the doors of the great Hall. More Drenai warriors ran from the battlements to aid them, but the Vagrians were too powerful and the Drenai were forced back into the Hall itself. There the enemy swarmed around the battling defenders, taunting them with their defeat. The Drenai formed a fighting circle and stood their ground, grim-eyed.

A Vagrian officer entered the hall and pointed at Sarvaj.

'Surrender now,' he said. 'It is over.'

Sarvaj glanced at the men around him. Fewer than twenty remained.

'Anyone feel like surrendering?' he asked.

'To that rabble?' replied one of the men.

The Vagrian waved his men forward.

Sarvaj stepped back as a warrior rushed at him, ducking under the sweeping blade to thrust his own sword into the man's groin, dragging it clear as a second warrior bore down on him. He parried a wild cut, then staggered as a lance clanged against his breastplate. A sword cut into his face and he fell, and rolled. Even then he stabbed upwards and a man screamed. But several warriors surrounded him, stabbing at his face again and again.

There was no pain, he realised, as his lifeblood rose up and choked him.

On the battlements above, Jonat – helmet gone, sword dulled – watched helplessly as the Vagrians swept over the ramparts. A warrior ran at him; he parried the blade and sent a dazzling riposte ripping through his throat. Dropping his sword, Jonat swept up the man's sabre and tested the edge. It was still keen and he grinned.

Drenai warriors backed away from the advancing enemy and fought a steady retreat down the winding stairwell to the next floor. From below Jonat could hear the sounds of battle and knew in that moment that the siege was over. Anger rose in him, and all the bitterness of his twenty-seven years washed over him. No one had ever listened. From the moment when, as a child, he had begged for his father's life, no one had ever really listened. Now was the final humiliation – to die in a lost war a mere five days after his greatest promotion. Had they won, Jonat would have been hailed as a hero and become one of the youngest First Dun officers in the Legion. In ten years he could have been a general

Now there was nothing . . . he would not even make a footnote to history.

Dros Purdol, they would say – was not a battle once fought there?

Once out of the stairwell the Drenai formed a fighting wedge in the main corridor, but the Vagrians were now coming from above and below. Karnak and Dundas emerged from the left with a score of warriors and linked with Jonat's group.

'Sorry about this, old lad,' said Karnak. Jonat said

nothing as the enemy charged from the left and Karnak met them with an insane counter-charge, his axe cleaving into their ranks. Dundas - beside him as always – fell with a spear through the heart, but Karnak's furious assault left him unmarked. Jonat cut and thrust at the advancing warriors, screaming his rage and despair. An axe hit his breastplate, careering up to crack sideways on against his head. Jonat went down, blood streaming from a shallow cut to his temple; he tried to rise but a Drenai warrior, his head cloven by an axe blow, fell across him. The sounds of battle receded and Jonat passed into darkness.

One by one the Drenai were cut down until only Karnak remained. He backed away, holding the great axe high as the Vagrians advanced with sword-points extended, shields raised. Karnak was breathing hard and blood ran from wounds in his arms and legs.

'Take him alive!' called an officer. 'The general wants him alive.'

The Vagrians rushed forward and the axe swept down. Fists rained upon the Drenai general and he slipped on the blood-covered floor. Booted feet thundered into his face and body and his head snapped back, striking the wall. His fist lashed out weakly, then finally he was still.

On the second floor the surviving priests of The Thirty had barricaded themselves within the Keep library. Dardalion listened to the hammering on the door, then called the priests to him. None of them was armed, save himself.

'It is over, my brothers,' he said.

Astila stepped forward. 'I will not fight them. But

I want you to know, Dardalion, that I regret not an action, not a single deed.'

'Thank you, my friend.'

The young Baynha approached and took Dardalion's hand. 'I regret the use of the rats against common soldiers, but I feel no shame at our battles with the Brotherhood.'

'I think we should pray, my brothers, for time is short.'

Together in the centre of the library the small group knelt, and their minds swam together. They did not hear the final splintering of the door, nor the crash of the barricade, but they all felt the first sword-blade that pierced Astila's heart, that cut Baynah's head from his shoulders, and the other sharp swords which plunged into unresisting flesh. Dardalion was stabbed in the back and pain swept through him . . .

Beyond the dying fortress, Kaem stood on the balcony of his quarters watching with barely concealed glee as the battle moved into its final stages.

The bald Vagrian general was already planning the next move in his campaign. Leave a powerful force to hold Purdol and move his troops through Skultik forest to root out Egel, before turning south to deal with Ironlatch and the Lentrians.

Something bright and dazzling caught his eye and he glanced to the left where a low line of hills edged with trees heralded the entrance to Skultik. There, on a splendid black horse, sat a warrior with armour blazing in the noonday sun.

Bronze Armour! Kaem squinted against the glare, his mouth suddenly dry. The warrior raised his arm and suddenly the hill seemed to move as thousands of riders streamed towards the fortress. There was no time to organise a flank defence – Kaem watched in horror as rank after rank of fighting men swept over the hill.

Five thousand? Ten? Twenty?

On they came. The first Vagrian soldiers watched them approach and stood transfixed. Realisation hit them and they drew their swords, only to be swallowed up by the charging mass.

All was lost, Kaem knew. Numbers meant nothing now. The enemy would drive a wedge through his ranks and his army would be sundered and dispersed.

The Bronze Warrior sat atop the hill, his eyes fixed on the fortress. Kaem saw his head turn towards the harbour and knew with a sudden chill that the warrior was seeking him.

Kaem backed from the window, thinking rapidly. His ships were still docked nearby – he could escape the destruction at Purdol and join his southern forces. From there he could plot a holding action until winter, with a new offensive in the spring.

He turned . . .

Standing in the doorway was a hooded figure, tall and lean, a black cloak over his shoulders, in his hand a small, black crossbow.

Kaem could not see the face under the hood, but he knew. He knew.

'Don't kill me,' he begged. 'Don't!'

He backed away to the balcony, stepping out into the bright sunshine.

The silent figure followed him.

Kaem turned and climbed the balcony wall, leaping for the cobbles thirty feet below. He landed on his feet, both legs snapping under the impact and his left thigh driving up through his hip into his stomach. He fell on his back and found himself staring up at the empty balcony. Agony seared him and he died screaming.

The hooded figure walked to the harbour and climbed down a rope ladder to a tiny sailboat. The wind was picking up and the craft skimmed over the waves and out of the harbour.

Inside the Keep, the Vagrians dragged Karnak along the blood-drenched corridors. His remaining eye was swollen and his lips were cut and bleeding. Down the steps they took him and through the carnage of the great Hall. Karnak struggled to walk, but his left leg was swollen and his ankle would take no weight.

Out in the sunshine the men stopped and blinked in surprise.

The courtyard was packed with Drenai soldiers and at the centre stood a man in the shining Bronze Armour carrying two swords.

'Release him,' ordered the warrior, his voice muffled and almost metallic.

The Vagrians stepped back.

Karnak staggered and almost fell, but the warrior in bronze moved forward to support him.

'The Vagrians are routed,' said Egel. 'The war has swung.'

'We did it?' whispered Karnak.

'By all the Gods, I swear it,' Egel told him.

'Kaem?'

'He killed himself.'

Karnak struggled to open his eyes, but tears swam in them.

'Take me away from here,' he said. 'Don't let anyone see me.'

Epilogue

With Kaem dead and the major Vagrian army surrendered, the war was over on the last day of autumn, when Egel and Karnak led the Drenai army to link with the Lentrian general Ironlatch on the outskirts of Drenan.

The following year, Karnak led the invasion of Vagria which saw the Emperor toppled.

The Drenai ruling houses refused all talk of monarchy and a republic was instituted, with Egel nominated to lead a government. The general refused, but took the title of the Earl of Bronze and returned to Delnoch, where he organised the construction of a mighty six-walled fortress across the Pass.

His adviser was a priest named Dardalion, who had been found seriously wounded in the library room at Purdol. Egel was much criticised for the expense of constructing Dros Delnoch, but maintained his faith in Dardalion's vision.

Five years after the success of Purdol, Egel was assassinated in his rooms at the fortress. In the civil war that followed, Karnak rose to rule the Drenai.

Jonat survived the siege of Purdol and became a general in the Legion. He died six years after the battle, leading a rebel force against Karnak in the civil war.

Danyal, with the gold Egel gave her for returning the Armour, bought a house in Skarta where she lived with Krylla and Miriel. But she was often seen riding in the Delnoch Pass and scanning the northern horizon.

Six months after the Vagrian defeat, she and the children vanished from home.

Two neighbours discussed the disappearance with the South Gate sentry.

'I watched her leave,' he said. 'She was riding with a companion. A man.'

'Did you recognise him?'

'No, he was a stranger. A waylander.'